PRAISE FOR KAREN COULTERS NOVELS

"Karen Coulters is my new favorite author! At once charming, vivid and delightful, *Hope from Daffodils* has a natural movement with a suspenseful build-up that kept me turning pages well into the night. Set on the seacoast of Maine, I could picture myself by the water, in the bakery, smelling the flowers and watching the events in the beautiful barn. I fell in love with the characters and miss them already."

~Jenny Bruck, Author, *52 Vitality Tools*

Hope from Daffodils brought me through a wave of emotions that kept me from putting the book down until I was done! Each character is so well developed and rich, you become invested in each of their outcomes. Thank you for the journey, Karen!"

~Caleigh Flynn, Amazon

"Hard to put down…I enjoyed reading every part of *Hope from Daffodils*. You really come to like the characters and before the book ends, they feel like old friends. Reading this book feels like a mini-vacation."

~One Girls Opinion, Goodreads

"I felt I knew the main characters as well as if they had been long time friends of mine. The conversations throughout were natural and never contrived, giving me the sensation, I was present as a silent partner. I was delighted that I never knew exactly where Coulters' was taking me, but I willingly turned the pages to find out!"

~Connie Evan – Author, *The Pine Tree Riot*

A grieving widow. A disillusioned attorney. Set along the idyllic Maine coast, *Hope from Daffodils* is about how we lose our way in the world and find our way back. Coulters delivers a romance both twisty and heartwarming. A charming debut!

~Lorrie Thomson, award-winning author of *A Measure of Happiness, What's Left Behind,* and *Equilibrium*

IAN Book of the Year Finalist

BOOKS By KAREN COULTERS

"York Harbor Series" Novels

Hope from Daffodils

When Cookies Crumble

Look forward to:
Patchwork to Healing

Published by Howland Press

Hope *from* Daffodils

May hope Always
Bloom in you!

Hope *from* Daffodils

A YORK HARBOR SERIES NOVEL

KAREN COULTERS

Howland
Press

Howland Press

18 Loudon Rd. # 494

Concord, NH 03302

This is a work of fiction. All of the characters, organizations, and events portrayed in this novel are either products of the author's imagination or are used fictitiously, and any resemblance to actual persons, living or dead, business establishments, events, or locales is entirely coincidental.

www.karencoultersauthor.com

Library of Congress Cataloging-in-Publication Data

Names: Karen Coulters, Author

Title: Hope from Daffodils

Description: First edition. | New Hampshire: Howland Press, 2019.

Identifiers: LCCN 2019902143 | ISBN 978-1-7336460-0-0 (softcover)

ISBN 978-1-7336460-1-7 (ebook)

Our books may be purchased in bulk for promotion, educational, or business use. Please contact your local bookseller or Howland Press via email @ HowlandPress@KarenCoultersAuthor.com

Cover & interior designed by: My Custom Book Cover

Editor: Clio Editing Services

Printed in the United States of America.

First Edition: 2019

10 9 8 7 6 5 4 3 2 1

"There came a time when the pain of remaining tight in bud was worse than the risk to blossom."

~UNKNOWN

PROLOGUE

Sophie rubbed the sleep from her eyes and stepped out of bed. The creaking of the wooden floorboards didn't wake Daisy, her rescue calico, who was curled up on Sam's pillow and seemed to be in the midst of a glorious dream. Coffee was first on Sophie's agenda. She pulled her robe up over her shoulders, looped the belt, and gave Daisy a rub on the head, at which the cat stretched and jumped off the bed with a thud. Sophie touched the indent on Sam's pillow and lay back down, placing her head next to where his warm pillow lay, convincing herself that Sam had just gotten up to make breakfast, or had just left for work.

Time ticked on, and the pillow became cold and damp from the tears that now covered the case. Daisy became impatient and began to meow until Sophie sat up once again. "All right, I'm coming. You'll get your breakfast."

In the kitchen, she selected the strongest blend and watched the steaming liquid fill her owl mug. Feeling the warmth of the cup in her hands and tasting the creamy sweetness temporarily washed away the ache that was building deep inside, helping her to relax for just a moment before facing the reality of this dreadful day. *Just put one foot in front of the other, Sophie.* She could hear Sam whispering in her ear, "One step at a time, Soph. You can do this; I'm with you." *Easier said than done; one sip at a time is more like it.*

Sophie rubbed her finger around the rim of the cup, recalling when Sam had given it to her. With a glimmer in his eyes and a sheepish grin on his face, he'd handed her the mug and said, "Whooo loves you, baby?" *You do, Samuel Anderson, you do.*

"Happy Anniversary, Sam," she whispered as tears dripped into the hollow of her neck, dampening the worn terry cloth robe that had become her best friend. The air was suffocating and closing in around her—tightening her lungs and strangling her resolve to make it through the day. Daisy wrapped herself around Sophie's leg as she slid to the floor and sobbed. *I'm sorry, Sam.* Daisy stepped into her lap, then stood with her paws on Sophie's chest, looking into her eyes as if to say, "I'm here, it's going to be okay." Animals always seemed to know the perfect time to comfort their humans. She stroked Daisy's fur between the teardrops that moistened the cat's back.

At last, Sophie wiped the tears from her cheeks. "Daisy, we need to get moving. Time's a-wasting, and we have important things to do today." She picked Daisy up, stood, and nuzzled noses with the cat before setting her down and making her way back to her bedroom, with Daisy leading the way.

Sophie opened the closet door and closed her eyes, deeply inhaling Sam's scent. She selected a sleeveless A-line dress with a sweetheart neckline and an overlay of lace in Sam's favorite color, which matched the blue in her eyes. He'd called them pools that he wanted to dive into, but right now, they were nothing but drained and empty. She slipped on her heels and made her way back to the kitchen.

While Sophie waited for her dearest friend, Emily, to pick her up, she refilled her coffee and stared out the kitchen window, watching the carefree life flittering around her bird feeders. In the distance sat the wrought iron love seat her mother had purchased for them a year ago. He'd placed it in numerous spots, never losing patience, until Sophie had been completely satisfied with its location. She recalled the many times they'd sat there listening to crickets and watching the moon reflecting on the water. She'd laid her head on his shoulder, and they'd talked about their future children running around catching lightning bugs. *Some things were never meant to be*, she thought sadly.

There was a hesitant knock at the kitchen door. Emily gently opened it, standing there with an unsure expression on her face and a hesitation that was completely out of character.

"Are you ready, Sophie?"

Sophie pushed the look of sympathy aside, set down her cup, and grabbed her purse, which she'd filled with tissues. "As ready as I'll ever be."

The church was about a five-minute drive along the shore road, but it seemed like an eternity. As she rode past the Simpsons' home, she could see the farmer's porch that Sam had built the previous summer. He'd spent hours drawing plans and tirelessly laboring in the heat until it had met his high standards. When he'd come home that day, Sophie couldn't wait for him to show her the finished project. She'd

avoided looking until he was done because he enjoyed showing projects to her himself. He'd puffed out his chest, and with
a broad grin, and stretched out his arms with a resounding
"ta-da." Seeing his proud smile was what she'd lived for. What
she wouldn't give to see it one more time. She swallowed the
lump forming in her throat.

The sunlight hitting the windshield was a blessing, allowing her to wear her sunglasses, which would hide the tears
that still flowed intermittently. Sophie took in the aroma of
daffodils and white, pink, and purple hyacinth that lined the
circular drive of the church entrance. It was quite fitting that
purple hyacinths would be in bloom here, she thought as she
recalled their meaning: *sorrow for a wrong committed.*

Emily glanced at Sophie and nodded. *It's time.* Sophie
collected herself, straightening her dress, which she was sure
most would deem inappropriate for the occasion. Her mother
had reassured her that Sam would like it, and that was all that
mattered. She wished more than anything that her mother
could be with her, today of all days. A gathering of family,
friends, and members of the community awaited her arrival.
She was grateful that she had Emily. Sophie looked at her for
support as Emily took her hand and gave it a squeeze. *One step
at a time, Soph...one step at a time.*

Sophie wobbled as they made their way down the cobblestone walkway, and Emily embraced her a little tighter.
They were greeted with sad eyes, a touch on the shoulder, and
a shake of the head as they made their way into the church.
Sophie's heart raced as she walked down the center aisle,
approaching her beloved. *One step at a time, I'm almost there.*
Then, Emily guided her to the front row and she was able to
take a seat.

How could it be that they had just been planning their tenth-anniversary getaway, and now she was facing the very same altar where they'd vowed to love one another until death, sitting amongst a sea of friends yet feeling utterly alone?

Music echoed off the cathedral ceiling, and Sophie felt the vibration in the pit of her stomach until Mr. Templeton got up to say a few words and others followed suit. She watched each person speak of her husband with words of tenderness and love. She could see their mouths moving, but she couldn't hear them. She was lost in her own thoughts, remembering walking down the aisle, surrounded by smiling faces as Sam waited for her at the altar, beaming with delight. He had been so handsome standing there with his boutonniere, rocking his feet from heel to toe. He always did that when he got excited, as if trying to resist the impulse to leap with joy—he took her breath away.

A slow, rhythmic strum of guitar strings snapped her back to the present. Within moments, a multitude of voices were singing "Amazing Grace." Sophie sat stoically looking straight ahead with her hands clasped on her lap. A soaked tissue was within her grasp, but there would be no more tears; she was empty and simply prayed that this day would soon be over and she'd wake up from this living nightmare called death.

Chapter 1

Sophie woke to the beeping sound of a delivery truck backing up her driveway. Knowing lemon cake for the Parishes' five-tiered wedding cake was on her partner's agenda for the day, and having lain in bed half the night, staring at the ceiling beating herself up, she'd decided she might as well dress and head downstairs to the shop. Normally, their delivery guy would let himself in, but she hadn't been much help to Emily since Sam's death, and she thought a little bit of mindless work would keep her nagging thoughts at bay.

Emily Vassure had been Sophie's friend since childhood. Proposals, a dream come true, wouldn't exist without her persistence and positive attitude. Emily had a sweet tooth and the ability to satisfy her cravings by making decadent pastries and cakes with the perfect amount of whimsy, sophistication, romance and beauty that tasted as good as they looked. Sophie's passion for gardening had flourished into beautiful blooms and arrangements that were the envy of every bride-to-be and were featured in bridal magazines up and down the East Coast. It had only seemed reasonable to partner up and create Proposals.

Sophie and Sam had purchased the run-down Victorian with panoramic views of the Atlantic, situated in the quaint village of York, Maine, within a mix of historic homes and shops. Sam had painstakingly rehabbed the home, restoring its original charm, and Sophie had contributed by revitalizing the long-neglected gardens with shrubs, evergreens, and lush flowers that surrounded the freshly painted beauty. Winding pathways, fountains, and secret places to escape gave the home a life of its own. There was a vast attached studio that had at one time contained an antique shop. It hadn't taken long for Sophie and Emily to realize that Proposals should and would be born there. With all she'd been through, Sophie was fortunate that she had Proposals to take her mind off her problems.

It was still a bit dark, as dawn hadn't quite arrived, and it had been raining profusely, which only added to Sophie's down mood. She placed the bulk of the delivery in the walk-in cooler, set the crate of lemons on the counter, and flicked off the lights. She was making her way back to the main house when she saw Emily's headlights cutting through the darkness.

Sophie held back, unsure if she wanted to make her presence known. Emily had a way of making her think and talk, and right now, she simply wanted to *be*.

She watched as Emily pulled into her usual space behind Proposals. She flicked on her overhead light in search of something, then dashed out of the car, stepped around the puddle at the back door, and stretched to reach the landing so she wouldn't soak her flats. As she entered the kitchen, Sophie could hear her inhale deeply; the aroma of lemon was palpable.

"Amen. Thank you, Lord, for small favors," Emily said with relief.

Thank you, Lord, for small favors is right, Sophie thought, realizing that she needed her best friend.

"It smells amazing in here, doesn't it?"

Emily jumped at the sound of Sophie's unexpected voice next to her. "Holy crap, Soph, you about gave me a heart attack. What are you doing here?"

"Couldn't sleep. I figured I could give you a hand. The Parish wedding, right?"

"Yep." Emily turned on the lights and removed her rain jacket. "Hey, wash up and grab a lemon. You can take some stress out on the juicer. It's always worked for me."

Sophie nodded in agreement. She washed and dried her hands, removed an apron from its hook, and waited for instruction.

Emily threw Sophie a pair of prep gloves and motioned toward the counter, then began pulling the ingredients from the shelves. "Fresh lemon zest and fresh-squeezed juice were a must. We need to prep enough for the center lemon-curd-and-buttercream frosting as well. Oh, and can you cut some mint sprigs and daisies as an added touch for my masterpiece?"

"You just think you're something else, don't you, Emily Vassure?" Sophie said with a slight giggle that seemed almost foreign to her.

"Why, yes, I do…I am the master!" She curtsied toward Sophie and the invisible audience. "Anything specific that kept you up? Anything you want to talk about?" Emily strained some seeds out of the juice.

"Slippery little buggers, aren't they?" Sophie stated, hoping to change the subject.

"Yes, but I am smarter than the average lemon seed and I shall be victorious!" She used the back of her gloved hand to wipe a squirt of spray that had gone to the outer corner of her eye.

They quietly worked together for quite some time, and Sophie's attempts to leave her thoughts behind while doing busywork were unsuccessful. She couldn't escape the weight of the knowledge that clung to her chest. The sound of Sam's last words to her rolled through her mind over and over like a broken record. "Anything for you, buttercup. You know I'd do anything for you." Sophie realized that she'd been holding her breath when she heard herself break the silence.

"I was thinking that if I'd had my tires rotated like he always told me to do each time I got my oil changed, we would have known we had a bad tire, and he wouldn't have gotten a flat and he'd still be alive."

"Wow, I can see why you couldn't sleep with all that guilt resting on your shoulders. Soph, we've gone over this a million times. Please don't do this to yourself. You know it's not your fault."

"Or, if I hadn't had him pick up the dried roses I'd ordered, he wouldn't have been there then. I could have had them shipped. But, no, I had him pick them up because I wanted to save a few bucks! He died because I wanted to save money, Emily!"

"He was already going to the city and he'd be right near there anyway. He offered, Soph." Emily stepped toward her dear friend, and Sophie fell apart in her arms.

"Don't you see, Em?" Sophie sniffed and wiped her cheeks. "He was picking…up…dried…white roses," she said with a quivering lip.

"Okay," Emily said inquisitively.

"Dried white roses mean…great sorrow! I brought this on myself." The weeping continued to the point of exhaustion. Emily guided her to the chaise in the back office.

"Sophie, you're tired. Why don't you lie down for a little bit? I'll get you a cup of tea and you can get some sleep." Emily left her to rest.

Sophie knew that Emily's heart was in the right place, but a cup of tea wouldn't soothe the ache that consumed her. Sam was gone, and it was her fault. Hearing that it wasn't, over and over again, didn't change a thing.

She heard the hum of the microwave circling as the tray turned, then the clink of the spoon hitting the inside of the cup as the sugar was being stirred. She recalled the infinite number of times that Sam had emerged from the kitchen with a cup of tea for her, perfectly prepared, just the way she liked it.

Sam had been a coffee drinker, which was fine by her as well, in the morning. For comfort, tea was her preference. Oh, how she wished that tea would make it all better—that she'd be able to sleep again, that she'd dream a beautiful dream and wake up with Sam on his side of the bed. Waking up was the hardest part. Facing another day without him was almost more than she could bear.

Sophie looked up as Emily gingerly approached with tea in hand.

"It's a bit too full," Emily said as she gently handed it over. Sophie took the cup and blew on the steam.

"Do you think they'll ever catch the person who did it?"

"Sure. They at least know what the car looks like, don't they?"

"Presumably, but who knows? I've been told that eye-witnesses are wrong about seventy-five percent of the time. Seventy-five percent!"

"I hear you. I really do, but didn't you say that this person seemed really confident?"

"Yes, but just because they say something confidently doesn't make it true. I just can't figure out what could be taking so long." Sophie sipped the hot tea, and her shoulders relaxed just a bit.

"They'll get him, you wait and see. For now, though, I have a cake to bake, and you have to get some sleep."

CHAPTER 2

Brady Owens would, by all accounts, be living the dream—
except for the fact that it wasn't his dream he was living. His
father had bigger ideas for him, and running the family's
construction business wasn't good enough for his only son.
Brady had been strongly encouraged to study law and make
something of himself. Right out of law school, Brady had
obtained a position as a low-level corporate attorney for a
small law firm. After a while, he'd convinced himself that his
father had been right and had thus put everything he had into
his career and his future. Before long, he was working as a
criminal attorney at the law offices of Lockwood & Hurst; it
was the place to be, smack-dab in the middle of Manhattan
and surrounded by a feast of clients. Brady was lucky to have
scored such a position at the firm, and being named partner
was surely in his future.

He wrapped the tie that Cynthia, his girlfriend, had
given him around his neck and tucked it under his crisp white

collar. Brady nodded his approval in the mirror as the knot slid to just the right spot. He carefully collected the jacket that he'd draped over the edge of the bed, then ran out the door and down the steps of his Midtown apartment. Brady grabbed a coffee at the corner before heading to his BMW, which was parked in his reserved spot, thanks to some perks from Lockwood & Hurst, and headed to work.

Traffic in the city was a typical mad dash to go, only to grind to a standstill. Brady's mind wandered, and he thought about where his life had taken him.

He was unhappy and underwhelmed with his career choice, but he'd worked too hard to get this far to walk away now. He resigned himself to sticking it out and making a success of it. He only had himself to blame—and the drop-dead gorgeous, knee-weakening woman that he'd *had* to get to know better.

He'd seen Cynthia often at the firm, and he'd finally gotten her attention at a company event. He was a charmer, and it came easily to him. Turning their heads—making them take notice—was natural. It was the keeping them part that he found more challenging. Cynthia Lockwood was no exception.

She was a woman of stature and prominence, not to mention stunning. Her long blond strands, sun-kissed skin, and deep green eyes would pull him in and make him take leave of his senses. Discovering that she was Henry Lockwood's daughter only made her more intriguing.

Brady's artistic side appreciated great beauty. The lines of a face, the curve of a hip, the slope of a bare shoulder were works of art to be respected and savored. He longed to take her picture, but that was a past-life hobby and this was now. To attain the prize of Cynthia Lockwood, he had to be a powerful, in-control, top-of-the-ladder kind of man. Most importantly, Daddy's little girl needed the approval of her father, and Brady was determined to gain that approval.

He approached the elevator and smiled with self-assurance as he pushed the button for the top floor. When he stepped out, Henry Lockwood sat behind a mahogany desk trimmed with gold leaf and leather. Most men would appear small behind the impressive desk, but Henry filled the space, exuding power and dominance. The impeccable space on the top of the desk would lead anyone to believe that nothing ever actually happened there, but Lockwood only needed to pick up a phone to make magic happen. His underlings did the work; Brady was one such underling.

As Brady approached, Lockwood peered over his wire-rimmed glasses and gestured for him to have a seat. Brady sank in the massive leather high-back chair, and his heart raced. The look on Lockwood's face robbed him of his confidence, and he waited with anticipation as to why he'd been summoned to the top floor.

"Owens, I have a case that is, let's say, very sensitive in nature and it needs my undivided attention right now. I need you to take over the Bishop case for me while I deal with the matter. As you know, Stevens can assist. He's already up to speed."

Brady swallowed hard and wiped away the moisture that was starting to form on his hands. He'd heard rumors about what a prick Bishop was as a client; winning the case would solidify Brady's standing with the firm.

"Yes, sir."

"That'll be all," Lockwood said, peering over the top rim of his glasses.

Brady stood up to leave but hesitated at the door. He'd mustered up as much confidence as possible, though his pulse was quickening and his nerves were nearly visible.

"Mr. Lockwood, I'll give it my best. You can count on it."

. . .

Cynthia poured herself another glass of wine and leaned over Brady's shoulders while he thumbed through the files. He wished she had just stayed home so that he could focus. The Bishop case was coming along nicely, and he was satisfied that he'd pull off the impossible. He could see light at the end of the tunnel, much to his relief. Bishop was guilty of insider trading and money laundering; of that, Brady had no doubt. But there was a chance that they'd come away with a not-guilty verdict, and he hoped he'd found it. He just had a few loose ends to tie up and he'd be ready for court.

"Why do you always have to be working?"

"Because it's what your father expects me to do, and we want your father to be happy, right?"

"I can't wait until your stupid case is over," she whined. "Daddy would understand that you need to spend time with his baby girl, now wouldn't he?" she said with a little whispery voice much like Marilyn Monroe's. It used to drive him wild; now it only grated on him. She'd become increasingly overbearing, possessive, and just plain off over the past few weeks; she'd changed, and not for the better.

"Cynthia, I have to finish this." Brady pushed back his chair with a swivel and faced Cynthia's pouting lips that quickly turned into a seductive grin before she leaned in for a kiss, sloshing the merlot over the edge of the rim, which caused her to giggle and stagger forward, barely missing at least the bulk of case files on his desk.

"Dammit." Brady scrambled to keep the stacks dry. "I don't have time for this," he said under his breath.

"You don't have time for what? Me? You'd miss me if I wasn't here, you know."

"Seriously, Cyn, I can't do this right now. I'm back in court tomorrow, and I have to get this done."

"Oh, I am serious, Braaady. You'd miss me." She downed the rest of the glass and sobbed while flopping on the sofa with excessive drama.

Brady set aside his laptop and tried to brace himself for another *you wouldn't understand* conversation. He slid his hand underneath her disheveled hair and brushed her bangs back to see her eyes, softening his words and slowing his anger, hoping to de-escalate the situation.

"What are you talking about, Cyn? What's going on?"

Cynthia turned her eyes away and bit her lower lip. "Daddy said everything will be okay, but I'm not so sure."

He pulled a tissue out of the box on the end table and handed it to Cynthia. "Tell me about it."

"Now you're just being condescending. You know how I hate that. Just forget I ever said anything." Hiccups surfaced along with the tears. She stood up to leave but lost her balance and fell back on the sofa with such force that it appeared the room had moved beneath her.

"I'm sorry. Why don't you just start from the beginning?"

"I can't." Another hard hiccup rose from her chest, and she pressed her hand to her temple.

"How can I help you if you don't tell me what's bothering you?" Again, she was quiet. His patience was wearing thin, and he needed to alleviate the problem. Otherwise, it was going to be a long night. "Cyn, I would suggest that you either tell me, or just go home and we can talk about it another time, when you're feeling better."

"You're not listening to me, Brady. I can't talk about it."

"Then why did you even bring it up in the first place? This is nuts." Running his fingers through his hair, he paced the den. Between his job, which was quickly sucking the life out of him, and Cynthia's erratic behavior, he'd had quite enough.

"You're right." Cynthia stumbled to her feet. "I've got to get the hell out of here." She seized her handbag off the entry table and fumbled for her keys.

Her hands shook while tears streamed down her face.

"Cyn, I'll take you home."

They made their way to his car, and she slid quietly into the bucket seat. Rain pounded on the windshield, and he tightened his grip. The sound lulled Cynthia to a drowsy sleep. Thirty minutes later, they were pulling into the entrance of the boss's estate, driving through the vestibule and into the back. Situated among well-manicured gardens was Cynthia's private guesthouse. The rain slowed as a fog arose to engulf the entry. He helped her to her feet and escorted her to her bed. He removed her shoes, silky sheath dress, and hair clip before he gently guided her to her pillow. There was a time when he thought he'd had a future with her, but seeing her lying among the billowing down of satin sheets, he only felt pity for her. He, too, had made this same kind of bed. A bed of self-pity and dreams of something better.

He covered her beautiful frame. "Good night, Cyn."

"Night, Brady. I'm sorry I couldn't—"

"Just get some sleep." He picked up her clothes and draped them over the ottoman, turned off the light, and retreated into the fog, headed for home.

. . .

Brady sat staring at the Bishop case files and the blotches of merlot. He stroked the scowl lines between his eyes and tried to focus, but thoughts of Cynthia kept creeping their way into his mind. He poured himself what was left of the wine. Deep notes of plum slid down easily. He licked the sweetness off his lips and tried to wrap his brain around what was happening with her. She'd always been high-maintenance and demanding, but in a managed, assertive kind of way. If he didn't know better, he'd almost think she'd become a bit unstable. He wrestled with that idea, then concluded that it was just his own pent-up frustrations. Something has got to change.

Morning came much too early. Brady stopped at Starbucks on the corner of Lexington and East Forty-Eighth Street for an espresso. *Caffeine, have your way with me.* He still couldn't get the drama with Cynthia out of his mind, and it had meddled with his subconscious throughout the night. She'd been so clingy, which wasn't in her nature, and the heavy drinking was completely out of character. At least, it had been until a few weeks ago. There was no doubt about it; he had to get to the bottom of what was going on with her.

But for now, his focus had to be on the Bishop case. He hoped to get accolades from Lockwood and climb up another rung on the ladder, and in doing so, he'd have more say in his future. A future that would make his job bearable. He'd hoped for a Hail Mary, or anything that would serve as his client's get-out-of-jail-free card, but he had his doubts.

Soon, Bishop's destiny would be out of his hands. If he could only shake the uneasy feeling of dread.

This day in court proceeded without too many interruptions and objections. He had done his best to prepare for the closing arguments; now all they could do was wait for the jury to reach their verdict.

The break was brief, which boosted his confidence. He, Stevens, and Bishop stood, and all eyes were on the foreman as each verdict was read.

"We the jury find the defendant, Reginald James Bishop, guilty." Those words were repeated for each count; Brady's body temperature rose, and nausea commenced. *Guilty on every count! No…damn it!* The courtroom roared with approval. The gavel pounded on the bench repeatedly.

"Order in the court!"

Bishop looked at Brady with contempt. "What the hell happened, Owens?" Before Brady had a chance to respond, Bishop was cuffed and removed from the courtroom.

. . .

Lockwood summoned Brady to the upper floor. The elevator climbed slowly. With each passing level, his heart rate increased. He could swear the pounding in his chest was audible. He kept his eyes straight ahead to avoid seeing the looks of pity he was confident were coming from those in the crowded compartment. The smell of spicy cologne mixed with new carpet and shoe polish made his stomach turn, and he couldn't get out fast enough. He made it to the men's room in time to splash cold water on his face, pull a few sheets of paper from the wall dispenser to dry his dripping brow and regroup. *Man up, Owens, for God's sake.* He shook off the debacle and entered Lockwood's office, trusting that he'd done everything he could to win but had fallen short. It just hadn't been in the cards this time. Lockwood would have to understand.

"Owens, what you showed in that courtroom was nothing short of brilliant!" *Brilliant? That's it, I made the man go insane.* "You pulled it off, my boy!" Lockwood patted him on the back with such force that it nearly brought up his lunch.

"I'm confused, sir. I lost."

"Damn right, you did, Owens. We've been wanting to get rid of Bishop for some time now. The partners have been, let's say…not pleased with the riffraff that he's been pushing on our firm, but we couldn't just refuse him because he'd ruin us. You see, Owens, between you, me, and this chair here, he owned us. We couldn't have done it without you, my boy. We built you up to be the best closer we had, and he trusted you. And he was smart to trust you. You nearly pulled it off a win."

Brady's mind reeled with the realization that he'd been played. The good old boys had used him. They'd bent him over hard.

"Don't you see? It had to look good…as if we could actually win. That way, Bishop and his cronies wouldn't think we were trying to get rid of them. I knew you were the man for the job, and you didn't let me down." Lockwood gave him a full-handed pat on the back. "You're going places, Owens."

The only place he wanted to be going was out. Out of Lockwood's sight, and out of this wretched profession that he'd begrudgingly found himself in.

. . .

Brady couldn't get his suit off fast enough. He felt strangled by it. Each button was suffocating. Brady threw his tie across the bed, dropped his pants on the floor, and pulled off each sock. Wadding them into balls and shooting them into the hamper had become a daily ritual, but today he did it with such force that the lid fell before the second shot. Those bastards used me! What the hell! They knew I'd fail but make it look good! That's messed up. He had to get out of here. Even his bedroom felt like a prison. He threw on his running clothes to relieve some stress. He opened the door, flew down the stairs, and accelerated his pace until he broke into a sweat. No warmup, just pure uninhibited abandonment, and it was liberating. The escape was just what he needed to clear his mind of this day.

. . .

Brady entered his apartment with a huff. He was sucking air and rested his hands on his knees to catch his breath when he realized that Cynthia had let herself in. He glanced around the room and assumed that she must be in the bathroom as she was nowhere in sight.

Water was boiling on the stove and shrimp were in cold water thawing. The table was set, candles were lit, and the room appeared dim in an effort to set the mood, with Mary J. Blige playing in the background. It wasn't the first time she'd done something like this, but this time he was in no mood for it, not even remotely. He'd hoped that the run would lessen his anger, but it hadn't. However, with the aroma of tossed veggies simmering, he could feel his stomach roll with hunger. He hadn't eaten all day due to the hectic trial and its aftermath.

It was nice to see that Cynthia had made such an effort for him. She'd been so self-absorbed for quite a while, and he hoped that she'd turned a corner.

A moment later, Cynthia burst into the room, wearing a low-back slinky dress. She was beaming ear to ear and ran to him for an embrace. "You're all sweaty...but that's okay." Cynthia picked up the dishcloth to wipe her hands, then quickly picked up the bottle of Sauvignon Blanc and shouted, "Congratulations!"

"For what?" Brady shook his head in disbelief, trying to make sense of her jubilation.

"I heard through the grapevine that Daddy was ecstatic about the trial today, and I wanted to give my Brady a proper congratulations."

Brady clenched his jaw, closed his eyes for a moment without saying a word, and proceeded to the bathroom.

The barrier of the door between them allowed him the space he needed. *The whole damn family is certifiable. I lost a client's case, and they're happy. What part of the real world does that happen in? I was manipulated and used, and that's a reason for celebration?* Brady turned on the shower and stepped inside, hoping that the water could wash away the filth that clung to him like a shroud.

He hadn't been in there for five minutes when Cynthia pushed the bathroom door open with her hip, the bottle of wine and two glasses in her hands. "Can I join you?"

"Cynthia, I can't do this right now. I've had a crappy day and I just need time by myself."

"But I made you dinner to celebrate," she whined.

"Celebrate what, Cynthia? The fact that your father treats me like his puppet?" He stepped out and slammed the glass door as water dripped off his body onto the floor.

"You're scaring me, Brady. Why don't you calm down and have a drink?"

"Calm down!"

"You're a hero at the firm. Daddy said that you sent a client away. It's unusual, I know…but this time, that's a good thing. Why are you acting like this?"

Brady's eyes went wide, and he shook his head. "I'm done. I've had enough of this heinous job. I hate it, Cynthia!" He knew he looked like a madman, standing naked and shouting at the top of his lungs.

"Don't you think you're overreacting?"

"You think I'm overreacting? You don't know the first thing about what your manipulative father puts me through every day. He's manic, Cyn. The man is sick!"

"So he bends the rules and uses the law to his favor. That doesn't make him sick; it makes him smart."

Brady wrapped a towel around his waist, ran his hand through his tangled wet hair, grabbed the bottle of wine, and stormed out of the bathroom.

"Just sit down and let me feed the bear. Okay?"

"I really can't do this anymore. It's not who I am. It's not what I want."

"Just relax, Brady, and let me make you feel better."

She pushed him into the dining room chair and opened his towel to reveal his manhood. Then she lifted her dress and climbed on, straddling his muscular legs. His mouth found hers and the feel of her warm tongue combined with his sweetness from the wine made him harden. She began to churn until his fullness entered her. Their breathing became heavy as he loosened the straps on her dress to reveal her succulent breasts. His mouth moved toward her enticing hardened nipples. She moaned with approval and arched her back to make his task easier. Taking hold of her hips, he moved her in rhythm. *No…no…no. I don't want this.* He was being played again.

"Stop."

She continued her pleasure to nearly a climax, then he pulled her off him.

"Brady, I wasn't done," she cried, trying to pull him closer.

"But I am, Cynthia. This isn't going to happen; not anymore."

"You don't mean that, Brady. Why don't you just be a good boy and let's finish what we started? You know you want to." Her whining and impertinence set him off once again.

"Apple doesn't fall far from the tree, now does it? What do you want from me?" He could barely contain his rage. "Do you want my potential? Does Daddy see me going places, and you want in on that?"

"Look here, Brady. You got exactly what you asked for: a position at my father's firm, a nice car, this place, and you even got me. Why are you making me out to be the bad guy here?"

"Honestly, Cyn, I don't even know anymore. All I do know is that I don't want this." He flailed his arms around to indicate everything around him. "You're right, I did ask for this. But I was wrong. I'm not happy." As he sat back down on the chair, he once again wrapped the towel around himself. "I'm not this kind of guy, Cyn. I'm pissed all the time and I hate it."

"You don't think we all have problems and hate life once in a while? The difference is that I know what I want and I'm not ashamed to say it." Cynthia's voice grew louder. "I want an insane amount of money, a gigantic house, a sweet car, and you." She pulled up her dress, tied the straps behind her neck, and turned off the stove. "Hell, I even want a cook! You're ruining everything, Brady!"

"We never had anything to begin with. It was all a ruse, Cynthia, and I even deceived myself." Cynthia gathered her keys and purse and readied to leave, and Brady walked away.

Her cell phone rang. "Hello, this is Cynthia." There was a long pause as Brady reentered in his sweats. "Yes, I understand," Cynthia continued with a concerned expression and hushed voice. "Have you spoken to my father, Henry Lockwood?" Cynthia's face flushed as she paced back and forth. Her fingernails found their way to her mouth and she bit her cuticles with a nervous energy. "I hear what you're saying, but you're not getting it. You have nothing on me. As my father has already stated and will state again, you have no evidence." Cynthia sat on the couch, listening intently to the voice on the other end of the receiver. "Am I going to be under arrest? No, I didn't think so. So, Detective, don't you ever call me again. If you have anything further to say, you can say it to my attorney." Cynthia hit the End button on her phone and then threw it at the wall, shattering it into pieces.

"Whoa, what the hell was that all about?"

"I killed somebody, okay! But it'll be all right, because Daddy will take care of it."

Silence filled the room, during which Brady's mouth opened and shut several times, before he finally muttered, "God almighty, Cynthia. You can't come out with, um, 'I killed somebody' and expect it to come off as though you... oh, I don't know, forgot to pay a traffic ticket! How? When?"

"Remember when we had that fight a couple months ago about you not wanting to move in with me?"

"Yes, so?"

"Well, when I left your apartment, I was heartbroken, Brady. So, I met up with one of my friends at her place, and I had a drink or two, or I guess a few…I don't know. Anyway, I got confused driving out of the city. So, I was putting information into my GPS. I didn't see him there. I looked up just as I hit him. He hit the front of my car and then my windshield. He must have been changing his tire or something."

"Did you call an ambulance or anything?"

"Of course. I called my dad."

"Your dad!" Brady was baffled. "Well, did you stop to see if he was okay?"

"Just long enough to see that I might have killed him. So, I got back in my car and left. No one else was there. I mean, what are the odds of that? So, who'd ever know, right?" she said matter-of-factly.

Brady threw his hands up in disbelief. "You just left him to die?"

"What else was I supposed to do? Besides, I don't know why you're so upset with me anyway. It was your fault," she said with a deadpan expression.

"My fault! You're blaming me for this?"

"Yes. If you hadn't gotten me so upset, I wouldn't have had too much to drink, and—"

"Oh, no, you don't, Cynthia. It is your fault—not mine, yours—and you need to make this right."

"Brady, I can't get caught. Don't you see? Daddy's reputation is at stake, and I don't want to go to jail," Cynthia stated with an eerie calm.

"Why didn't you tell me about this? I mean, was I hiding under a rock or something? How could I not have known that something this horrible had happened?"

"What good would it have done, Brady?"

He considered everything she'd been saying. He recalled when she'd asked him to drive her around because she hated paying to ride with strangers. Surely her car had to have evidence of damage. "Where's your car?"

"I reported it stolen. I can't believe you don't remember that."

"Right...where is it, then?" He was afraid of her response.

"Daddy had it taken to some salvage dump on the docks. I think it was somewhere on or near Long Island. I don't really know for sure." She waved it off as if were irrelevant.

"Do you hear yourself?" *That's it...the whole damn family is certifiable.* "Don't you even care about the poor man that you killed? Or have you even thought about his family?"

"What good will it do? It won't change anything."

"Cynthia, I think we should call it a day today, and every day after. I'm going to give my notice, and I think I need to head out of the city for a while."

"But we can't. I was told that I can't leave the city."

"Not you and me, Cyn. Just me."

"You can't mean that!"

"Oh, yes, I can." It was the most sure he'd been about anything in months. A sudden peace washed over him, and he was resolute in his decision.

"No...you can't. What do you want me to do? Whatever it is, just tell me, Brady. I'll do anything. Don't you see? I need you!"

"I'll tell you what you can do. You can confess to killing

that poor man. If you want me, Cynthia, then make things right. Confess."

. . .

Brady paced in his apartment, tossing his phone up in the air and catching it over and over. He knew she wouldn't confess; deep down he knew. She only looked out for herself, and he was confident that her father certainly wouldn't "allow" her to do that.

He cursed at himself for getting wrapped up with the Lockwoods. He'd let money and power go to his head, something that he'd never desired. Now, with one phone call, he'd be throwing it all away. Thinking back, he realized that he'd wanted to make his dad proud, but the angry man he'd become certainly wouldn't have been what his father wanted.

He sat down and stared at the number he'd punched into his phone. There would be no going back once he hit Send. Everything he'd worked for and accomplished would be thrown away, but he knew this was the right thing to do— the only thing to do. Besides, maybe, just maybe, it could be the best thing to happen to him. He'd been unhappy for a long time anyway, he concluded.

Brady tapped his finger, which dialed the number of his buddies at the precinct. Within moments, he was transferred to Detective Sykes. Because of his position at Lockwood & Hurst, as well as his relationship with Cynthia, he was able to convince the detective to keep his information confidential. Brady told him that she'd confessed to killing a man and had added some additional details that filled in the blanks.

Sykes shared how Cynthia Lockwood had reacted when they'd initially brought her into the precinct. She'd denied that anything had happened. They'd even told her that they had a witness who'd identified her vehicle leaving the scene, but all she'd done was shout about how she'd sue them and demand that they call her father.

"Yeah, that sounds like her," Brady interjected.

Sykes continued, "Lockwood came into the precinct like he ruled the place." Brady imagined Lockwood with his height, broad chest and barrel-like midsection filling the room. He'd seen it before and knew it could be intimidating, but knowing Sykes like he did, Brady was confident that he had stood his ground. "He said we didn't have any grounds to hold her. He bellowed it through the whole precinct. You should have seen it. We even told him that we had a witness. He went on about not having proof that it was in fact her car or that she was the one driving it, because her car had been reported stolen. He was right, Brady. We didn't have anything to hold her on, and they left."

"Damn," Brady acknowledged.

"I kicked my chair and it broke and splintered beyond repair. I about broke my damn foot. I swear I could hear her laugh echoing the whole way down the hallway. I don't know how the hell you live with that."

"Me neither, Sykes. Me neither."

Detective Sykes suggested they tell her they had additional credible information, which wasn't a total bluff, as they'd located her vehicle. They hoped it would convince her to confess. Brady hung up, feeling relieved yet anxious, knowing a shitstorm was about to take place.

CHAPTER 3

Two months had passed since Sam's death, and wedding season was still in full swing. Proposals needed her, and the distraction was welcome. She was sick of acting like a victim. She had never been the type to feel sorry for herself, but unfortunately, she'd allowed it to happen.

Sophie set up a production line of pink and white peonies and garden roses, lilies of the valley, ivy, and satin ribbon. Carefully arranging each stem for the upcoming shabby chic wedding in Boston required mindless concentration. The meaning behind each bloom that went into the cascades of beauty brought her comfort and a sense of purpose. Ivy for fidelity, love, and affection. White roses for purity and innocence. Pink for grace, admiration, and joy. Sophie inhaled the scent of the lilies with longing. *Return of happiness*. The meaning cast a sense of melancholy on the task at hand, to which she'd become quite accustomed.

Sophie's cell phone rang in the pocket of her apron,

startling her. *Dammit.* Pruning shears and jumping unexpectedly didn't go well together. Juggling to answer the phone with one hand while catching the droplets of blood dripping from her fingertip in the other was a challenge at best.

"Hello, this is Sophie." She stuck her finger into her mouth to suck out the sting of the cut and stop the flow. The voice on the other side brought her to a sobering halt. "Jackson?"

"Yes, Mrs. Anderson, it's Jackson," he said, his tone sounding serious. This call was different than the usual updates of non-information. Sophie's pulse quickened, and her armpits quickly turned moist. "Sophie, we've found her."

The room started to whirl, and she found a stool to sit on. *Her?*

"Really? Who is it? Where is she? What did she say?" All the waiting, wondering, and hoping was coming to a head. She paced in her small space, excited to hear the answers.

"We're still getting the details, but she confessed to the hit-and-run. An anonymous tip was called in. It's over, Sophie. Sam will get justice."

An anonymous tip, she pondered. There were still good people in the world, she thought, wishing she could thank the person who'd turned the woman in. The momentary excitement ushered in a dash of loss. The closer they were to justice, the closer she would be to moving on with her life. She'd counted the days until they caught the person who'd changed her life forever. Now it was all happening too fast. She wasn't ready to move on, not yet. She still expected him to come walking through the door. The last thing she wanted was to close it... forever. She picked up the lily and inhaled deeply. *Is it possible, my love? A return of happiness?* This was just another step along her journey, and she concluded she should be grateful. They'd found Sam's killer, and she'd choose to be happy.

Sophie dialed her mom to tell her the good news, but the call went directly to voicemail. Sophie shook off her disappointment and went in search of the one person who had never let her down.

Emily was cashing out a customer in the bakery when Sophie walked in. Emily's eyebrows rose with question, and she rushed the transaction. As soon as the customer walked out the door, Emily turned to her. "You're grinning, Soph! Do you have something that you'd like to share?"

Sophie unloaded in a string of excitement. "Can you believe it, Emily?" she concluded.

Emily gave her a big hug, and they bounced around in circles like schoolchildren. The day Sophie had hoped and prayed for had finally come. The word *justice* rolled around her tongue, and the mere sound of it brought Sophie a profound sense of peace. She wanted to see this woman face-to-face, then watch her walk away in shackles.

CHAPTER 4

Sophie was grateful that her dear neighbor, Agnes Templeton, and Emily came all the way to New York with her. Having them with her for support during the courtroom proceedings was a huge blessing, but she continued to watch the door in search of her mother. Her mom was out of the country traveling and hoped that she'd make it, but Sophie quickly erased that expectation…again. She loved her mother dearly, but the woman was seldom dependable. She just wished that, for once, her mom would be with her when she needed her. Sophie swallowed the lump in her throat and gave her dear friends one more embrace.

Sophie hadn't laid eyes on Cynthia Lockwood, and the anticipation of seeing her weighed on her. She'd prayed that she would be able to keep her composure, but the closer the time came, the more anxious she became. Sophie placed her hands on her knees to keep them from shaking, which was a futile task. Adrenaline rushed through her body, and she found it hard to control the trembling.

The doors opened and there she stood: the woman who had killed her beloved Sam. Sophie had expected to see a woman full of remorse or fear, but when she entered the room, she was smiling as if she were a celebrity, clearly enjoying being the center of attention. Sophie wanted nothing more than to stand up and scream at her and tell her what a horrible human being she was, then slap the grin off her face and bash in her teeth.

"I don't understand. How could she be smiling?" she asked Agnes in a whisper. Agnes patted her hand and gave it a gentle squeeze.

As the proceedings continued, Sophie would learn more detail regarding Sam's death. The depth of depravity that Cynthia Lockwood possessed was immeasurable. Sophie pictured Sam lying in the street in pain, watching the car drive away into the night, leaving him to die. How long had he been there, alone and afraid? Sophie's lip quivered, and she fought back a wave of nausea. Agnes provided an embroidered hanky to dab her eyes while Emily placed her hand on Sophie's back and gave it a tender rub.

This can't be real, she thought. This was a bad dream, and she'd wake up any minute. But it was all too real. Her kind, sweet husband had been left to die in the street, and she would forever be alone. The words *forever alone* played over and over in her mind like a sad melody. Her tears had dried up, and she focused on seeing this through with grace and making her husband proud.

By the time the proceedings ended and the gavel came down, the woman was sobbing, about which Sophie was pleased. Seeing Cynthia Lockwood being escorted out in shackles was a vision that she hoped would stay with her for a very long time. Sam would finally have justice, and redemption was sweet. *It is done, my love. It is done.*

Agnes held Sophie's cheeks with her weathered hands and peered into her eyes to reassure her. Sophie nodded back in understanding and walked out of the courtroom with her chin up, ignoring the reporters that were clamoring for a statement. Emily shielded her friend as they made their way to the car for the long drive home.

. . .

It was a cool day on the harbor with a light sea breeze as Sophie and Emily arrived back at the house. To stretch their legs and get some fresh air, they decided to walk toward the pier, where happy people gathered. Or were they? Sophie imagined all the stories that each seemingly "happy" person might be hiding, putting on a false face for their friends to see but inside being torn apart. *Sam, I miss you.*

"Do you want to get a drink?" Emily asked to break the quiet.

"How about the coffeehouse? I'm still a bit queasy. My stomach just hasn't been that great for a while. It will be good to find a new normal and feel like myself again."

"You've had an upset stomach just about every day. Maybe you should see a doctor."

"It's just the stress of everything. It will pass. A cup of tea will help." They continued to walk without saying a word to one another until they arrived at Grounds. Steam covered the windows from the espresso machines working overtime. The aroma of coffee and vanilla beans was palpable. Music from a strumming guitar in the background helped Sophie to relax. They picked out a mug from the basket and waited their turn in line. Jillian, the owner of Grounds, stood at the counter. Her smile was contagious and instantly made them feel welcomed.

"Hey, you two! I didn't expect you here today." Jillian leaned over to give Sophie a quick hug.

"We were nearby and couldn't resist," Emily replied.

"How are things going, Sophie? I've heard through the grapevine that you've had a rough go of it."

Sophie was reserved in her response. After all, how did one convey the gravity of what had been happening? She just knew that she didn't want to see sad eyes looking back at her.

"Could be worse and could be better."

Emily jumped in to say that Proposals was doing well, thanked her for the referral, and ended the conversation.

"It's my pleasure. What can I get for you?"

Emily ordered a vanilla lavender latte, and Sophie got a large black tea and one of Emily's famous cinnamon twists, compliments of Proposals.

"Don't you ever get sick of those?" Emily asked.

Sophie could see a bit of pride in Emily's face. Her cinnamon twists were a local favorite. Crispy, flaky twists rolled up with sugary coated pecans and powdered sugar.

"Never," replied Sophie. "They've been making my tummy happy, and I need any kind of happy I can get."

"I still think you should see a doctor."

"If I'm not better in a few days, I'll make an appointment."

"Promise?"

"Pinky swear." They both let out a little giggle, something they hadn't done together since Sam had died. Sophie couldn't help but feel a bit guilty about that. *Too soon for laughs.*

CHAPTER 5

Brady sat in the spectator area, just out of view from Cynthia and her counsel so he wouldn't be noticed. Judge Stanton sat on the bench. He was a fair judge and ruled his courtroom with the dignity that one would expect. Brady couldn't help but notice the woman with long auburn hair, a porcelain complexion, and a petite build who was taking a seat behind the State's bench. As she turned her head, he could see her striking blue eyes. She was stunning, a natural beauty who didn't need makeup. The tip of her nose turned up just a bit and was red from an obvious bout of emotions. As the proceedings continued, he learned that she was Mrs. Anderson, the woman whose life Cynthia Lockwood had destroyed—the widow of the deceased, Sam Anderson.

He'd been shocked when Cynthia had initially come into the courtroom. He'd heard about people just snapping, and Cynthia certainly had. He couldn't wrap his head around her behavior and hoped beyond all hope that he had nothing to do with it. He was repulsed that he'd been involved with her for as long as he had.

The pang of guilt rose like bile in his mouth. If he did have anything to do with Cynthia's behavior and the death of that poor man…no, he wouldn't do this to himself. He wasn't to blame, and yet he still felt responsible. He'd been working too much and not paying enough attention to her. If he'd just given in about moving in together, then the auburn-haired woman would be enjoying her life with her husband right now instead of enduring the spectacle of a smiling murderer.

The proceedings continued without complication when Cynthia finally began to show an ounce of remorse. Brady soon realized, however, that her grief was for herself and not for what she'd done. She broke down in tears as she heard the crime she was being charged with: involuntary manslaughter, which carried a penalty of up to ten years in state prison and fines. Cynthia Lockwood entered a plea of guilty, and Henry Lockwood would soon lose the most important case of his life, as his daughter would, indeed, be sent to prison.

Brady weighed his options. If he was going to make the necessary changes in his life, he'd need to leave the firm, or at least take a sabbatical of sorts. Law was a noble profession, and he'd gained immeasurable influence and skill within the field. He'd earned a good reputation, which wasn't easy in that cutthroat environment. He'd made some great friends at the firm, but it just wasn't enough. He was lost, as though he was treading water in a sea of unrest, and that was the bottom line. He needed to get away—from his field, the rat race, and his volatile relationship. He needed to find peace and get back to the Brady that he'd lost along the way.

After leaving the courtroom, Brady walked until he

found himself in Central Park. He was sitting on a bench when he made his decision. He raised his eyes to the heavens. *I hope you're not too disappointed in your boy, Pops. I'm sorry that I let you down.*

. . .

The Maine coast provided Brady the opportunity to dust off his camera and test his rusty skills. He gathered up his camera bag along with a bottle of water and headed to downtown Portsmouth, New Hampshire. He sat in traffic as the drawbridge was raised. A tall ship made its way up the Piscataqua River with the help of a tugboat. Knowing he'd be there for a bit, he removed his camera from its case, stepped out of the car, and walked to the edge of the bridge to get a shot. The light cast a perfect reflection on the water. *Beautiful.* Capturing the historic buildings and the steeple of the North Church provided symmetry and context for his object.

The ease of the tug gently guiding its charge to safety gave him a sense of romance. It was a dance of gentle movements, balance, and purpose as the tug took the lead. The bones of the tall ship danced back and forth, giving the carved figurehead mounted on its bow an air of confidence and stature. He looked on with a longing for romance and purpose in his own life. As the ship made its way under the arches, he went back to the car, took a swig of water, and advanced to find a parking spot.

After collecting his belongings, he found an open bench on Market Square, tipped his head back, and closed his eyes to take in the sun. The laughter of children stirred his relaxation but provided him the perfect opportunity to capture the image of a bridal party stepping out of the North Church, directly across from where he was sitting. The bells chimed with congratulations. He zoomed in just as a kiss fell upon the forehead of the bride, causing a silhouette effect. *Priceless.* Brady continued to take shots as her bouquet twirled in the air and landed in the hands of a hopeful bridesmaid. Laughter and cheers arose from the crowd gathered around them. *Happiness, sheer unadulterated love and happiness. Oh, how I needed this day.* He looked up at the sky and thanked God for the reminder that it was possible. He'd have to remember to thank his old friend again for allowing him to stay at his nearby cottage in Cape Neddick, Maine.

After a few hours of exploring Portsmouth and getting what he thought were some great shots, he headed back up Route 1 toward his retreat. *It was a good day.*

The cottage was surrounded by other seasonal homes, with activity going on all around him and a pathway that led just a few steps away from the rocky coastline with a dock, a small boat, and a private beach. A view of the Nubble Lighthouse stood only a short distance away. He had learned that Nubble was the most photographed lighthouse in America. Seeing it for himself proved to be the perfect opportunity to try out his new purchase, a Canon Mark III.

Photography was his secret passion and had been since he could remember. His pictures were for his eyes only and had become a diary of sorts. He found it exhilarating being behind the lens, capturing moments in time that could never be repeated, and he realized he was smiling for the first time since he could remember. *This is what happiness feels like*, he thought as he clicked the shutter.

CHAPTER 6

Sophie arose early, feeling more refreshed than she'd felt in a long time. She broke open a bag of Tasty Vittles and alerted Daisy, who came running at a faster pace than Sophie could have imagined considering that, moments before, she had been curled up on her pillow, sleeping. *To have your energy, kitty; I forget what it's like.* She spooned some yogurt and cut up some strawberries for her own breakfast and gazed out the window.

There had been a light rain throughout the night, and everything seemed extra green and lush. The purple clematis climbing its way around the window frame was in full bloom, and it cast a purple hue across the kitchen. *A beautiful new morning*, she thought. *A fresh new beginning.*

Daisy jumped up on the counter to give Sophie a kiss. For a moment, Sophie felt content. "I love you too, Daisy Mae, but you're not allowed up here." She set her on the floor and made her way to the bathroom to get cleaned up and dressed for the day.

Sophie had a spring to her step and was looking forward to a productive day. She'd be making centerpieces with white birdcages filled with sprigs of wildflowers in peach, coral, teal, and yellow. Thinking of some added little touches she'd like to apply to the centerpieces, Sophie began to brush her teeth. About ten seconds into the task, a wave of nausea overcame her, and she dashed to the toilet to expel her breakfast. She sat on the floor, holding her hair back with her hand, and thought she'd better keep her word to Emily. *I'd better call the doctor.* She pushed back the idea that anything could be truly wrong with her, believing that God wouldn't be that cruel; however, she'd been feeling awful most of the time and needed some answers.

Emily's tires moved along the gravel driveway, alerting Sophie that she was there. She made a second attempt at brushing her teeth, washed her face, and ran a brush through her hair. As soon as she felt a little better, Sophie met Emily in the drive. Emily had been busy unloading supplies.

"Good morning, sunshine," Emily said with enthusiasm that quickly turned into concern. "What's the matter, partner?"

"Not feeling so good. I just wanted to let you know that I've made an appointment with my doctor and that I'll be in as soon as I'm done."

"Don't rush. I'll be in the kitchen all morning. It's all good."

"Super, see you in a bit." Sophie hopped in her car and headed out, again imagining all the things that could be going on with her. She hadn't been eating right because of a lack of appetite. She'd been stressed out, depressed, tired—the list could go on and on, but she'd thought she'd turned a corner.

An hour later, Sophie walked out of the doctor's office

feeling overwhelmed, tearful, emotional, and utterly alone in the moment. *Sam, I need you. I can't go through this alone.* Unready to head home, she drove past the house and proceeded toward York Harbor Beach. It was still early, so she'd be able to be by herself to collect her thoughts and allow the news to sink in. She turned off the car, removed her sandals, and walked toward the water. Seagulls roamed the beach along with her as tears streamed down her face. The seafoam rolled over her ankles as she watched her toes sink deeper into the sand with each small wave. She shivered with the icy water numbing her skin as she approached a large boulder that she'd frequented over the years. Sophie climbed up, had a seat, and prayed. "God, why now? Of all the times, why now? This isn't fair! I'm tired, I'm afraid, and frankly, God, forgive me, but I'm pretty mad at you right now."

The sun had warmed her feet, and she brushed off the sand that had collected between her toes, then stepped onto the rocky path that would bring her back to the grass. Sophie sprawled out and watched a lonely cloud roll by, considering how she'd break the news to Emily. A half an hour later, she'd be home.

. . .

Emily looked up to see a puffy-eyed, red-nosed, slumped-shouldered, defeated friend standing in the doorway to the bakery. "Sophie, what's wrong? Are you okay?"

Sophie looked at Emily and responded in the only way that she knew how: directly. "I'm pregnant."

"Oh my…well, that's quite a surprise, now isn't it? Congratulations?" Emily gave her friend a long embrace, then stood back, keeping her hands on her Sophie's shoulders.

Sophie looked back into Emily's eyes, knowing she was waiting for a response. She searched herself for her truth. On one hand, she was thrilled to know that she held life inside her. Sam's baby would be an extension of him and their love, but there was a side to it that saddened her at the same time. They had tried for several years to conceive, without success. The months of disappointment had taken a toll on them emotionally. They'd blamed themselves, blamed each other, lifted each other up, and then resigned themselves to believing that it wasn't meant to be. Why now, when he wasn't there to enjoy this moment together? It should have been cause for celebration, but she felt only fear and sadness. How could she do this without him?

"I'm happy." Tears welled in her eyes, and her bottom lip quivered. "Oh, Emily, Sam would have been so thrilled."

"Yes, he would have been, and you should be now." Emily's brown eyes grew wide. "Just think about it, Soph. You have life growing inside of you—a life that you always wanted! Sam will live on through a child that you never thought you'd have. This is awesome news, my friend…the best news ever! So, wipe those tears and let's celebrate!" Emily walked behind the counter to retrieve two of Sophie's favorite cinnamon twists. She handed one to Sophie and raised hers in the air as if preparing to make a toast. "Here's to baby Anderson and the soon-to-be best mommy on the planet."

Sophie raised her pastry in the air and touched Emily's with a gentle tap.

"I'll eat to that," she said with a giggle. "I can do this, can't I? I mean…women do it all the time, right?"

"You bet your cute little ass you can, sista!"

"If I keep eating these, there will be nothing cute about

it. But it will be worth every pound." Laughter filled the room as they tapped their cinnamon twists together again.

"Hear, hear."

The door chimes rang, and an adorable, googly-eyed young couple entered Proposals. Emily and Sophie scurried to collect themselves. Emily set her treat down and removed her flour-covered apron while Sophie excused herself to wash the smudged mascara off from under her eyes.

"Welcome to Proposals!" Emily said with enthusiasm. "How can we help make your day special?"

Chapter 7

Brady silenced his phone. This was the sixth call that he'd refused to accept from the Bedford Hills Correctional Facility, the women's state prison in New York where Cynthia was being held. Brady had washed his hands of her, and he wasn't about to go back. Being away from the city had given him a new lease on life. For the first time, he was content without a woman in his life. He approached the day invigorated and motivated to pursue his love for photography.

Henry Lockwood had tried to convince him to come back to the firm, offering incentives that most people in their right mind would never reject. Thinking that a peer could convince him of his idiocy, they'd sent Stevens, who'd insisted that Brady was making a huge mistake and that by not going back immediately, he'd be destroying his reputation in the legal profession forever. All that didn't matter. Brady was done with law—that much he knew for sure.

He'd made the decision to look for a new place of his own, as the Maine coastline suited him. He was close to the cities of Portsmouth, Boston, and Portland as well as small seaside villages. The area had a bit of everything, which pleased him.

The cool morning had a slight sea breeze, but the sun was shining, which gave him all the more reason to go on an adventure. He pulled a gas can out of the shed—*Full. Do wonders ever cease?*—and made his way down the slippery path to the tied-up boat. He stepped into the fourteen-foot boat, added the gas to the outboard, squeezed the bulb to give it a little prime, and pulled on the rope starter. After a few quick pulls, it started. He revved up the motor as it sputtered and spat in the water.

Feeling confident that the boat was sound, he killed the motor and walked up the path again to retrieve oars, a life preserver, his camera, and a few other necessities. When he returned, the boat started right up again, and he was off to see the coast from the water side. There was no better way to look at waterfront real estate than by boat, he'd concluded. He made his way around the Nubble Lighthouse, Short and Long Sands Beaches, and the tip of Eastern Point to the entrance of York Harbor.

He'd driven down Route 1A just about every day since he'd arrived in Maine and found the picturesque village to be welcoming and scenic. The homes were impeccable, with great history and charm. He imagined the technique and skills of the craftsmen who had built them. *This will be a good place to start.* He slowly proceeded around the harbor and entered the York River, taking pictures of rental signs for properties that held a bit of interest.

Time seemed to get away from him, and his stomach growled with hunger. He skipped some waves back toward the harbor and then guided the boat gently onto the edge of the beach and tied it to a rock to secure it. Brady was convinced that there was a pub of sorts just up over the hill. A cold beer and a burger would hit the spot. Brady meandered up the stone path toward the main road. At the top of the crest, he sighed with relief to see a familiar sight—the pub he'd remembered was across the street.

Brady opened the heavy door that led into the brick tavern with exposed beams and wide pine floors. He was greeted with a smile and ushered to a seat next to a window that overlooked the manicured lawn and pathways. While he waited for his food, he scanned through the photos and made some notes. He'd call a real estate agent in the morning to set up some showings.

Brady wasn't hurting for money, as he'd received a comfortable inheritance from his father. His work at Lockwood & Hurst had only added to his net worth, and the fact that he lived well beneath his means provided him the ability to pursue what he wanted in a home. But for now, a rental would do the trick. No need to put down roots just yet.

The beer went down easy, and the burger was sure to sustain him for a bit. He gathered his belongings and made his way back to the boat. He climbed in and pushed his way off the rock using an oar, then pulled the rope to start the motor. He tried several times, with no luck. Frustration turned to dread as the boat listed in the water and began to follow the current along the rocky shoreline.

. . .

Sophie was famished. After leaving her breakfast in the bathroom and only eating a cinnamon twist, she needed something more in her stomach. She put together a ham sandwich with fresh tomatoes and decided to take it to her sanctuary.

The large flat rock awaited her once again. *Twice in one day. We have to stop meeting like this.* She sat down, opened the bag that housed her sandwich and took a bite. It was truly a beautiful day, she thought, not a cloud in the sky. But for the annoying seagull that kept trying to snag her sandwich, she felt…happy and a bit excited about her soon-to-be new life. Sophie laid her hand on her belly and giggled at the idea of there being a tiny human inside her.

Sophie's interest perked up at the sound of a motor that sputtered on and off, then on and off again. She could see the small boat off to her right. The man in the boat took out an oar and began to paddle in her direction. Moments later, he stepped out of the boat, missing his mark, and sank knee-deep into the water. He appeared to be frustrated yet capable. He removed his shirt and threw it in the boat, his perspiration gleaming in the sunlight. Sophie looked on, secretly appreciating his physique. He must have been at least six feet tall. Slender at the waist and broad in the shoulders. Through his now-wet jeans, she could tell that his legs were strong. He brushed his dark brown hair with his fingers as he stood there looking at the motor.

Sophie placed her trash in her bag and made her way toward the man in distress. "Are you out of gas?" The man took a step back and looked in her direction. Sophie yelled a bit louder and waved her hand in the air to get his attention. "Are you out of gas?"

The man squinted his eyes and covered his brow with his hand to block the sun. He walked through the water, pulling the boat behind to greet her as he responded. "No, I still have gas. I just filled it not that long ago. It must be a spark plug or something." They circled toward the boat. "I don't get it. It was working fine."

"How old was the gas? Did you buy it new?"

His shoulders rolled forward, and he looked at the motor with disdain. "I got it out of my buddy's shed. It's his boat and he's letting me use it for a while."

"It's the old gas."

"Yep…I bet it is."

"You'll need to flush it out and replace it. My husband had that happen once. It went along just fine for a while and then it stalled out and wouldn't start until he changed it out. It should be fine afterward, though."

"Sounds good, but as you can see…I'm kind of…well…"

"I have some supplies at my house that will help, if you'd like." She didn't normally invite strangers to her home, but with the shop open, Emily and customers would be around. "It's not far, and I'm happy to help."

He sighed with relief. "Thank you, Mrs.…"

"Sophie. You can call me Sophie." He gave her a broad warm smile, and she reached for his hand.

"Thank you, Sophie. You can call me Brady," he said with a wide smile. They shook hands, and he followed her up the path toward her home. By the time they arrived, Brady's jeans had soaked up sand, salt, and dirt. His pant legs had been brushing together making a swooshing sound. Sophie imagined that he'd have to be pretty uncomfortable.

"There's a fresh can of gas, a small siphoning hose, and

a jug in the shed. Feel free to get them, and I'll grab a pair of shorts for you to wear."

"Oh no, it's not necessary. My jeans are fine."

"Don't be silly. You're going to have to stand back in the water anyway. It's no trouble." She stuck her nose in the shop to tell Emily what was going on, then headed to her bedroom. She opened one of Sam's drawers and withdrew a pair of Nike drawstring shorts, then held them up for inspection. Sam had been notorious for wearing his shorts long after holes had formed. Noticing they were intact and presuming that they'd fit, she headed back outside.

Brady had removed the items from the shed and sat on a wrought iron bench in the garden area outside the back door of Proposals to await Sophie's return. She watched as he got out a camera and snapped a few photos of hummingbirds washing and dipping in the rain-filled birdbath.

Sophie took in the scene before her. *What an interesting man you are. I wonder what your story is.* She cleared her throat to get his attention and handed the navy-blue shorts to Brady. "There's a restroom in the shop if you'd like to change."

"Sounds great. I'll be right back."

Sophie sat on the bench and took over the work of watching the tiny little hummingbirds. She formed her hands together to create a circle and put them up to her left eye envisioning what he might have been seeing through his lens just as the tiny bird flew away.

Brady strolled back with a strong, confident gait. As she saw him in Sam's shorts, it momentarily took her breath away.

"That was quick." Sophie jumped to a stand too quickly and wavered on the cobblestones beneath her feet. Brady reached out and braced her elbow with his hand steadying her. He had kind eyes and a gentle touch that lingered. Not in an awkward way, she realized, but in a protective way. She pulled herself away from his gaze. "Now, let's say we get that motor running. We need to get the boat off that beach sooner rather than later, so you don't get a fine. It's really not supposed to be there."

"Oh, didn't know. Thanks…Sophie. But I don't need to trouble you any more than I already have. I can take care of it from here."

"Right…sure. You know, it's probably better that way. Proposals looks pretty busy, and I should get in and get back to work."

"Would it be all right with you if I bring all your stuff back sometime tomorrow? I'd like to wash these first."

Sophie studied the tight-fitting shorts, surprising herself with a flutter in her chest, and swallowed hard. "Not necessary, but of course."

Brady collected the items, thanked her once again, and headed to leave.

"Brady, if it doesn't start, come back up and we'll see if we can get you a ride home." She wondered where home was. He had a hint of a New York accent and concluded that he was one of the thousands that chose Maine for their vacation spot.

"Will do, Sophie. If that's the case, I might have to trouble your husband so he can show me his trick."

Sophie's heart skipped a beat, but she was able to maintain her composure. "I'm sure you'll do just fine."

Brady gave a wave and a smile and was gone.

CHAPTER 8

Sophie entered Proposals and greeted Mrs. Bennington for their afternoon appointment. Margo Bennington was from what they called the upper crust. She was known in the area for her snobbery and seemed to have her nose in everyone else's business. But today she was at Proposals in order to make arrangements for her one and only daughter's upcoming nuptials.

"You won't believe it, Sophie. The venue that we reserved months ago has decided that it will be going through renovations at the same time as my Penelope's wedding. This is unacceptable!" she said with such anguish that Sophie thought she might swoon right then and there. "What am I to do? They say that it shouldn't interfere, but I hardly call having filthy old construction equipment within view anything but interfering. Don't you agree?"

"Maybe there's a way that the equipment could be moved for the day?"

"They can't promise that. I told them that I must insist, and all they would do was offer me my money back. My poor baby is in tears about this."

"I'm sure she is. It was a lovely place, but surely you can find someplace even nicer."

"You're quite right, I'm sure. But it was just perfect. It had breathtaking views of the water, lovely gardens—much like yours, Sophie. Why, it even had a lawn for the chandelier tent."

"Mrs. Bennington, there's a gorgeous spot just up the road across from the inn that would have the same kind of views, and they have a space for the tent too. Perhaps you could look at that?"

"Everything is booked. Everywhere I've looked is booked well into next year! What are we to do?" Mrs. Bennington's arms were raised up in the air, and she spoke with such a booming voice that everyone else at Proposals looked to see what the fuss was all about.

"Mrs. Bennington, why don't we step outside to get some fresh air?" Sophie suggested, hoping to remove her from the eyes and ears of the other customers.

"Splendid idea, Sophie."

Sophie escorted her out the door and walked her through the arbor and to the gazebo to have a seat. "Can I offer you some lemonade, perhaps, Mrs. Bennington?"

"Why, yes, dear, that would be most kind of you." Sophie left her to get the lemonade. Upon her return with a tray, she found Mrs. Bennington was wandering around the garden, muttering to herself. Sophie set the lemonade tray down and approached her with a bit of apprehension, handing her a glass.

"Mrs. Bennington, is everything all right?"

"Splendid, Sophie, simply splendid!" she said, wide-eyed and smiling from ear to ear.

"You seem to be in much better spirits. Did you come up with a place?"

"Why, yes, I did. I most certainly did!"

Sophie searched her mind to try and figure where she could have thought of in such a short amount of time.

"Well, how wonderful for you, Mrs. Bennington. What have you found?"

"Here! Right here at Proposals. Isn't it brilliant?"

Sophie began to choke on her partly swallowed lemonade. "Here, Mrs. Bennington?"

"Yes, it's perfect! You don't have any bookings to worry about because you don't have events here. Which in and of itself is beneficial, as the Benningtons will be the first to have such an event here. Why, it will be the talk of the town. Anybody who is anybody raves about your gardens and views. The tent can go right here. Why, you could even open up the carriage house for a bar, as I'm sure it wouldn't be too much trouble for you. Don't you see? It only makes sense. After all, the floral arrangements and cake are already coming from Proposals. Wouldn't that just make it easier that it's all right here?"

"Mrs. Bennington, I appreciate the fact that you would find our place suitable for your daughter's wedding, I truly do. But you're right, we've never done an event here, and Proposals isn't set up for such an extravagant affair as yours."

"Well, right now it's not, but by September it can be. Oh, please say that you will, Sophie. You must!"

Sophie was both honored and terrified. *Could we pull it off?* "I'll talk with Emily and see what we can do. I'm not making any promises, but we'll think about it and get back to you just as soon as possible."

"You are a gem, my dear girl, an absolute gem! The Maddoxes will be so jealous. Isn't it just delicious?"

"Let's not get ahead of ourselves. I really must talk with Emily first to see if it's possible. But for now, let's go back inside and finalize Penelope's floral arrangements, and then we can select the flowers for yours and Mr. Bennington's anniversary celebration."

"Wouldn't it be simply spectacular, Sophie?"

"Yes, it would, Mrs. Bennington. Yes, it would."

. . .

Brady was finally moving along the waters toward the cottage. He'd been taken aback by Sophie's generosity and hospitality toward a complete stranger. That just didn't happen in the city, or at least it had never happened to him.

There was something familiar about her, but he couldn't put his finger on it. Her hair had been tucked up under a wide-brimmed hat, and she had worn sunglasses, masking her features. It was only after he changed and gone back outside to see her that it had really started to gnaw at him. She'd turned her head toward him when she'd stumbled, and he'd seen her eyes. There was something about those eyes that he just couldn't shake. He looked forward to seeing her again.

Back at the cottage, Brady secured the boat to the dock. He was anxious to develop the photos he'd taken with his old camera. Afterward, he'd review the rentals he'd captured with his new one.

After throwing his jeans and the shorts that Sophie had lent him in the wash, he closed the door to the back bedroom, shut the makeshift black curtains that he'd made of trash bags and secured them with Velcro, turned off the light and turned on the red light over his developing table.

He found the rhythm of developing film therapeutic. There was something special about taking a blank paper, moving it around in chemicals, and seeing an image appear. Sure, he could have used his digital camera with all the bells and whistles to add contrast, color, and enhancements. However, Brady preferred to look through a lens and create. Film couldn't be manipulated and edited, and it left him with an element of surprise. This was making raw art, which he had greatly missed.

The mindless motion caused his thoughts to stray again. He was overtaken by the beauty and the detail of Sophie's gardens. There were cobblestone pathways, a gazebo, and an archway with mature roses weaving between the slats. He was happy that he'd had his old faithful camera with him and hoped that he'd captured some good shots.

As he moved each paper in the developing liquid, he watched it until the image and color were just right, then move it into the stop bath, fixer, and wetting agent. Lastly, he hung each image up to dry.

There was one photo that captured his interest the most. This one was special.

. . .

It was midday when Sophie came out of the office. Her hair was in a sloppy bun held together with a pencil. She had her reading glasses on, and no makeup since morning sickness had already washed it off twice. She looked out the window to see a BMW with New York plates pull toward the back, and she grinned with satisfaction while she watched Brady unload the borrowed equipment and place it back in the shed. He was wearing Sperry shoes, a pair of navy knee-length shorts, and a pale blue button-up shirt with the sleeves rolled up just below his elbow.

"Hey, Soph, something yummy just arrived," Emily said, snapping her out of her trance.

"What? Wait...I thought you already got your order delivered today, but I'll never turn down yummy."

"I was referring to the stud muffin." She gestured toward the door.

Brady was standing in the doorway with a small package in tow and wearing a smirk on his face. "I hope this is a good time."

Sophie shot Emily an if-looks-could-kill glare. "Oh, hi, Brady. It's a fine time. I was just doing office work. It's not very glamorous, but someone's got to do it." Sophie pushed the stray hair that had fallen away from her makeshift hair tie.

Emily waited for an introduction, but the awkwardness lasted a bit too long for her liking. "Hi, I'm Emily, Sophie's business partner who doesn't like doing office work." She extended her hand as Brady responded in kind.

"Nice to meet you, Emily. Looks like you have a pretty sweet setup here," he said with a wink.

"Aw, I see what you did there," she snickered. "Would you like to try something? I just finished some sinfully chocolatey cupcakes."

"Sounds sinfully delicious. I'll take two to go, please. And how about one of those cinnamon swirl things? They look awesome."

"Sure thing." Emily threw Sophie a quick look.

Sophie interjected, "So, you must have made it home all right. And the boat?"

"Safe and sound. Thank you again for your generosity." He handed the shorts back to Sophie, along with a gift-wrapped package.

"What's this for?" She couldn't imagine what it could be.

"It's just a little thank-you."

"You really didn't have to. You would have done it for me if I'd been in the same boat," she said with a grin.

"Aw, I see what you did there," he said as he flashed a big smile.

Sophie responded with a giggle as warmth crept up her throat and on to her cheeks. "Should I open it now?"

"Sure, go ahead."

Sophie walked over to the wrought iron bistro set by the window, and Brady followed. She laid the package on the table and carefully opened the wrapping. The image in the frame was stunning. "The hummingbird from yesterday?"

"Yes, I thought you might like it as a token of my appreciation."

Sophie looked at the beautiful, delicate image. The bird's wings were almost a turquoise with red and yellow tips, his belly and head were a deep teal, and the wings were a blend of fuchsia and purple. The lovely creature was in midflight. His sweet reflection was cast in the water of the birdbath, and he was surrounded by a blurry background of color from the gardens.

"It's breathtaking, Brady, just breathtaking."

"I was hoping you'd like it. Some people say that they're a messenger of joy."

Sophie reeled with its meaning. "One could never have

too much joy," she said as she tried to hold it together. "Thank you."

"You're most welcome." Brady got up to leave, with some hesitation. "Well, I better let you get back to your office work, knowing how much you like it." Before she could respond, he'd nodded a goodbye. Sophie watched on, grasping "her joy" in her arms.

CHAPTER 9

Sophie really needed to get back to Mrs. Bennington, and it nagged at her continually. She'd been waiting almost a week, but they'd only have a few months to get it ready, and they were right in the middle of wedding season.

She, Sam, and Emily had planned on converting the barn and carriage house someday anyway. They could tackle the carriage house without too much trouble. Once it was cleaned out, it just needed a new roof, some paint, and a few structural repairs, and it would be good to go.

They could hire some more help for Proposals, and that way they could focus on getting the carriage house redone, knowing that it would be great for revenue. And it *was* a long-term vision of theirs. But she could see at least three obstacles. One, she was pregnant and felt like…pregnant, so she wasn't sure how much she could help. Secondly, they really couldn't afford the additional labor right now. Thirdly, Mrs. Bennington was distraught over the construction at the old location and worried that they might not get it done.

Sophie peeked her head into the kitchen just as Emily was pulling a tray of muffins out of the oven. The image and aroma of blueberries instantly brought back a clear-as-day memory of her mother. She'd been around ten years old and they'd baked blueberry muffins together. She remembered her mom removing the top and watching the steam rise into the air. She'd placed a pat of butter in the middle and it had instantly melted. She could almost taste the sweetness. It was one of the few childhood memories she had of spending time with her mother, and she cherished it.

"Earth to Sophie," Emily chimed.

Sophie snapped out of her daydream to see Emily staring at her, waiting for a response.

"Well, hello there, partner. Glad to see that you could join me," she said as she tipped the tray of muffins over, tumbling them onto the cooling rack.

"Sorry. Those smell incredible. I knew that my sense of smell could be heightened, but wow. Can I have one?"

"Knock yourself out."

Sophie pulled up a stool and shared the thoughts she'd been having regarding the project. The more she spoke, the more pessimistic she sounded.

"Sophie, this isn't like you. Where's the positive, can-do Sophie that I know and love? We have always pushed ourselves beyond what we thought might be possible. We can do this, Soph."

"I know, I know, it's just that…I don't know. I mean, I really want to, but what if—"

"What if we don't, Soph. What if we don't even try? You'd just be spouting how we should have, and you know it."

Sophie chewed on the tip of her index finger and imagined the possibility. "We've got to be crazy, Emily. Let's do it!"

As soon as Sophie uttered the words, she regretted it. Seriously, she hadn't even come to terms with the fact that she was going to be a mother, and now she was adding on to their business. She looked up at the heavens, hoping for a miracle. *Proposals, your wedding destination.* Could this be happening? Two of the dreams she and Sam had shared were coming true—without him, but happening nonetheless.

. . .

Brady awoke well before dawn. He lay awake, restless and unable to quiet his mind. *May as well get up.* The transition from working insane hours in a high-pressure job and having a high-maintenance girlfriend and a high-society social life to becoming a man of leisure was a bit unsettling. Being alone with his own thoughts had been fine for a while, but lately he was finding himself quite bored.

He threw on his running clothes, laced up his shoes and headed down the drive with no destination in mind; he'd just see where his legs would take him.

The gravel beneath Brady's feet gave way just enough to keep him from gaining traction. He stepped tentatively until the damp pavement began, then he opened up. Running had always been a form of therapy for him. The cool, fresh salty air was invigorating to the senses.

It was early in the morning, with very little traffic on the roads. There was nothing like feeling as though he had the world all to himself. It was quiet but for the seagulls squawking for their breakfast, the crashing waves hitting the breaker walls, and his feet pounding in a rhythmic cadence that coincided with each breath.

Brady made his way down Route 1 along Short Sands. The night before, it had been alive with tourists and locals meandering through the streets. Music had played at the different nightclubs, and laughter and shouts of joy could be heard from partygoers. But now, the town was sleeping, and Brady was grateful for the peace.

The pounding of his heart, the expansion of his lungs made him feel alive. His stride was long and easy. He checked his distance and saw he had already gone three miles. From his calculations, he'd be at York Village in another mile or so.

The sun was beginning to rise. Soon the world would awaken.

Brady was momentarily startled by the blaring of a car horn as it passed by. He couldn't make out the driver but recognized the Proposals logo on the back window immediately. The Subaru Outback, as he recalled, had been parked behind the shop when he'd been there. Practical and safe, just what he'd picture Sophie driving. However, honking at him didn't seem like something she'd do. Not that he knew her well by any means, but it just didn't fit. Although lately, his ability to judge character had been off considerably.

Flashes of Cynthia ran through his mind, and it pissed him off that he missed her. Maybe not so much her specifically, but he missed being in a relationship. What he didn't need was a spoiled, high-maintenance crazy person like Miss Cynthia Lockwood. He'd vowed never to let his sexual urges control him again. If he ever started to waver from that vow, he'd recall the feeling of utter disdain and pity he'd felt for her as she'd sat in the courtroom.

What was I thinking? To think of the life he might have

had with her was enough to make him celibate. Thank God he'd finally woken up from that nightmare. He was disgusted with himself that it had taken a two-by-four upside his head for him to see the error of his ways.

Brady shook off the thought and turned around to head back, stopping briefly to take a gulp of water and proceeding to dump the last of the bottle over his head. He'd have to get back before it got too hot.

As he passed the entry of Proposals, the thought of Sophie flowed through his mind. He wished he could place how he might know her. She was kind and giving—a woman who seemed confident yet reserved, not overbearing. He found her intriguing, in a mysterious kind of way. It must be the auburn hair. *The hair! Oh my God, she's Mrs. Anderson. No, she couldn't be.* He must be mistaken. After all, Sophie was married and living in Maine, not New York. He shook off his momentary deliberation and simply resigned himself to finding out more about her. He was mildly amused at the prospect of diving into this little quest. *Hmm, who are you, Sophie?*

. . .

Daisy purred and kneaded Sophie's breast as she lay sleeping, trying to wake her for her morning vittles.

"Daisy, it's too early, girl. Go back to sleep." Daisy wasn't having it; she rubbed her nose under Sophie's neck and circled her head on the pillow. "Okay, girl, you win." Sophie sat up, placed her feet on the floor and wiped the sleep from her eyes as Daisy leaped off the bed. "I'm coming."

Morning had come way too early for her liking. Sophie had tossed and turned most of the night as her mind raced from one thing to the next—the expansion of her business, and the soon-to-be expansion of her belly. *I need you, Sam.* The words played over and over in her head.

She threw on some sweats and proceeded with her morning ritual, then took the stairs to the kitchen. Daisy circled her ankles until her need was met. Sophie pushed the button on her Keurig and plopped in a decaf coffee, which didn't really satisfy her need for caffeine, but at least she could be comforted by the warm cup. After taking a few swigs, she pulled on her rain boots and ventured out to water her potted plants.

The sun was just beginning to rise. Normally she'd feel content, as this was her favorite time of the day. Today seemed unsettled, though, and she was exhausted. Sophie rubbed her belly, wondering if this was going to be her new norm for a while.

While moving from container to container to give her flowers a drink and pluck off the dead blooms, she ran through her to-do list in her head. She crossed the damp grass to reach the driveway entrance and the plants that surrounded the Proposals signage. New life was sprouting in the planters. Before too long, light blue, purple, and white cupid's dart and shasta daisies would be showing their lovely faces.

Sophie saw Frank Templeton collecting his morning paper at the end of his driveway. He was already fully dressed for the day, per usual. "Good morning!" she yelled. He tipped his cap, as a gentleman would do. She smiled, embracing this ritual of normalcy.

Emily pulled into the drive and gave a quick beep on the horn, causing Sophie to jump. Emily waved and smiled, looking quite proud of herself. She rolled down the window as Sophie removed the hand from her heart. "What planet were you on this time?" Emily asked with a satisfied giggle.

"You're a brat, Emily Vassure!"

"Yeah, that's what my momma always said. See you soon, partner," she hollered, then rolled up the window and proceeded up the drive to the shop.

Sophie looked on, grinning. *You're a brat, but I love you.*

Sophie walked in several minutes later, holding two mugs of coffee. She snatched a blueberry muffin from the display case. "One decaf for me, and one caffeinated for the oh-so-lucky one. What are those?" She pointed to the bridal-gown-shaped sugar cookies cooling on the counter.

"For the Clarks' shower. I'll be adding white icing, piping and silver detail once they're cool. Hey, you'll never guess who I ran into this morning."

Sophie pondered for a mere millisecond before Emily interjected with the answer.

"Your boat guy! Well, I didn't physically run into him. He was running through the village and was my first startle honk of the morning. I don't even think he knew who I was, which made it all the more glorious."

"You are incorrigible, Em."

"He was looking pretty sexy…great legs." She leaned back against the counter, her eyes glazing over. "Nice ass, too."

"Emily!" Sophie said with amusement.

"What? You can't tell me you haven't noticed his ass."

"I honestly don't think I have." All she'd noticed was Brady wearing Sam's shorts…just the shorts…and his legs, she confessed to herself.

"Well, you missed out, my friend," Emily said with a sheepish grin on her face. "But I sure didn't."

"On that note, I'll let you get back to your cookies. But first you better wipe the drool off your face."

Boutonnieres and corsages for Mr. and Mrs. Bennington were Sophie's morning task. She headed for the cooler to select the flowers. A deep red rose for love, and petite white stephanotises for happiness in marriage, with a touch of greenery and a string of pearls for Mrs. Bennington. They'd be celebrating their thirty-fifth wedding anniversary, and as Mrs. Margo Bennington would say, "It must be spectacular." The centerpieces would be tall fluted glass vases filled with crystals and red roses, draped with strings of pearls. Emily would complement the floral arrangements with a decadent red velvet cake, decorated with white pearled frosting and roses, which, as Mrs. Bennington would conclude, would be the talk of the town. At least, that was their hope.

As she stood in the walk-in refrigerator, Sophie momentarily thought about the prospect of another man in her life. She'd always pictured herself with Sam in their golden years, definitely still flirting with one another. He'd always had a way of making her blush, but secretly it had made her feel sexy and wanted; she'd adored him for that. Now that he was gone, being single would most likely be her future, and she'd just have to get used to it. No one would ever compare; of that she was certain.

Sophie peered through the potted and cut flowers when a leather glove caught her eye. It was one of Sam's that was haphazardly lying next to one of the pots. He'd been looking for it one afternoon, and they'd searched high and low without success; now, here it lay. She picked up the worn leather and brushed off the dried soil. After years of use, it had molded to the shape of his hand, and she ran her fingers across it, imagining his strong hand inside.

The cold air brought goose bumps to her skin, and she

shivered. She made her floral selections, tossed the glove in the basket along with the flowers, then shut the door behind her with a firm push of her foot and a loud thud.

Chapter 10

Brady arrived back at the cottage and downed a tall glass of chocolate milk. Stripping off his drenched clothes, he lay on the floor to stretch. The ceiling fan overhead softly blew the beads of sweat that had accumulated across his body. He closed his eyes, stretched out his arms as if preparing to make a snow angel, and took in the sounds of crashing waves and the distant rolling thunder. The temperature of the air coming through the screened-in windows changed quickly, and the coolness ran across his body. Feeling refreshed, Brady stepped into the shower and prepared for Jane Winslow from Coastal Properties to show up for their appointment.

Jane arrived twenty minutes later with listings to peruse. The homes were from some surrounding towns that he'd driven through on numerous occasions over the past couple of weeks. They were all waterfront homes, located in areas of varying affluence, but without *really* knowing the area, he was hesitant to make appointments and waste both of their time. No, he'd research a bit more and then follow up.

Brady said goodbye, and Jane went on her way. He opened the refrigerator to see nothing that seemed appealing. He grabbed his keys and the paperwork, then hopped in his car in search of something a bit more pleasing than a day-old half-eaten Italian sub and soggy french fries sitting in a Styrofoam container.

Leaving the driveway, he flipped an imaginary coin and headed south. Within minutes, he was once again passing by the entry of Proposals. Without thinking it through, he slammed on the brakes, turned the wheel hard to the right, and drove toward the back entrance of the shop. He saw the Subaru sitting in its usual spot, along with a few other vehicles. Running his fingers through his hair, he climbed out of the car and walked toward the arbor entryway just as the sky opened up. Within seconds, he was drenched. Brady picked up his pace, and his shoes slid across the granite step as he reached for the knob. Suddenly the door opened, and with his momentum, he spilled across the floor with a thud.

"Welcome to Proposals. How can we make your day special?" Emily tried to say in a serious tone but could barely hold it together. She and Sophie looked down at Brady splayed out on the floor.

Brady looked up to see them both staring down at him. "I can see by the looks on your faces that you find this quite amusing."

"Why, yes…yes, we do," Sophie said in a fit of laughter. "I'm sorry, but if you could have seen yourself…"

Emily joined in, laughing uncontrollably. "It was like slow motion, only it wasn't."

Brady picked himself up and brushed some of the water

off, leaving a puddle. "I'm glad that I'm able to provide the entertainment for your afternoon," he laughed.

Sophie grabbed some paper towels from behind the counter and instinctively dabbed the water off his arms. "Are you okay? I mean, you really took quite a fall."

"I'm fine. My ego is extremely bruised, but otherwise, I'm just fine." He thanked Sophie as he took the towels from her and wiped his face. "Do you have a mop so I can wipe up this mess?"

"Already on it," Emily said as she wiped up the floor. "We wouldn't want anyone to fall or anything."

Sophie responded. "I'm really sorry; I saw that you were coming, and I pulled open the door to be helpful. I guess that wasn't the best move."

You're adorable. "Thank you for your hospitality," he said with a wink.

"Seriously, though, are you really okay?"

"Seriously, I'm good, but… I could still use your help."

"Sure, what is it?" Sophie asked with concern.

"Well, you see, you're about the only person I know around here. I have some real estate listings to look through, and I don't know the area that well. I thought I could show them to you and get your feedback, if you didn't mind. You know, like the neighborhoods…stuff like that."

"Oh, sure. That actually sounds like fun," Sophie said with a couple of quick little claps.

"I see you're a glutton for punishment." The thought of looking through listings was hardly what he'd call fun, but he appreciated the enthusiasm and willingness to help. Besides, spending more time with her wouldn't be a bad thing.

Brady picked up the dampened file folder off the floor

and placed it on the table while Sophie took a seat. As she reached for the folder, he couldn't help but notice her hands, and the finger that wore a wedding band. He wished he'd done his homework on the net prior to seeing her again, but he hadn't planned on this impromptu meeting.

"So, does your husband also work here at Proposals, or is it just yours and your partner's venture?"

Emily approached the table before Sophie had a chance to respond. "Just the two of us and some staff. Would you like something to drink? I was just going to grab a club soda."

Sophie inhaled, then exhaled deeply before responding, appearing to collect her composure. "Sounds great. Thanks, Emily."

"Sure, thanks." Sitting back in the chair, he observed a look between the two of them. Guessing the question he wanted to ask was out of bounds, he pulled open the folder and decided to table the conversation for another time.

Brady spread a handful of properties across the table. "I picked the ones that I found most intriguing. Part of me wishes that I could just start from scratch and build something, but you can't duplicate these locations."

"You're a builder?"

"No, not really. My dad was, though. A damn good one at that, so I know the business. I used to go with him to job sites as a kid. Once I hit high school, and during college summers, I worked under a couple of his foremen to earn a few bucks. I'd hoped that I would take over the construction company once he retired, but my dad felt differently, and being the dutiful son that I was, I complied." Brady couldn't believe that he'd just rattled off his life like a smitten child. What was it about her? He'd acted like that once before, and it had ended in a disaster.

"A man of many talents."

"Yep, a jack-of-all-trades," Brady said with a shrug. "Maybe someday, I'll figure out what I want to be when I grow up."

"Until then, why don't we find you a place to live?" she said with a grin.

"Sounds good."

Sophie gave detailed input on each listing, which helped him to narrow down the possibilities. He'd be looking at four places to potentially call home.

The rain came to an end, and Brady's stomach began to churn. Being with Sophie had made him forget why he'd headed out in the first place; he needed to eat. "So, I was going to grab some lunch somewhere, and I thought, since you know everything there is to know about the area, you might have some suggestions?"

"Better yet, I'm famished. Mind if I join you?" she asked, then her posture stiffened. "I'm sorry, I don't know what I was thinking. I didn't mean to—"

"That'd be great! I'm thinking seafood. Does that work for you?"

Sophie grimaced and shook her head no as her hand rested on her stomach.

"I take it you don't like seafood."

"It just hasn't sounded good to me lately. How about something from the kitchen? I have some grilled chicken in the fridge, and I could throw together a salad."

"Perfect!"

"Emily, we're going to the kitchen for a bite. Can I bring you back anything?" Sophie said with a bit of hesitation in her voice.

"Umm, nope, I'm good," Emily replied as Sophie's cheeks turned pink. "You kids go ahead. I'm up to my armpits in brides and grooms."

"Well, now, that image just made your cookies sound atrocious."

"Just trying to keep you away from my sweets. A girl's got to do what a girl's got to do."

Brady picked up the empty glasses from the table and brought them to the counter. "Thanks for the drink, Emily. I owe you one."

"Yep, I'm keeping a tally," she said, her bobbed brown hair tipping to her shoulder as she nodded.

Brady sat at the marble island, with the sun breaking through the clouds and casting its rays across the countertop. He could feel the coolness of the marble on his palms and the warmth of the sun across the backs of his hands. Such a contradiction of feeling, much like the stirring of his mind as he watched Sophie rinsing fresh basil. Her hair shimmered, and he imagined running his fingers through the strands. Her movements had an element of grace as she plucked each leaf from its stem and arranged them on the platter of sliced tomato and mozzarella. She was beautiful. Not like the superficial beauty of Cynthia, but genuinely beautiful from her core. It radiated from her eyes, her movement, and her long delicate fingers. She looked like a porcelain doll, and he was captivated.

He watched as Sophie squeezed a lemon into two glasses of ice water, popped a slice of cheddar into her mouth, and added a rosemary cracker for good measure.

Brady touched his lips to wipe the imaginary salt off as Sophie mimicked his actions. She licked the salt off her fingertip, and he couldn't keep his eyes off her. She was a seductress and didn't even know it.

"Everything looks fantastic," he said, a hidden layer of meaning behind his words.

"So, you're really going to make York your home?"

"Sure. It's as good a place as any, and it speaks to me."

"Oh? How so?"

Brady took a moment to collect his thoughts. *Why does it suit me?* "Well, it's quiet, and it's conducive to reinventing myself."

"Reinventing yourself...interesting. Who were you before—a serial killer?" She giggled. "What do you see this new you doing with your life?"

"I can assure you that I'm definitely not a killer, just a lawyer. I'm just getting back to when life was simpler and I was happy."

"What makes you happy?"

"Well, for example, when I actually had the time for my photography. Nature is beautiful, right?" Sophie nodded in agreement. "But to capture a moment so that it can live on forever...well, let's just say it makes me feel alive." In his enthusiasm, Brady got more animated by the second. "It takes a scene and freezes it in time. You get to see great detail and intricacies that we normally miss when we only take a cursory look at things."

"I see what you mean. It's like in the photo you gave me of the hummingbird. I had no idea of the multitudes of colors that one little tiny bird could have."

"Exactly! Especially when taking shots of people." Brady paced in the kitchen, using his hands and arms to express himself as if performing on a stage, his actions exaggerated and dramatic. "You can see right through their eyes, and it makes you wonder what they're thinking, what their story is… you know? Are they wearing a mask to hide pain? Do they feel beautiful? Proud? Oh man, the list goes on. And nature shots are glorious regardless of their circumstances." Brady placed his hand on Sophie's shoulder and guided her to the window.

"Take that tree out there, for example. No matter the time of day, the time of the year, or the weather, it has a story to tell. From a leaf's birth to its eventual death. The creatures that live in it and feed from it. It ages, it withers, it bends to the sun, and its leaves flip to prepare for rain. It aches from the weight of ice and snow, but it still thrives. When I zoom in, I can capture a bird's nest, and even the nest has a story to tell. Each twig, feather, and thatching of mud brings a timeline and a beauty to it. You can see so much more than meets the eye. There's always a story to tell."

Brady sensed that Sophie was now watching him, and was yet again surprised at how easy she was to open up to.

"I can certainly see why you have a love of photography. Nature in any medium is a thing of beauty for sure," she said in a hushed voice, then turned toward the stool and took a seat. "I hate to think what you see when you look at me."

"I think I see what you want me to see."

"But you see more than that, don't you?" she replied.

"I see a strong woman that has a beautiful heart."

"You don't see that." She looked away.

"Oh, but I do."

Sophie took a long sip of water. "You really need to clean your lens."

Time moved swiftly as they devoured their lunch. Brady gathered the dishes while Sophie topped off Daisy's water dish. They worked silently together, filling the dishwasher. The rhythm came naturally to them, as if they'd been together for years.

"Well, I suppose I should let you get back to work. I've monopolized enough of your time for one day."

Sophie hesitated for a moment. "Do you think I could trouble you with something?"

"Sure. After that lunch, your wish is my command."

Sophie proceeded to the den, where large pages of plans were sprawled over a desk. Brady looked around as Sophie calculated where to start.

"I'd like your opinion on our expansion of Proposals. You have an eye for beauty, my husband had an eye for structure, and I lean toward function. I keep looking at the renderings of the barn, and I can see how it works, but I think we could do better with bringing in some natural light. But I'm not seeing how. Any thoughts?"

Brady surveyed the plans. They were quite detailed, to include the exterior landscaping. "Your husband drew these?"

"Yep. He did these quite a while ago. Took me some time to find them, though. I can't tell you how relieved I was. The thought of hiring someone to do them all over again—well, you can imagine, that would be quite a task. And the timing to complete the project would have been a nightmare."

"I haven't met your husband. I hope you don't mind my asking a personal question, but are you separated or divorced?" Brady held his breath, waiting for the answer. If her husband was who Brady thought he was, he knew he couldn't see her again. There was no way she'd want anything to do with him. If he was still in her life, he couldn't see her again, because the temptation was too great and he wouldn't ruin a marriage.

Either way, he was screwed. He just hoped that it was a crazy coincidence that the name on the plans was the same as the man his ex had killed and that she also happened to have the same hair color. In his heart of hearts, he knew this to be wishful thinking. He couldn't bring himself to investigate it. He hadn't wanted to know the answer. He'd just hoped that he was wrong.

Sophie looked down toward the plans. Her hand rubbed the edge of the desk in a slow, methodical motion. After a moment, she looked directly into Brady's eyes. Brady instantly felt like he could see into her soul.

"My husband, Sam, is dead. He was killed in a hit-and-run. I'm sorry that I didn't let you know. I can only imagine what you might have been thinking of me if you thought I was still married." Sophie looked once again at the desk.

Brady stepped away and ran his fingers through his hair, then hesitantly rested his trembling hand on her shoulder. He took one look at her and felt the urgent need to hold her. Her tear-filled eyes gazed up at his, and she let loose. He grabbed her and held her tight. She pressed her cheek to his chest and wore his embrace like a swaddling blanket as she wailed like a baby.

He could hear steps quickly approaching and then the door flew open wide with a bang.

"Get your hands off her, you son of a bitch!"

Brady turned with a start to face Emily. Before he even knew what was happening, she grabbed him by the shoulders with both hands and kneed him in the groin. Brady went down with a loud thud and a deep-throated moan. Sophie froze as Emily ran to her.

"You're in shock. What did he do to you? Are you okay?"

Emily took a blanket off the sofa to wrap around Sophie's shoulders. "Sophie, sit down, I'm calling the police."

"Emily, no! It's not what you think. I'm okay!"

"Hello, my name is Emily Vassure and I'd like to report a…" Emily turned to Sophie. "Sophie, did he try to rape you?"

"No!"

"Did he assault you?"

"No, Emily!"

Emily spoke urgently into the phone. "I'm sorry, ma'am, I'm trying to find out what happened. Sophie, just tell me what happened."

"He was hugging me, Emily."

"Officer, the man was hugging her!" Her face turned red, and she stammered, "Ma'am, I'm very sorry, there's been a misunderstanding. I'm sorry to have bothered you. Yes, ma'am, everything is fine. Thank you and have a good day."

Emily hung up the phone carefully and looked at Sophie, then at Brady, who was cradling himself on the floor as he rocked back and forth, his pain excruciating.

"My bad."

Sophie let out a giggle, then an all-out laugh, which turned to snorting. That made Emily laugh. Sophie's tears of sorrow turned into hysterical tears of laughter. It was contagious as he pulled himself up from the floor.

Through intermittent laughter, Brady said, "Twice in one day, I've ended up on the floor, looking up at the two of you laughing. I don't think I can take any more!" The three of them were uncontrollable as Sophie crossed her legs and stated that she'd peed a little, which started the snorting and squealing all over again.

A few moments passed as they collected themselves.

Sophie explained to Emily that she'd asked Brady to review the plans to see if he might have any suggestions or recommendations. Brady drew on the plans with his finger and viewed the options that he'd laid out. "Opening the first floor of one full side of the barn and inserting beams with glass garage-style roll-up doors would provide an indoor-outdoor capability. In addition, if you built a patio with a pergola just outside of the roll-up doors, then the gardens and views would feel like one continuous space."

Emily leaned in close, studying him. "So, when would you be able to begin construction?" she joked.

"If you can get me a list of contractors, I'll be happy to oversee the work and lend a hand. I can start right away. Would that help?" Brady responded without hesitation.

Emily and Sophie looked at each other with astonishment. "Why would you do that?" asked Sophie.

"Why not? It's not like I have anything else to keep me out of trouble. Besides, you're going to look at some real estate with me."

"I am?" inquired Sophie.

"Oh, did I forget to tell you that? It must have slipped my mind after Emily attacked me. My bad," he said with a grin.

"If you're sure you can still swing a hammer after I assaulted you and dropped you to your knees," Emily replied with a smirk.

"I'll just have to do the best I can, won't I?" he said as the shop bells rang to announce that a customer had arrived. Emily suggested that Sophie take a few minutes and then retreated to the shop.

"Thank you for being willing to tackle this project, but are you really sure you want to do it? You were kind of put on the spot, and I wouldn't blame you if you wanted to change your mind. I'd completely understand," she said with pleading eyes.

"I wouldn't dream of backing out. It'll be fun." He watched Sophie's face relax. Even with puffy eyes and a red nose, he found her captivating, and a pang of guilt seized his heart. He abruptly turned away to study the plans as if dismissing her. Silence filled the room until Sophie broke the quiet.

"I guess I'll just leave you to it, then. Take your time in here if you want. I'm just going to freshen up a bit...unless you need anything?"

"No, I'm good. You can go," Brady said in a dismissive tone. He realized that he had turned into the persona of Henry Lockwood, and that realization repulsed him. Again, silence fell over the room. Sophie backed out of the room and closed the door between them.

The realization that Sophie Anderson was indeed the widow of the man Cynthia had killed finally sank in. He owed her...big-time. That wonderful woman had lost so much, and helping with the barn renovations would at least ease a smidgen of his own guilty conscience. Besides, he really was going a bit stir-crazy. Staying occupied was essential, and being close to Sophie Anderson would be a bonus.

That's it...I'm a selfish ass, he thought, tossing his hand in the air in defeat. She was a sweet, kind, and vulnerable woman. She wasn't there for his amusement or to absolve him of his guilt, and certainly not for his lustful pursuit. *No*, he countered, *I need to do this for her.*

As he stood there alone, looking at the plans that Sam Anderson had painstakingly created for his wife's future, his cell rang in his pocket. Lost in thought, he answered without looking to see who was calling. "Hello, this is Brady."

"Brady, my love, why haven't you been answering my calls? I was beginning to think that something had happened to you. You haven't even visited me…not even once." There was a long pause as Brady cursed himself for not paying attention to the caller ID. He felt as though he'd just gotten punched in the gut, again. "Brady, are you still there?"

"Yes, I'm still here, Cynthia. *Unfortunately.*"

"Why haven't you come to see me? I don't think I can last much longer without you. Daddy said that he's pulling some strings to get me out, an appeal or something, but I'm scared it won't work. I can't live like this, Brady. I just can't!"

Brady could hear an argument ensuing in the background that continued to get louder by the second. Whistles began to blow as Cynthia shouted, "It was my turn, you bitch!"

"Lockwood, to your cell now!"

"Brady, I've got to go…please come. I need you, baby," she said in a rush. Then the line went dead.

Brady shook his head in disbelief. Needing to remove any thoughts of Cynthia from his mind, he rolled up the plans, stepped outside and took a deep breath of the salty air. With a million and one ideas floating through his head, he climbed into the BMW and tossed the plans into the backseat. He grabbed his camera and proceeded to capture the angles, lighting, and structure of the barn so he could do his homework. His shoes soaked up the dampness from the wet grass, which formed small pools here and there. *This will have to be fixed.* He could picture guests in their formal attire and dress shoes walking through the muck; it simply wouldn't do.

CHAPTER 11

Sophie climbed the stairs and shook off Brady's abruptness. Her hormones were all over the place, and she didn't want to overreact or read too much into his reaction. She chalked it up to his excitement about studying the plans.

The realization had hit her like a ton of bricks. Hearing the words *Sam is dead* coming out of her mouth had set her body in motion. She was humiliated at the thought of losing it in front of Brady, but she hadn't said those words out loud to anyone. Her throat once again tightened up as her eyes filled with tears. She sat on the edge of her bed and let the tears fall. She could taste the salt on her lips for the thousandth time since Sam's death. This time she deserved it, as she'd enjoyed Brady's company too much. She was comfortable with him and had let herself forget, if only for a little while, that Sam was gone. *I'm so sorry, Sam. Please forgive me, my love*, she said to the heavens. Yes, she concluded, she deserved this.

Sophie washed up her face and applied fresh makeup in an attempt to remove any signs of crying. It was near impossible, as her eyes were puffy, her lips were plump, and no amount of concealer could remove the red from her nose. She had hoped that the laughter that had followed her tears would have taken care of it, but no such luck. She hadn't cried like that since his funeral, not even when she'd found out she was pregnant. Her emotions were raw, and her hormones were in overdrive.

Daisy entered the bedroom and carefully leapt up onto the vanity, avoiding the items strewn about. Sophie gently stroked Daisy's soft fur as the cat stepped onto Sophie's lap and purred softly in the arms of her human. She could feel the warmth of Daisy's breath and underbelly. Moving her hand back and forth over her furry companion was so calming. *Just you and me, Daisy. Do you think we can do it?* Realizing that it would be three of them, she added, *Don't worry, my girl, no one will replace you.* She stroked her furry friend's back. The thought of holding her and Sam's baby gave her a renewed determination. *One step at a time...just one step at a time.*

A shadow caught the corner of her eye as she passed the window. Brady was wandering around the barn, taking photos. She watched his movements. He had a tentative gait, as if approaching a rabbit that he didn't want to scare away, and he took a few shots before stepping down the cobblestone path. His stance was strong and his shoulders broad. A ray of sunlight put him in full silhouette; he was a picture of perfection. Soon Sophie felt the heat rising to her neck and cheeks, but she blamed the hot flash on baby hormones, quickly rejecting the notion that it could be Brady causing her internal temperature to rise. She placed Daisy on the floor as Brady opened his car door to leave.

Back to work I go, Daisy. Mommy loves you.

Sophie took one last look in the mirror, shook her head in defeat at her poor attempt to remove the signs of crying, before heading out of her room and making her way into Proposals' kitchen. Covered in flour, Emily was trying as she might to get a wisp of hair that had escaped its secure hair tie out of her face without using her hands. Sophie reached out to Emily's abandoned tresses and tucked the strands behind her ear. With an upward glance of thanks to her friend, Emily rolled out the sugar cookie dough.

"How great is that that Brady's going to help us out?"

"Yep, it's pretty great." Sophie watched on, mesmerized by the familiar motion of Emily's hands rubbing flour on the wooden rolling pin while pressing corner to corner over the dough to make a perfect circle.

"Did he say anything more about what his next step is?"

"No, not really, but he was just out taking pictures of the barn."

"Yeah, I figured that. He was putting his camera in his car just before he waved goodbye."

Relieved to know that he was good, Sophie was quick to change the subject. "What will you be cutting today, partner?" Sophie asked with enthusiasm.

"Phlox flowers with fuchsia centers and light pink petals."

"Aw, one of my favorites... union of souls. It's a beautiful meaning for a beautiful wedding. The Rocklands, right?"

"Yep. They want them for the bridal party luncheon as part of their thank-you favors. The mini cake will also be in the shape of a phlox, with small phlox surrounding the base and a fondant cluster on top with raspberry filling."

"I'll be pairing the pink phlox with white gardenias for the ceremony bouquets. Combining the meaning of clarity, trust, and unity of souls seems fitting. I've never seen two people more perfect for each other."

"You say that about all our couples."

"I know. I'm a romantic at heart. What can I say?" With that, she turned away to get to work. "Make an extra cookie for me, please!" she said as she retreated.

"I always do!"

CHAPTER 12

Sophie could see that Brady was stressing out over the barn construction, and she could hear the crew's discussions regarding the pitfalls during their breaks. Brady rarely took breaks himself. He usually paced around and ran his hand through his hair, which she'd concluded was a nervous tic, while mumbling to himself. Occasionally he'd nod with approval at the solutions that he'd arrived at in his head. She tried to avoid him as much as possible, as she didn't want to put more pressure on him. He was doing a great job, and the crew seemed to have confidence in his oversight, so she didn't worry. Emily, on the other hand, was continually wanting to see what was happening. It was all Sophie could do to keep her in the kitchen. Each time they'd go out and interrupt, it would just slow the progress down, and they had a deadline quickly approaching.

Sophie stood on the back porch, leaning against a pillar while Daisy darted back and forth chasing a chipmunk. He was a good-looking man, and from what she could tell, he was skilled at his tasks and his approach to the workers. He was firm yet kind, which in her mind was a good character trait. Brady truly did appear to be a jack-of-all-trades.

Sophie tipped her head back, closed her eyes, and allowed the sun to hit her face, recalling how she and Sam tended to do home projects together—which had been wonderful, but it had its drawbacks as well. Sometimes, it was nice to know that the work was getting done while she focused on other things she wanted to accomplish. This, she concluded, was refreshing, and she surprised herself by remaining so calm with everything going on around them. Fortunately, the crew went out of their way to avoid interfering with the customers. She was confident that Brady had a lot to do with that.

"Okay, Daisy, our break is over." Sophie scooped Daisy up into her arms, opened the house door and gently dropped her inside before heading into the shop. The customers were all abuzz about the goings-on. Brady had thoughtfully prepared some of the final designs and posted them on display so that the customers could see what was taking place. What Sophie and Emily weren't quite ready for were the reservation bookings.

The Getchels, one of the well-to-do families that were great friends with the Benningtons, insisted on booking their anniversary celebration at Proposals. Sophie could only imagine the competition between the two families. However, the Benningtons could always say that they'd had the very first event held at Proposals.

Emily and Sophie blocked out time during the days to interview candidates for a much-needed staff. A booking agent would be their first position to fill, followed by waitstaff, bartenders, valets, setup and cleanup crews, design crews, groundskeepers, and so on.

The more Sophie thought about paying all of these people, the more she worried the costs would be way more than anyone would be willing to pay. A quiet panic set in. Secretly, she feared it would be a huge investment, and a waste of time and money. What if it was a complete and utter flop? She'd be the laughing stock of York.

Initially, they'd thought they'd be able to handle most positions with their current staff and their own blood, sweat, and tears. But with her pregnancy advancing and the current buzz, they needed to be prepared.

While Sophie was deep in thought, Emily pushed her way through the swinging doors in the floral assembly room. "Sophie, best news ever! Well, not ever, but still pretty awesome. We just got a call. They want to run a feature segment about us on Channel 6!" Sophie's eyes grew wide, and she grimaced as her panic grew. Emily didn't slow down. "They heard about the construction and want to do a feature on the project for free!" Sophie was still trying hard to still her heart and remained silent. "Soph, did you hear me? Free."

"Um, yes, I heard you." She was fast becoming overwhelmed. Everything was a mess out there right now, and it seemed more like a demolition zone than a construction site.

"Brady can run them through the actual project. All we have to do is talk about what we've always done and how it's only going to be better! And—this is doubly awesome—they want to come back and do it again, when it's all done!"

Sophie was trying her best to stay positive, but the doubt was slowly creeping in. "Emily, don't you think it's all getting a bit out of control? We haven't even had our first event, and it seems like expectations are so high, and what if—"

"What's with you and the what-ifs? What if it's a huge success, Sophie?" Emily was looking for a response and getting nothing. "Okay, so if it flops, which it won't, we can never say that we didn't try—or the dreaded words that you so eloquently just said…*what if.*"

"You're right, I know you are. But aren't you even a little bit anxious?"

"Of course I am. But I've learned to turn that anxiety into positive energy." Emily pressed her hands on either side of Sophie's face and looked into her eyes. "Embrace it, my friend. We're going to be amazing."

. . .

Emily and Sophie prepared Brady for the upcoming television spot. He was more than happy to oblige. Camera shyness was not a concern of his, since he had often been on camera and faced jurors and the press at trials. To Brady, this would be a piece of cake. He was certain to give the crew a heads-up.

"So, here's the game plan," Emily said as she laid a spreadsheet across the table in the bakery. She set three coffees down, being sure to place a decaf in front of Sophie. "I've got it all under control. The TV crew will be arriving at seven a.m. and Sophie will begin by explaining who we are and what our mission is. She'll show them around and proceed to the construction site. Brady will give a tour of the work site. Then Sophie can—"

"Hmm, and what is it that you'll be doing, Em?" Sophie interjected with a suspicious smirk. "As it happens, I don't see you on this spreadsheet anywhere." Sophie looked at Brady for validation.

"Seems right to me, Sophie. I'm not seeing it."

Emily stuttered and stammered to find her words. "I'll serve the crew drinks. A pastry, even. I've done the back end of things. I even did this spreadsheet," she said, looking a bit flabbergasted and distraught.

"Emily, you need to be with me and contributing. We're partners."

"Yeah, about that… what do we say I'll just be the silent partner?"

"I can't believe this," Brady said with a laugh. "You're afraid!"

"No. I'm not afraid," Emily said in a childish, unconvincing manner.

"Emily's a scaredy-cat, Emily's a scaredy-cat," he teased.

"You're a jerkface, Brady."

"Sticks and stones, Emily, sticks and stones," he countered as the laughter continued.

"Fine! All right! I'm only terrified," she said, defeated. "I want to do it. But the more I think about it, the more terrified I get. I'm happy to do anything else, but there is no way I'm going to talk in front of a camera."

Sophie sat back and watched the spectacle before her. She'd never known Emily to be like this. But, come to think of it, she'd never been in this position before. Sophie thought Emily would be a natural in front of the camera.

"Em, you've always told me to be positive, that I can do anything, and that we'll get through anything because we have each other. I cannot do this without you. You are my other half, the yin to my yang."

"There's some tricks that I learned at my law firm. I could teach you. It would be fun."

Emily wasn't convinced. "I'd feel ridiculous."

"Seriously, it'll be fun."

"I'm not going to picture you without your clothes on, if that's what you're getting at. I'd have nightmares."

"Now that's the Emily we know and love," he said as he patted her on the head.

"You are such a jerk!" She punched him hard in the chest.

Brady faked being stricken by pain and collapsed on the chair.

"All right, I'm not going to promise anything, but I'll give your stupid 'lesson' a try."

Sophie jumped up with a clap. "You're going to do great, partner. Now would you look at that? I'm helping you to be positive for a change. I could get used to this."

Emily picked up the spreadsheet and ripped it in half. "I guess I'll have to redo the stupid thing, then."

"Or better yet, why don't we just wait and see what they'd like us to do and do that?"

"Sounds like a plan. I'll pop over after I'm done for the day to show you my tricks," Brady said as he took his last gulp of coffee. He turned to head back to the site, then retreated. "Thanks for the joe, Em. Mind if I grab a twist?"

"You're going to eat us out of our profits, but sure. Go ahead." Finally, a smile crossed her face. "But if you laugh at me or make fun of me, I'm done. Capiche?"

"Capiche."

. . .

The TV crew arrived shortly before 7:00 a.m. They unloaded two vans of cameras, lighting, and sound equipment. Jessica Phelps, the host of *In Your Neighborhood*, stepped out of her car wearing a white button-down chiffon blouse, a pale pink floral pencil skirt, and a matching pair of pink pumps. She stood about five eleven with the pumps and had a slim build. Her hair was a light golden hue that cascaded in light curls that flowed across her shoulders. Her makeup was pristine, and she had a perfect smile. She walked with confidence and an air of sophistication toward Sophie and Emily.

Emily took one look at Sophie and laughed. "Are you kidding me? We have to stand next to that!"

Sophie giggled. "I've never felt so frumpy in all my life."

"Tell me about it. At least you're tall. Not as tall as Lurch there, but tall. I'll be looking into her breasts the whole time. A short, fat-faced troll. We'll be the new Beauty and the Beast."

"Stop it. You're beautiful in your own adorable way. Besides, knowing Brady, he'll make her put on a hard hat, which won't work with her outfit, at all." They shared a giggle as Sophie continued. "Now, what do you say we do this, partner?"

"Lead the way."

The morning went by quickly. They were surprised at how easy Jessica made it. In spite of her appearance and popularity on television, she was very down to earth and made it quite easy on them.

Brady was in his element. He flourished in the role of "cohost." If Sophie didn't know better, she'd think he was smitten. As the morning continued, she had to fight off jealousy. He was available, good looking, and talented. They would make a pretty great couple, like Ken and Barbie.

He had Jessica eating out of his hand. Of course, he was considerate enough to bring Sophie into the conversations, but she was becoming more convinced that he was interested. She felt like a schoolgirl on the inside while trying to be a professional businesswoman on the outside. What snapped her out of it was Emily. Apparently, Brady's trick of not looking at the cameras but focusing on Jessica and the surroundings was all she needed. Sophie couldn't have been prouder of her. The recordings would be edited and aired on the morning segment. All in all, she'd call it a wrap.

. . .

The fresh aroma of coffee wafted through Grounds, adding a sense of peace to Sophie's morning. She had planned on roughing out the details of the upcoming weddings here, having found that she was easily distracted at Proposals, whether she was inside her home or in the shop. A change of scenery would do her some good, and she hoped it would give her renewed creativity.

She found a cozy spot in the corner and sat in a comfortably worn leather chair. The table was made of an old coffee shipping crate and gave her plenty of room to spread out a few of her files, in order of urgency. She wasn't one to procrastinate, and getting the tough stuff out of the way gave her something to look forward to, as a bit of a reward for herself. She pulled out her laptop, extended the cord and reached behind a bookshelf to plug it in. Lastly, her sketchpad and pencils made their way out of her satchel. Sophie preferred to sketch out the flower arrangements that floated around in her head. It made it much easier to describe things when her clients could actually see what was in her mind. Frankly, it usually sealed the deal.

Now all I have to do is get a cup of decaf and my day can officially begin.

Jillian came bubbling over with an unusually cheery disposition. "Well, well, look who's here!"

"Hi, Jillian."

"What can I get for you? The usual?"

"Amazingly enough, I'm going to have actual coffee today and not my usual cup of tea."

"Okay, then. Aren't you just full of surprises these days?"

"Oh?"

"Everyone is buzzing about the news clip that was on television. We have a celebrity in our midst."

Sophie couldn't help but blush as Jillian continued, "It looks like it's going to be very nice, very nice indeed."

"I hope so…"

"With all the *new developments*, you must be beside yourself with excitement." Jillian emphasized *new developments* as if the words were some kind of secret code.

"We are excited but, honestly, a bit overwhelmed. So much happening so fast."

Jillian looked as if she was ready to bust. "So, tell me the juicy details."

"I hardly think a construction project allows for much in the juicy details department."

"Oh, come now, Sophie. It looks like you and Brady seem to make quite a team."

"Jillian," Sophie said, a bit taken aback, "I can't imagine that you'd be implying that Brady and I are…together."

"Well, aren't you?" Jillian said, looking confused. "You both completed each other's sentences, he couldn't take his eyes off you, and you seemed so comfortable together. Not to mention, based on the way you kept putting your hand on your adorable little baby bump, that you are expecting…I just assumed."

Sophie felt the room closing in on her, and it seemed as though the entire audience was watching a scene being played out before them. "You assumed wrong. Most utterly and completely wrong. Now, if you'll excuse me."

"I'm so sorry, Sophie. I don't know what to say."

Sophie clumsily stood to gather her belongings. "I would suggest that if you don't know something to be true and just make assumptions, you might consider keeping your thoughts to yourself and your mouth shut." She said it much louder than she had intended, and those in attendance looked on, half of them embarrassed for her and the other half anxious to see how the show would play out. Sophie stacked her files, pulled the power cord out of the wall, and frantically began shoving her things into her bag so that she could quickly exit the scene stage left.

As Sophie crossed the threshold, she could hear Jillian apologizing, but she couldn't breathe. She needed to get away as fast as possible.

She was completely mortified. *They think I'm having Brady's baby? I know I made myself clear when they were recording...didn't I?* She'd have to watch the segment again.

Tears didn't come, but she could feel her pulse quicken through her veins until she felt her head would explode. Sophie walked toward the harbor to sit on her faithful safe place—her rock.

As the morning fog burned off, a haze developed. Not only was her internal temperature rising, so was the external. The sea breeze ceased, and she felt her feet swell. *Maybe this wasn't such a good idea after all.* Before she knew it, she was slipping into a dizzy, confused state. Her feet weren't going the direction that she intended, and her satchel felt like a load of bricks. The next thing she knew, the ground was fast approaching. She felt damp sod on her cheek, and all went black.

CHAPTER 13

Brady didn't want to say anything to Sophie and Emily, but the barn conversion was much like the children's story If You Give a Mouse a Cookie. Every time he tackled one of the tasks on the project, it began anew. He felt distracted and pulled in many directions, and it seemed like he wasn't making as much progress as he'd hoped to by this point.

They'd gotten past the work of fully supporting the roof. To allow enough open beams in the ceiling, they'd needed to add structural supports under the foundation. In order to put in the supports, they'd dug up part of the foundation, and in order to access the foundation, they'd needed to remove a mound of granite. It had been one of the many stumbling blocks that had come their way.

Each time Sophie or Emily came out to investigate how things were moving along, he had to put his attorney poker face on so he wouldn't worry them. He'd grown concerned that he wouldn't pull it off in time after all. He'd been asked to relieve them of the burden of overseeing the project; the last thing he wanted was to let them down. So, here he stood at the top of a ladder, with hammer in hand, pounding nails in order to help speed things along.

Off in the distance, but approaching quickly, were the sounds of sirens. Just as Brady noticed them, Emily yelled at the top of her lungs, "Brady, come quick. I think something might be wrong with Sophie!"

Brady placed his feet on either side of the ladder rails and slid down as if it were a fireman's pole. He was at Emily's side in less than thirty seconds. "What's wrong?"

"I don't know for sure. Jillian from Grounds just called me, looking for Sophie. Apparently, Sophie left Grounds upset and hasn't returned home yet, and now I hear sirens. My instincts are telling me something is wrong."

"Let's go, then! I just hope that your instincts are wrong, Em."

"Yeah, like they were the last time I thought something was wrong with Sophie and I punched you in the nuts."

Brady tried to stay positive as they ran up the road, but he did in fact feel like he had been punched in the nuts. *Please don't let it be Sophie…please let her be okay.*

As they rounded the corner, they could see an ambulance pulled over, and a bystander was directing traffic.

Both Emily and Brady stopped dead in their tracks. Auburn hair spilled out and was flowing from a gurney. It was Sophie.

Emily sank to her knees as she shook uncontrollably, and Brady felt stuck. He couldn't move. He bent down to hold Emily. She put her forehead on his chest and sobbed. "I don't see a car. I can't lose another friend."

"She wasn't driving a car, Emily. She was walking, remember?"

"Maybe it was another hit-and-run!"

"Emily, Sophie needs us. We need to get up and see how we can help her. Okay?"

With that, Emily pulled herself up with Brady's support and they hesitantly approached the scene. Sophie wasn't moving as the EMTs lifted the gurney into the vehicle.

"Where are you taking her? What happened? Is she okay?" Emily stuttered as a strong-jawed man in uniform surveyed the two of them.

Brady intervened. "We're Sophie's…family. Please tell us what happened. We need to be with her."

"She's being taken to York Hospital for observation. Can you tell us if she's allergic to anything, or anything else that might be helpful to know?"

Brady looked at Emily with a blank stare. He suddenly realized that he really didn't know much about Sophie. "Um, Emily can answer, right, Emily?"

"No, she's not allergic, except for feta cheese and your typical ivy and oak stuff. Oh, and she's four months pregnant. Does that help?"

"Yes, ma'am. Thank you." With that, they jumped in the van, shut the double doors in Brady and Emily's face, and drove away.

Brady was stunned. "Sophie's pregnant?" he said quietly, hoping Emily didn't hear. He'd suspected it but hadn't dared to broach the subject. After all, what if he'd been wrong? That wouldn't win him any points, and he knew he was already down more than he'd care to count.

Without further delay, he turned and double-timed it

back toward the house. "Well, let's go!" he called back to Emily.

Emily followed quite a distance back, huffing and puffing. Brady was already in his car and driving down the driveway as Emily reached the base of the drive. He stopped so she could hop in.

"So, where the hell is York Hospital?"

"Head to the center of town…it's back in on the left." Emily gasped for air. "Crap, I really need to work out more. That was pathetic." She'd opened the door for some kind of sarcastic retort, but Brady was focused on getting to Sophie.

By the time they reached the hospital, which was just a couple minutes away, Emily had gained her breath back, and her pulse had settled. "You really like her, don't you?"

"Of course I do. Doesn't everybody?"

"That's not what I meant."

Brady knew what she meant but wasn't about to talk with Emily about something that he himself hadn't even come to terms with, especially not when Sophie was in the hospital with God only knew what wrong with her. He chose to ignore her last statement and increased his gait to the emergency room receiving desk.

"A woman by the name of Sophie Anderson was just brought in. We'd like to be with her."

The desk clerk looked up through wide-rimmed purple glasses that made her eyes appear magnified. "Please fill out this form and take a seat, and I'll let them know you're here. We'll let you know when and if you can go in. Okeydokey?"

Brady took the clipboard, filled out the questionnaire, and sat facing the door separating him from Sophie. The minutes ticked by mercilessly slow as the ramblings of Fox

News played in the background. Brady ran his fingers through his hair as he observed mothers holding sick kids, listened to the moans of a man with severe back pain, and watched a woman grimace as she held an ice pack and bandage around a bloodied hand. He couldn't help but think that everyone had a story. What would Sophie's be? He wasn't much of a praying man but felt the need to ask the big guy upstairs to intervene.

Finally, a nurse opened the double doors and peered about the room, "Mr. Owens, Ms. Vassure." Brady and Emily jumped to attention. "Please come with me."

They followed her and waited cautiously as the nurse approached a heavy curtain and slid it to the side. The room was dimly lit, and Sophie lay there with an oxygen mask over her face and an IV stuck into her hand. Steady beeps pierced the quiet. As they approached the bed, Sophie opened her heavy eyes, and a small smile broke on her face.

Brady found his voice. "Hey there."

Sophie reached her hands out to the two of them. They each took a hand.

"What's going on, partner?" Emily asked.

The doctor stepped in and closed the curtain behind her. Emily guessed her to be in her midfifties, with dark blond hair cut to her chin, and she radiated a calm demeanor. "Well, look who has company," she said in a kind-hearted voice. Her nose crinkled and her eyes squinted with a smile.

Brady was finally able to breathe.

"What happened, Doctor? What's wrong with Sophie?" Emily asked.

"We're still running some tests, but it appears at this point that Sophie was dehydrated, and her blood pressure was low, which caused her to faint." She turned to Sophie.

"We're giving you some fluids, and we'll need to continue to evaluate you for a little while longer."

"Is everything all right with the baby?" Brady said in a whisper.

"Her heart rate is strong, and she seems very happy in there. Everything appears to be normal."

"Her?" Sophie said with a renewed strength, removing the oxygen mask. "I'm having a girl?"

"Yes…you didn't know? I'm so sorry. I shouldn't have—"

"You have nothing to be sorry for. You've taken good care of me and my little girl," Sophie interrupted as her eyes filled up with tears. She looked at Emily and Brady, then squeezed their hands. "I'm having a girl."

Emily couldn't contain her excitement and let out an enthusiastic "woo-hoo!" to the chagrin of the nurses at the nurses' station. Emily and Sophie let out a giggle as Brady grinned from ear to ear.

"How soon can we celebrate?" asked Emily.

"I'd give it until tomorrow. I'd like to see her rest when she gets home, drink plenty of liquids—and to clarify, the non-celebratory kind. But she'll need to stay here for a bit longer. Sound good?"

"Sounds great," Sophie said with relief.

. . .

Sophie arrived home late in the afternoon. Brady walked with her up the stairs as her legs were still a bit wobbly. Emily went to the kitchen to prepare a tray of fruit and cheese to serve with water and cucumber slices.

Sophie sat on the edge of the bed as Brady removed her sandals. "I'm not a complete invalid, you know. I can certainly take off my own shoes." She secretly loved every minute of the attention, and the feel of his warm hands.

"I know, smarty-pants. Now, you'll have to tuck yourself in all by yourself."

She pulled her legs up and tucked them under the blanket. Brady leaned over to kiss her forehead and then, turning to leave, reassured her by stating, "I'm glad that you're home safe and sound."

"Thank you, Brady," she said, still feeling the warm kiss he was leaving her with.

Brady paused on the steps and looked back empathetically at Sophie. "Aw, don't mention it. You would have done the same for me."

"Will you be here tomorrow to celebrate?"

"You bet, little momma. Now get some rest."

She lay comfortably in her bed as the sun fell. *What a crazy day.* She replayed the day back. Jillian had really pushed her buttons, but why? It had been innocent enough, and she was confident that Jillian hadn't meant to be judgmental. But to think that people would be assuming that she and Brady were an item and that she was carrying his baby was just too much. Had she been flirtatious without realizing it? No, she didn't think so. She hadn't even come to terms with how she felt about him. *How do I feel about him?*

She confessed that she enjoyed his company. He made her laugh, which was a plus, as laughing hadn't come easily to her since Sam's passing. A grin appeared on her face and her cheeks burned at the thought of him in the physical sense. He was truly a good-looking man. Warmth between her legs was a clear indication of how she felt about him. She tried to brush the thought aside as Daisy pounced atop her duvet.

"We're going to have a little baby girl, Daisy. What do you think about that?" she said with a tenderness that put Daisy at ease. Sophie could tell that Daisy knew something had been wrong and gave her a few extra strokes for good measure.

Sophie's mind began to wander as she drifted off into a dreamy sleep. Brady consumed her subconscious. He reached out for her hand, and they whirled around a dance floor. She was wearing a long flowing gown of pale pink as onlookers cheered. The music got louder and louder and faster and faster, until she was spinning out of control. The walls closed in on them as the cheers became jeers. Brady's suit became running gear as he escaped the falling walls. She could see him running away, and then came the sound of glass shattering on the dance floor all around her, and she was left standing alone, watching Brady retreat. The last sound she heard was a woman's sadistic laughter.

She awoke sweating and breathless, panic running through her body. Sophie fumbled in search of the nightstand lamp. Grabbing her robe at the foot of her bed, she climbed out from under the covers in search of a glass of water and a dose of reality. *One foot in front of the other, Soph. One step at a time.*

CHAPTER 14

The sound of Brady's cell rang in the recesses of his mind to awaken him from a deep and peaceful sleep. "Hello," Brady said sleepily.

"Good morning, handsome," Cynthia said in a seductive voice. "I bet you miss me waking you up. Of course, I can't give you my personal touch this morning, but we can still have some fun over the phone."

"Cynthia, you need to stop calling me. I am not your boyfriend, lover, or friend. I've told you numerous times to leave me the hell alone."

"You should know that you can't escape me, Brady. I have friends in high places, remember?"

"What do you want from me?" he said with an anger that cut to his core.

"You're silly."

"You're out of touch with reality. I am not available for the taking, Cynthia."

"Brady, don't you see? I'm just like you. I always get what I want."

"I repeat, I'm not for the taking."

"Oh, but you are, Brady...you'll see."

Brady threw the phone against the wall, and the protective cover, along with the phone, shattered into pieces. He ran his hands through his bedhead and cursed himself for letting her get under his skin. *She-devil!*

He picked up the pieces and set what remained of the phone on the kitchen counter. He threw a K-cup in the coffeemaker, pushed start, and then sat down with a thump. It infuriated him how she could get under his skin and turn him into everything that he hated. He decided to contact Stevens at Lockwood & Hurst to do a little digging.

After a quick run to blow off some steam, followed by a shower, he took a drive across the border into Portsmouth in search of a new phone and a gift. He had to laugh at the thought of purchasing a girly baby gift. He liked this side of himself much more. Sophie was good for him, that much he knew, and he'd be damned if he'd let the likes of Cynthia Lockwood get to him again.

Brady searched his now-upgraded iPhone for Stevens's number and tapped Send. "Hey, buddy," he said when Stevens answered.

"Hi, Brady. You do know I have a first name...right?"

"Of course, Stevens. But you'll always be Stevens to me."

"You sure know how to win friends and influence people, don't you? What's up?"

"I was hoping you'd do me a solid."

"Okay...I think."

"I need you to see what's up with Cynthia. Is Lockwood getting her out or something? Or is she still just delusional?"

"He keeps pretty closed-lipped about her, but I'll do some asking around to see what I can find out. Is that it?"

"You sound surprised. What did you think I was going to ask you to do? Something nefarious?"

"You? Never," he said with a laugh. "Not that it's any of my business, but I was under the impression that she was out of the picture for you."

"On the contrary. I never thought I'd say this, but she's becoming more of a pain in the ass than before she was behind bars."

"Get a restraining order on her."

"Nah. It's not like she's threatening or anything. Besides, what would I say to a judge? My ex is calling me from prison and driving me nuts, and I can't handle it? They'd laugh me out of the court."

"I see your point. Change your number."

"Nope, not going to do that either. At least not yet. I have too many contacts, and it's such a hassle. She used to call me collect, but I stopped accepting the calls. Now, who knows how she calls out?"

"I'll check it out. Maybe you could take a trip to the city and we can grab a beer so I can fill you in on what I get. You do remember where the city is, right? It's that place with really tall buildings and—"

"Always the wise guy. I should be done with my project before too long. If the timing's right, that sounds good."

He had to admit that it had been a long time since he'd had a beer with one of the guys. He hardly recognized himself.

. . .

The weeks were flying by and the new venue was taking shape. Masons were finishing up the last details of the stone fireplace. The granite hearth and mantel provided a focal point for the far end of the barn. Sophie could envision floral arrangements and candles on the mantel, and a roaring fire below. She had ordered a custom iron screen for its opening that had double wedding rings linked together in its center. Her checklist was getting shorter, and she was beginning to feel like her dream was actually going to be a reality much quicker than she'd imagined.

The sun had been beating down on Brady's back all morning long, prompting him to remove his sweaty T-shirt. Sophie admired the sight of Brady in his jeans, bare-chested, toolbelt below his six-pack abs as she brought him a tray of lemonade for a much-needed refreshment break.

"Making progress. We'll finish up the windows and the six-panel glass lift-style garage doors for the east side today," he said with pride and satisfaction. Sophie was beyond excited to hear it. The project was moving way ahead of schedule, and her enthusiasm was quite evident.

"When will the chandeliers be going up?"

"Soon, very soon. The four five-foot chandeliers are here already, and the eight-foot one for the center should be arriving this week."

Sophie beamed and felt like a child as she jumped up and down with a few claps.

"Careful there, momma, you wouldn't want that little peanut to get too shaken up in there." He pointed to her belly with a grin.

"That reminds me," Sophie said hesitantly. "I've wanted to ask you something since I was in the hospital." She looked like a child, playing with her fingers and rocking back and forth as she stared at the ground.

He lifted her chin carefully with one hand and looked deep into her eyes. "What is it, Sophie? Go ahead."

"You didn't seem shocked or act surprised. How long have you known...and how did you find out that I was pregnant?"

"You forget, I'm an observer of nature in all its glory. You've been protecting your little one for quite some time now, but I didn't want to say anything. I figured that you'd tell me when you were ready. I admit that it wasn't confirmed until Emily told the EMTs bringing you to the emergency room."

She was relieved to know that she wasn't continuing to be the brunt of rumor and gossip. "It was that obvious, huh?"

"Only all the time," he said with a gentle smirk. "You must be feeling better."

"Finally. I never thought the nausea would pass. Since I've been able to keep my fluids down, I feel like a new woman. The next time that hospital sees me will be to welcome my little one into the world."

"Glad to hear it, Sophie." She loved how her name rolled off his tongue. It had an emphasis on the *ph* with a lingering *e*.

"Well, I better let you get back to it, then," she said with a stutter. *Stop it, Sophie. You're being ridiculous.*

"Okay, chief." He rested his glass back on the tray as a few clouds rolled in to give them a break from the beating sun.

The sound of backup beeps broke through the moment as the lift drove up the driveway carrying the focal point for the new entrance. Sophie went inside to get Emily so she wouldn't miss the event.

Within a short time, Brady and the construction crew were lifting the massive stained-glass kaleidoscope window up to the second story, over the tracked double-door entry of the barn. The copper-foiled lead seams, mixed with the beveled crystal, champagne, and blush tones, combined beautifully to create an image of intertwined double wedding rings. The light shining through the glass reflected across the stonework of the adjacent fireplace, and it took Sophie's breath away.

Sophie and Emily watched as Brady and the team hoisted the frame into place. The painstaking measurements had to be perfect for it to fit. With one final adjustment, it slid into place just as the clouds rolled away and the sun hit the glass, sending a shimmer of light cascading in every direction. Sophie soon realized that she'd been holding her breath. Emily squealed with delight as the two of them embraced.

"Better than I could have ever imagined, partner," Emily said as they locked arms and witnessed the moment.

Tears of joy formed in Sophie's eyes. "Better than ever, partner."

Chapter 15

It was a gorgeous September morning as a whirlwind of activity abounded in preparation for the big day's event. The Bennington wedding was in fact the event of the season; Mrs. Bennington had made sure of it. There would be a full spread in the *Yankee* magazine and *The Knot*, as the who's who of Maine, New Hampshire, Connecticut, and Massachusetts would be in attendance.

As the caterers set up buffet tables for the hors d'oeuvres, the bartenders stocked the bar outside under the ivy-covered pergola that extended the full length of the open side of the barn. Chairs and stands for the musical ensemble were arranged on the stage at the far corner of the barn. White satin tablecloths were draped over each table. Gold chargers and white china with gold-rimmed plate settings were laid at each seat. Blush satin ribbon was being tied on the backs of each white wrought iron chair.

Sophie was in her element, placing gold-and-crystal candelabras dripping with blush-colored Sahara roses detailed with crystal buttons at their centers. Seeded eucalyptus and cascading blushing bride protea with glimmering blush-colored ribbon hung from the beams over each table. Sophie placed ivory taper candles with crystal detail and set three tall hurricane vases with the same bouquets at each table, along with gold satin napkins and gold-rimmed crystal stemware.

Emily was busy putting the finishing touches on the four-layer cake. Each layer had light pink icing, embellished with pearls, and rhinestones that surrounded the bottoms. The top of each layer featured gold-and-white roping. The flowers, which Sophie had supplied, wrapped around the cake from the top layer and then cascaded down to the front with rivers of lace woven in with the flowers. A gold monogram topper was gently placed on top for the final touch. As always, it looked too beautiful to eat but would be devoured anyway. A crystal plate with a gold fork and cake knife was placed next to the cake, and a gold satin napkin in the shape of a rose was carefully set atop the plate, all awaiting the bride and groom.

The outside was also in motion as the staff placed white guest chairs, facing either side of the last of three archways that overlooked the horizon. Each archway sat astride the stone tile aisle and had cascading flowers flowing from it, keeping with the same theme as the inside.

Finally, all was ready. Sophie and Emily changed into their formal wear and touched up their makeup, gave each other a hug and took a deep breath. The valets, dressed in black tie, stood at the circle drive approaching the barn, awaiting their charge. The first person to arrive pulled up in his BMW. Brady stepped out wearing his tuxedo, and Sophie's knees buckled.

She glanced at Emily. "He wanted to take some photos. Besides, Mrs. Bennington said he worked so hard to get it ready that she thought he should be here."

Emily gave her a look of understanding.

"You go ahead, Emily. I forgot to get something." On her cue, Emily made her way over to greet Brady.

Sophie took another look in the mirror, then sat down and bowed her head, saying a little prayer. She really needed everything to go exceedingly well; so much was on the line. All the anticipation, hard work, stress, and hype had been weighing on her. She hated to admit it, but she was scared to death.

. . .

Brady picked up the two black duffels with ease and approached the main house to leave some of his extra camera equipment. Just as he was about to step inside the entry, he saw Sophie praying. He couldn't take his eyes off her. She was stunning. Her auburn hair was up in a twist. Her long milky neck was adorned with a simple crystal choker. She wore a dress of deep green satin that sat low on the shoulders. His heart was racing; she was perfection. As she stood, she straightened her pleated gown. Her little treasure protruded from under her high waistband. Brady cleared his throat as he began to enter; he didn't want to startle her.

"Brady, you're here! Now don't you look handsome?"

Brady set the duffels down. He couldn't resist—he sauntered toward Sophie and reached for her hand. Bowing, he gave it a kiss. "You look breathtaking, Sophie. A picture of perfection." Her cheeks instantly turned pink. "May I escort you out?"

"Sure," she said with a smile that radiated utter beauty.

"No, wait!" Brady opened one of the duffels to retrieve his camera. "The lighting is hitting you just right. I want to take your picture. Okay?"

"All right," she agreed, not seeming to know quite what to do with her hands.

"Just relax, Sophie. It will be painless. I promise."

"Well, you haven't broken a promise yet. Click away," she said with a shy giggle.

Moments later, they exited the house to start the evening.

Brady was blown away by the attention to detail. He snapped photos from every angle, inside and out, both close-up and distant shots. There was a gentle breeze, and the air was unseasonably comfortable. He took shots of a violin leaning against one of the wrought iron chairs, a simple rose, and the reflection on the table as the sun shone through the stained-glass window. He took shot after shot of the arrangements, cake, trays of fruits and cheeses, champagne flutes of bubbly, and the shimmering water through the arches, along with the floating roses in a birdbath.

This was a first for him. He'd never photographed a wedding before. Knowing that he wasn't the official hired photographer allowed him to relax and just have fun. Sophie had been so great to mention his photography skills to Mrs. Bennington, and Mrs. Bennington had been happy to oblige. He just needed to avoid encroaching on the paid professional's space.

The guests arrived at a fast pace as the ensemble played in the background. A harpist was stationed off to the side with the ocean as her backdrop as the sun slowly descended beneath the horizon.

It was time. Emily and Sophie stood back to take it all in. They'd done all they could do, and now it was out of their hands, except for being available to assist where needed.

Mrs. Bennington greeted each guest with a kiss on the cheek, a look of pride on her face. She was escorted down the aisle to take her place in the front row to await her one and only child, her precious Penelope.

Brady hesitated, watching Sophie look on as Penelope walked down the aisle toward James Ashworth. James stood tall and proud. A warm smile spread across his face as she took his open hand at the altar.

Mrs. Bennington shifted in her chair just enough that Brady could see her wipe a tear from her cheek; he snapped the shot.

"I hope you got that, Brady," Sophie said in a whisper. "I didn't know that Mrs. Bennington could be so sentimental."

"Me either," chimed Emily. "This is why we do what we do, Sophie; it gets me in the feels every time." Emily wrapped her arm around Sophie and gave her a squeeze.

"It sure is, and I doubt it will ever get old."

They watched the exchange of vows, and as the words *until death do us part* crossed James's lips, Brady saw Sophie give Emily a return squeeze and gesture that she was going to head to the barn. He could see by the look in Emily's eyes that she understood; then she gave a nod and let her go.

Within a short time, the new Mr. and Mrs. Ashworth would be announced, accompanied by a rousing cheer.

Emily made certain that the bartender and hors d'oeuvres were ready to go for cocktail hour as Sophie made the rounds inside the barn in order to make sure that every last detail was perfect and ready.

Brady clicked away on his shutter, capturing the special moments during the ceremony. While the wedding party lined up for their grand entrance, he could see Sophie signaling to the MC. She appeared confident, as if she'd been doing this for years.

Brady made himself invisible as he worked his way around the room with his camera in hand. He could hear the chatter among the guests. The Benningtons had accomplished their goal. They had become the talk of the town, and Proposals was the place to be.

CHAPTER 16

Sophie pried her eyes open. She couldn't remember a time when she had been this exhausted. Daisy was in her usual spot, curled up next to Sophie's belly.

Emily and Sophie had decided to close today. After the event the night before, they knew that there was no way they'd be able to aptly function. They were sure their patrons would understand.

She picked up her cell phone to see the time and was surprised to see how early it was. Going back to sleep would be the wise thing to do, but now Daisy had stirred and wanted her breakfast. Sophie sat up and dangled her legs over the side of the bed, searching for her slippers with her toes. She grabbed her robe, which was draped over the corner of the footboard.

"Okay, Daisy. Goodness, you don't have any patience this morning, do you?"

As Sophie made it to the bottom of the steps, she heard tires crunch on the gravel drive. "What on earth is Emily doing here, Daisy? We're taking today off, for Pete's sake."

She heard the car door shut, and in a moment, there was a knock at her door. Puzzled by this turn of events, she turned the porch light on and saw Brady standing there. *Good Lord…I haven't even brushed my teeth yet.* She quickly did a once-over in the mirror and opened the door.

"Good morning, sunshine!" His jovial demeanor took her aback.

"And what did I do to deserve your presence this morning?"

"I couldn't wait. I hope you don't mind, but I wanted to be with you when you saw this." He held up a rolled-up newspaper. "But first you need to sit down."

"You're making me nervous, Brady."

"No need to be. Trust me, you'll be happy."

Sophie and Brady walked to the living room, and she made herself comfortable in her favorite cushy chair. She turned on the standing lamp, and Brady plopped down on the arm of the neighboring couch. He thrust the paper into her hands. Right there on the front page of the *Portsmouth Herald* was a photo of the barn entrance all aglow. The new Mr. and Mrs. Ashworth sat in a horse-drawn carriage, with a sign reading "Happily Ever After" held by the flower girl and ring bearer. The caption read, "Proposals Exceeds All Expectations."

Before Sophie could continue reading the review, she jumped up and squealed with delight, then placed her hands on either side of Brady's stubbled cheeks and planted a kiss on his lips as if it was the most natural thing in the world to do. It was so quick and unexpected that Brady became unbalanced on the arm of the couch. His eyes widened as he fell backward onto the cushions with his legs flailing in the air. Gathering his dignity, he came to a stand as Sophie continued in her celebration.

"I feel like dancing!" Sophie twirled in a circle, her arms outstretched wide with the paper in one hand. Brady stood back and watched her uninhibited joy. She wasn't embarrassed or shy about it. She was happy. She stopped just long enough to read aloud the rest of the review, which was accompanied by an array of photos, courtesy of Brady Owens.

Sophie grinned with pride. "Brady, all the effort paid off, and I can't thank you enough. We never could have pulled it off without you. You are an angel sent from heaven." Then she gave Brady a lingering hug, which he returned. The embrace felt good and right, if only for a moment. She broke away and felt the familiar warmth grow across her cheeks.

"I'm happy that I could do it for you, Sophie."

She glanced down at the paper once again to study the photos. "How did you do this?"

"I'm full of mystery, Sophie. I'll never give away my secrets."

"Okay, fine. Honestly, I don't care how you did it. I'm just glad you did." With a realization, she said, "I hope the other photographer won't be upset!"

"I doubt it. He's the one that got paid."

With that conclusion, Sophie rubbed her protruding belly and said, "Do you want some breakfast? We need to eat."

. . .

It was late morning as he headed home. He was overjoyed to see Sophie so happy, and he wanted nothing more than to continue to make her happy.

After being up most of the night detailing his photographs of the wedding for the newspaper and spending the morning with Sophie, Brady finally succumbed to his exhaustion.

The full-size bed tucked in the tight space of the cottage bedroom sounded like heaven; a catnap was in order. He kicked off his Sperrys, tugged off his jeans and sweatshirt, dropped his boxer briefs to the floor, stepped out of them, and flipped them in the air with his toe. Catching them, he shot for two toward the hamper in the corner of the room. *And the crowd goes wild!* He bowed to his imaginary spectators. *I really need to get a life.*

He had resigned himself to staying at the cottage for the foreseeable future. Work at Proposals had consumed most of his time and derailed his plans to look for a more permanent residence. As he lay on the softness of the down comforter, he took in the sound of the waves crashing on the rocky shoreline and smelled the salt air and the pine panels that lined the walls of his tight quarters. Some would call it quaint; he'd call it good enough for now. Contentment permeated his mind for a few minutes before the inevitable thoughts of Sophie once again consumed him.

Her uninhibited joy regarding the article conveying their success had been amusing, to say the least. Sophie was usually more reserved and serious. Yes, they'd shared a few laughs over the past couple of months, but most of the time, she was focused and to task. He found this side of her refreshing and outright adorable. He couldn't get the feel of her out of his mind. Holding her was a surprise that he'd fantasized about for far too long. He recalled the hint of lavender he'd smelled in her hair, and how it had taken everything in him not to kiss her back. Visions of her paraded through his mind, until at last sleep found its way.

When he awoke, Brady felt refreshed and ready for whatever the rest of the day would bring. He flipped through a few channels on the TV, then scrolled through his phone mindlessly when it rang in his hands. It was Stevens, with news he didn't want to hear: Cynthia was getting out.

Brady informed Stevens that he would head to New York, right away. He was grateful that it was a perfect time to head out. The construction was complete, and he didn't have a good excuse to hang around. Maybe the time away would clear his mind of Sophie and bring him to his senses.

The drive through Connecticut was always congested. No matter what time of day, I-84 through Hartford became a parking lot, but he was making pretty good time regardless.

Stevens had let him know that he'd heard through a reliable source that Cynthia Lockwood would indeed be getting a parole hearing, which in and of itself was pretty unprecedented. She should be in for no less than three-fourths of her sentence; something was definitely up. He was confident that Lockwood had had something to do with this. She had said that she and her father had friends in high places. If this played out like Stevens thought it would, she'd have to be out on probation and therefore wouldn't be able to leave the state. However, being released would certainly make it easier for her to indulge her stalking tendencies. Brady needed it to stop, regardless of his relationship with Sophie. The thought struck him. *Relationship? Are we in one?* There had to be something he could do to entice Cynthia to leave him alone—or perhaps he could find something on her that would force her to stop bothering him.

Kyle Stevens hadn't been happy since Brady had left the firm. Apparently, Lockwood had taken Brady's resignation pretty poorly, and Stevens had become his new puppet. Lockwood had become more conniving, and the slimebaggery was hitting an all-time high. Maybe it was because his precious princess was in prison, and that had pushed him to be more of a bastard than usual.

Brady had agreed to meet Stevens at a scotch bar in Midtown that they had frequented in the past. It was out of the way enough that he wouldn't be likely to run into someone they knew from the firm, but close enough for convenience.

Stevens sat at the bar, adding a drop of water to his glass of Talisker, when Brady walked up behind him and poked him in the side. "Easy there, killer. You almost made me spill my drink."

"We can't have that. That would be a crime punishable by you paying the tab." Brady and Stevens gave each other a quick one-armed hug, then Stevens gathered his drink, folder, and jacket.

"Why don't you go order, and I'll find us a table that's a bit more private."

Brady surveyed the bar as the Scotsman behind it placed a glass in front of him. "What'll it be? It's been a while. Thought you'd be gone for good."

"Yeah, it has been a while. I'll have an Aberlour. Keeping it on the lighter side today, Duncan."

"I give that one to the lasses, ya Sally."

"I've missed you, Duncan. Now would you just give me the damn drink?" he said with a humorous tone.

"Aw, shut up. Here's your damn drink; now leave me the hell alone." Duncan walked off with a swagger.

Brady joined Stevens in the corner near the window. The streetlights had just come on, their light shining across the folder that Stevens opened.

"You managed to piss the Scotsman off again, didn't you?"

"Damn right I did. He had it coming," Brady said with a grin, then pulled out the chair and had a seat. "What do you have for me, Stevens?"

"Not absolutely sure just yet, but I'm working on a pretty solid lead." Stevens turned the folder toward Brady, then leaned back in the chair and rested his hands behind his head. "Take a look."

Brady pulled the file closer and began to read the contents. Occasionally he ran his hand through his hair and let out a *hmm* or a *ha*. "This might just do the trick, if we can prove it."

"Oh, I know we can prove it if we can get one of them to talk."

"That's a pretty tall order. We'd have to get the judge or someone on the parole board to confess to accepting bribes," Brady said with a deep scowl. "If we're wrong, we'll be blacklisted. Now that I think of it, I'm already in the shitter, so I haven't got anything to lose."

"Another angle would be the warden," Stevens said before taking a good long sip.

"Good call. The only way I can think of that she'd be able to have a parole hearing at all is if the warden was in on it somehow."

"Good behavior to the nth degree. Perhaps he got a little somethin' somethin' on the side from the princess, if you follow my drift."

"Or Lockwood paid him off. Maybe I should pay a little visit to our princess."

"Are you out of your mind, Brady? You can't encourage a woman like that. She's messed up."

"I can't think of a better way. She sang like a bird when she confessed to killing Sam Anderson. Maybe she'll sing again." Saying Sam's name out loud caused him to feel guilty, but for what? He hadn't done anything wrong. But he felt the pang of guilt in his gut just the same. He'd have to do this; it was the only way.

CHAPTER 17

It was a beautiful day for a walk along Long Sands Beach. The tide was out, but a sea mist was still prominent along the breaker wall. It was a cool afternoon, which was typical for a mid-September day. The change in temperature was a welcome gift for Sophie, at five months along. Fall was usually a difficult time for Sophie, and she typically fell into a bit of melancholy. Not much bloomed naturally outside. Sunflowers, mums, coneflowers, and sedum were staples around Proposals' grounds, but so much would fall into a deep sleep in preparation for winter. Intellectually, she knew it was necessary, but she found it regrettable just the same.

Sam had always loved fall. It was his favorite time of year. He found the crisp air, the smell of fallen leaves, and the unending task of fall cleanup invigorating. Sophie would watch him as he raked, mulched, and planted. Oh, how she missed him. Sophie held back her tears as best as she could when she saw Emily approach.

"Hey, partner. Sorry I'm late."

"It's all good. Shall we?" She wiped a tear from her eye, careful to make sure that Emily wouldn't notice. They had too much to talk about without getting sidetracked by her issues.

"You set the pace," Emily said with a gesture toward the hard sand near the water.

Sophie and Emily needed a change of atmosphere for planning an open house at Proposals. Since the television spot and the Bennington wedding, they had been inundated with future customers wanting to see the setting in person. The website just wasn't enough. Holding an open house would help eliminate the multitude of tours that had been taking so much of their time. Baking and arranging had to be their priority, but tours were necessary.

Having girl time outside of Proposals was a welcome treat. They really hadn't had much time to catch up on life. Even though much of the time was spent talking about work, it felt good to simply take a walk with their best friend. After the plans were arranged, a comfortable silence fell over them that neither of them felt the need to break.

Sophie reached out to take hold of her friend's hand. The reassurance of knowing she was a constant in her life gave her a sense of peace. She needed some consistency with everything that had happened over the past six months. Feeling Emily's hand in hers was surely different than Sam's. His were strong hands, callused and rough. It was an ongoing task to apply hand cream to the back of each hand and rub it in. She'd circle them, apply pressure to his palms, and massage each finger. It wasn't much, but she knew he'd enjoyed it. He'd worked hard for her and would joyfully do anything she asked without excuses. He was a good man.

Lost in their own thoughts, they were both taken by surprise when a kite came crashing down in front of them. Two teenagers ran to retrieve the dragonfly that had taken a nose dive in the sand between them. "Sorry," the young man said as his girlfriend breathlessly giggled at his side.

"It's all right," Emily replied. "What a great day to fly a kite."

"Yes, ma'am," the girl said as they ran off.

"Young, in love, and carefree. Wouldn't it be great to be them right now?" Sophie said wistfully.

"Are you kidding me? Never! I wouldn't relive my teens for all the money in the world. It was hard enough the first time."

"I wonder what I would do differently if I could do it all over again."

"Nothing, Sophie. You don't live with regrets. You're the one who's always saying that we are who we are today because of what we've been through in the past. We can choose to allow our past to make us stronger or let it defeat us. You, my friend, grow stronger, and you are beautifully and gloriously made. Don't you ever forget that."

Sophie pulled her collar up over her neck to block the chilling wind. The salty air, mixed with the brisk wind, began to bite at her ears and her cheeks. It was time to turn back. The image of the dragonfly kite was a good sign, she thought. Her mother had told her when she was a child that a dragonfly symbolized a change of perspective on oneself and a deeper understanding of life. Sophie's wisdom and adaptability had been instilled in her by her mother, and adapting was all she could do right now. *One step at a time.*

"Have you thought about a name?"

"Not yet. Sometimes it still doesn't seem real. I can't

believe that I have a little tiny baby girl growing inside of me." A tender caress inside her belly brought a smile to her face. "Oh, she just kicked! Do you want to feel it?"

"Does a seagull shit in the sea?" Emily placed her hand ever so carefully where Sophie guided. The baby rolled from one side to the other, and Emily quickly withdrew her hand. "Oh, my heart! That's amazing! I've never felt anything like that."

"Pretty incredible, isn't it?" Sophie's mind instantly shifted to what it would have been like for Sam to feel it for the first time. He would have been ecstatic and shouted something splendid for the world to hear. He was a corny fool, but she loved every ounce of him. Before she could bring herself to the point of tears again, Emily snapped her out of it.

"I wonder if she'll have a lot of hair. Or, I wonder what color her eyes will be. I bet they'll be blue, like yours."

"Or green, like Sam's. His eyes were like windows to his soul, you know what I mean?"

"Honestly, I never really looked that intently into his eyes. That was your job."

"Good point," Sophie said with a nod of agreement.

. . .

The days were moving by quickly and the open house was upon them. Sophie was relieved to some degree that Brady had been away. She didn't need the gossiping tongues to speculate about them any longer.

They staged Proposals as if a wedding were taking place. The bartenders were on hand to sell alcohol and serve complimentary soft drinks, coffee, tea, and mulled apple cider. On the stage, a small instrumental ensemble played quietly in the background to set the mood. They'd chosen smaller high-top round tables with champagne linens. Pumpkin centerpieces sat atop each table, with cascading dahlias, sunflowers, and chrysanthemums in yellow, orange, and burgundy, complemented by a pop of tiny white star-shaped bouvardia, to signify enthusiasm.

A long table sat in the center of the room with a couple half bushels of apples, additional pumpkin arrangements, and a cornucopia of pears, grapes, pomegranates, apples, and mixed nuts. A variety of cheeses, nuts, chocolate, and crackers were arranged on pieces of barn board that lay atop small bales of hay. Tiers of cupcakes sat among the fruit and cheeses. Emily had created the magical assortment of cinnamon-spiced caramel apple, pumpkin, and maple cupcakes, each garnished to perfection.

Even though it was early in the evening, with the sun still shining, Sophie and Emily lit carefully displayed candles throughout. Lanterns lined the outdoor wedding location. Pumpkins, hay bales, and squash announced the entrance. An archway of grapevines, covered with flowers coordinated with those inside, was the focal point, helping the guests envision what could be.

The maple trees that lined the property burst with red, bright orange, and yellow. Some of the leaves had already started falling, completing the scene.

The timing had worked out perfectly for the open house as the Templetons, her sweet elderly friends, would be celebrating their fiftieth wedding anniversary by renewing their vows the following weekend. This helped both the Templetons and Proposals, as they could share in the cost of the flowers and anything else that could be used again.

The Templetons had been like another set of parents to Sophie and Sam over the years. Agnes Templeton would often stop by for tea as Sophie gleaned from her the subtleties of marrying different pollination techniques to create the most beautiful species of flowers. Her hands were tanned from years of exposure to the sun. Wearing gloves, she'd say with a hint of mischief, was for sissies. The lines of her hands were stained with soil and clay. She wore an apron most days, the pockets bulging with snips, shears, a spade, and miscellaneous weeds popping out the top. She usually adorned her wide-brimmed straw hat with a flower wedged under the floral ribbon band.

Frank Templeton would often meander about the wide expanse of the grounds, suggesting pruning methods and transplanting ideas and explaining the proper way of dividing each type of perennial. Sam would take it all in and ask a million questions. Frank was always steady and thorough in his response. He had been a college professor in his younger years, and his teaching style remained part of his charm. Sam never grew impatient, as Frank had a way of making the process of dividing a hosta captivating.

Sophie and Sam owed much to the Templetons for the way Proposals looked today. Offering to split the costs of the open house had been the least Sophie could do, as the Templetons were proud and that was the most that they would accept.

As Sophie stood back to take in the scene before her, she was once again moved by the product of two minds working in tandem.

Emily stepped up next to Sophie. "We did good, didn't we, partner?"

"Indeed, partner, we did." And with that, they opened the doors to an onslaught of potential clients and nosy neighbors.

Sophie and Emily greeted each guest while handing out trifold brochures explaining each area of interest, option, and package that Proposals offered. Each brochure had a detachable comment card and was carefully wrapped in a champagne-colored ribbon. A small peach-colored rose that symbolized appreciation was tucked into the ribbon.

Mrs. Bennington was sure to pay a visit to express her gratitude once again for hosting such a fine wedding for her Penelope. She arrived with a booming voice as if to announce her presence to all of York Village. She always wore her position in the community as a badge of honor, regardless of the occasion. After all, she was *the* Mrs. Bennington.

Within moments, she was asking about Brady. "Where is your gentleman friend, Sophie?" she said with a sideways glance and a wink. "You've sure snagged yourself a handsome one." She tapped Sophie on the shoulder. "I simply must see him again to congratulate him on the beautiful spread that was in the paper, and I've got to get my hands on any other photos that he took of Penelope."

Sophie was aghast. "Mr. Owens isn't here today, Mrs. Bennington. He's in New York on business."

"Oh, why the formality, Sophie? His name is Brady, isn't it?"

"Yes, um, it is…but, Mrs. Bennington, he's not my—"

Just then, Mrs. Bennington caught the eye of one of the other socialites in town. "Well, look who's here! Clara, darling, how are the twins?" With that, she waltzed off.

Sophie had a fondness for Brady, but why was everyone so convinced that there was something more to it than mere friendship? She'd have to put some distance between them, that much she was sure of.

The taste and sound of the event were just what Sophie needed. She had been born for this, she realized, and she cherished every moment. It was especially nice that she and Emily only had to please themselves today. No mother of the bride, bride, or bridezilla, for that matter, would be hovering about, panicking over the simplest of non-issues. This was their time to enjoy and take it all in. It was the aftermath of the event that wouldn't be as enjoyable: paperwork and meetings.

CHAPTER 18

The booking desk at Proposals was stacked with inquiries and contracts. The dates were filling up through the following year. Sophie had been working on interviewing an assistant who would step in while she was on maternity leave. Granted, Sophie would only be a few yards away and thought that she could handle the workload, but she felt strongly that the bonding period with her little one was more important. She had vowed to be the best mother she could be, one who thought of her child before herself. She'd be a mom that was dependable. Still, she had her doubts and hoped beyond all hope that she wouldn't let her little girl down. An assistant, she concluded, could help her to achieve that. They could focus on the putting the arrangements together and placing the florals on the cakes and at the site, and she would establish the vision based on the wishes of the parties involved, with the support of her assistant. But it had to be the right one.

There were many nuances to the way Sophie saw the arrangements. Each piece was a work of art. Hers was an artistic eye, and no two artists were the same. As such, each arrangement could be very different, even when the same flowers were chosen. Sophie was known for a certain style, and she needed to pass that on to another so that her reputation wouldn't suffer while she stepped away. As she only had a few short months for training, she needed to find someone soon. Rebecca Mills came as a highly recommended floral designer. Sophie and Emily had already gone over Rebecca's resume, and Emily had given her blessing, so long as Sophie thought she was a good fit.

Rebecca was prompt and professional in appearance. Sophie's first impression of her was positive. She had a slender build, thick brown hair drawn up into a loose bun and almond-shaped deep green eyes. Her lips were full, and her smile was striking. She shook hands with a firm, confident grip and put her other hand on top of Sophie's to reinforce the connection.

"Thanks for coming, Miss Mills," Sophie said with an encouraging smile.

"Oh, please call me Rebecca," she replied sincerely in a pleasant tone.

Sophie knew right away that it would be a good match but conscientiously proceeded with a formal interview that lasted close to an hour. According to her resume and references, Rebecca was hardworking and skilled; she didn't complain, and while she took pride in her work, she was open to constructive criticism to improve her craft.

"Are you up for the challenge, Rebecca?"

Sophie could tell that Rebecca was ecstatic, but her response was carefully managed. "I sure am. Thank you."

Sophie made a mental note that Rebecca could be read like a book, and that somehow pleased her. "Welcome to Proposals," Sophie said, reaching out her hand.

"I'm a hugger," Rebecca said with enthusiasm and appreciation. "May I?"

Sophie responded by opening herself up for the hug.

Sophie and Rebecca entered the bakery, with Sophie taking the lead. "Emily, please meet our new team member. This is Rebecca Mills."

"Nice to meet you, Rebecca. Welcome to Proposals."

. . .

Brady arrived at the Bedford Hills Correctional Facility. He filled out the appropriate forms, as Cynthia had already approved him as a visitor when she was first incarcerated. But on this occasion, he would enter as her legal counsel; this would allow them more privacy, and there'd be a greater chance of her spilling the beans.

It wasn't the first time he'd been there as legal counsel for a client, but he still felt uneasy. The women were just as bad as the men when a member of the opposite sex was there. It was as if they could sense the testosterone level increase as soon as he entered the hallway, just beyond the locked doors. The women whistled and showed their excitement with gyrations and lip smacking. The guard yelled, and the inmates yelled back. Brady was brought to a private room to await Cynthia's entrance. There were strict rules against touching, for which Brady was quite grateful. She'd be in cuffs and sitting on the opposite side of the table. A guard would be nearby.

Cynthia entered the room with a sullen look on her face. Her eyes were downcast, her blond hair had dark brown roots, and she wore no makeup. Brady would have never believed that he'd see her looking this way in his lifetime. He'd imagined that even on her death bed, she'd be on point. It wasn't until she actually sat down that she took note of who was on the opposite side of the metal table.

"Brady! It's you, my love!" she said with delight. "It's really you! I thought you'd be another one of Daddy's stooges. When they said my visitor was my counsel, I just assumed." The realization of her appearance finally hit her. She tried to tidy her hair, to no avail, as her cuffs prevented such a move.

"I don't know why they have to put these damn things on me. Honestly, it's not like I'm some kind of criminal. You must think I'm a beast, looking like this."

Brady couldn't believe his ears…actually, yes, he could. She was incapable of remorse or of seeing reality as it was. But he knew he would catch more flies with honey than with vinegar.

"You'll always be beautiful, Cyn." Saying that out loud made him feel ill.

"I never gave up on us, Brady…never. I knew you'd be back in my life."

"I hear you're up for parole." He'd decided that the direct approach was best.

"Yes, I am! I never dreamed that it would be so soon. I mean, no one ever gets a parole board meeting as quickly as I am."

"Yeah, it's pretty amazing. So, how has it been in here?"

"Dreadful, just dreadful. I share a cell with a Neanderthal and a snitch. It's all I can do to stay sane."

Brady could barely keep his composure. *She thinks she's sane; how cute.* "Have they caused you any trouble? Have you been hurt?"

"Of course. What else would you expect from a beast that wants to control your every move? And every time I plan to do something about it, the scrawny little snitch opens her piehole. But I've figured out how to beat the system. I get in just enough trouble so they put me in solitary. I get privacy, so no one bothers me. I honestly don't know why solitary confinement gets such a negative rap. I still get the same food, I get time alone outside, and I don't have to deal with the population. On top of that, the guard is even nicer."

None of that made sense in Brady's mind; everyone knew solitary confinement was horrific. No one would purposely put themselves in there. "What's the room like in solitary?"

"It's pretty nice, really. Since there's no other beds besides mine, I have more room for shelving, a table with a chair—oh, and my bed's more comfortable."

"It does sound better than I would have thought. I can't say I blame you for getting into trouble so you can be there. If I were you, I'd pick fights just to get moved there."

"Oh, I do!" Cynthia said as if she were proud of herself. "In the beginning, being here was really scary. My roommates were terrifying, and I cried all the time, which made things worse. But Libby—oh, he's one of the guards—gave me a few pointers that helped me out a lot."

"Really, Libby? A guard helped you?"

"Yes, he's one of the newer guards in my block. He also told me to act really furious and fight when they bring me to solitary. He said that the other inmates would see that and think I was strong and tough and not mess with me as much. So, I play the part and then I get to stay where I like it better. Right now, though, I'm in with the Neanderthal, which, I admit, scares me so much that I can't sleep."

"Hopefully you'll be getting out of here really soon and you won't have to deal with this nightmare anymore, Cyn," he said with as much sincerity as he could muster.

"Daddy said it will be really soon, too."

"Does your dad visit you often?"

"All the time. He said he'd always be looking out for me and that he would never let me down again," she said with a pout. "He did really let me down, you know. I shouldn't be here in the first place; it was an accident. It's not like I purposely ran over the man."

It was inconceivable that she couldn't understand the consequences of her actions, and it made Brady's blood boil.

Without missing a beat, Cynthia completely shifted gears. "What shall we do when I get out? We could take a long drive or go to the theater. Oh, no…let's eat at our favorite Italian place, then afterwards we can bring a bottle of wine up to the roof, look at the stars, and make love! Sounds perfect, doesn't it?" she asked with a squeal.

Brady shook his head. "Whoa, let's just see when and if you get out of here before we start making plans." A look of dejection flashed across her face, and Brady took her hand. "I wouldn't want you to get your hopes up, only to get hurt," he reassured her. She gave a toothy smile.

The guard pounded on the door and peered through the small window with a stern face. "No touching," he mouthed.

"You can't be serious!" Cynthia screeched. "It's not like we can do anything in here. I'm cuffed, for crying out loud!"

Brady tried to quiet her without success.

"He's come all this way to see me and he can't even touch my hand? This is ridiculous…you are ridiculous!"

Brady could hear the keys turning in the door. The guard

approached the table and took a firm stance. "Time's up, Lockwood. Back to your cell."

"Already?" Cynthia said like a petulant child. "But we didn't finish our business. You can't do this!"

"Keep it up, Lockwood, and you'll end up back in solitary."

Cynthia looked at Brady and flashed a smile. "See you soon, my love."

Brady was left speechless and getting more furious by the moment. He'd wanted more answers; he'd needed more time. His mind was racing as an escort guided him through the corridors toward the exit. With one last buzz and clank of the door, he was back in the parking lot, in search of his car.

He was on the road for an hour-long drive back to the city to meet up with Stevens. He'd have to find out more about this so-called guard, Libby. What was his connection with Henry Lockwood? How was he able to provide a special room with special treatment under the noses of the other guards and the warden? Then the realization hit him. *The warden is* definitely *in on it!*

CHAPTER 19

Sophie decided to start Rebecca off with Agnes and Frank Templeton's vow renewal, since it was pretty much mapped out already. Rebecca seemed to catch on rather quickly and was able to make some modifications to the arrangements that added charm and expressed the couple's personality. Sophie was quite relieved. The Templetons had been so kind and understanding when Sophie had approached them with the idea of having someone else take over the planning. Agnes had been thrilled to play a part in the growth of Proposals, while Frank, on the other hand, hadn't cared one way or the other. He was a bit lost without Sam, as Sam had given him purpose. He went along with the ladies and anything they thought best. Frank was much happier wandering the grounds, poking about here and there. Since Sam wasn't around to see to things, he took it upon himself to do what he could and contribute in the only way that he knew how.

Neither Agnes nor Frank were ones to gossip. They minded their own business unless they were invited to offer advice, a shoulder, or a strong pair of hands. Frank had mentioned that he'd seen Brady at Proposals for the last several months and assumed that Sophie hired him to help out since she was in the motherly way, and that things were well under control. Having a reason to be on the property, he'd recommended that they prepare for the winter, as nothing had been done, and he knew darn well that Sam would never have allowed that.

Rebecca sat and had tea with Agnes to do a final run-through of the floral side of things. Agnes seemed to be pleased with everything and told Rebecca as much.

"You've known Sophie for a long time, haven't you, Mrs. Templeton?"

"Oh, yes. Seems like yesterday when she and Sam moved in. They were hard workers from the beginning. They were wet behind the ears, but Sophie always had a green thumb." She chuckled with an impish little grin and squinted eyes. Rebecca responded with a kind smile, fond of Agnes already.

"I don't mean to pry," said Rebecca with some hesitation, "but do you know what happened to her husband? She never speaks of it, and I don't want to ask. It's just that I don't want to say something that could be…well, you know, awkward, without meaning to."

Agnes placed her hand atop of Rebecca's and tapped it gently. "It's not for me to tell, my dear. She'll share if she sees fit."

Emily had entered the room as Agnes was responding to Rebecca. "Anything I can help you with, Rebecca?" she said curtly.

"Um, no, not really. We were just finishing our tea so I

can get back to work."

"That's right, dear. Just finishing our tea." Agnes stood up to leave.

"Mrs. Templeton, it was enjoyable spending some time with you today. Please let me know if you have any questions."

Emily responded under her breath, "Seems to me you're the one with all the questions."

"I'm sorry, Emily, did you say something?" Rebecca knew full well that Emily wasn't pleased with her.

"Nope, nothing important." Emily turned away and headed toward the kitchen.

"Well, I'm off," said Agnes. "I've got to see what Frank is up to. For all I know, he's fallen in a hole somewhere. You think I'm joking, but it wouldn't be the first time," she said with a sparkle in her eyes and walked out the door.

Sophie met Agnes at the door and held it open for her. They greeted each other with a hug. "It's getting a bit harder to wrap my arms around you, dear. You couldn't be more adorable with that belly of yours."

"I'm not feeling so adorable these days, but thank you for the sentiment. Is Rebecca taking good care of you?"

"Oh, yes, she's a peach." With that, she was on her merry way.

There was an awkward silence as Sophie entered the room. Both Emily and Rebecca were in the bakery. Rebecca was wiping down the small wrought iron table and chairs that she and Agnes had shared while Emily was placing more apple tarts and banana muffins in the case. You could cut the tension with a knife. Sophie was in no mood to intervene; they ware adults and could handle whatever the problem might be, so she decided to ignore the obvious situation.

"Hey, Sophie. When's Brady coming back?" Emily said with more of a change-the-subject manner than actual curiosity.

"I'm not really sure. I would imagine any day. I received a text from him a couple of days ago. He said he had a surprise for me that he couldn't wait for me to see."

"Sounds intriguing…any ideas?" Emily said with a hint of "Sophie's got a boyfriend" humor.

Sophie was taken aback by Emily's quick turnaround but was relieved just the same. "You can get whatever little thoughts you're having out of your head." Sophie turned away, as she could feel her cheeks turning pink.

"Where did you say Brady went again?"

"What's the wanting-to-know-all-about-Brady thing happening here?" Sophie decided to turn the tables. "Does someone miss him? If I didn't know better, I'd think somebody was missing him."

"Yeah, yeah, that would be a great big no."

"I don't know…you seem to be awfully curious about him."

Emily picked up her apron and strutted toward the kitchen. "Okay, fine. I admit I miss him a teeny-weeny bit. I need someone to pick on, and it just doesn't feel right picking on a prego."

"I can't believe you just called me a prego! Emily Vassure, you're a brat!"

Brady opened the door and stepped inside with a grin. "Did I just hear you call Emily a brat?"

"You bet you did," said Sophie with a scowl, her hands on her hips.

"And I thought I was the only one who thought that," Brady said laughingly.

"Okay, enough from the two of you. Doesn't anyone ever

work around here? This brat is going to bake a cake." Once she was in the kitchen, she yelled, "Glad to have you back, Brade, man!"

"It's good to be back, Emily!"

It *was* good to have Brady back. Sophie had grown accustomed to him being a fixture around the place. She hadn't realized how much she'd miss him until he was gone.

"Were you able to take care of the business you needed to get done?"

Brady avoided looking directly into Sophie's eyes. "Um, I have a good start to it. I'll be taking a few more trips, but hopefully it won't be much longer."

"That's good."

"Oh, hey! How did the big open house go? Was it a success?"

Sophie was pleased by his inquiry. Most men wouldn't even remember, let alone ask about it. "It was great. We honestly couldn't have asked for it to go any better."

"Fantastic. Wish I could have been here to join in on the fun." A grin began to form across his face. "Would you like to see what I brought you?" He started easing his way backward out the door.

"What do you have up your sleeve, Brady?"

He seemed a bit nervous, yet excited at the same time, Sophie thought.

"I'll be right back. It's in the car. I didn't want to bring it in because I wasn't sure you'd be in here."

He turned and jogged to the car, opened the back, and took out a large flat box. Sophie watched from the window with anticipation. As he got closer, she opened the door. Brady took a leap onto the landing with a huge grin.

"I hope you'll like it."

"Maybe we should go into the main house. You know, in case a customer comes in." Not knowing what it was could prove to be embarrassing should she open it in front of Lord knows who.

"Sure, lead the way."

"Let's go to the den." She almost felt giddy with curiosity.

"Sounds like a plan." The light shone through the windows, and he brought the package to the table that sat within the round nook. Full-length ivory sheers edged the large windows, whose many small panes allowed the sun to flood the room. Sophie cleared the table of some magazines while Brady lowered the package onto the table.

"I hope you like it. I went to quite a few shops until I found what I was looking for."

Sophie moved one of the chairs to the side, stood at the edge of the table, and carefully pried open the lid of the box. She reached her hand in and touched a soft foam wrapping and gently slid the item out. Setting the box on the floor, she looked up at Brady before proceeding.

"Go ahead," he urged.

Sophie unwrapped each layer of paper until it began to show a chestnut-colored wooden frame. The frame itself was a work of art, intricately detailed with carved flowers of different sizes and depths. Sophie's heart began to race, and her hands shook with anticipation of what lay beneath the tissue. She lifted a corner and carefully pulled the tissue away. Sophie gasped as it revealed a photo of herself from the night of the Benningtons' wedding. She was wearing her green gown. The crystal choker around her neck sparkled just a touch as she stood at an angled profile. Her head was turned to face Brady as he took the shot, which elongated her neck and showcased her tresses. Her auburn hair glowed with golden highlights from the lighting in the room. The background was a blur of copper and pearl.

What took her breath away, though, was her little baby girl wrapped within the embrace of her hand atop her protruding belly. She was mesmerized by this portrait. Her fingers caressed the details that passed before her eyes. Her mind swirled with the memory of such a beautiful evening, the beauty of her surroundings, and thoughts of herself as a mother-to-be. Brady had made her look beautiful too. She blinked, and a tear ran down her cheek.

"I love it, Brady. I absolutely love it."

Brady stood behind her and rested a hand on her shoulder. "I thought you might."

"Thank you so much." She turned to give him a hug. "So, this is what you went all the way to New York City for." Without waiting for a response, she retreated and picked up the portrait. "Where do you think it should go?"

Brady looked around the room, nodding as if this really was the perfect place for it to be. "How about right there over Sam's desk, between the bookshelves?"

"Perfect. That would be simply perfect." She wiped the damp drops off her cheeks.

"Now, how about you telling me who the new woman behind your counter is?"

"Oh, I completely forgot! Her name is Rebecca Mills and she's my new assistant. She's really delightful."

"Delightful," he said with a nod of agreement.

CHAPTER 20

Brady sat on his porch, overlooking the vastness of the gray Atlantic. He wore a hooded sweatshirt that was torn at the cuff, a relic from his alma mater, Cornell. The old wooden rocker creaked with each motion, causing an uneven rhythm as it combined with the loose wooden decking. The moon cast a gloomy reflection upon the water, but the moon itself wasn't distinguishable behind the storm clouds that were rolling in. Brady was thrilled that Sophie loved the portrait. He was pretty proud of it, as he usually took shots of places and things. There was something about shooting a portrait that stirred something in him. He enjoyed capturing the moment and being able to see into the soul of an individual. The resolution on his camera could take in every fine line and detail, down to the hues of their eyes. It was as if he could sense from the participant an unspoken truth. Of course, he could brush out the fine lines, but the truth of the person could live on to tell a story. They were here, they were real, and they mattered. The problem with this particular portrait was that it only caused him to see the untruth that he was harboring within himself.

He was fond of Sophie Anderson, and that fondness had only grown deeper. He cared for her, wanted what was best for her, and felt a deep yearning to protect her. Brady knew that the New York trip wasn't just about justice, and it wasn't completely about revenge. He just knew Sophie mattered.

His secret was gnawing at his gut. It wasn't right, he knew that, but it was what was needed. Maybe someday he would tell the truth, but not anytime soon. He wanted the time he had with her to last for as long as it could, but he couldn't shake off the eerie feeling that crept over him. He brushed off the urge to go inside to escape. Stretching out his leg to retrieve his phone from his pocket, he pressed the number for Stevens. Brady was just about to leave a message when he picked up.

"Hey, I was just about to call you. Are you sitting down?" Stevens asked in a winded gasp, as if he'd run to answer.

"Umm, yeah, I'm sitting. What's up?"

"The parole board approved her for parole, Brady. She's going to be getting out in a few weeks." It was all Brady could do not to chuck his phone over the cliff. He stood up and began to pace.

"How did Lockwood do it, Stevens? Did you find out more about the guard, Libby?"

"I sure did. Adam Libby is Lloyd Becker's son-in-law."

"Who the hell is Lloyd Becker?"

"The warden, Brady. He's the warden."

"Dammit! How the hell did I forget that?" Brady was steaming. "Adam Libby is the warden's son-in-law!" He slammed the door behind him as he went inside, realizing that his anger was loud enough for the neighbors to hear.

"Apparently he'd made several attempts at being a police officer but couldn't pass the psychological or fitness testing. Becoming a guard was the next logical step, especially considering his father-in-law is a warden. Seems his finances had started to dry up, and he couldn't wait out the lag time until the next testing block."

"Sounds like someone pretty susceptible to a bribe to me," Brady said after taking a swig of a beer that he'd grabbed from the fridge. "But what's in it for Lloyd Becker?"

"That's what I've been trying to figure out as well. Do you think Lockwood has the influence to remove him from his position? He's in pretty tight with the governor and the attorney general. I'm not saying they have anything to do with this, but he could have thrown his weight around and threatened Becker. It would have been easy for Becker and Libby to work together to make Cynthia look pretty good to a parole board. Exceptional, even."

Brady ran his hand through his hair and paced the kitchen, then stopped for another gulp of beer. "We need proof, Stevens. This is all speculation. Plausible and more than likely factual, but we need to find the proof somehow."

"Not sure how we can get it, and if we can, I can't imagine how we could get it before she's released," Stevens said doubtfully.

"Do you think any of the parole board members are in on this? Seems hard to believe that they'd be unanimous; she hasn't been in that long. At least one of them would call that into question, wouldn't you think? This just doesn't happen—ever."

Stevens hesitated. "There's some dirty play going on, that's for sure. I've got a friend that can do some snooping around. I think we should see if any money changed hands. Lockwood has some really deep pockets and some political connections. Maybe there's a trail."

"My guess is that he's too smart to leave a trail, but this is his little girl we're talking about—he might have slipped up." Brady leaned against the counter, twirling the beer cap. "See what your friend can do, and I'll pay another visit to Cynthia." With that, he flicked the cap across the room, aiming for the trash can, and scored.

. . .

Sophie arose with a yawn after hitting snooze on her phone for the third time. She was missing the usual spring in her step, which wasn't surprising, since she had been awake half the night. Trying to get comfortable in her third trimester was becoming a bit of a nuisance, but she was grateful for the discomfort. Sam's little girl was growing, and it was worth any sacrifice, even if it meant losing sleep. She stepped into her slippers but skipped the robe. Sophie had enough body heat to wilt her flowers.

Daisy jumped off the bed in search of her breakfast, making her impatience loud and clear. "I'm coming, Miss Daisy. I'm a little bit slower, but I'm coming." She popped in a K-cup of decaf and listened to the drip while working out the sleep from the corner of her eyes. Looking out the window at the blanket of frost covering the grounds, she heaved a sigh of relief that a lot of the fall cleanup had been done; Frank Templeton had made sure of it. With Sophie's permission, he'd hired a crew to take care of the heavy lifting, but he had been sure to supervise.

Sophie had hoped that Brady might be here to help with the cleanup, which she knew was presumptuous of her. After all, he wasn't her personal handyman. She'd just gotten accustomed to having him around, as he was always willing to pitch in to help. Normally, she would have contributed to the task, as she loved getting her hands dirty, but it was simply out of the question; she feared she wouldn't be able to get back up off the ground.

The scent of spice cake wafting from the bakery was welcoming to the senses, and she was joyous that it didn't cause her to feel ill. All the morning sickness was over, and for the first time in a long time, she felt like herself, even given her much-expanded waistline.

Sophie shuffled toward the den with her coffee, careful not to trip over Daisy. She picked up her laptop along the way and brought it to the desk. She'd look over her to-do list and read the news before she truly started her day. Swiveling in her chair, she had a full view of the portrait that Brady had taken of her.

"He is really good, Daisy." Daisy jumped up onto the desk and circled around the pencil holder and her computer before curling up into a ball on her mousepad. "What do you think?" Sophie bent down to be nose to nose with her furry companion. "Do you think I should talk with Emily about hiring Brady as an in-house photographer?"

He would be the perfect fit, she decided. He was quite skilled and was making a name for himself without even trying. Everyone loved him, as he had a way of helping people relax. Making the subject feel at ease was key to a good portrait, and Brady had a knack for that, as she'd had the pleasure of witnessing firsthand.

He'd been unspeakably handsome the night he had taken her portrait. She'd grown accustomed to seeing him in jeans and a work belt, which she still found quite attractive. However, when she'd laid eyes on him in that suit—well, the thought of taking it off had crossed her mind. She'd enjoyed the feel of him being in his arms, and she still couldn't believe that she'd kissed him. Sophie closed her eyes, recalling the taste of him and yearning for intimacy again in her life.

Sophie gazed at the portrait again. She hoped he'd seriously consider her proposition. With the project done, he'd been so busy in the city, and she'd had her doubts. He'd seemed secretive as of late, which wasn't like him, and her curiosity was getting the best of her.

As if Brady had read her mind, there was a tap at the door. "Hello, Sophie. Are you in here?" Brady said in a quiet voice as if not to wake her should she still be sleeping.

"I'm in here, Brady!"

Daisy jumped off the desk with a thump and ran toward the squeaking door to where Brady stood.

"Hey, kitty, kitty. You're a good girl, aren't you, kitty? Yes, you are," Brady said in a baby voice. Sophie found this quite endearing and was lost in her thoughts of the pleasure of having him here when Brady approached the doorway to the den.

He stood tall and filled the space with his broad shoulders. His jeans were tight, showing his masculine form. He wore a beige pullover sweater with a brown leather pull zipper at the neck, which was unzipped enough to show the collar of his pinstriped oxford shirt. His dark hair was windblown and his cheeks were pink from the chill in the air. Sophie took in a breath and felt her hormones go into overdrive. She'd read about this symptom of pregnancy but had never dreamed it would happen to her. After all, she was single and without a love interest. The intensity of her arousal took her off guard, and she wasn't sure how to respond to it.

Suddenly feeling extremely exposed, she stuttered to speak and knocked her coffee over, spilling it all over her laptop. She jumped up to avoid getting wet, which caused her to lose her balance. Within seconds, Brady was there to catch her before she hit the floor.

"What happened? Are you all right?" Brady asked with confusion written all over his face.

"I, umm, I don't know, I was just, just…umm." Sophie was mortified. She didn't even know where to begin as she couldn't explain it to herself, let alone to Brady Owens. "No, umm, I'm fine. I was just…I saw a spider! Did I ever tell you how much I hate spiders? Nasty beasts with their creepy, hairy legs."

Then, she quickly came to the realization that she, too, had hairy legs, coffee breath, and an extremely sheer nightshirt on. She tried to cover her hardened nipples and exposed legs, which was a difficult task at seven months pregnant. The whole experience suddenly brought Sophie to tears, which was also an unexpected surprise. She stood there with a determined expression, gathered herself to a stern stand, and let the tears fall, while pretending that it wasn't happening.

"I do believe that I killed it. I'm fine now. Is there something you wanted, Brady?"

Brady was momentarily speechless. "Maybe I should come back another time?"

"No, it's fine. I'm just going to my room for a minute. Why don't you go get yourself a coffee, refill mine—decaf, please—and, oh, why don't you grab a couple of cinnamon twists? By the time you get back, I'll be...umm, dressed. Okay?" Sophie said with tear-stained cheeks.

Brady nodded and turned to leave without another word. Sophie brought her palms to her face and covered her eyes. "They're going to put me in a nuthouse, Daisy," she said, laughing so hard that she had to cross her legs to avoid peeing herself again.

. . .

As he centered her cup under the K-cup dispenser, Brady replayed in his mind the oddity he'd just witnessed. He stirred in the sugar, added a touch of cream to each cup, then went to pay Emily a visit to get the cinnamon sticks.

"Well, well, look who the cat dragged in," Emily said with a snicker.

"Emily, have you noticed anything different about Sophie lately?"

"Besides the fact that she walks with a bit of a waddle? No."

Brady shook it off and retrieved the twists. "They're for the baby!" he declared.

"Pretty soon you'll have to contribute to the overhead, Brady. You're eating my profits."

"Seems to me I've done enough around here to eat my way into the next few years."

"Okay, you may have a point there. But don't let it go to your head." The oven timer went off. "Hey, hang on a sec, I'll be right back."

Brady saw a car pull up and knew it was too early to be a customer. A tall attractive woman got out of the car and withdrew an armful of packages from the backseat. As she approached the door to the bakery, he stepped out to give her a hand when it registered who she was.

"Oh, thank you. Brady, right?"

"Yes, that's right. And you must be Miss Mills, the one that's helping Sophie."

"One and the same," Rebecca said with a wide smile. "It's nice to meet you." As she escaped into the floral shop, Emily returned.

She wiped her hands on her apron and put them on each one of his shoulders. "So, what's the deal with going to New York all the time?"

Brady swallowed hard. "You've never been one to beat around the bush, have you, Em?"

"Short and sweet; that's the way I like it."

"Just some work that I'm involved in. Some stuff that I used to handle back at my old job that they needed some help with is all." Brady could feel his heart rate pick up. "You know, I really should get back to Sophie. Her coffee will be cold by the time I get it to her. Thanks for the cinnamon twist, Em. You're the best."

. . .

Sophie was back at the desk with a cloth, cleaning up the coffee spill, when she heard Brady's phone ring. She pulled the chair out of the way and found it on the floor. She picked it up and saw *Bedford Hills Correctional* on the screen as Brady entered the room with the coffee and sweets.

"You must have dropped this when you caught me." Sophie handed the phone to Brady and he abruptly ignored the call. "Brady, why would someone be calling you from the Bedford Hills Correctional Facility? Do you know someone there?" Just seeing that place on his phone, knowing that that was where Sam's killer was, removed all semblance of her former state.

"It's just a job that I'm helping out with," Brady said in such a matter-of-fact manner that Sophie felt a bit uncomfortable that she'd even questioned him. After all, he was an attorney; he must know a lot of people that could be associated with that correctional facility.

"I'm sorry. It's none of my business. I shouldn't have asked," Sophie said with a bit of reservation. "I just haven't been myself lately, and my emotions are all over the place. Any little thing seems to set me off into one strange mood or another. Crazy, isn't it?"

Sophie sat down on the couch, took a sip of coffee, and asked Brady to have a seat.

"Glad you got that nasty spider. Otherwise, I would have had to kill it, and they give me the heebie-jeebies." His eyes squinted as his smile grew big. And just like that, Sophie's mood had changed again.

She smiled back with a wicked little grin as she recalled what had happened to her when he'd stood in the doorway earlier. The warmth and tiny throbs between her legs began anew.

He leaned close to her and kissed her. Sophie's world was spinning. His warm, full lips pressed upon hers with tenderness as he swept her hair back in order to hold her face in his hands; she didn't resist. His tongue moved gently, gliding between her upper lip and her teeth. Sophie leaned back to expose her neck as he worked his way down her throat. He licked and kissed the length of her neck until he rested just above her breasts. She held his thick locks and pressed him to her. She ran her fingers through his hair and squirmed as his head lowered within the crease of her breasts. She could feel the warmth of his mouth upon her and once again her hormones suprised her. She let go and quivered beneath him. Brady brought his lips to hers and kissed her with passion and carefully guided force. Oh, how she wanted him—all of him—but she couldn't; she wouldn't.

Sophie's breathing settled back to its normal rhythm and he released her. She lay back on the couch with her eyes closed. He leaned over her and softly kissed her forehead. Sophie's eyes opened with a lazy seductive gaze. She felt amazing and didn't want it to end.

"You're beautiful, Sophie Anderson."

"You're not so bad yourself, Brady Owens."

"Are you okay? I'm sorry if I—"

"You have nothing to apologize for, Brady."

Sophie wiggled and shifted until her head lay on his chest. She could feel the rhythm of his heartbeat. As Brady held her in his arms, she wished the moment would never have to come to an end, but it did. She was about to doze off as he brushed her hair from her eyes.

"Sophie," he whispered.

"Yes," she said sleepily.

"I hate to say this, but I've got to go back to New York. I won't be gone long; maybe just a few days."

"Do you have to leave right now?" she asked, moving to a sitting position.

"Unfortunately, yes," he said, taking her hands. "If you need me, though, for anything at all, promise you'll call me, okay?"

Sophie was too content to let this news break the smoldering warmth that she still felt. "It's okay, Brady, I'll be fine.

Go do what you need to do."

He leaned in for a kiss. "I'll miss you."

"I'll miss you back."

CHAPTER 21

Brady had decided to take the train to New York so he could use the time to work on the way. The train hadn't arrived at Boston's South Station yet when he arrived, so he bought a large coffee and sat at one of the metal tables. The chair was cold on his legs, and a draft blew in as the doors opened to the boarding area. A shiver went down his spine and he tried to shake it off. Holding the coffee with both hands, he blew into the opening to cool it down, but also to take in the steam; it felt good on his face.

A couple about his age pulled their carry-ons through the atrium. He watched as they struggled to walk with their arms around each other's backs. They laughed out loud as they stumbled. Approaching a table adjacent to his, they released one another so he could pull out her chair. He then took her order request and retreated to Dunkin' Donuts. She sat and longingly watched her lover walk away. She had a kind look on her face, a gentleness about her. They were in love.

Brady longed to be in love. He'd come to realize that he'd always been in lust, and to date, it had failed him miserably. He'd thought he was happy several times, only to be disenchanted by short-term relationships of selfishness, superficiality, and dread, as in the case of Cynthia Lockwood.

He couldn't get the thought of Sophie out of his head. What had possessed him to kiss her, and how in God's name had it gone as far as it had? He was pissed at himself for allowing that to happen; that was the old Brady that he wanted to leave behind. However, she had been willing, and that was more than he could have ever hoped for. The need to seize the moment had appealed to his ache and desire for her, and therefore he'd let his lust control his mind. He knew he couldn't let it go any further. *She's a good woman, too good for me.* He felt sick about what he'd done. Being in New York would help. He needed to get his mind off Sophie Anderson and focus on the task at hand. Cynthia could be out very soon, and he needed to know more.

The announcement of his train sounded. He gathered his belongings and filed in to board the Acela. The lovebirds walked the length of the train in front of him, holding hands and carrying on like newlyweds, which they most likely were. Perhaps they were on their way to their honeymoon. A grin arose on Brady's face. He could picture how Sophie would have been with them at Proposals. She would be smiling from ear to ear through the course of the wedding and reception. He enjoyed watching her in her element. She was everything he now knew he wanted, but also knew he couldn't have. The couple slipped into the side door to general seating as Brady proceeded further up the walk to board business class, suddenly feeling a sense of urgency to his mission.

. . .

Sophie gathered astillbe, antique roses, seeded eucalyptus, privet berries, and sea lavender of cranberry, mauve, and ivory. She pondered the meaning of this combination—secret bonds of love, passion, and "I will be waiting for you." Little did her customers know that the secrets of her heart were those very things. Sophie had thought she'd regret her passion and display of impulse with Brady, but she didn't. She yearned for his return as she placed each stem in its position. His touch, the warmth of his mouth and hands, was something she had missed since Sam passed away.

Sam had been a passionate lover, and they'd had a healthy sex life. He had pleased her in every way imaginable, and the thought of never having that again was something that she believed she'd have to come to terms with. It was a sobering thought, but she'd put her energy into her business and the little one that was growing inside of her. The prospect of a new relationship, of ever finding someone that would even come close to what she'd had and adored in Sam, would be close to impossible. She hadn't been opposed to the possibility but was pretty confident that it wasn't in her future.

Sophie continued to create the arrangements one by one as she recalled the first time they'd met. Between her junior and senior year of high school, she'd gotten a summer job at a restaurant in Kennebunk, Maine, to earn money for school, and Sam had been spending his summer vacation with his family nearby. He had been seated in her section; she'd seen him the second he'd walked in.

He was the cutest guy she'd ever seen. He walked with a bit of a strut—not cocky, just a gait that was unique to him.

His hair was a bit long and parted on the side, so he had to tilt his head to keep it from getting in his eyes. As she approached the table to take his order, he looked up to her, and his smile took her breath away. He teased and made corny jokes. She was smitten with him immediately. Sam visited every shift she worked, and they became inseparable for the rest of the summer until he headed back home and she went off to school. He was devoted to her, and she never dreamed of betraying his trust. They'd married after she'd graduated, and she'd never been with anyone else before him; she never dreamed that she'd fill the emptiness she felt not having him at her side.

Sophie was, by all accounts, a romantic. She'd always been captivated by romance, which was, in large part, why she'd found her way in her professional field. She recalled a few of her favorite movie scenes: the tender balcony scene in Zeffirelli's adaptation of *Romeo and Juliet*, the tantalizing scene of Jack Dawson sketching Rose DeWitt Bukater in the nude in *Titanic*, and the intertwining hands forming a clay vase in *Ghost*. *Passion, romance, and love are what makes us human. It makes us feel and yet makes us forget.* Sophie didn't want to forget Sam, nor replace him. He was irreplaceable as far as she was concerned, but she knew she needed to keep moving forward in life. She hadn't realized how alive Brady made her feel until he'd been gone.

She placed the last of the flowers in vases and stood back to inspect her work, moving this one and that one here and there until the arrangement met her high standards. Then she began to pull the ribbon from the spool.

Rebecca entered the room. "Do you need a hand? I'm free for a little bit."

Sophie glanced at the time. "Sure, you have perfect timing. I was just about to make bows. I have an appointment to get to, and I didn't realize it was getting so late. Would you mind taking care of them for me?"

"Of course I don't mind. Emily told me that you had a doctor's appointment this afternoon. I'll finish these up and get them in the cooler, then go help out front. Oh, and please don't feel like you need to hurry back. I'll be fine."

She was delighted that Rebecca was working out so nicely. It was liberating to take time away from the shop without the pressure of needing to be back.

Sophie ran by Emily in the bakery to let her know she was ready to go and waited restlessly for Emily to finish up so they could be on their way. Today she'd get to see her little girl, and she was jumping out of her skin to get there. Emily had insisted on driving her, which she felt was ridiculous, until an idea had popped in her head. Emily coming along would be perfect.

Within moments, they were off to the ob-gyn. "It's getting pretty real, isn't it, Soph?" Emily asked.

"Yep, we just need to get through the holidays before this little pumpkin shows her cuteness." Sophie rubbed her belly to calm the kicks while trying to get more comfortable. Sitting with the seat belt on was getting more challenging each day. "It's so much easier to stand. She's getting under my ribs already. I'm afraid to think of what it will be like in a few more weeks."

Emily reached out and took hold of Sophie's hand. "You've got this, chicky."

"Thanks for bringing me. I feel spoiled." Sophie counted her blessings again for the dearest friend she could ever have.

"And you should be. Besides, you're buying me a chai at Grounds. The least I can do is drive your waddle butt to your appointment."

"You, my friend, are incorrigible; adorable but incorrigible."

"I'm happy that you and Jillian have patched things up. I was going through withdrawals. I can sacrifice many things for you, but my Grounds fix was beginning to affect my work," Emily said with a smirk.

"I'm glad to know that I have that much influence over your addiction. I wasn't avoiding going there because I was angry with her. I just felt like an idiot to have gotten so upset the way I did. My hormones were out of whack, and I was overly emotional. But honestly, why does she have to be such a gossip? They should call Grounds the Rumor Mill. It would be more fitting, don't you think?" The thought of her and Brady as a couple had affected her. She knew deep down that she'd been attracted to him but didn't realize how obvious it was to others. She pictured everyone thinking horrible things about her. Sam hadn't been gone that long, and here she was lusting over another man.

"Your chariot has arrived." Emily pulled up to the door. "I'll park and meet you in the waiting room when you get done."

"Would you like to come in with me?"

"You mean, like, in the actual ultrasound room with you?" Emily said it with such excitement, and Sophie was thrilled that she wanted to be a part of this experience with her.

"Yes, up close and in person. We'll get to see what she looks like together, my friend."

"Okay. Don't let them take you in without me. I'll park really fast."

"Don't worry, I wouldn't dream of it."

Sophie exited the car, feeling excited and anxious. She was glad that Emily would be by her side. A pang of sorrow washed over her for a split second as she thought about how Sam would be right now. She shook off the thought. *This is supposed to be a happy moment, Sophie Anderson. Don't ruin it for yourself.* She opened the door and went to the counter to check in. Emily would help her through this. *She always has.*

. . .

Emily and Sophie were giddy with excitement. They went to Grounds, as they were too wound up to head right back to work. As Emily opened the door, steam escaped into the air. It was an unseasonably chilly day, and the warmth of the shop and the aroma of the coffee were welcoming to the senses. Sophie pulled the 3-D images out of her handbag to gaze upon the sight of her little girl again.

"I can't get over it. She's perfect, Emily. Just look at her." Seeing the little human sucking her thumb and kicking her feet was an experience that neither one of them would ever forget.

Sophie could see that Jillian was hesitant to approach. It seemed she was still a bit apprehensive. "Hey, Jillian, would you like to see a miracle?"

"Who wouldn't?" Jillian grinned and exhaled as if to release all the unnecessary tension she had been holding inside since she'd seen them come through the door. "What do you have there?" Sophie handed her the pictures. "Oh my goodness! Would you look at that? I wonder if she'll have red hair or brown."

"Or any hair at all!" Sophie said with a giggle.

"Bald is beautiful," Emily exclaimed.

"What can I get you? It's on the house!" Jillian asked giddily.

Emily hesitated, waiting for Sophie to respond, but she was in another world, gazing upon the pictures. "I think we've lost her." Emily motioned. "She'll have a decaf tea and I'll have a chai. Thanks, Jillian."

Jillian bounced off in her usual fashion. "Gotta make some drinks with some extra love," she shouted to the barista.

"Extra love coming up!"

Sophie and Emily sipped from their cups as open mic began. The sound of an acoustic guitar played in the background, which made it possible for them to have a more private conversation.

"So, Brady asked me if you were all right."

"Sure, why wouldn't I be?" Sophie replied quickly.

"I don't know…he just seemed concerned. Are things working out with your new helper?" Emily asked.

Sophie took a careful sip before responding. "She catches on pretty quickly, and I feel like I made a pretty good choice. Why? Don't you like her?"

"I don't really know enough about her to answer that."

"Have you seen something? Heard something that I should know about?" Sophie asked cautiously.

"No, not really."

"Then come on, Emily. Why would you ask that?"

"Oh, I don't know. No…that's a lie." Emily fidgeted with her napkin. She started to speak but hesitated. "She's really pretty, isn't she?" Sophie didn't interrupt and allowed her to continue. "It's just that you and Brady seem to be hitting it off. Aren't you afraid that she'll change that?"

"What am I? Chopped liver?"

"No, I—"

"I'm kidding you." She took another sip, set the cup down, and looked into Emily's eyes. "Seriously, though, she is beautiful, that much is true, but Brady is welcome to pursue anyone he chooses. Yes, he is attractive, kind, funny, and available. However, he certainly wouldn't want to be tied down with a woman who's about to have a baby. I have no interest in fostering a relationship with him beyond what we have now. We're just friends."

"I'm not convinced. I think he's into you."

"You're a crazy person, but if he were into me, which he's not, then you shouldn't be worried about someone else, now should you?" Sophie could feel her cheeks turning the telltale sign of pink and her neck starting to blotch. "Now, with that being said, I'm going to go pee." Before she could get up from the table, Emily sat back and grinned.

"I know you too well, partner, and you're not being honest with me."

"What is it with this place? I am not interested in Brady Owens," Sophie said in a low, strained voice before gently yet forcefully placing her cup on the table and retreating to the bathroom.

Secretly, Sophie wanted that more than anything, or at least the idea of finding love again and not being alone. She also hoped that her little girl would have a father figure in her life. However, as much of a friend as Brady had become, he was just that: a friend. He was just being a guy, with an urge, and she was a willing participant with hormones galore—nothing more.

. . .

Brady grabbed a yellow taxi outside Penn Station. He gave the cabbie the address that Stevens had given him and texted that he was on schedule. Stevens and his friend, an investigator, would be waiting for him to arrive.

Frank Sinclair was a meek-looking man. He had small features, a pointed nose, a narrow jaw, fair skin, and an untamed cowlick. His dirty-blond hair was laced with gray, and Brady suspected him to be in his mid- to late sixties. Brady was surprised that his voice didn't match his outward persona. He had a deep tenor, and he spoke firmly, with obvious confidence and authority. Instantly, Brady knew that Sinclair was the type to walk lightly but carry a big stick. He was already feeling much more positive regarding finding the truth and keeping Cynthia in prison where she belonged.

Brady listened as Sinclair reiterated what Stevens had told him; Brady only needed to fill them in on the latest. "I've convinced Cynthia that we have a future together, and I think she'll spill it in regard to her father, but it's going to take more time."

"Time we don't have," Stevens said as he tapped his pen on the table—ticktock, ticktock, ticktock went the rhythm of the pen.

"We need to get Cynthia to vouch for you—convince her that you admire her father and maybe help you get back in his good graces." Sinclair was asking a lot.

"I don't think I was ever in his good graces to begin with. Besides, what would that accomplish?"

Sinclair stood up and sauntered over to the window. It

was starting to sleet as he watched a pretzel and roasted peanut vendor close up shop. He turned, then leaned against the sill as Brady and Stevens looked on in anticipation. "You need to see who his friends are, and you need to build his trust. Maybe then he'll slip up."

"That's a tall order. He's a powerful, unforgiving prick," Brady chided.

"You tell me that Cynthia has him wrapped around her little finger. He'll let you in. He's powerful, but he'll let you in. You wait and see."

"I'll give it my best shot," Brady said with a shrug.

"Your best is all we can ask. In the meantime, I'll talk with my connections to see if I can get access to Lockwood's phone records and bank accounts. They might tell us quite a bit."

"You can do that?" Brady asked, astonished. "This isn't an official investigation."

"It will be our little secret."

Brady looked at Stevens as if he'd burn a hole through him as Stevens nodded in understanding. Their knowledge of the law kicked into high gear. "We have to do this aboveboard, Sinclair. If this goes where I think it could go, we'll need it to be by the book," Brady said firmly. Stevens concurred.

"Not to worry. I've got friends, too, and we have a very big book."

Brady's gut felt good. Stevens's connection to Sinclair would pay off; he was sure of it. It was himself he doubted. That was the problem.

Sinclair threw on his coat, put on his wool herringbone fedora and stepped out into the slush as a yellow cab pulled in as if it had been waiting for him.

"What did I tell you? He's going to be quite an asset," Stevens said with gusto.

Brady couldn't help but agree. His enthusiasm was overshadowed by the task at hand. *Get into Lockwood's good graces…Lord have mercy.*

CHAPTER 22

It was evening, and Sophie could hear the gusts of wind blowing leaves as they hit the windowpanes. There was a full moon that reflected off the water in the distance. She was curled up with a stack of books and her favorite fleece blanket, wearing a pair of Sam's sweatpants and his shirt. Her hair was in a sloppy bun that was adorned with a highlighter.

The wonders of childbirth were both fascinating and terrifying. Each page she turned reminded her that the large bundle of joy within her needed to come out.

"I've suffered more than delivering a baby, haven't I, Daisy?" She stroked her furry friend. Sophie could feel the rumble beneath her hand as Daisy's purr calmed her. *Everything will be okay.* "Next up, a book of girl names. What do you think, Daisy Mae...Buttercup, Petunia, or Whiskers?" Daisy rolled over to expose her underbelly. "Okay, Whiskers it is." Sophie highlighted a name here and there, but nothing quite hit her.

Picking a name was just the beginning. There was a nursery, car seat, stroller—basically a never-ending list of things to research and purchase. These items were completely foreign to her, as she'd never had a baby brother or sister. She was an only child, and babysitting had never been her thing. She was quickly realizing that she had a lot to learn and wished her mom hadn't become a world traveler. Her expertise would be most helpful about now.

Sophie closed the books, removed the highlighter from her hair, and took the last sip of tea from her cup. Sleep would come easy tonight. Her eyes were already heavy from reading, and knowing Brady would be returning from New York in the morning gave her comfort. He'd promised that he'd wallpaper one of the walls and help her paint the nursery in the morning.

She'd decided on a theme that was near and dear to her heart. When she was a little girl, she'd discovered a world of wonder, mystery and fantasy. She'd discovered herself, as an adult, by looking back to when her life path was born. Sophie had been enchanted with the story of *The Secret Garden*. It was only fitting that the new life in her home would mark springtime in her lifetime of new growth; it would be a time of blossoming for both herself and her little baby girl—but most importantly, a time of healing.

Sophie could envision the pink vintage rose wallpaper on two walls, blush-colored paint on the others, an ivory rocking chair with floral cushions and a quilted throw rug to match. A wrought iron arbor that she'd found at an antique shop along Route 1 would go against the adjacent wall and be intertwined with silk flowers, just out of reach of little hands, with a white crib nestled inside. Pink drapes, stencils of ivy, and butterflies. A small crystal chandelier would adorn the center of the room, and an open birdcage mobile with circling birds would hang above the changing table. Sophie was almost giddy with excitement to see her vision become a reality. Brady had brought a vision to fruition once, and she was confident that he would do it again.

. . .

Brady arrived to the scent of bacon and blueberry pancakes. "Aw, I love the smell of bacon," he said as he opened the door. He was dressed in paint clothes that consisted of jeans, a T-shirt covered by an old paint-spattered navy-blue Nike sweatshirt, a pair of Converse sneakers, and a New York Yankees hat. Sophie grinned as she snatched the hat off his head. "Hey!"

"Not in this house. You are welcome here, but a Yankees hat, never." She giggled as she hid the hat behind her.

"I guess, if it's a sacrifice that I have to make for bacon." He greeted Sophie with a peck on the cheek and lugged his toolbox up the stairs into the nursery.

"Do you like your bacon crispy or bubbly?" Sophie hollered up the stairs.

"Fall-apart crispy, if you don't mind," he said, taking the steps by twos in order to join Sophie that much sooner. Within a moment, he was standing at her side.

"You sure do know how to ruin a good piece of bacon," Sophie teased.

"I beg to differ." He kissed the nape of her neck.

Sophie grinned, and he was relieved that there wasn't any awkwardness between them, as he'd feared.

"Is everything going well for you in New York?"

Brady plucked a piece of bacon before responding. "Yeah, as well as can be expected. But let's not talk about that. You mentioned that you had a request for wedding photography. The date should work, and I'm psyched to do it."

He pictured a December wedding on the grounds of Proposals. Whether there'd be snow or not would play a role in what shots he'd take. Regardless, he envisioned black-and-whites, highlighting the red accents of the flowers. Sophie had filled him in on the details in an email while he'd been in New York. Red was such an obvious and predictable choice for a December wedding, but he knew they'd make it unique and spectacular.

His greatest concern—outside of Cynthia Lockwood—was Sophie's well-being. She was quickly approaching her due date of New Year's Day, and he wondered how she'd pull it off. He was constantly impressed with her drive. Fortunately, November was a slow time of year for weddings, and being able to focus on the nursery was a great distraction for them both.

Brady poured the orange juice and took a cutting board with fruit away from Sophie's grasp. "Let me help."

Sophie relinquished the cutting board and knife. "Here you go. Is there nothing you won't do for me?" He knew full well that there wasn't anything that he wouldn't do for her… except being truthful, which was eating him up inside.

"I'm not saying I'll do it well, but you have bacon to attend to," he said, tossing his ache aside.

Sophie gasped when she saw black smoke billowing up from the frying pan. She pulled the pan from the burner and opened the window to prevent the smoke detector from going off. "You said you like it crispy, right?"

"The crispier the better," he said with amusement.

She gave him a slap on the arm.

"Careful, now. I do have a knife in my hand, you know."

"It would serve you right. Why didn't you say something?"

"I thought I did."

"So you did. Coffee?"

"Yes, ma'am."

Brady grazed over the bacon while Sophie placed fried eggs on the plates. He slid the chair out as she adjusted herself in the seat.

"I need longer arms," Sophie said with a groan. "I still have more than a month to go. How is it possible that my belly can get even bigger than it is? I might starve to death, because I won't be able to reach the table."

"You could use your belly as your table." With that, Sophie gave him a punch in the arm. "Ouch! You better watch it. That's my painting arm, you know."

"Suck it up, Brady. You deserved that one."

"So I did." Brady adored this woman. She wasn't like anyone else he'd ever known. She was a genuinely good person who deserved someone better than him.

Brady devoured the breakfast before him, then cleared the table. Sophie placed each dish in the dishwasher while Brady washed the skillets in the sink. "Look, Sophie—a blue jay." It was singing atop the wrought iron bench just outside the window. They didn't feel the chill in the air with the window open as the melody of the bird and the waves crashing in the background were warming to the soul.

Brady quickly dried his hands and bounded out the door and down the steps. Within seconds, he had retrieved his camera in order to capture the moment. The bird tucked his head as a flurry of snow encircled him. It was the first snow of the season and unexpected. Brady zoomed in and clicked away. He'd experiment with black-and-whites while bringing out only the stark blue contrast of the blue jay. This would certainly help him prepare for the wedding shots he wished to take.

The blue jay took off with purpose and was out of view in a blink of the eye. The symbolism of the blue jay wasn't lost on Brady. Since childhood, he'd had a fascination with birds. They resonated faithfulness and truth, could endure much, were loyal, and mated for life. It was significant; he ached with the realization that he'd been living a lie with Sophie. The truth needed to come out, but not until the time was right.

It sickened him to think about the love she'd had for her husband and the pain she'd had to suffer with the loss of his life. She had endured too much. He'd have to make this right. He must make this right. She meant too much to him; he didn't want to be the cause of any future pain, but he knew it had to be done. In the meantime, he'd do everything he could for her. Most importantly, he wanted to get justice for Sophie and Sam. If she wouldn't forgive him, so be it—and truthfully, he knew he wouldn't deserve it. It was her well-being that he cared most about, not his. For the first time in his life, he truly cared for someone other than himself, and that scared the hell out of him, yet felt incredible at the same time.

Sophie turned his face toward her. She had a tenderness to her eyes, or perhaps a look of worry. "Are you okay?"

He couldn't respond; he just returned her gaze. He knew he hadn't been himself around her. He hadn't much liked himself, but he hadn't realized that it was becoming obvious. She wanted to help him, but it was his secret that he needed to bear.

"I'm fine, Sophie, but thank you." Then he leaned down and kissed her on the tip of her nose.

"Well, now, the paint isn't going to go up by itself."

"Umm, that's right." Then he plopped his Yankees hat back on his head.

"Let's get rolling. Did you see what I did there?" she said with a little giggle that was enough to melt his heart.

"Yes, yes, I did, you witty woman. Let's roll."

. . .

Every free moment that Sophie and Brady had was spent preparing the nursery, but Brady's responsibility the next morning, according to Emily and Rebecca, was to keep Sophie distracted. Of course, he was happy to oblige but was at a loss as to what to do. He let the hot, steamy shower flow over his chest as an idea came to him. After drying off with a towel and wrapping it around his waist, he snagged his phone off the counter. He was still amazed each and every time that he awaited her enthusiastic hi on the other end. His heart would pick up its pace just a bit with anticipation of hearing her voice.

"Hi, Brady. What's up?"

"I'd like you to come to my place in the morning. I'd also like you to bring a few outfits that make you feel beautiful. Do your hair, put on your makeup, and whatever else women do to get ready for a photo shoot. Can you do that for me, Sophie?"

Sophie was momentarily speechless. "Yes, I'd love that."

"Great! I'll have a green screen set up, lighting—well, you get the idea. We can take some shots inside, and the weather is going to be beautiful, so we can take some outside as well.

We can take a walk to the dock and have you strike a pose on the beach. We'll have fun."

"Sounds wonderful. I'm looking forward to it."

"I figured after we're done, we could grab lunch or something," Brady said, relieved that Sophie said yes.

CHAPTER 23

Morning came slowly for Sophie, who tossed and turned as Daisy kneaded the bed. Daisy seemed as restless as she was. Sophie didn't want puffy circles under her eyes for the photo shoot, but the more she didn't want them, the more she kept herself from falling asleep. Thank goodness Brady was a professional and could touch up the photos to remove her imperfections, she thought as the time slowly ticked by.

Darkness filled the room as the sun waited to announce that morning had arrived. Still resting her eyes, she reached for the alarm on her phone, ending its final interruption of her slumber. The familiar sound of tires on the gravel drive gave her comfort. Emily had arrived, and the smell of bread and confections would soon be wafting through the air.

Daisy bounded off the bed in search of breakfast. Sophie gathered her robe from the foot of the bed, wrapped it around herself to remove the chill from her skin, and slid on her slippers. As she walked past the nursery, she popped her head inside. The freshly painted and papered walls made the room come to life. She instinctively gave herself a hug and envisioned a bright side of her future. After yesterday, with Brady, she'd dared to dream of this giving, kind man in her life and looked forward to spending her day with him.

Sophie grabbed her owl cup from the cabinet and placed it in the Keurig. She pushed the button, then waited as the mesmerizing, tranquil sound of drips filled her cup.

Emily popped her head in. "Good morning, sunshine. I saw your light was on. What's got you up so early?"

"Brady is going to do a photo shoot with me. I want to make myself photo ready, which is near impossible. I look like death. See these dark circles? There's not enough makeup in the world to cover this mess."

"You, partner, are beautiful in every way," Emily said. "I wish I had your skin. And your hair. And your height. And your—"

"Enough already," Sophie said with a bashful glance. "Besides, you're just saying that. But thank you. Do you want a cup?"

"No, thanks. I have too much to get done today."

"I thought you were all done for this weekend's client. I was hoping you could relax a bit. You've been out straight."

"Umm, I just want to get some prep done and experiment with a few things. I'm thinking cupcakes today."

"Yummy, I love cupcakes. Save one for me, will you?"

"Sure thing. Now go make yourself gorgeous, and I'll leave you alone. Maybe later today, you can show me some of the shots, if Brady is willing to share them before they're perfect."

"If I tell him you've made cupcakes, it might just be enough to persuade him." Sophie picked up her cup. "Time to go get pretty. See you later, partner." Daisy led the way back up the stairs.

The sun was just beginning to peek through the darkness as Sophie stepped out of the shower. The warmth of the water eased her aching muscles. She massaged her neck and rocked it back and forth to relieve the stress, then arched her back. The reflection of herself in the full-length mirror stopped her momentarily. She stood to the side to see a profile angle of herself. Sophie was astounded by the miracle growing inside of her. She pulled her hair up off her shoulders, wrapping her long locks up into a twist to show her full body. Her breasts were swollen, and the coolness in the air made her nipples tight. Each curve of her body took her breath away. She didn't recognize herself. Who was this woman standing before her? Her hands cradled her belly as she dipped her head to say, "I love you." A tear ran down her cheek as the overwhelming feeling of joy tried to escape.

Daisy curled herself around Sophie's ankles with a purr. "You want to be in the pictures too, don't you, girl?"

Sophie dressed in an ivory knit tunic and a pair of skinny jeans. Sitting on her hope chest at the foot of the bed, she worked diligently to bend over, pull on her brown Frye boots over her ivory boot cuffs, zip one, take a breath, and zip the other. Taking one last look at her face and hair for any touch-up needs, she picked up her packed bag and turned to leave. She heard a quick little knock on the door and turned to see Brady, once again standing in one of her doorways. Sophie gasped at this vision. Sam and Brady's images blurred together as she recalled the many times that Sam had stood there watching her dress. But now it was Brady who stood leaning in the doorway with a seductive grin. Remarkably, she thought, she was okay with that.

"I'm sorry, I didn't mean to startle you. Emily suggested that I pick you up. Said you'd have enough luggage for a week away."

"She's exaggerating! I only have one suitcase and my makeup bag." Sophie gestured to the bag in hand, then quickly recognized that it was in fact a full-size suitcase. "Okay, fine. She made her point. I couldn't decide what to bring, so I grabbed a lot of options. I can certainly handle the bag myself, you know. See? It has wheels."

"I'm sure you can, but Emily will give me grief if I don't carry it."

"She's sweet but a bit overprotective. I'm sorry she dragged you all the way over here to drive me. Now you'll have to bring me back, too."

"It's okay. I have some things I need to do afterwards anyway, and you'll be on the way." Brady placed his hand on her back to guide her out the door. "The lighting will be perfect at my place, but we'll need to get a move on."

In all the time she'd known Brady, Sophie had never been to his place, and she was curious to see what Brady's world was like. As they made the many turns toward the cottage, she saw views of the ocean, a glimpse of the Nubble Lighthouse, the rocky shores, and cliffs. The homes were set fairly close together, but they were picturesque and charming. They seemed to be tucked in for the winter season. Piles of lobster traps were stacked up in yards, and various-sized boats were covered tightly with white covers like shrink wrap.

Brady slowed as he took a corner that led to a narrow drive of crushed seashells. She could see a cottage with gray cedar shake shingles and a wraparound covered porch at the end of the drive. The place was set privately, with a sloping yard, and lined with rose bushes that were determined to continue blooming until the first heavy snow. A small boat-house sat near the bottom of the lawn, which led to a rustic yet sturdy-looking dock.

"In all the years I've lived in the area, I never knew a place like this existed. It's...well...it's adorable."

"It's small, but it suits me. I'm just glad it was available."

"Me too. It's perfect," Sophie said with her eyes wide, and they progressed closer to the entry door.

"I think it will work well for some great shots. Although, I think if we were at the town dump, you'd make it beautiful," Brady added as casually as he would discuss the weather. Sophie was amused and flattered.

. . .

Brady was mesmerized by Sophie. He looked through the lens and was captivated. Her personality shined through and came alive with each pose and each outfit. She was a natural and had become comfortable with his direction as the day went on. She played the part of a relaxed everyday woman in her initial jeans outfit, the role of a teacher as she read a children's book entitled *Guess How Much I Love You* while sitting cross-legged on the bed. She was free-spirited as she wore a white chiffon gown with a long pink satin ribbon, the sun shining around her on the end of the rustic dock. Her hair glowed in the light as it silhouetted her figure. He drank it up as she spread her arms high and wide if to say she was on the top of the world.

"Can we go inside now? I'd like you to take some of my bare belly, and I think it's getting pretty cold out here for that." She opened the wrap of her gown to expose her belly with a giggle.

"Your wish is my command, my princess." He took her hand to escort her back into the cottage and asked her to wait for a minute before guiding her into the bedroom. Since the room was so small, he staged the bed with fluffy light pink pillows of various textures and a sheepskin rug he had been able to scoop up the day before. The light cascaded across the bed as he adjusted the curtains to cast just the right amount.

Sophie beamed. "I can't wait to see how these turn out. How would you like me?"

Brady knew exactly how he'd like her. He wanted her in his arms. He wanted to feel her lips on his and wanted her completely and fully. "Stand in front of the bed and turn your profile to me, please. Open your gown to expose your belly, then put one hand on the top of your little girl and the other one on your back. Look at you, Sophie. You take my breath away." He snapped shot after shot, moving from one position to another. "Now, just do what feels natural."

"Turn your head, Brady. I want to try something." Brady obeyed. "Okay, you can turn around now," she said after a few moments.

Brady turned and inhaled, nearly forgetting to exhale. Sophie had removed her gown and set it on the floor. She lay on the bed, propped up on the pillows. She had placed the pink satin ribbon across her, positioning her legs just right to hide the velvety warmth between her thighs.

"Stunning. You have captivated my heart, Sophie Anderson."

Sophie's cheeks began to turn their usual blushing pink, which only made the image even more enticing. Brady captured this moment in his mind as well as in his camera. He was humbled by her ability to be an innocent precious mother-to-be and a sexy vixen at the same time.

"I have an idea. I'd like you to stand up next to the window." He moved toward the window and took hold of the cream-colored sheer curtains. "Can you stand between them and drape them around you?" He watched on as she attempted to do as he asked. "May I?" he said in a hopeful voice.

"Of course, Brady. It's okay."

Brady set the camera down on the bed. His hands trembled as he gathered the layers of sheers and draped them just so. "Bend your knee, and hold the curtain at the top of your leg with your left hand. And use your other hand to hold it up to your chin. Tip your head back."

The folds of the drapes covered her private areas perfectly. He zoomed in to show only from just above her breasts to the middle of her thigh. As the sun filtered through the window, it cast an angelic glow around her body. He captured the perfect moment in time. Sophie closed her eyes, her breathing shallow and her breasts heaving with each breath she took.

Brady was grateful for the lens between them. It was a false barrier, but it was all he needed to contain himself. He could see a change in her as he took each shot. She dropped the sheers, and a lock of hair fell to cover her face. He set the camera down to adjust the curtain and tuck her hair back. As his hand brushed her cheek, Sophie turned her gaze to him. Her seductive blue eyes bored through him, then she closed them and tilted her head back to expose her long neck.

He couldn't hold back anymore. He leaned in and kissed her ivory throat as she moaned. He stroked her hair back as he held her. Her skin was warm and silky to his touch, and he could feel himself getting hard.

"Kiss me," she said in a raspy, breathless voice. "Please."

"We…shouldn't…do this," Brady said with each kiss that he gave her. "We…should…stop."

"Yes, we should," Sophie whispered as she groaned with pleasure.

In the distance, Brady's alarm sounded. It got progressively louder and louder until it was unavoidable.

"Can you make it stop?"

Suddenly, he remembered why his alarm was going off. "We've got to go, Sophie."

"No…really?"

"Yes, I need to be somewhere. I'm sorry, but we really have to go. Now."

The moment was lost. "All right, I'll get dressed and get my things." She took in a deep breath, then began gathering her belongings, seeming annoyed.

"What can I do to help?" Brady asked, looking around at everything scattered about. "I know. Why don't you go get cleaned up, get dressed, do your hair, makeup, or whatever else women do, and I'll pack up your stuff."

Within a few minutes, they were heading to the car. "This must be an important meeting. Anything to do with what you've been doing in New York?"

"No, absolutely not!" he said a bit too emphatically.

"Oh, okay. I didn't mean to pry."

"No, you're not prying. I just can't be late…it's a time-sensitive thing that I have to do."

"See? That's why I should have driven myself. Now you have to bring me home first instead of just getting to your meeting."

The minutes went by quickly as they made the drive back to her place.

"What's going on? Why are there so many cars here?" Sophie asked, sounding concerned. "I hope I'm not forgetting something. Emily never said anything about this."

"Hmm, can't imagine." Brady parked the car near the bakery as Emily came running toward them.

"Sophie, you won't believe what happened! You have to see this." Emily grabbed her by the arm to help her out of the car.

"What is it, Emily? You're scaring me."

"It's better to show you than to tell you. Come with me." Emily led the way toward the barn as Brady followed. "Brady, would you mind sliding the other door while I get this one?"

"My pleasure." With that, they slid the doors apart and a chorus of women shouted, "Surprise!"

CHAPTER 24

Sophie was stunned as she looked upon the gathering. So many of her friends were there: Mrs. Templeton, Jillian, Mrs. Bennington and her daughter Penelope, Rebecca, but most importantly, the auburn-haired lady with the sparkling blue eyes that stood front and center, looking back at her. Sophie's mom was a picture of grace. Her smile bore the years of laugh lines that showed the depth of her character.

"I can't believe you're here, Mom! When did you arrive?"

"This morning...surprise!" She gave Sophie a generous hug and leaned back to take in her growing belly. "I wouldn't miss your special day for the world." Sophie had always wished that her mother had been a grounding force, a source of strength, a rock unmoved in support of all Sophie had ever done in her life, but she wasn't. Her mom always meant well and desired to be there for her, but her follow-through was quite lacking. Regardless of her flightiness, though, Sophie knew that her mother loved her deeply. She'd missed her greatly and didn't realize quite how much until she was standing right in front of her.

"You told me you were headed south."

"I am. I'll be flying out in the morning, but I'll do my best to be back for the arrival of this little love." She gave a tender squeeze to Sophie's belly.

"I'm so happy you're here. I've missed you." They embraced, then Sophie turned toward all the others who were there to share this special moment.

Sophie was overwhelmed by the show of love emanating from the room. "Thank you so much. This is such a surprise! I had absolutely no idea!" She gave Emily a hug.

"Rebecca helped too."

Sophie gave Rebecca a big hug as well.

"This is too much. I can't believe you went to all this trouble for me."

"And we couldn't have pulled it off without Brady keeping you occupied." The crowd cheered and whooped.

Sophie turned to face Brady, who stood back. "You brat! You knew all along, didn't you?"

"Yep. You are my most important time-sensitive meeting, and I knew I'd get cupcakes," he said with a sheepish grin.

Sophie wasn't used to being the center of attention and was never quite comfortable in the spotlight, with the rare exception of her photo shoot, but today, she soaked it all in. She was open to all the belly touching as she greeted each guest. Sophie was beaming with joy, and her arms were open for the show of love she was receiving. Her cheeks were covered in a myriad of lipstick colors from the multitude of kisses laid upon her face.

Pink balloons and streamers hung from the rafters, a clothesline of baby dresses and a pair of adorable bib overalls were draped over the hearth, and pink tablecloths with white place settings and crystal stemware filled with pink champagne adorned the tables. A pyramid of cupcakes sat on the table in the center of the floor. The table skirt was lined with tulle to create a full-length pink tutu, and strands of pink petals fell from the chandelier above. There was a table overflowing with gifts. Pink lemonade punch was flowing at the fountain table as a lavish buffet lunch was served.

. . .

Brady stood back and took witness of Sophie and her mother. He could see now where she got her beauty and countenance. He had been sure to capture the look of surprise on Sophie's face when she saw her mother, as well as their embrace. She never really spoke of her mother, much to his surprise, seeing their obvious love for each other. He sauntered around the room, trying to remain invisible while taking candid shots. The camera loved Sophie. Her porcelain skin glowed, her eyes were bright and alive with excitement, and she was giddy. She had a childlike joy that was bubbling out of her, and it was contagious. The ladies showered her with gifts as the unending exclamations of *aw*, *cute*, and *how adorable* filled the air.

This moment of innocence, sweetness, and kindness erased the angst and bitterness he'd been harboring since his return from New York. Cynthia was truly off her rocker, and he knew she'd be released very soon. He wanted to protect Sophie from pain. He'd have to find a way to send her back to prison, along with her father. He knew in his heart what they had done, and he wouldn't rest until he accomplished his goal. He would never give up.

An incessant buzz went off in Brady's pocket. When he couldn't ignore it any longer, he pulled the phone out and anguished over having to answer, but he knew he should. Taking a controlled breath, he tapped to answer.

"What do you want?" he asked impatiently, finding a quiet spot near the restrooms. Brady paced as he tipped his head and massaged his temples.

"Don't sound so petulant, Brady. I'm only calling to ask you to pick something up for me before you come to get me out of this horrid place."

"I won't be able to do that."

"But you don't even know what I want you to pick up," Cynthia said plaintively.

"No, I mean I won't be able to pick you up. Besides, there's no guarantee that you'll be getting out anyway." Brady hoped beyond hope that she wouldn't.

"What? Are you serious? Of course I'm getting out. Brady, I've been counting the days—no, the seconds until you could hold me again. I need you to be here when I'm released!"

"I wish I could, Cynthia. I know you're disappointed. I am, too, but I have work to do." Brady rolled his eyes. "I'm sure your father plans on picking you up, anyway. We don't need him to know that I've been visiting you. Remember, we know how he feels about me. It has to remain our little secret."

"How could you let me down like this? Am I nothing to you but an inconvenience, a distraction from your work? Am I not a priority? I would think that you'd be counting the days as well. I miss you, Brady, and I need you at my side."

Brady managed to keep his voice calm despite his growing anger. "I miss you too, Cynthia. I'll be there as soon as I can." He pulled the phone away from his ear and made a motion as if he were heaving it into the fireplace, then placed it back to his ear. "I can't wait to start our new life together either, but I'm working right now, and I have to go." With that, Brady hung up and headed into the men's room.

A couple of minutes later, he stepped out into the adjoining alcove and nearly ran into Emily. "Hey, Em, looks like we pulled it off." He showed his broad smile.

"Yep, you've succeeded in pulling a fast one, that's for sure." Emily's response was given with a slight snarkiness. He was used to her sarcastic sense of humor, but it had never presented itself in anger. This felt different. He wondered if Sophie had told Emily of their little rendezvous this morning. He could definitely sense her disapproval if she had.

"You really did a great job here, Emily. You've created a lasting memory for Sophie; she sure deserves it."

"Lasting memories, that's what it's all about. And I couldn't agree more. She deserves to be treated with love." Her bitter tone took Brady aback.

"You know, I should get going. I've lingered long enough with the ladies. Would you mind letting Sophie know that I'll be back in the morning to bring all the gifts into the house? I know she'd like to get the nursery completed. I have to head to New York again soon, and I don't want to let her down by not finishing."

"Sure."

"I'd tell her myself, but she's having too much fun, and I don't want to interrupt."

"I guess you better go, then."

Again, he detected a coldness to her words. "Are you all right, Emily?"

"Of course I am. Why wouldn't I be?" Emily asked with a touch of suspicion in her voice.

"Oh, I don't know. You seem a bit…um, not your usual self is all."

"I don't have any idea what you could be referring to. I told you that I'm fine…just super."

"Okay, if you say so. See you tomorrow, Em."

"See ya."

Perplexed, Brady collected his belongings and retreated outdoors. There was a bitter bite in the air. A storm was brewing. He could feel it.

. . .

Brady was up until the wee hours of the morning, determined to finish a few of the portraits he had taken of Sophie. He pored over the shots until he knew each one intimately. Her eyes went through every emotion that a soul could feel. Bashful and unsure in the beginning, an innocence, a twinkle of daring and curiosity, then they shifted to a soft wondrous love for the life that was growing inside of her. He was fascinated by that look. He couldn't help but think that she was going to be an amazing mother, reflecting on the image of Sophie with her mom. Sophie must have been raised with that same love and affection that showed in her eyes, he concluded. It was familiar to her.

Brady didn't recall ever feeling that kind of love from his own mother. She was more or less a stranger to him, as she'd left when he was only twelve. He remembered knowing that she was a beautiful woman but that she was ugly on the inside. He'd been a mistake, and not a day had gone by that she hadn't reminded him of that fact. Her appearance was everything to her. Knowing that he'd caused a stretch mark was enough for her to resent him before he was even born.

Brady continued to sort through the progression of shots. Sophie's images left the sweet, tender love and then moved toward mischief. He could see that she was gaining confidence as he clicked each frame. The thumping of his heart quickened as he remembered watching her move, uninhibited. She was breathtaking as her cheeks and nose became red from the cold. Her blue eyes, red cheeks, and auburn hair had burned vibrantly as she'd raised her arms in glorious wild abandonment. He was enchanted by this creature.

Brady touched up and edited the images, saving the best for last, knowing that he would never finish the others if he moved on to the sensually seductive Sophie that had inspired and amazed him first. He touched the image before him and closed his eyes, imagining the feel of her next to him: the warmth of her lips brushing his, her skin like silk as his fingers glided down her long beautiful neck. He wanted her in his arms…he needed her in his bed.

CHAPTER 25

Emily arrived early in the morning and greeted Sophie with a Grounds decaf coffee. Sophie was sleepy-eyed but dressed for the day.

"I never dreamed I'd see you at this hour. It's your day off," Sophie said with an inquisitive expression. "You were here so late."

"I wasn't expecting it either, but I woke up energized and thought, what the heck, I could spend more time with your mom and see if there was anything I could do for you today. Maybe help you sort through your gifts. I could wash the tiny adorables you got."

"Aw, that's so sweet. But my mom's already gone. She had to catch an early flight."

"I'm so sorry, Soph. But she was here. That's good...right?"

She sipped her coffee. *Finally.* "There was so much going on last night that we really didn't get to visit, but yep...she was here and yes, it was good."

"Okay, then, put me to work. What do you need?"

"You already did too much. You threw me an awesome shower, helped clean up, and carried everything upstairs. What more could I possibly ask of you, Em? Oh, and you got me a coffee—lavender vanilla at that. Thank you, by the way." Sophie waited for a response of some kind, but Emily seemed a million miles away. "Em, is everything okay?" Still no response. "Emily…earth to Emily."

"I'm sorry, Soph…did you say something?" Emily replied.

"Emily, what's going on? Are you all right?"

The familiar sight of Brady's car appeared in the driveway.

"What on earth is he doing here at this hour?" Sophie asked in astonishment.

"Oh, right. I forgot to tell you that he was going to be here early this morning to help bring everything in from last night," Emily said nonchalantly.

"What a shame. You didn't need to work so hard bringing it all in yourself since Brady had already planned on doing it. I feel bad. He came here for nothing."

"You know what? Why don't I run out and let him know that it's all done before he gets out of the car and everything? That way he can just head back home."

Before Sophie could respond, Emily was running out the door. Sophie looked on with curiosity as Daisy curled around her legs. Sophie picked up the cat to caress her head and back.

"Emily seems to be acting mighty peculiar, Daisy." She could see that Emily was becoming quite animated. Her back was to Sophie, and she couldn't make out what was being said, but Brady's response was calm, with a slight look of concern on his face. He reached out to touch Emily's shoulders, but Emily jerked away in a huff and entered Proposals with the door slamming behind her. Brady braced himself, seeming to brush off whatever it was that had infuriated Emily. He looked toward the window into the kitchen, where he must have assumed she might be, then carefully approached the door.

Sophie greeted him with a pause. "I'd say good morning, but it doesn't appear as if it is. What's going on, Brady?"

"Apparently Emily overheard a conversation that I had with…a client last night on the phone. It was heard out of context, and Emily misunderstood it. I think she just needs a little space right now. She's not convinced." Brady didn't seem to be affected by the ordeal, and Sophie read the situation as one of the kneejerk overreactions Emily had been known to have.

"I should go check on her," Sophie said hesitantly.

"Maybe it's best if you just let her be. She'll be back to herself soon, I'm sure."

Sophie could tell that he tried to sound persuasive, but she doubted that Emily would let whatever this was go anytime soon.

"I don't feel right about that. You don't deserve to be treated that way. You know…I sensed something wasn't right when she got here this morning. Now I see she was just waiting for you to get here. She didn't forget you were coming—she tried to prevent you from coming!"

"Sophie, she thought she was doing the right thing. It's okay, really. She'll come around. Now, let's start again, shall we?"

"Start again?"

"Good morning, beautiful." Brady leaned in and kissed her. "Mmm, a hint of vanilla. You are tasty this morning."

Sophie's knees went weak as she melted into his embrace. "Good morning."

"Oh baby."

"I could get used to that," Sophie said in a sultry voice.

"I would have to think so by now. It must happen all the time. Does it hurt?"

"Does what hurt?"

"The baby." He saw the blank look on Sophie's face. "When it kicks…does it hurt?"

"Oh, baby! Not *oh baby*. You meant the baby." Sophie's babbling took Brady by surprise, and laughter slowly started and built to a full-on belly laugh.

"I'm sorry. I don't know why I'm laughing. It's just that you're so darn cute." He covered her face with kisses, then moved to her belly and covered it with kisses as well. "You both are, for that matter."

Sophie was ticklish and squealed, trying to wiggle her way out of his grasp. "Stop it, Brady! I mean it…stop!" Laughter filled the air. "I'm…warning…you! I…can't catch…my breath."

Brady embraced her as if he would never let go. "What do you say we get crackin' on the nursery?"

"I say let's get crackin'." Sophie gave Brady a peck on the tip of his nose and started for the stairs. "Emily helped bring up the boxes and bags already. Oh, right, I guess you already know that." When Sophie opened the door, she was astonished that so much of it was unpackaged and in some semblance of order. Clothes were untagged and stacked by size, the rug was down, the mobile hung, baby wipes and diapers were stacked, and the butterfly lamp was on with a note leaning against it. Sophie opened the note.

Dearest Sophie,

I couldn't sleep last night as you were heavy on my mind. I hope you don't mind that I did some unpacking for you. It brought back such sweet memories.

Seeing you surrounded by your friends, I couldn't help but be proud. I'm proud of what you have done with your life and the home that you have created for yourself and my little granddaughter. (That sounds incredible to say.) Thank you for the gift of making me a grammy.

You, my precious girl, will be an amazing mommy. You are kind, loving, and giving. You are stronger than I could have ever hoped to be. You inspire me, Sophie...my Sophie...my beautiful baby girl.

When I think back, your dad and I would look at you with such wonder. You could light up a room by just your very presence. We'd often dream about the kind of woman you would become. You've exceeded our expectations, Sophie. It's the goodness you carry inside of you and the generosity of your love that we adored. You have planted roots that ground you and nurtured a support system that will help you flourish in your new role as a mother.

I know that I don't need to worry about you, Sophie, but you will always be my baby. Soon you will know full well what I mean by that. No matter the distance, I am with you, I am for you, and I love you beyond measure.

There is a gift for you and our precious little one. Your grandmother made it for you when you were born. It only seemed right that another generation should have it.

With love,

Mom

Sophie wiped the tears from her cheeks. Her mom could be fickle and had been absent for much of her adult life, but when she showed up, it erased the void that she often felt... until the next time, anyway. After her dad's passing, her mom had never truly reconciled what to do with her life and had become somewhat of a nomad. Seemed her mom's roots didn't run too deep, Sophie concluded, but she knew she was loved still the same.

Sophie noticed the package with a pink ribbon tied to perfection sitting atop the ottoman. "It's from my mom."

Brady nodded in understanding. She sat in the rocker, carefully opening each end and sliding out the box. The lid pulled off easily. Lying inside was a folded quilt. Each square had a different flower embroidered in ornate detail. Her hands glided across the multitude of textures. Her grandmother had used satin ribbon and cotton and silk threads and yarns. The 3-D images were each labeled with the name of the flower and its meaning.

"I forgot all about this. It was my garden." Sophie's hands worked their way slowly and carefully over each flower. "My grandma would tell me about each one." Sophie closed her eyes. "I can still hear her sweet voice. 'This is a Bird of Paradise and it reminds me of you,' she'd say. 'It means joy and magnificence.' I even remember trying to say magnificence. She called me her sunshine and told me that beautiful flowers wouldn't grow without sunshine." Sophie held the memories tight across her chest and rocked quietly as Brady knelt down next to her to feel the fabric as well.

"It sure sounds prophetic. It's as if she knew who you were going to be before you were even born."

"Maybe it's why I became who I am."

Sophie heard her phone ring in the other room and chose to ignore it to savor the moment. Brady's phone buzzed in his pocket a few seconds later. He glanced down at it.

"Baby, I have to step out for a minute."

"It's all right. I wouldn't mind some alone time to play in here anyway. I want to take another look at all the cuteness and do some organizing myself."

Brady gave Sophie a kiss on her forehead and left the room. He went downstairs and opened the den door in order to have some privacy.

Sophie held the quilt tenderly and traced the flowers. Growing up, her grandmother had been a nurturing soul, and Sophie prayed that she'd be more like her than her own mom. Sophie's hand rested on her belly and caressed her moving child within. She feared being a single working mother. Owning her own business consumed her time, and raising a child, by herself, on top of it seemed near impossible.

"I don't want to fail you, little one." With a kick to the palm of her hand, she vowed always to be present when she was needed.

. . .

Brady stepped into the hallway, made his way toward the den and dialed Stevens. Pacing the floor, he could hear the rings until it went to voicemail. Brady ended the call.

"What the hell, Stevens? You can't say 911, then not answer the damn phone." The phone rang in his hand. "Yes, what is it, Stevens?"

"She's out, Brady. Just got released a few minutes ago."

Brady felt sick.

"Dammit! I'll head out there within the hour. I should make it there around one." Brady disconnected, then sat on the couch, carrying the weight of his head in his hands, to think.

When he got up again, he took the steps two at a time. The tune of "Hush, Little Baby" was coming from the nursery. Sophie stood leaning against the crib as the butterflies whirled around and around. He cleared his throat. "Baby, I have to head to New York again."

"Aw, so soon? Brady, is everything all right? You look like you've seen a ghost."

"Um, yeah, everything is fine. Just hit a snag with that case I'm helping out with." Again, the agony of lying to her turned his stomach.

"How long will you be gone? Oh, goodness, I hope you'll be back before Thanksgiving."

"I'll do my best. You know there's no place I'd rather be than here with you…right?"

"I don't know about that…you seem to be running away an awful lot lately." Brady's face dropped. "I'm kidding! Go! I'll be here when you get back."

He held her face and planted a big kiss on her lips, then turned and ran down the stairs. Before he hit the bottom step, the words *I love you, Sophie Anderson* fluttered through his thoughts, as if in a dream.

CHAPTER 26

Sophie was conflicted about Brady's leaving. She had no hold over him. He was a free man, and she acknowledged that she didn't have any right to persuade him otherwise. However, his absence left her feeling very much alone. She felt alone with her mother always being gone and with Sam's passing. Then she looked around the nursery, taking in the fullness of what would fill that void; she wouldn't be alone for much longer, and that thought lifted her spirits.

She gathered all the little outfits and placed them in the hamper, examining each one and savoring the moment. Lifting the basket was easy, and she giggled at the number of tiny outfits that she could carry without any trouble. As she descended the first stair, her phone rang again. Reaching around the corner to her nightstand, she picked up her phone. *The prosecutor for Sam's case?*

"Jackson. To what do I owe the honor?"

"I'm not sure how to tell you this, so I'll come right out with it. I don't know how this happened. It's unprecedented, but Cynthia Lockwood has been released from prison." Sophie had taken the first few steps as the basket slipped from her grasp. She sat on the staircase as colorful pink outfits and bunny rabbit, flower, and Mommy Loves Me onesies tumbled down the flight.

"How can that be, Jackson?" Sophie took a hard gulp, trying to grasp the situation.

Jackson was clearly shaken by the unexpected turn of events. His typical matter-of-fact, calming demeanor had abandoned him. "I confess, I am in disbelief myself."

"You really mean to tell me that you had no idea that this was coming?" Sophie's blood was pumping at a rapid pace and shook with rage. "How could you have allowed this to happen? Shouldn't I have had a say?" Jackson was silent on the other end, allowing her the time she needed to vent. "This can't be legal! You've got to fix this…make it right, Jackson! Sam deserves better than this! I deserve better than this!" Sophie stood at the top of the steps to pace and think. Time ticked by, and still Jackson waited. "I'm sorry, Jackson. I know it's not your fault. It's just that—"

"You don't need to explain. I can only imagine how you must be feeling."

"Is there anything that can be done?" she asked, feeling defeated.

"No. At least, nothing that I know of. She was paroled with some conditions after her release. Maybe it was because of overcrowding or good behavior or both. I don't know, Sophie. I've never seen anything like this. It's too soon, way too soon. Honestly, I don't even know how this can be legal."

"I'm going to go now, Jackson. I…I can't…I just can't talk anymore right now." Sophie hung up the phone and once again sat at the top of the steps, staring into space, just as Emily entered the room below.

"Okay, partner, taste test time!" she yelled toward the upstairs. "I know you're knee-deep in baby mania, but I need your opinion on these cake fillings." Emily rounded the corner and stopped abruptly when she saw the garments strewn all over the stairs. "Sophie?" No reply. "Sophie, look at me…what happened?"

Sophie gazed in Emily's direction. "A killer has been set free."

. . .

Horns blared around him. He was deep in thought when the light turned green. Brady looked in the rearview mirror in time to see a middle finger fly in the air. "All right already. It's not like there's anywhere to go, anyway," Brady said in a futile effort to feel better, knowing his words couldn't be heard. He pressed the gas, only to brake seconds later. "I hate this city!" He pounded the steering wheel and tossed his head back, hitting the headrest as his phone rang through the car speakers. It was a number he'd hoped he wouldn't see for many more years to come.

Brady pushed the answer button on the steering wheel. "Well, there's my girl."

"I'm out! Can you believe it, Brady? Isn't it wonderful! I'm so excited."

"Pretty amazing, Cynthia. Your father sure is a miracle worker."

"You have no idea. He's my savior! Do you want to know

the first thing I did? I took a long bath and used actual bubbles and body wash. I blow-dried my hair, put on makeup, and now I'm wearing jeans and a cashmere sweater. You wouldn't believe how much I've missed this—the things we take for granted. When will I get to see you, Brady…when?"

"Umm…I was going to surprise you, but I suppose I should've asked first. I'm not sure how your father will take it if he sees my car in the driveway. Am I safe?"

"He'll get over it. Besides, I already told him that you are part of my life whether he likes it or not."

Brady couldn't imagine her talking with her father like that. She was more likely to sweet-talk him while batting her eyelashes. "Do you think that was wise? I wouldn't want to stand between you. I know how much he means to you."

"It'll be fine. Honestly, he seemed a bit indifferent about it, actually. I guess he's just happy that I'm home."

"Great. I should be there in about a half hour or so—lots of traffic."

"Perfect! You can stay for the celebration. Daddy's arranged for a dinner with some of our closest friends and some of his colleagues. It's not a huge event. Daddy thought it would be best to keep it more intimate. He doesn't want the press to get wind of my getting out and ruin my privacy. You know how dreadful they can be."

Brady's mind reeled with the prospect of who might be at this gathering: it was a party he couldn't miss. "Sounds great, but I didn't bring a suit. You know what? I'll swing in to see Stevens. We're the same size, and I'm sure he wouldn't mind helping me out."

"Why don't you just go back to your place and get one, silly? It's not like we live a million miles away from each other."

"You're right. What was I thinking? Just excited to see you, I guess. I'll see you in a bit, okay?"

"Looking forward to it, lover." Cynthia sent kiss noises and hung up.

Dammit, smarten up, Owens! He'd sublet his apartment, never dreaming that he'd be back in the city anytime soon and certainly not reconnecting with Cynthia Lockwood. He'd have to prevent her from going to his place. With enough time, Brady would head to Stevens's and borrow a suit and still make it to Lockwood's in good time. He dialed Stevens to give him the heads-up.

CHAPTER 27

Brady drove up the long winding drive to the inner sanctum of the Lockwood estate. He proceeded around to the back, where Cynthia awaited him. He felt sick in the pit of his stomach as the tires rolled across the cobblestone pavers. He could see a broad smile and hand waving ahead. *God help me.* Brady pulled into his usual spot. He stepped out as Cynthia ran skidding in her heels with arms open wide.

"Whoa, easy there. You're going to break your neck in those things."

"Heels, Brady, actual heels! Isn't life grand?" Cynthia landed an open-mouth kiss that took Brady off guard. "Don't you feel yummy." Her hands squeezed his biceps. "I want to take you into my place immediately and have my way with you, but I can't. Daddy wants to see you right away."

The pout of her mouth and her puppy-dog eyes were more than Brady could take. He'd have to figure out a way to avoid her advances. Images of Sophie passed through his mind. He'd have to hold on to that to keep up this charade.

"Your father rules around here. Better not upset him." Brady nudged Cynthia away to allow some space between them. "Let me look at you." Cynthia twirled around to give him a full view. "Looking great as always, Cyn."

Cynthia batted her eyes.

"Do you find me irresistible?"

"Oh, you don't know the half of it. Words cannot describe how I feel right now." Cynthia giggled with delight. "We'd better get inside. Don't want to keep him waiting." She took his arm, and they walked carefully across the patchy ice covering the cobblestones to the back entrance of the main house.

"Daddy, look who's here," she called. Lockwood sauntered into the room with a bourbon in hand and stopped short of Brady's reach. Brady stepped forward to shake his hand, but Lockwood looked him in the eyes with a steely glare, then gulped his bourbon, effectively snubbing him. Brady stepped back, placing his hands in his pockets.

"Owens." Lockwood eyed him up and down.

Brady stood his ground, held up his chin, and looked Henry Lockwood in the eyes. "Mr. Lockwood."

Instantly, he was pissed with himself for stooping to saying mister. In Lockwood's presence, he had instantly reverted to his former submissive self. The control Lockwood had over him was immeasurable. *Resist him. He's a piece of shit: a vile, slithering slug to be brought down. Now suck it up and play the game.*

"You must be thrilled to have Cynthia back home. I have to say, I don't know how you did it, but I, for one, am impressed. You're a miracle worker, Mr. Lockwood, and I only hope to gain a small measure of your talent and abilities."

"Good to have you back, Owens." With that, Lockwood approached and gave him a slap across the back, then grabbed him around the shoulder to give a sideways embrace. Cynthia was beaming at the camaraderie. "What can I get you, my boy?"

The fireplace was ablaze with embers of blue and orange, each flame licking the monogrammed andirons of H & L. Lockwood picked up the stogie that was resting in a leather-and-brass Cohiba ashtray sitting atop the mantel; with a Lenox crystal glass in his other hand, he took a deep inhale. Tipping his head back and forming his lips into a circle, Lockwood puffed out rings of smoke that grew large, then vanished. Brady could see the brazen satisfaction of a job well done. *Such a pompous ass.*

"So, Owens, what have you been doing with yourself since you left my firm?"

"Photography."

"Pictures? You've been taking pictures? You're wasting your talent. You could have been a great lawyer, Owens, and you're spending your time playing with a camera?"

"Needed a break from law, I guess. You know, how we lost Cynthia here, it knocked me for a loop." He hoped that Lockwood wouldn't be able to see his tells. He was known for reading body language and had won hundreds of cases because of his keen instincts. Brady fought to find some truth in his words, to hide the lies. *Look him in the eyes.*

"Daddy, Brady's been heartbroken over me being away. He couldn't even see me locked up there because it was too upsetting for him. He sure surprised me when he finally came. I think it's the sweetest thing ever."

Lockwood gave him a look that penetrated to his core and sent shivers down his spine.

"Hmm, never took you to be a candy-ass, Owens. But my girl here can make people do or not do things that they'd never dreamed of before; she's that special. Don't ever let me see you, or hear of you, forgetting that again."

"No, sir. I'd never dream of it."

"Daddy, we have more guests arriving." Cynthia shuffled over to the window and peered out. "Oh, it's the governor and his wife! I didn't recognize the car. They usually arrive in a limo."

Brady was shocked that the governor would be careless enough to associate with the Lockwoods, especially under the circumstances.

"Come with me, Brady, and I'll introduce you. Isn't it great how he wants to see me?" Cynthia gave Brady a tug on the arm and led him like a puppy. Brady picked up the pace to walk beside her. He needed to save at least a meager sense of dignity as he met the governor and the First Lady of New York.

"I had no idea you and your father were friends with the governor," Brady whispered nonchalantly.

"Oh, yes, Daddy's firm has been his legal counsel for years. I can't believe you didn't know that," she said with a shrug. "I don't think he'd even be governor if it wasn't for my daddy."

"How's that?"

"With his money, silly. Daddy is one of his biggest donors. He doesn't like to make that known to too many people; he's really humble like that, you know."

He almost laughed out loud at the thought of Henry Lockwood being humble. She was delusional.

"It's so good of you to come, Gwen." Cynthia and the governor's wife exchanged a kiss on the cheek. "You look as beautiful as always. Unfortunately, I'm looking more like a hag. I do wish Daddy had waited until I could at least get to the spa before throwing me a party." Cynthia took the governor's hand. "Thank you for taking the time out of your busy schedule to come and see me."

Brady stood there, invisible, until Cynthia remembered his existence. "Governor, Mrs. Palermo, I'd like to introduce you to Brady Owens. He's my….my…boyfriend for now. I'm sure before you know it, we'll be celebrating our engagement. Won't we, Brady?"

Dear Lord, the woman is certifiable. "We never know what the future will hold, my sweet. Governor, Mrs. Palermo, it's an honor to meet you."

The afternoon progressed into the evening. They were treated to a five-course dinner of prime rib and lazy man lobster, then were entertained by a pianist who took requests. Cynthia was chatty, per usual, as she soaked up the attention. Brady was puzzled that this particular gathering of people would welcome her back with open arms. She was an ex-convict who'd served time for killing someone without remorse. It was true that money, power, and influence could make people do anything.

. . .

Standing back, Sophie admired the nursery. She had placed a rose-patterned valance over the window, tucked in the matching crib sheet, and added the final touch: a small ivory frame with a bird's nest holding one tiny robin's egg.

"It's beautiful, Sophie," Emily said, bringing up the last set of baby clothes from the dryer.

"It is, isn't it? I can't believe that soon I'll be holding my little girl, rocking her in that chair, and placing her in that crib. It just doesn't seem real, Em."

"It's as real as can ever be, partner. You're going to be a wonderful mom, and I will be the best auntie ever!"

Sophie could see that Emily was trying hard to snap her out of her melancholy mood, and she loved her for it.

"Couldn't you just see Sam with her? He would have been a great daddy." Sophie swallowed the lump that formed in her throat.

"He would have been amazing. It will be our job to bring her up so she knows every wonderful thing about him. Now, let's go get a bite to eat. It's late and I'm starving."

"Let's stay in. I'll heat up some beef stew."

In the kitchen, Sophie grabbed a copper pot from the overhead rack as Emily removed the container of stew from the refrigerator. "Oh, I made some bread today. I'll be right back." Emily escaped into the bakery as Sophie stirred the pot, getting lost in her thoughts.

Emily returned to remove two bowls and a breadboard from the cabinet.

"Emily, do you think Sam would approve of Brady?"

"Umm, well, in what regard?"

"I don't know…as someone important in my life, I guess."

"I would imagine that he'd want you to be happy, Soph. That's all he ever wanted for you. Does he make you happy?"

"Sure, I guess."

"You don't sound too convincing." Emily sliced the bread as Sophie ladled the stew.

"It's not that he doesn't make me happy. I mean…I feel content around him, like I can be myself, you know?"

"So, he's a good friend, then?" She poured tall glasses of milk and waited for Sophie's response.

Sophie hesitated. "More than that, I guess. Honestly, I'm not sure what we are. It's not like we've made any kind of commitment to each other or anything. But I do miss him when he's gone, and I'm always happy to see him. Part of me can't help but feel a bit guilty; is it too soon?"

Emily took a few bites and tore her bread, dipping it into the stew. "Only you can answer that, Sophie. Are you falling in love with him?"

"I think I am. I know...you can pat yourself on the back and say *I told you so.*"

"Who, me? I wouldn't dream of doing that."

"Who are you kidding, Emily? I know you too well."

"But how well do we really know Brady? We know he came from New York and was—*is* a lawyer. We know he takes great pictures and is a task pro. Outside of that? I don't know."

"Yea, I guess you're right," Sophie said reluctantly.

"I mean, why did he feel like he needed to leave New York and his profession, anyway? Haven't you wondered?"

"Sure I have. But it's not like it's the first time that someone's wanted to make a simpler life for themselves. I don't begrudge him that."

"Of course not."

"Besides, he's technically still working there...doing the law thing." Sophie watched as Emily stirred the remnants of her stew, clinking her spoon against the inside of the bowl. "Okay, out with it. What's eating you?"

"How do you know that he's really going there all the time for work? Aren't you curious to know if he had or even has a girlfriend or anything?"

"I guess I never really thought about it."

"You have to wonder why he's been spending so much time back in New York. I know I do."

"He's helping someone with a case. I know it's a pretty tough one, too, because he gets really upset when he has to leave, and it takes him quite a bit of time to relax once he's back. I guess that's why he left the legal world…too much stress."

"Maybe you're right, but just take it slow, Sophie. I don't want you to get hurt."

"I know you don't, and you are adorably sweet to think about me, but I'm fine. So, tell me, what got you so worked up this morning? I got the impression that you didn't want Brady around to help."

Emily looked down at the empty bowl and got up to scoop another ladleful. "I don't know. I was just, umm…wanting to help you myself. Maybe I was a teeny-weeny bit jealous because I wanted to help you finish the nursery." Emily turned to sit back down, still not making eye contact.

"Why didn't you say so? I would have been happy to have you help. I'm sorry, I didn't realize—"

"Because I was being ridiculous. Just forget I ever mentioned it."

Sophie could tell that something was still eating her but knew her well enough to know that when Emily was ready, she'd open up with the truth. She just hoped that she wasn't disappointing her by having feelings for Brady while she was carrying Sam's child.

. . .

Lockwood's boisterous laugh carried through the house. "I'd like to have seen the look on the prosecutor's face when he found out that Cynthia was out."

"I bet he shit himself," said the bald, round man that was going on drink number four.

"Before or after he spoke to the widow?"

"Both!" Laughter filled the air. Each man was sucking on a stogie and holding a pool cue. "My guess is that she told him he had shit for brains…he was an embarrassment to the field of law!" Lockwood was in his element.

Brady took a long burning swig. That was rich, coming from the man who'd lost to him in court. Brady had once dreamed of being a part of the boys' club, thinking that it would be proof that he'd *made it* and make his father proud. *Good God, how in the hell could I have ever wanted this?* Listening to this crap was killing him. Keeping his cool was proving way too difficult. Hearing them joke about Sophie's counsel only meant that Sophie would, in fact, be hearing of the news at any moment, if she hadn't already. Wanting to be with her, at this time, was impossible to bear. However, gaining some insight as to how Cynthia had been set free would be worth their separation.

"So, Palermo, when are you officially throwing your name in the ring for US Senate?" the bald man chimed in.

"That depends. How much support will you give me?" The governor rubbed his fat fingers together. "Lockwood here has thrown his support, and I'd expect you to do the same!" The room erupted with booming cheers. "In that case, I'll be making the announcement soon—very soon."

Cynthia and company entered the room with a chatter. "What's all the excitement, gentlemen?"

"Palermo here has just announced that he's in for running for the Senate," Lockwood said with his chest out like a proud rooster ready to crow.

"Well, it's about time!" Gwen ran over to embrace her man. "I've been trying to get him to make the decision for weeks. I should have known that you'd all convince him. He's going to be a fabulous senator."

Cynthia raised a glass. "Let's make a toast!"

"Hear, hear!"

"To the great governor of New York. You will be missed at the statehouse as you head to the Hill!"

Brady raised a glass but couldn't take a drink.

The celebration continued well into the evening. Cynthia staggered down the hallway, limping with one shoe on, the other dangling in her hand. The powder room was approaching as she maneuvered gingerly around a table that sat in the center of the rotunda leading to the other wings of the mansion. A cornucopia of fresh flowers, fruits, and nuts sat atop the table, beckoning her. Cynthia groped for a handful of nuts, then tipped her head back, trying to find her mouth in one clean swoop. The floor suddenly found her. She lay splayed on the floor, surrounded by the mixed nuts that had missed their mark. Her shoe slid across the marble tiles and found its final resting place against the bathroom door. The loud thud of her failed attempt was soon followed by giggles that echoed throughout the halls. Cynthia tried to stand.

Brady stood back to witness the spectacle. Disgust permeated to his core, but he was consumed with relief all the same. There would be no need for making up excuses to stay the night elsewhere; Cynthia had solved the dilemma. Per habit, he carried her to her bed, tucked her in, and exited into the night.

CHAPTER 28

Stevens poured two steaming cups of coffee and slid two fried eggs out of the frying pan and onto Brady's plate. "I'm surprised you're up so early. You got in pretty late."

"Thanks for having me, Stevens. I appreciate it."

"It's all good. Besides, I was looking forward to hearing all about Miss Cynthia. Wish I'd been a fly on the proverbial wall."

"Trust me…you don't." Brady cut the whites from around the yolk with his fork, scooped up the runny yolk, and popped it into his mouth.

Stevens stood with elbows propped up on the island opposite Brady and breathed the steam in. "Learn anything?"

"Maybe. We need to look into campaign contributions for our 'great' governor." Brady's eyes rolled to the back of his head. "I'd like to find out how often and how much Lockwood has contributed. He's running for the Senate, you know."

"Who, Lockwood?" Stevens asked, standing up in amazement.

"He may as well be the next senator. He'll be pulling all the strings if Palermo gets elected. But no, I think he's funding the campaign. Most likely most of it—bending the rules here and there."

"Sure, I'll look into it."

"Can you also find out who Palermo's appointees are? I'd like to know if any of our parole board members were appointed under Palermo's watch. Kind of a shot in the dark, but something tells me there's more to the Lockwood-Palermo relationship than we may realize."

"I don't know, Brady. I'm not so sure that the governor would stick his neck out and show his face at Lockwood's estate so soon after Cynthia's release if he had anything to do with it."

"Thing is, he showed up in an unmarked car. No escort, no limo or Caddy. Cynthia herself said she didn't recognize the car and was surprised to see it was the governor."

"Okay, I'll check it out. When are you heading out?"

"I want to pick up a couple of frames, follow up on a few possible leads, then I'm heading back. I heard that Sophie's attorney found out the news, and I don't want to be away any longer than I have to be."

"You've got it bad for her, don't you, man?"

"Not sure what I've got. Just want justice for someone I've grown fond of." Brady gulped the coffee down as if stuffing down his true feelings for Sophie Anderson. "Gotta head out." Brady got up and grabbed his coat hanging by the back door. "Thanks again for the stay. Call me if you find anything." The door squeaked and closed with a bang. Brady put his head down and lifted his collar to the wind, excited to see Sophie again, despite his dread.

Brady was on the interstate, heading out of the city, when he turned the radio off. The silence was a welcome treat, allowing him a chance to think. As quiet as his surroundings were, the noise in his head was deafening. His mind raced from Sophie, Cynthia, Lockwood, and the governor to Thanksgiving and photography.

So long as he continued this charade, Cynthia would expect him to join her for Thanksgiving. At least she knew that he was trying his hand at professional photography; he could always use this work as an excuse, even though she hadn't been very tolerant of sharing time with his career in the past. Knowing her, she'd drink herself into a stupor again and wouldn't even miss him.

Brady ran the images he'd taken of Sophie over and over in his mind. She was perfection in every way. The thought of her caused his pulse to quicken. Sophie had won his heart, and he knew he finally had to admit it. He'd continue to wait until the time was right to confess it to her. *Confess what, you idiot! That you're in love with her and that you've been lying to her since pretty much the moment you met her? Brady, you're a piece of shit! You wouldn't want yourself after that, so why the hell would you expect her to ever want you?* Brady slammed his fist on the leather steering wheel. *Dammit, I should have told her from the start.* He was more resolved than ever to make sure Cynthia Lockwood and her overbearing and insufferable father were held accountable for whatever the hell it was they had done to get her out of prison. Maybe that would be his saving grace if he ever had a remote chance of earning Sophie's heart.

Noticing the time on his dash, Brady figured Cynthia would have finally woken from her hungover slumber. It was midafternoon, and the day had really gotten away from him.

He hoped he wasn't already too late to call. He spoke the command and could hear the ringing of Cynthia's phone.

"Well, it's about time I heard from you. Where are you, Brady?"

"I didn't want to wake you. Besides, the phone goes both ways, Cyn. If you wanted to know where I was, you could have called me." Brady tried to keep the disdain from his voice.

"Oh, sure, now you're being considerate."

"Cynthia, why don't you just relax—"

"Relax! I have a raging headache. You've left me, and you want me to relax?"

Brady took a deep breath, "Sweetheart, I brought you to bed late into the night. It was the first time you've been in your own bed in months. I thought you'd enjoy being able to sprawl out and rest. We'll have our time." Brady bit his lip. "I promise."

"But I need you now. Where are you?" she whined in the singsong voice he'd grown accustomed to loathing.

"I'm on my way back to Maine. I have some work that's time-sensitive, and it can't wait any longer."

"What! You're going to Maine! For what work? Oh, let me guess—for your ridiculous photography hobby! That's what you're calling work?"

"Yes, my work." Seething, Brady continued, "I was going to tell you last night, but I didn't want to spoil your homecoming. I did everything I could to be there for you, but today I have to head back."

"How can you think that your pictures could possibly be more important than time with me?"

"Trust me, Cyn. Nothing could be more important than 'time' for you, and I'm doing everything that I can to make that happen."

"When will you be back?"

"As soon as I can."

"Fine. I'll be waiting for you, but you better put some serious thought behind your cute little picture phase. I trust it will pass soon and then you can get back to doing real work. Daddy and I are expecting that you'll do the right thing."

"Cynthia, I'm done talking about this right now. I will see you when I'm ready. Now, why don't you drink a bloody mary and go back to bed."

Brady ended the call. His blood was boiling; he was tired and getting hungry, and he knew he wouldn't be seeing Sophie tonight. He was in no mood now. Cynthia had once again infuriated him to the point of self-contempt. He hated this side of himself and refused to have Sophie witness it. *No, tomorrow will have to do.*

CHAPTER 29

Sophie woke abruptly, her sheets damp, her heart pounding.
Clumsily and frantically reaching for the nightstand lamp, she inadvertently tossed Daisy to the floor. She looked around the room to make sure it was safe. Grabbing her robe, she turned on her cell phone flashlight and turned the doorknob as quietly as possible, then lifted up on the knob as she opened the door to avoid the creaking noise that the hinges made. She tiptoed into the hallway, peeked into the nursery, then picked up the pace down the stairs toward the front door to be sure it was locked. Her hands fumbled with the chain as her speed hastened, fearing she wouldn't secure it quick enough.

The dream had been so real that she needed to be sure that it actually wasn't. Feeling ridiculous, she advanced to the stairs to head back to bed. *Nope, can't do it.* She turned toward the kitchen but then stepped into the den. She could see the embers still burning in the fireplace. The heat of the floorboards brought warmth to her bare feet. She checked each window's latch, then moved on to the kitchen to be sure to secure the lock there as well. The creepy-crawlies didn't abate as she could feel Cynthia Lockwood near. In her dream, Cynthia had said, with a twisted grin, "I killed one. Now I'll kill the other."

Sophie couldn't shake the feeling of dread and fear. She got a glass of water and rechecked every window and door as she made her way once again toward her bedroom. Fear still found its way back to her mind as soon as she clicked off the lamp.

Sophie reached for her cell. *Only one thirty!* Realizing that she had the duration of the night to endure, she tapped Brady's number. If he didn't answer, then she'd be relieved that she hadn't woken him. However, if he did, she'd be relieved just the same. Hearing his voice would bring her comfort. The phone rang several times, and she was just about to hang up as his deep, raspy voice answered.

"Hello."

"Brady, I'm sorry it's so late…but…"

"Sophie! Are you okay? Is it the baby?"

"No, everything is fine. It's just that…well, I feel like an idiot telling you this, but…I had a stupid dream and I'm a little freaked out. I thought if I could talk to someone that I'd feel better. You know, get my mind off it. I'm really sorry that I woke you. You know what, never mind, I'm good. Just go back to sleep and please forget I called."

"I'll be right over." Before she could respond, the phone went dead.

Well, I didn't even know he was back in town, but I guess he'll be right over and that's that. Sophie paced back and forth in her room. Seeing herself way too many times in her full-length mirror gave her a shudder. *At least brush your teeth and put a comb through your hair, Soph. You look like something Daisy dragged home.*

Her nerves were shot, and she trembled while applying the paste onto her brush. The water ran cold, awaiting the intrusion of her toothbrush. The mirror reflected her internal struggles as puffy circles expressed the anger at her current situation. Sam's killer had been set free. She'd vowed not to lose sleep over her again, and yet here she was.

Kitchen lights blazed in the night. After filling the water container to the coffee machine, she sat and waited. Brady would be there any moment, much to her surprise. A different form of nerves crept their way into Sophie's being. Her palms were sweaty and her nightgown felt damp under her arms. The anticipation of Brady's arrival seemed to drag on as each second felt like minutes. Headlights beamed up the driveway. He was here, and all would be well.

Brady sprinted to the back door and pushed to open it. The house shuddered as the chain held. Realizing she'd forgotten to unlock the door, she dashed to remedy the situation. Daisy beat her there and bolted out the door through the crack.

"Are you okay?" Brady wrapped his arms around her as she snuggled her head deep into his chest.

"Yes, I'm okay. Just feeling a bit embarrassed. Do you want any coffee or anything?"

"No, thanks, I'm good. Do you want to talk about it? Being able to talk about it has always helped me." They took a seat at the kitchen counter.

"Sure, I guess. But I have to back up before I get to the bad dream part. I got some horrific news while you were gone."

"Oh?"

"Sam's killer, Cynthia Lockwood, was released. I'm blown away by that fact. She was released way too early. Even Sam's attorney doesn't understand how that could have happened. It's as if she slipped through the cracks or something." Brady listened on intently. "Anyway, I dreamt that that woman was in my house! She'd said she'd 'killed one and now she'd kill the other.'" Sophie got up to pace, tapping her fingers atop her protruding belly. "Who is the other? Me, my baby, or…this is crazy, isn't it?"

"It was a dream, Sophie—a very real-feeling dream, but you are safe and I am here. Nothing is going to happen to you. This woman will get what she deserves. You can be confident in that."

"But how? It's like it's the best-kept secret. It's not on the news or in the papers. It's as if it didn't actually happen. If it wasn't for Jackson, the prosecutor, I wouldn't even know about it. Something isn't right."

"It does sound pretty unusual, and I can see why you'd be perplexed. I would be, too." He stood to take ahold of her hands. "I think the best thing that you can do right now is to get some sleep. I'll stay with you for a while if you want me to. What do you say?" She nodded in agreement.

The wind was kicking up again and the windows panes rattled with each gust. "Daisy! I forgot to bring Daisy in."

"I'll get her. Why don't you go ahead and get yourself tucked in? I'll be right up."

. . .

Brady took a moment to collect his thoughts. His throat was tight and his head pounded. Coming clean right now had to be avoided; it wasn't the right time. However, the feeling of avoidance was eating at him. He'd no sooner opened the door than Daisy ran full bore into the kitchen and skidded around the counter, through the living room, and bounded up the steps. He secured the door, turned off the multitudes of lights with a grin, then ventured toward Sophie's sanctuary, reflecting on what a difference a day could make. The comparison of tucking Cynthia into bed to Sophie was a complete 180-degree pivot—one that he was most grateful for.

He caught Sophie climbing into bed and pulling the blankets up high under her chin. Daisy jumped up and curled up next to Sophie's head, taking up a third of the pillow as Brady stood in the entry. "Now that's quite a picture to put in my memory bank." He leaned against the open doorway, crossed his arms, and grinned with amusement. He got a kick out of seeing the raised mound under the quilt, Sophie's sparkling eyes peering out the top, wearing a calico headpiece.

"It's how we roll," Sophie said with a snicker. "Are you sure you don't mind staying for a while? I'm even willing to share."

"Do you think Daisy will allow it?"

"Not sure…it will be a first since…umm. We'll just have to see."

Brady, not sure quite how to proceed, stood on Sophie's side of the bed, did an extra tuck, and kissed her on the forehead for good measure. "I'll just…keep watch on the other side."

"Keep watch!" Sophie's eyes widened.

"It was just a dream, remember? Sorry for the poor choice of words."

He sat on the other side of the bed and removed his shoes, then lay on the bed. He flopped onto his side to face

Sophie. Propping his head up onto his elbow, he surveyed the intimate perspective. She gazed into his eyes, and he wished he could dive in. He touched her lips with his hand as she gave him a kiss.

"Good night, Sophie. Sleep well."

He turned off the light and waited until his eyes adjusted to the darkened room. He could see that Sophie had already fallen asleep. Daisy watched the intruder by her master's side. Before long, Brady had drifted into a much-needed slumber as well.

. . .

Brady lay awake, looking at Sophie's silhouette as the moon shone through the window. They had moved to a spooning position in the night, and his hand rested on Sophie's unborn child. This little one wasn't sleeping either, and he could feel the subtle movement and kicks from within. Off in the distance, the sound of a slamming car door piqued his interest. After gently rolling over from atop the bed, he gathered his shoes and carefully retreated into the hall, so that he wouldn't wake this woman who had seized his heart.

Dammit! Seeing Emily's ride, he now knew the reason for the slamming car door at this hour of the morning. Forgetting that Emily arrived to work before the sun came up, he realized that he should have left much earlier, but the drive back and forth from New York was wearing on him, and he had been more exhausted than he'd thought. Falling into a sound sleep on Sophie's bed was unexpected. He'd intended to stay only until he knew Sophie was comfortable and resting; now he'd been caught. He was confident that Sophie wouldn't have minded in the least, but he knew that Emily hadn't been herself lately, and he didn't want to cause added stress to Sophie's life right now. Not to mention the fact that he was close to getting caught in his lie and didn't want to poke the bees' nest.

Brady flicked on the kitchen light in search of paper and pen. He removed the notepad stuck to the side of the fridge and retrieved the small pencil attached.

Good morning, Sophie,

I'm glad that you were able to get some sleep. You looked so peaceful this morning that I didn't want to wake you. I have some things to catch up on today. Not sure when I'll see you next, but I hope it's soon.

Thanks for calling me last night. I'm glad that I could help a damsel in distress…I've always wanted to play the hero. Thanks for making this guy's dream come true. Hope you have a great day.

Love, Brady

PS. Emily was already here when I left…just thought you might like a heads-up.

. . .

Sophie awoke to Daisy kneading her pillow, then finally settling into a cozy spot after circling a time or two. It took a moment to register that Brady had been there.

Her hand grazed the empty pillow to her side; seeing the indentation brought a smile to her face and not the sadness that usually crept over her. She recalled Brady's arm around her and his warm kiss. Oh, how she'd missed tender moments like that. It had been just she and Daisy in this bed, and that had become her new normal. Never had she expected Brady Owens to step into her life. The thought of him stirred emotions she'd never dreamed she'd ever feel again, and somehow, it felt right. She lay there picturing Brady standing in her doorway, seducing her with his sultry eyes. *Seriously, what are you thinking? You're an expectant mother, Sophie Anderson!* She shook off the thought amazed at how rested she was, considering the unsettling night she'd had, came as a surprise until she looked at the time. *I'm late…ridiculously late!*

In no time at all, she was showered and dressed for the day. "I'm famished, Daisy. How about you, girl?" Sophie dropped a decaf in the Keurig and pushed the button for a large cup. She tapped her fingers on the counter impatiently as it seemed to take an eternity to fill. She opened Daisy's canned breakfast and watched her eat. She was peeling a hardboiled egg when Brady's note caught her eye.

"Of course he left a note, Daisy. I should have known." Flipping open the note caused her heartbeat to quicken a bit. "Let's see what it says, shall we?" Daisy jumped up on the counter and stuck her nose onto the paper; Sophie gave her a kiss. "You've got to let me see it to read it." She took her time to read his scrawling, then folded the paper and brought it to her chest. "Seems we have a hero, Daisy." Determined not to let a possible conflict with Emily spoil her great mood, she entered the shop ready to start her day.

Sophie was pleased that Rebecca had been able to piece together several arrangements before she made it down to the shop. Having Rebecca there certainly gave her more time to start the day without too much stress. Upon entering, the scent of mouthwatering apple and pumpkin pies wafted through the air.

"Aw, you see, this is why Thanksgiving is my favorite holiday."

Emily looked up with exasperation. "Easy for you to say. This holiday is literally for the birds. It's exhausting, and I can officially go on record to say that I hate apples—everything about them." Sophie's laughter carried through the shop.

"Good morning, Sophie," said Agnes Templeton while partaking in an apple turnover fresh from the oven.

"Good morning to you, Agnes. I see you're starting your day off with a little sweetness."

"We could smell the apples baking from our place. Frank insisted that I get something to bring home. He doesn't know that I usually buy three. One for now, then one each for when I get home. Let's keep that little secret to ourselves, shall we?"

"I wouldn't dream of telling on you, Agnes. We gals need to stick together."

Agnes popped the last morsel into her mouth and licked her fingertips, savoring every last bit of sugar. "Sometimes... just sometimes, secrets help to keep a relationship stronger." She got up from the white wrought iron chair and gave Sophie a goodbye hug. Emily stayed behind the counter. She wasn't a hugger, which Agnes knew full well. "Emily, delicious as always. You might not be liking apples right now, but they love me. I am quite grateful. Now, you ladies have a wonderful day." She drew her knit hat over her ears and headed out the door.

Sophie watched Agnes tread along the pathway to her home—her galoshes, woolen socks, coat, and hat all wrapped up her short, round stature, painting a picture of days gone by. Sophie continued to look on, lost in nostalgia, until Agnes was out of sight.

"You're looking refreshed this morning, Soph. Sleep well?"

"Actually, no. I had a terrible night's sleep. It wasn't until early this morning that I was able to finally drift off. Looks like you could use some shut-eye, too. I don't expect Brady to be back again today, so if you need to, feel free to go in the house and take a nap. Rebecca and I should be fine." Sophie nonchalantly plucked a dying flower from a bouquet that sat in the center of the table where Agnes had been sitting and motioned to Rebecca that she'd arrived.

Emily's blank stare spoke volumes. Sophie had been sensing Emily's disapproval recently, which added to her feelings of guilt, but she hadn't done anything wrong, and she'd be darned if she'd let Emily make her feel otherwise.

Emily continued to sputter incoherently when the timer blared in the kitchen, which snapped her out of her fumbling. "All right already!" she shouted toward the kitchen, "I'm coming!" Within moments, Emily turned off the timer and pulled another group of apple pies from the oven. "That's it, I'm done with you. No more apples today." She placed the pies on cooling racks, turned off the oven, and removed her apron.

Emily threw on her coat and shouted through the shop, "I'll be back in a bit…need to run an errand."

CHAPTER 30

Brady was focused as he went about developing the shots he'd taken of Sophie. He was excited about the results so far and looked forward to finishing the last batch. He was, however, distracted by the crunching sound of tires rolling toward the cottage. Brady paused to listen more intently when the distinct creaking of the floorboards on the porch became clear. He quickly finished pulling a photo from the bath with his tongs when the anticipated bang on the door began. Removing his apron, he looked around the room to make sure that everything was protected before he made his exit. The impatient banging continued, growing louder, until Emily's familiar voice rang over the pounding of the door.

"Brady, I know you're in there! Open up!"

"In a minute," he responded from deep inside the cottage. Panic washed over him with this unexpected visit. *Bang, bang, bang*, went her fist on the door for the last time when Brady breathlessly answered.

"Emily! Oh my God, is everything okay? Is it Sophie?"

"Yes, it's Sophie." She barged into the cottage without hesitation.

"Why didn't you call? If something's wrong—"

"Yes, something is wrong. It's all wrong. I don't know what your intentions are with Sophie, but I'm putting you on notice. She is not to be toyed with. She is a vulnerable woman right now, and you are taking advantage of her." Anger raged on as Brady turned and walked away toward the back of the cottage. "Don't you turn your back on me, Owens!"

Brady continued on. "I'm kind of right in the middle of something right now. Why don't you follow me? You can keep talking while I finish up."

"How do I know you're not some kind of crazed lunatic that's going to lock me in a cooler or something?"

"Good Lord, Emily! Where is this coming from? Frankly, Em, you're the one acting like a lunatic right now, and I have to say, I'm getting concerned for you."

"Don't try to turn the tables, Brady. I know your kind," she said through clenched teeth.

"I'm going to my darkroom. I'm in the process of developing some photos, and I don't want to mess up the timing. They're too important to me to screw up. Please just come with me so we can have a conversation. I'm happy to answer any questions or alleviate your suspicions, but I really need to get back in there."

"Fine." It took a moment for their eyes to adjust to the darkness before he pulled the chain and the glow of a red light filled the small space. The room appeared hazy at first. Then images appeared one by one, hanging from a sort of clothesline. Sophie's face peered through the darkness and Emily gasped. "When did you take these?"

"The day of her shower. It's how we killed time until it was time to bring her back to Proposals."

"Oh, right. They're stunning, Brady. She looks so beautiful."

"I think so, too," Brady said as he looked upon Sophie's images with love and adoration while a silence fell over the room. He watched Emily walk carefully from one to another until she turned to face him.

"You surprise me Brady, I came here to…well, give you a piece of my mind, and then I see this. I can't figure you out."

"Emily, why don't you have a seat, and we can start from the beginning? What seems to be the problem?" He dipped some paper into the chemicals with tongs, apprehensive about what she was about to say.

"I'm worried about her, you know. She's my best friend and partner, and I can't have you hurting her."

"What makes you think I'd hurt her? Have I ever given you the impression I'd do that?"

"It's just that she needs someone in her life that she can count on to be there. You're always running to New York, doing God knows what."

"What is it you think I might be doing there, Emily?"

"I don't know! You could be living a double life for all I know. You have a girlfriend there, don't you?"

"No, I do not have a girlfriend there," he countered with certainty and without hesitation.

"I'm sorry, but I don't believe you. The conversation that I heard you having was too intimate to be a 'client' of yours. She was obviously someone that pushed your buttons. I've seen that before in men, and I know a volatile relationship when I see one."

Brady considered his possible responses. He processed the last of the images, hung them on the line to dry and pulled up another barstool to face Emily straight on. "Emily, I need you to listen to me. Not just hear me, but actually listen to me. It is critical that you fully listen. Please hear me out completely and don't interrupt. I can assure you that it won't be easy to hear what I have to say, but you must. I give you my word that when I am done, you can ask me anything and I will respond honestly. What I need you to understand is that I love Sophie and I would do anything for her. Can I have your word that you will hear me out?"

Emily looked into his eyes as he watched the crease between her eyes grow deeper as if she were trying to read his mind. "Yes, I give you my word," she said cautiously. "I will hear you out."

Brady gently took Emily's hands. He could feel them tremble but gave her a reassuring squeeze. "It's okay, Em... really." She nodded her approval and assurance. "Meeting Sophie was, I believe, far more than a coincidence...it was meant to be. The first time I ever saw her, and it was only a glimpse, was in New York. I felt sorry for what she had gone through, and although she was a stranger to me, I hoped that she would feel vindication for the loss of her husband." Emily tried to tug her hands from his grasp, but he held on. "Hear me out, Emily." She nodded in agreement. "You see, Cynthia Lockwood, the woman that killed Sophie's husband, had been my lover." Emily broke the hold and jumped up from the stool. Brady gave her some space. "Shall I continue?"

Emily once again nodded in agreement. "I worked for Cynthia's father at Lockwood & Hurst. Henry Lockwood was her attorney, and I was the one that turned her in, but neither she nor her father knows this. I'd broken it off with her as soon as I found out what she did and how she did it.

"I wanted to start a new life—one that wasn't self-absorbed and cruel. I needed to escape that rat race and find some peace. Then it happened—the serendipitous day that I met Sophie. As time went on, I came to realize that she looked familiar to me, and by the time I put two and two together, we—you, me, and Sophie—had become friends, and I was looking for the right time to tell her. I've been a coward, I guess."

Emily once again took a seat on the stool opposite Brady. She had a stern look with crooked pursed lips.

"Go on," she said, still looking as though she needed some convincing.

"I've been going to New York to get justice for Sophie, because I love her, and because it's the right thing to do."

Emily reached her hands to take his and gave them a squeeze. "Can I talk now?"

"Yes."

"So, the conversation that I heard you having was with Cynthia Lockwood, right?"

"Yes."

"Does she know that you and Sophie are…friends?"

"No."

"Does Cynthia still love you?"

"Yes."

"You're going to put her away, right?"

"Yes…and her father."

"Her father?"

"He's corrupt and he did something—I don't quite know what just yet, but he did something to set Cynthia free, and I will not stop until I have them both sent to prison for a very long time."

Emily sat quietly, looking down at the floor. Her hands were to her sides, gripping the stool, while her foot tapped relentlessly on the floor. Brady held his breath in anticipation of her response. After what seemed like an eternity, Emily pulled her head up and looked intensely into Brady's eyes.

"How can I help?"

Brady exhaled. "You can help by trusting me and allowing me to tell Sophie myself, when it's the right time."

"But—"

"Em, it sucks that I have to ask you to keep a secret, and I hate having to do that to you. Once I have proof that can put them behind bars, I can come clean. Sophie doesn't need this in her life right now with the baby coming. She should focus on hers and the baby's well-being."

"She's not an invalid or a frail woman. She can handle it. She's a big girl."

"If you truly believe that, then why are you here fighting her battle? Why didn't you tell her what was on your mind so that she could confront me herself?" Emily looked away. "Hmm?"

"I don't know. Because she's my best friend, and I wanted to protect her. She's been through enough."

"Exactly. Don't you see that's what I'm trying to do too?"

"I don't know. It just doesn't feel right."

"I'll make it right, Emily. I promise."

Emily threw her hands up in surrender. "Fine, you win. But, for the record, I object."

"Duly noted."

"Good." Emily paced about the confined room. "Are you sure there isn't something more that I can do besides keep quiet and trust you? I want to really help, Brady."

"Trusting me is going to be hard—harder than you might think. I have to get close with Cynthia again to develop her trust, and so that her father can also trust me. I need them to talk."

"You're not going to get too close, right? I mean, you're not going to—"

"No! A kiss here and there, if necessary, but I will not ever sleep with that woman again. I confess, it's difficult to keep her at a distance. The excuses aren't going to hold up much longer, which means that I'll have to work that much harder to get to the truth. Thankfully, I have Stevens, a former colleague and friend of mine, helping me out and doing most of the digging in New York. I just go there when absolutely necessary, which, unfortunately, has been far too frequent as of late in light of the fact that she's now out of the damn prison."

"I get what you're saying. Thanks for laying it out there for me."

"I suppose you better still allow me to piss you off per usual so Sophie doesn't suspect anything."

"Trust me, that will be the easy part. I can pull my weight in that regard, because you generally piss me off."

"Glad you won't disappoint," Brady said with a grin.

Emily gazed again at the photos hanging around her. "What are you going to do with these? Did you build a shrine in the back or something creepy like that? You don't have candles and statues, or a doll dressed up in Sophie's clothes or anything, do you?"

"How does that stuff even enter your head, Emily? I truly worry about you." Brady shook his head in dismay. "I really do need to get back to it, though. But, before you leave, why don't you tell me which three you like the most. I want to frame one—maybe two or three—for one of the walls in the nursery. Do you think Sophie would like that?"

"You're kidding me, right? Of course she'll like it…she'll love it!" Emily thought about it as she took in the images. Gently, she touched the corners of three: one of an adoring mother looking into the camera as if she were an angel looking at her beloved child, another of a loving mother at a profile hugging her belly with head bowed, and, lastly, one of Sophie reading a children's book.

"Thank you, Emily. Those are some of my favorites as well."

"Fine…good. Okay, I'm leaving now. I have to go back and start deceiving my partner and best friend. You suck, Brady Owens." She gave him a quick awkward embrace and exited.

For a moment, Brady was suspended in a reality that he wasn't quite sure of. He and Emily had become allies and co-conspirators. Brady ran his fingers through his hair and sat back down on the stool, surrounded by photographs of Sophie. A pang of guilt struck as her eyes pierced into his. For his sake, he needed to bring closure to the situation and fast. He was on the brink of loving someone so much that it hurt, and now he'd involved Sophie's best friend in his deceit.

A distant ring came from beyond the door. Brady thought for a moment to ignore it but couldn't take the chance of missing something important. The lights were still low as he jumped from his stool and forcefully slammed his knee into the doorjamb. Brady cursed as he hobbled into the bedroom, where he'd left his phone to charge. By the time he arrived, the phone had gone silent. "Missed Call from Stevens" glowed on the face of the phone as a text alerted him. A 911. Brady pressed to dial, and Stevens answered after the first ring.

"Owens...you called it!" Stevens's excitement made it hard for Brady to understand.

"What...what did I call? Contributions, the campaign, what? Speak to me."

"Are you sitting?"

"Enough of the sitting crap, Stevens. Cut to the chase."

"The governor appointed two parole board members in this term. And get this: someone at the New York Department of Corrections central office told a senior parole board member that one of Palermo's new appointees was the lead commissioner presiding at Cynthia's hearing. Coincidence? I think not."

"What you're telling me is—because of perfect timing—the governor was able to stack the cards for Cynthia to be released. My guess is that he was going to get a sizable contribution for his Senate bid from Lockwood to do so. We need to find out more about these board members. What could the governor have over them to get them to play his game? There's got to be something in it for them. Either they're just as corrupt as the governor and Lockwood, or they're being pressured or provided incentives like our friends Adam Libby and Lloyd Becker."

"I'll keep looking. Anything more from Cynthia?"

"Nope, not yet."

"Well, get to it, man. The clock's ticking."

"I hear you, and I'm working on her."

"Okay, then. I'll let you get back to whatever it was you were doing. I've got some parole board members to learn about."

"So you do. And, hey, thanks for the work you're putting into this."

"It's what I do, my friend. It's what I do. But, you're welcome."

Brady ended the call, grabbed a bag of ice from the freezer, and placed it on his throbbing knee.

CHAPTER 31

The last of the Thanksgiving desserts had been picked up, along with the multitude of floral arrangements. Sophie and Emily turned the Closed sign around and took a deep breath. A mini vacation was desperately needed for both of them. Rebecca had been good enough to stay long enough to get them through the rush before she flew home to be with her family. The rest of the staff had just left, and it was just the two of them looking through the door to the outside. It was quiet, and that was good.

Sophie had tried her best to put on a happy face but had fought melancholy throughout the day, knowing that she was about to experience her first Thanksgiving without Sam. Thanksgiving had always been his favorite holiday and she'd promised him, even in his death, that she'd save him a piece of pumpkin pie, recalling that he liked it loaded with whipped cream. Sophie nodded to herself with the knowledge that some things didn't have to change.

Emily placed her hand on Sophie's shoulder. "Penny for your thoughts."

"Just wishing he could be here."

"I know, I wish he could be here too."

"It is what it is," Sophie said with a tone that wasn't quite believable, lifting up her chin.

"I'm sure he tried everything he could to be here."

Sophie blinked and raised her eyebrows at Emily's response, not sure whether to be pleased that she was referring to Brady or disappointed that she was actually thinking of Brady and not Sam. Sophie shifted gears in her response, concluding that she didn't want to make the situation worse. "I'm sure he did. It's not like he promised he'd be here or anything. Really, it's all right." Sophie began to shut off lights in the shop when the realization hit her that she wished Brady could be with them too. Shaking off that conflicting realization, she thought it best to change the subject. "Want a cup of tea?"

"Nope. How about I make us some mulled cider?"

"Perfect."

"I was hoping you'd say that." Sophie stepped back as Emily took the lead into the main house after grabbing a wicker basket of fixings from behind the counter.

"What's in there? It looks so inviting."

"Just a little of this and a little of that." There was a forest-green ribbon holding together two gold-and-bur-gundy brocade napkins. Within the napkins were two large mugs filled with spices and cinnamon sticks, two apple turnovers with sugar glaze, and a small pumpkin with an ivory taper candle in the center. A couple of ivory plates with hand-painted fall leaves trimmed the rims. Sophie picked up the mug that Emily had placed in front of her; it had a message on its face. *Life is sweeter knowing someone loves you.*

"Emily, this is so sweet! No pun intended," she said with a giggle. "Thank you."

"Sappy, I know, but I'm trying to step out of my comfort zone. I just thought you could use a little something special." Emily heated up the apple cider and threw in a sack of spices that she had tightly tied up with string, then plunked herself next to Sophie at the counter. "Why don't we light a fire in the living room and put our feet up?"

"I think I'll throw on some comfies first. I'll grab some sweats for you too."

"Cool, I'll get the fire going."

"It'll be like a mini girls' retreat. I'm so excited!" Sophie waddled toward the stairs with a little spring to her step. Within a few minutes, they were flopped on the couch, sipping cider. Sophie had placed the plate carefully on her belly and was stabbing individual sugar crumbs with a moistened finger and licking her fingers clean.

"Looks like you liked the turnover. I can get you another one if you want."

"No, thanks. This was just enough." Sophie popped her finger into her mouth one last time.

The fire flickered and snapped while they both got lost in thought. Sophie broke the silence. "It's sure going to be different having Thanksgiving dinner with Agnes and Frank. I feel funny only bringing flowers and dessert."

"They insisted that we not bring anything else. Frank said Agnes was the best cook in the county and that cooking for us was giving her purpose and she couldn't be more excited. You should have seen him; he was so proud talking about her."

"They're so stinking cute together," Sophie said. She sipped her cider and became quiet. As the silence continued, a tear rolled down Sophie's cheek. Emily gave her hand a squeeze. "It's the first big holiday without him, Em. I pictured us aging like Agnes and Frank. We would have been cute together too."

"I know, and yes. You would have been adorable." Emily carefully wiped the tear from Sophie's cheek. "But we have each other, and we'll get through it together."

But I want more, Sophie thought as the sweet cider washed down her throat. Brady once again permeated her thoughts. Was it Brady she wanted, or was it the idea of not being alone? She tossed it back and forth with the vision of growing old. She closed her eyes, envisioning who was sitting next to her on her bench. Was it the memory of Sam, her dearest friend, or was it Brady Owens? The faces blurred together in her mind's eye, and she prayed for clarity. *One step at a time, Sophie, one step at a time.*

. . .

Brady hated leaving Sophie for Thanksgiving, but knowing that she wouldn't be alone gave him a little peace of mind. He had batted around the idea of staying instead of venturing off to New York again but knew it was for the best to leave. Emily having his back was an added benefit, to be sure.

His focus was pulling off the highway in search of a coffee. He'd been fighting to keep his eyes open for the past few miles. He'd cracked the window open, thinking the cold air on his face would keep him alert. He slapped his face and cranked the radio as a last-ditch effort when he saw a familiar orange-and-pink sign for Dunkin' Donuts ahead. He was tired and had to piss like a racehorse.

Brady pulled the car into a parking spot near the side entrance and bolted from the car in order to reach the restroom, hoping to make it in time, all the while cursing at himself for cutting it so close. He cleaned up, then placed an order for a large coffee. He reached for the wallet in his back pocket, only to remember that he'd taken it out and set it on the dash. Traveling back and forth to New York so much was wreaking havoc on his back, and the wallet in his pocket didn't help. The kid behind the counter repeated the price in anticipation of payment.

"Can you hold on a minute? I've got to get my wallet out of the car." Without waiting for a response, Brady ran out to the parking lot to find a young man retreating from the driver's side of Brady's car.

"Hey! What the hell are you doing?" The man took off, sprinting into the darkness. "Son of a bitch!"

Brady peered into the open car to see both his wallet and cell phone were gone. Brady slammed the car door, shouted at the top of his lungs into the night sky, and pounded the hood of his car for good measure. With gritted teeth, he went back in to the cashier.

"I was just robbed."

"Can't say I've ever heard that one before. That's a good one."

"No, seriously. My car was just broken into and my wallet was stolen."

"Whoa, that sucks," said the pimple-faced teen.

"Yes, yes, it does. Do you think you could call the police for me?"

"Sure. Oh, and hey, take the coffee…it's on the house."
Brady's adrenaline was pumping and he didn't think he
could sleep for a week at this point, but the coffee gave him
something to do with his hands. Stepping back outside, he
noticed a couple of guys around the same age as the one that
had taken his stuff.

"Don't suppose you saw what happened here?" He gestured toward the car. The two men ignored him completely.
"I said, did you see what just happened?" No response. "You
mean to tell me that you stood ten feet from my car while it
was getting robbed and you didn't see a thing?" Still getting
ignored, Brady took the nearly full cup of coffee and threw
it to the ground between the two young men. "Did you see
that, you pieces of shit?"

"Forget you," said one of the guys as the other approached
Brady with a fist ready to punch.

"Bring it on," Brady said out of sheer anger, assuming that
these assholes were probably in on the whole thing.

"Sure thing, old man." With one powerful punch to the
face, Brady went down. Scrambling to bring himself to a stand,
he dove and tackled the guy around the knees and landed hard
on the pavement. Brady straddled the guy and landed one
punch after another while the other one took off running.

Brady hadn't realized that cruiser lights flashed behind
him, and within seconds he was being lifted by a cop, tossed to
the side of the cruiser, and then cuffed.

The bloodied guy lay sprawled out on the pavement
moaning and spouting off. "That man attacked me for
nothing!"

"Officer, they were in on a robbery. Someone, probably
one of them, stole my phone and wallet—"

"I want you to arrest that crazy-ass old man for assault and battery or something. The dude is messed up!" Brady could hear the other officer calling in for an ambulance.

"Officer, I'm fine. Everything's okay. I just want to get my things back. I won't press charges and we can all go about our business."

"Mr.—"

"Owens, Brady Owens."

"Mr. Owens, your nose looks like it could be broken, your hand is swollen, and you're bleeding all over my cruiser, and that's just you. I need to get you both checked out, bring you both in, then we'll see what happens from there."

The kid chimed in. "Hey, Officer, no…I'm good. It's all good. No need to go in. I won't press charges either. Let's just say we call it a night."

"Let's say we don't." With that, the kid was also placed in the cruiser to await the ambulance.

CHAPTER 32

Hours had gone by while Brady sat in the jail cell. He had a bandage on his right hand and a splint across the bridge of his nose, which was also covered by bandages. His eyes were already turning black and blue, and his head pounded. He had no ID besides a car registration, for which he was grateful. Brady's driving record and ID were able to be pulled, proving his identity, and the cashier at Dunkin' was able to validate that Brady had been robbed.

Brady considered calling Stevens to rescue him from this nightmare but resolved himself to calling Cynthia instead, knowing that her precious daddy would be able to get him released relatively easily. Besides, they were just a little under an hour away, and he was headed to their place for Thanksgiving anyway.

The community cell was a collection of characters: a drunk, what appeared to be a heroin addict, a teen that looked to be in shock with a friend that wouldn't stop crying, and a bad-ass guy who resembled a bouncer from the World Wrestling Federation, if there was indeed such a thing.

Brady only had himself to blame. He had known he was tired. He didn't want to be going to New York, he was already agitated that he had to be away from Sophie for Thanksgiving, and he was growing angrier the closer that he got to the Lockwoods'. He'd handled the whole situation poorly. He'd lost his temper in a big way. Brady sat on the bench, tipping his head back to rest it on the wall, looking toward the ceiling with a clenched jaw. *You frickin' dumbass. You could have just drunk your coffee and waited for the police like any civil human being. But, no, you had to turn into a dumbass lunatic.*

"Owens. Time to go." The cell door opened with a clank and squeak, and Brady was led down a short hallway with windows on one side that looked into the police precinct. He could see Lockwood laughing with the police chief. Brady sucked in his breath and closed his eyes just long enough to let out a long exhale. Lockwood looked up to see Brady approaching.

"There he is!" Laughter continued. "It seems you've got quite the left hook, my boy."

Brady peered into Lockwood's eyes and with assured condemnation said, "If you say so."

Without any recognition of Brady's attitude, Lockwood smacked him on the back. "Let's get you to the house. It's getting late."

Brady took another deep breath and, with a clenched fist that he fought to relax, said, "Thanks for coming and getting me out."

"No thanks needed. Thanks are for the weak. Besides, that's what family does."

Brady knew his reaction wasn't well disguised, and he felt that Lockwood picked up on his subtle shock at being called family.

. . .

Time stood still as Brady watched the grandfather clock slowly click by. He could hear talking from every direction around the table. Cynthia's incessant yapping in his ear, Lockwood's boisterous vibrato bellowing into the kitchen, demanding more pinot noir, Mrs. Lockwood's monotonous chattering about the latest fashion, and numerous other ramblings.

"Well, what do you think…Brady!" Cynthia's face was within a few inches of his. Her eyes were glaring and her mouth was cocked to one side. "Do you not see me? Are you blind? You didn't hear a word I was saying, did you?" she asked, seething.

"Someone's in trouble," Mrs. Lockwood said with a hiccup and a giggle. "Cynthia, darling, Brady had a very trying night last night, from which I'm sure he hasn't quite recovered."

"He had a trying night! I had months of trying nights and you didn't give a damn about me. All you cared about was yourself." Brady grinned at the irony of her statement. "Tell me, Mother, did you chip a nail while I was locked up? Or, did your housemaid forget to turn down your bed and you weren't able to have a restful night's sleep?" Cynthia was screeching as everyone fell silent. "Maybe, God forbid, you broke a heel on a pair of your Christian Louboutin stilettos! Is that why you never came to see me? Just let me guess, you were too ashamed that I ruined your perfect image, Mother! Now, you roll out the red carpet for Brady because he had a bad night! Even he can't manage to give me the time of day.

Can't you see that all he's thinking about is himself, too!" Brady stiffened as Cynthia turned toward him. "Well, aren't you?" She looked at Brady with malice. "Is it your handy camera work that you think about all the time? Is that what brings you to an orgasm now? Because it's quite obvious that you don't need me for that!"

"Cynthia Marie Lockwood, that is quite enough!" Mrs. Lockwood shouted from the far end of the table as she stood with authority. "You reap what you sow, my child. This is one area that your daddy can't fix. He has stuck out his neck far more than you know, Cynthia, and it's time you grow up. I, for one, will not condone another second of his irresponsible prosecutorial actions for one spoiled-rotten, ungrateful brat!"

Cynthia bolted from the table and pounded up the stairs with the temper of a shrew and slammed the door for good measure.

"Please excuse our daughter while she carries on with her temper tantrum in her childhood bedroom, which, I might add, is quite fitting for the occasion." She cleared her throat, took another swig of pinot noir, and sat back down in her chair as if nothing had ever happened. Lockwood raised a glass.

"Here's to better days."

Brady took his leave as soon as dinner ended, refusing the mountainous desserts. He was relieved that Cynthia didn't come back down, giving him an excuse to get out of the city without saying goodbye, again.

CHAPTER 33

Sophie and Emily hugged Agnes and Frank farewell, then gathered their excessive amount of leftovers. The early-afternoon dinner had gone on into the evening. They'd stayed to help clean up and listen with fascination to endless stories of Agnes and Frank from days gone by. Sophie was content and at peace with the day; she'd had a wonderful time. Emily turned on her cell phone flashlight to guide them along the pathway home. Their merriment continued as they approached the back door to the house. The kitchen lights were on, smoke was coming from the fireplace, and music was playing in the night air. Sophie turned back to see Brady's familiar BMW in the driveway, and her heart skipped a beat.

"You go on in, Soph. I'm going to get home and get my leftovers in the fridge. You two have a good night."

"Are you sure? You can come in, too."

"Yep, I'm sure." Emily leaned in to give Sophie a peck on the cheek. "Happy Thanksgiving, partner."

"Happy Thanksgiving."

Sophie placed her leftovers on the counter and followed the sound of music coming from the den. She could see Brady's silhouette sprawled out on the couch and heard a light snore, indicating that he'd fallen asleep waiting for her to return. She tiptoed back into the kitchen to put the food away, then turned off the lights and locked the door. Sophie stoked the fire and retreated to her bedroom to change into a nightgown and brush her teeth. Before too long, she was kneeling next to Brady and stroking his hair out of his eyes.

"Mmm, you're home," Brady said in a raspy voice.

"Yes, and I'm ready for bed." Sophie took Brady by the hand and led the way to her bedroom as Daisy followed obediently.

. . .

Morning broke with a frost covering the ground. The smell of fallen leaves and the night's rain remained as he let Daisy back in from her morning exploration. Brady could hear Emily coming up the drive and recalled Sophie mentioning that she'd be arriving early to bake some bread and make some kind of wedding cake thingamabobs. He went to task, rummaging through the fridge. To his delight, he spotted the leftover pumpkin pie, his favorite. He'd just taken a massive bite when Emily abruptly pecked on the kitchen windowpane and surprised him.

His eyes grew big with alarm, until he saw Emily's big smile grinning like a Cheshire cat through the glass. With the pie pan in one hand and the half-eaten piece of pie in the other, he struggled to open the door. He stuck the piece in his mouth in order to unbolt the door with his free hand. Emily entered with a giggle and a quick thrust and shoved the rest of the pie into his mouth, spreading the excess all over his whisker-stubbled face and nose. She doubled over as Brady removed the pumpkin filling from his swollen nostrils. Meanwhile, pieces of crust and filling landed on the floor, which the calico licked with caution and delight.

"Holy crap, Em. You had to get the nose, didn't you?" As pain shot across his face instantly causing his eyes to water and his nose to throb.

Emily was taken aback. "Don't get your nose out of joint. It was just a piece of pie, for crying out loud." Stepping back, she took notice of Brady's swollen nose and black eye. "What the hell happened to you?" she asked as her hand covered her mouth.

"It's a long story. Let's just say I was an ass, ended up in the slammer, and had to eat crow for Thanksgiving."

"Alrighty, then. Sounds like an unforgettable Thanksgiving. Fun times had by all in New York?" A smirk plagued Emily's face.

"That's one way of putting it." He dampened a towel and proceeded to clean the remains of the pie from his nostrils and chin.

Sophie slipped in with a yawn. "Morning." She opened the fridge and reached for the orange juice, grabbed a glass and gulped down her prenatal vitamin before truly taking in the scene before her. "Oh, my, gosh, Brady! What happened to you? How did I not notice this before? Are you okay?" She gently stroked the rim of his nose and cheekbones. "You look terrible." Without thinking, she leaned forward and kissed the softness under his eye.

"It's better already. Thank you," Brady said with a

tenderness that filled the room.

"Um, I better get in there and press some molds. Sugar leaves can't make themselves," Emily said as she clumsily backed out the door.

. . .

Sophie watched Emily run to the shop. "I don't know what's gotten into her. Don't get me wrong, I'm happy that she supports our...um...relationship? Right? Are we in a relationship?"

"Yes, we're in a relationship," Brady said, then leaned forward, dropped his head, and kissed her on the tip of her nose.

"Okay, then. That's good."

"It's very good." At least he hoped the hell it was.

"So now that we're in this relationship, are you going to explain all of this?" she asked with a whirl of her hand around his face.

"I was robbed, but I'm okay," Brady said with a calm that relaxed Sophie at once. She breathed a sigh of relief, then wrapped her arms around his waist and gave him a squeeze. He kissed the top of her head and held her tightly. Feeling movement from her belly against him, he was content—more content than he had any right to be.

Sophie reluctantly released herself from his embrace. "I've got to eat something and head into work. Want anything?"

"No, thanks, I'm good. Had some pumpkin pie already. Besides, I have to head home and get some work done myself."

"I don't like this adulting thing. I'd much rather play hooky. Will you be home for a while, or do you have to go back to New York again?"

Not wanting to think about New York, he caressed her

cheek. "I kind of like doing the adulting thing," he said with a smirk that broadened into a large grin.

Sophie's cheeks instantly turned bright pink. "I guess you've got a pretty good point there."

"Sophie Anderson, you little she-devil." Brady grabbed her once again to embrace her; he gently grabbed her butt cheeks and gave them two quick squeezes. Sophie playfully did the same to him in return.

"Now get out of here, Brady Owens. We have work to do."

He found her mouth again, and the warmth of her tongue intertwined with his. His breathing became heavy, and his touch became stronger.

"Seriously...I...can't," she said, panting as she responded to his touch. Steam was forming on the kitchen window from the heat they were creating between them.

Just then, Emily pushed open the door in haste, which knocked both Brady and Sophie off balance. They landed with a bang against the wall. Pain seared through Brady's nose as his face smashed into the door frame. His eyes watered again, as he tried to catch his breath.

When Emily peered cautiously around the door to take in the scene before her, Sophie and Brady were in full embrace, smashed between the wall and the door.

"Oh my gosh. I'm so sorry. I had no idea you were there. Are you all right, Sophie? I didn't hurt the baby, did I?"

"I'm fine...we're fine."

"Yep...just fine here," Brady said with his chin high as he tried to hide the pain, to no avail.

His eyes watered, and blood was beginning to drip out of his nose and over his lip.

"Why the hell aren't you wearing a brace on your nose or something? It's not my fault you aren't protecting yourself, so don't go blaming me for being an idiot."

Sophie quickly grabbed paper towels, dampened them, then placed the wad on his face. "Apply pressure, if you can. It will stop the bleeding."

"Do you hear me complaining about anything?" he mumbled. "No, you don't. I guess I wasn't planning on someone charging through a door and smashing me into a wall. Call me crazy, but I actually thought that I'd be safe to take the damn thing off. But no…'Emily beware' signs should be posted around this place."

Emily huffed. "How was I supposed to know that you'd be right there? I couldn't see anything through the glass. The whole damn thing was steamed over," she stammered.

"That would have been a clue, don't you think?"

"No, smart-ass, it wouldn't. Sophie makes tea all the time and the windows steam up, but she isn't usually standing behind the damn door, now is she?"

"Well, it's about time you two started to act normal again. You had me worried for a while there," Sophie interjected.

They blankly stared at Sophie as if noticing her for the first time. Sophie began to giggle with satisfaction. "All is well with the world now. My two favorite people are arguing once again." Sophie leaned back on the counter and crossed her arms, grinning ear to ear. "So, Emily, do tell, what's going on?"

Brady and Emily looked at each other, then back to Sophie. Brady cleared his throat and looked toward his feet. Emily just stood there dumbfounded.

"Well, I'm waiting," Sophie said, now with an irritated

tone. Still no response. "Emily, seriously. I'm not a mind reader, and you're worrying me now." The look of concern grew tenfold in a split second. "Why did you came bursting through the door, Emily?"

"Oh, that! Geez, I forgot all about that." Emily sighed. "The police department called the shop asking for you, Brady. I put them on hold while I came to get you."

Sophie placed her hands on Emily's cheeks. "I love you, my friend, but sometimes, my sweet, you really take the cake."

"They've been waiting all this time on the phone?" Brady proclaimed.

"It's not like I meant to forget."

Sophie and Brady now exchanged wide-eyed glances.

"I smashed you into a wall; there was blood…there was a pregnant woman. Well, don't just stand there looking at me. Go answer the damn phone!"

Brady dashed out the door, swearing a blue streak.

"He can be a real ass sometimes. I don't know how you can put up with him," he heard Emily say as he retreated.

. . .

A few minutes later, the brass doorknob turned and opened ever so gently. Brady stuck his head in the slowly growing crack, then yelled, "Hello, is there anybody on the other side of the door?"

"If I wasn't so sweet, I'd punch him in the damn face. You are such an ass, Owens."

Brady ignored her taunts. "Seems they found my phone and a pretty empty wallet a few blocks from where I was robbed. They were able to trace it to a dumpster. Pretty cool, huh?"

"That's great!" Sophie said. "What a shame, though. I hope nothing too important was taken. Well, besides credit cards and stuff."

"It's all good. I'll have my wallet…love my wallet. It's all worn in perfectly."

He didn't mention that a small folded note that said *Thinking of you. Thank you. xoxo* would still be tucked in one of the slots. It was the only time that Sophie had handwritten anything to him. He'd found it one hot afternoon, on a tray of lemonade that she'd brought out to him; to his surprise, it was tucked under the pitcher. She could have written anything else, but knowing she was thinking of him made him feel good, and the sentiment had struck him. The kiss-hugs added an innocence and charm that encompassed who she was and what he'd grown to love about her.

"I'm surprised they threw your phone out. What was the point of taking it if they were just going to get rid of it?" Sophie inquired.

"I had a security feature on it. They wouldn't have been able to access anything, and when I got to the police station, I enabled the feature. It would have been impossible to get into it, and even if they did, it was already emptied into my cloud."

"Didn't know that was possible," Emily said. "You're smarter than the average bear."

"You think so, Em?"

"Dammit, did I say that out loud? I could have sworn I said that to myself. Must have slipped out." Sophie grinned widely and sipped her tea.

CHAPTER 34

Cynthia hung up the phone and shoved it into the comforter that was balled up on top of her bed. She had tossed and turned all night and had yet to hear back from Brady. His phone continued to go to voicemail. She was now venomous with anger. She had no other way of reaching him besides his cell phone. Knowing that it had been a holiday weekend seemed to have zero impact on her reasoning. *He must have gotten a new phone by now, so why isn't he answering?* Gathering her robe tightly, she stomped out of her bungalow toward the main house for a bloody mary and some eggs.

Lockwood was sitting at the table with his glasses balancing on the brim of his nose. Looking up from the *Times*, he could see his angel was in a devil of a mood. "What is it, pumpkin?" he asked as he set the paper down.

"He isn't answering my calls, Daddy."

"He was robbed of his phone, my sweet. Give him some time. I'm sure he'll call soon." Taking his glasses off and carefully setting them down, he yelled to the cook in utter impatience. "Catherine!" He waited a beat before he yelled once again. "Catherine! Are you killing the chicken to get to the eggs, for God's sake?" Then he calmly reached his hands out to gather Cynthia's small fingers in his. "Dearest Cynthia, I hate seeing you unhappy. I'll take care of it; don't give it another thought."

"Thank you, Daddy. I knew I could count on you." Catherine came running and skidded into the dining room with a halt.

"Miss Cynthia, I didn't realize you were here. Your usual?" She laid the plate in front of Lockwood with a curtsy.

"Yes, and make sure the eggs aren't runny this time. Dry—I want them dry. You know how runny egg whites make me want to vomit."

"Yes, ma'am." Nodding her head, she backed out of the room, then turned with haste.

"Daddy, Mother really needs to do a better job with her hires. The incompetence of her choices is reaching an all-time high."

Lockwood rang the police department and asked to speak to the captain. Within moments, he was on the other end. "Captain Hastings, Lockwood here." Cynthia could hear a murmured response. "Yes, it was a great time with you and the missus. We'll have to do it again real soon." Lockwood rolled his eyes, then put his forced smile back on. "I'm looking to contact Brady Owens. He was at your precinct, a robbery resist incident." He winked at Cynthia as she leaned forward to get a better listen. "Seems he hasn't obtained a new phone as of yet, and it's imperative that I reach him. Did he happen to leave a number or address with your officer?" There was a muffled response. "Sure, I'll wait."

"Daddy, what would I do without you?" Cynthia asked as Mrs. Lockwood entered the room.

"Seems to me you wouldn't be able to take a pee unless your dear daddy was there to hand you the toilet paper." She swilled her mimosa, which contained more champagne than juice.

"Don't be vulgar, Mother. It doesn't suit you."

Lockwood's eyes perked up. "Proposals, you say. In York, Maine. Of course, I should have known. Thank you, Hastings. Be sure to tell your lovely bride that I said hello, won't you? And give 'em hell out there."

Cynthia was perplexed. "Proposals? What in God's name is Proposals?" She thought for a moment as a tall bloody mary was placed on the small dish in front of her. "Oh, Daddy. Brady's planning our wedding!"

"What wedding?" Mrs. Lockwood said with alarm. "I should certainly have been told if our daughter was getting married. Do I not even get the courtesy of knowing something this monumental?"

"Mother, he hasn't actually proposed yet. But we will be married. I can assure you of that."

"Oh dear God, Cynthia, must we go through this again? What is this, Henry…the third or fourth time that she's said she's *going to be proposed to*?"

"Now, dearest, Cynthia could be right this time."

"Thank you, Daddy. I need to check out this place. Proposals, you say, in York, Maine?"

"Yes, my sweet."

"Yes, my sweet," Mrs. Lockwood mimicked under her breath.

"Have another mimosa, woman, and get the broom out of your ass." He slipped his glasses back on and lifted the paper.

"You smug son of a bitch. You don't want to get on my bad side any more than you already are, or I'll—"

"You'll what, Elizabeth? Divorce me? Prenup, my dearest. You'd be penniless, so stop wasting your breath and drink your damn drink. You're giving me a headache."

She downed the glass and smashed it on the floor, then stormed out.

"Sorry, Daddy. Mother can be insufferable." She gave him a peck on the top of his head then headed out the door.

CHAPTER 35

Brady sifted through the mounds of records that Stevens had emailed him, trying to connect the dots. The two new members of the parole board, Julie Barrows and Charles Denning, appeared by all accounts legit. There had to be a connection, but where? He drank down another strong coffee. He could feel the caffeine kicking in as his stomach turned a bit and his hands began to jitter, but eating wasn't an option right now. He needed to find something, anything.

Julie Barrows was an attractive woman with a prominent nose, high cheekbones, and a stellar smile. Her hair was blond with a hint of gray that splayed delicately around her face. Brady studied the photo on one of the New York Correctional Parole sites, as if waiting for it to answer his questions.

Charles Denning exemplified prestige. His suit was of good design, he was well groomed, and his stature was lean and tall. He was handsome, but Brady speculated that Denning was a bit of a dandy and quite full of himself.

Brady paced around his dining table. A fire crackled and reflected on the screen he'd been staring at for the past several hours. Leaning over the table, he scanned through article after article. He compared his notes, files, and numerous websites—and then he found it. Charles Denning had been a staffer for Mark Palermo years earlier, back when Palermo was district attorney, and Julie Barrows had been an intern within the same department. Case studies showed signatures, affidavits, and other documentation to verify his findings.

He'd made the connection, but he wasn't satisfied. *What did Palermo hold over you, and how did Lockwood play into all of this?* Brady knew he was close to something big, but what? It had to be right in front of him.

His frustration was eating at him as well as his stomach, which ached as his head began to pound. He tapped his pen in rapid succession upon the table. *Food...must have food so I can think.*

The refrigerator door swung open, and Brady grunted in disappointment. He couldn't remember the last time he'd gone shopping. He lifted the lid of several containers, then pitched the contents into the trash when his phone rang. Stevens's name showed on the screen; food would have to wait.

"Hey, good timing. It's good to hear from you."

"I heard you got your ass whooped. You healing up okay?"

Brady groaned. "Yeah, yeah, my ass was handed to me, but I got my share of licks in. He'll be taking a lot longer to recover than me, I can tell you that."

"I'm sure you did. Enjoy your Thanksgiving?"

"You're kidding, right?" Brady said, laughing.

"So, were you able to make any sense of what I sent you?"

"You bet your ass I did."

"Oh?"

"They all worked together back when Palermo was a DA."

"No shit! I can't believe I missed that."

Brady gave him the rundown on his findings. "Now, we just have to figure out what Palermo has over them."

"Anything come out of Turkey Day with the Lockwoods?"

"Yep, a lot of screaming and yelling. Never realized the dynamics there. Seems the missus loathes both her husband and daughter about as much as we do."

"Could work to our advantage, Brady."

"I see what you mean. Now that I think of it, she did say something that struck me as pretty fantastic at the time, but I lost sight of it with all the venom that was getting thrown around."

"Oh?"

"Liz Lockwood said that she wouldn't condone another one of Lockwood's prosecutorial actions."

"What the hell was she getting at?"

"She knows a lot, Stevens, I'm sure of it. I've got to head back to the city to pick up my wallet at the police precinct, and when I do, I'm going to see if the missus will join me for a drink and a little chat."

"Careful, I don't think the apple falls far from the tree. You don't want two batshit-crazy Lockwood women chasing after you."

"Actually, Stevens, I'm kind of counting on that."

"Now look who's batshit crazy."

"If it can work, it will be worth it. I'll be back as soon as this next photo opportunity is over."

"You really like that gig, don't you?"

"Yep, I like it a lot. Livin' the dream, my man. Livin' the dream."

CHAPTER 36

White lights were draped across every beam in the barn, and white birch tree branches were clustered in corners, hugging the walls, with various-sized Christmas trees sporadically interwoven among the birches, tiny white lights wrapped around the branches and boughs. Gold, silver, and red decorations adorned the pines, and snow blankets curled around the bases, completing the winter wonderland theme for the upcoming wedding.

Sophie smoothed the red satin tablecloths and placed garlands of winterberry, fir, pine, gold, silver, and red ornaments so that they lay down the center of each table and then draped over the edge. White pillar candles wrapped in birch bark were staggered amongst the garlands, and gold napkins were formed neatly into the shape of Christmas trees and propped upon each white plate, which rested on a gold charger.

Sophie took a step back from her garland task to watch Brady, in his frustration, curse while he fought with a snow-blowing contraption hidden on top of the beams just overhead. She wanted it perfectly centered over where the groom would kiss his bride. He straddled the beam and stretched in order to reach the mounting bracket. He got the nut just where he wanted it, then managed to drop the nut to the floor for the second time.

"Fffuu…stupid thing."

Sophie grinned, knowing that he'd been trying to curb his swearing. He said that there were little ears listening and big girl ones too. She touched her earlobe with the memory of his kiss.

"Make sure it's really tight up there, Brady. We can't have it falling," Emily hollered.

"Okay, Em, I'll get right on it," Brady said sarcastically as he fumbled around in his pocket for another nut.

Sophie intervened. "Emily, would you mind putting the garland on the mantel for me? I'm not feeling too steady on the stool, never mind that I can't even see my feet to climb the two rungs." Brady looked down with a grin, and Sophie replied with a scrunch of her nose.

Before too long, the finishing touches were added to the cake, the candles were lit, music filled the air, the logs crackled in the fireplace, and all was ready for the happy couple and guests to arrive.

Prior to dressing for the event, Sophie suggested that Brady take advantage of the surroundings without everyone there. She leaned back against the back wall and watched as he draped his extra camera over his shoulder and snapped shots with the other, taking in the scene before him. He was wide-eyed as he looked around. Sophie was happy with the results as well, but seeing Brady in his element brought her even more joy.

"The honored guests will be blown away, Sophie. I just hope that a light glistening snow will fall on cue and that I'll be able to capture the moment, as well as the guests' surprise at the unexpected sight."

"You did a fine job setting it up, Brady, and I have no doubt that your shots will be brilliant," Sophie said as she pulled up a chair, careful not to wrinkle or skew the seat cover and bow attached to the back. Standing in front of the seat, she reached back to steady herself, then slowly lowered herself to a sitting position as best as she could. She felt a sense of satisfaction at having accomplished such a big task. She looked forward to resting up and contributing in a less physical way until the baby came, feeling a bit of excitement for the change. Yet a pang of fear and a hint of sadness set in at the thought of Proposals running without her controlling every detail. Emily reminded her frequently that she was a control freak and needed to delegate more. She now recognized that her friend might have a point.

Rebecca's training was going well. Sophie had made the decision that it was time for her to run an event on her own but recognized that she still didn't want to fully let go. She vowed to give her the next appointment and let her run with it. After all, she was only a few steps away if needed. Feeling a bit more confident in her decision, Sophie sat back and watched Brady in action, looking forward to seeing what he'd capture through the lens. Her heart raced as she said a quick prayer that the feelings he stirred in her would never grow old.

"Are you ready to do this thing, partner?" Emily said with excitement as she approached Sophie sprawled out in the chair.

"Yes, ma'am. As ready as I'll ever be. I'm tired, my feet are swollen, and this little girl isn't ready to nap anytime soon. She's become quite happy playing kicking games with my rib cage. But, yes, I'm ready. You just need to help me out of this chair first."

"Nope, I want to see you get up on your own; it's incredibly entertaining to watch. You just have no idea."

"You are incorrigible, Emily Vassure."

"And that's why you love me."

"Indeed. Now help me up, please. I'm getting a cramp in my butt."

Brady approached. "I keep telling her that she's a pain in the ass, but she doesn't believe me." Emily sneered, then stuck her tongue out.

"Good heavens, you two. How am I ever going to manage three children? Seriously, though, I have a cramp in my butt." They both grabbed a hand and pulled her up. "Now that's more like it…cooperation. That's how big kids do it. Shall we get changed and do this thing?"

They walked out the door as "All I Want for Christmas Is You" came through the overhead speakers. Brady placed his arm around Sophie's expanded waistline and gave her a squeeze. Sophie responded in kind.

. . .

Sophie tried to hide how uncomfortable she was and had been for most of the day. The event the night before had worn her out.

"Maybe you should consider calling it a day, Soph," Emily said with a worried look on her face.

"I'm fine. Why would I do that?"

"You're not fine. You've been grimacing much of the day. I can see you from the counter."

"It's nothing. I think they call them Braxton Hicks contractions."

"Contractions! Good Lord, Sophie, why didn't you tell me?"

"They're not real contractions, just practice ones."

"How do you know? Maybe they're the real thing. It's almost time and—"

"I just know. Besides, I still have a long way to go until she's due to arrive. But, if it makes you feel better, I think I will go grab a tea and put my feet up for a bit."

"I knew it; you're not feeling well."

"I'm fine, really. Go bake something already."

"Go bake something…crap, I've got to take my cake out!" Emily scurried to the kitchen, mumbling, "Crap, crap, crap."

Sophie slipped into the stockroom in search of Rebecca and finally admitted to herself that she really did need to take a break. Her ankles were swollen, and she was crampy and just plain miserable. As she was turning a corner, her belly bumped into a stack of storage boxes. They teetered as she grasped one in hopes of saving it, but to no avail. The more she tried to prevent them from falling, the worse it got. Sophie was unaware that Rebecca had been standing on a step stool behind the stack of boxes until she heard a scream and the clank of the stool, followed by what sounded like shattering glass.

"Oh my God!" Sophie said repeatedly.

"I hear you, Sophie. I'm coming," Emily shouted from

the basement just below the kitchen. "I knew it…you're in labor! I'll get Rebecca to watch the shop, and I'll get you to the hospital. Then I'll text Brady to have him meet us there with your bag of baby labor stuff." Panting, she stopped to grab her breath while beads of sweat began to form above her lip and brow. "Don't worry, Sophie, I've got this under control." Once she caught her composure, she stood up. Rebecca and Sophie peered at her from behind the fallen stack of boxes and glittering glass fragments.

"Rebecca," said Sophie in a now-calm voice. "You appear to be okay. Am I correct in that assumption?"

"Most definitely. I'm perfectly all right. It just scared me is all."

"Good." Sophie nodded, then acknowledged Emily's existence. "Rebecca, do you think you could fill in for me for a while? I'm going to put my legs up. These Braxton Hicks contractions are wearing me down a bit." Sophie once again looked at Emily in hopes that she'd finally understand her overreaction.

"Sure thing. I'd be happy to, just as soon as I clean this up."

"Don't be silly. Emily wouldn't mind cleaning it up, would you? You see, Em, I bumped into these and knocked Rebecca off the stepladder, which made her drop the box of vases. Now, I would feel terrible if she had to clean it up after my having made her fall, and with her being so willing to fill in for me and all. Wouldn't you agree, Emily?"

"Oh, fine. But in all fairness, you were yelling 'Oh my God' like a bazillion times. What else was I supposed to think?"

"Touché, my sweet friend."

"Well, go put your feet up already," Emily said with satisfaction. Sophie leaned in for a hug.

"I will, right after I catch my breath."

Rebecca interjected, "Emily, I've got this. Please don't worry about it; you're busy."

"Oh, please. I was just rummaging in the basement. I can't seem to find my...whatever, it doesn't matter. Truly, I don't mind at all. My cake is out and I'm waiting for it to cool anyway. This will fill the time just as well as what I was doing."

Rebecca carefully shook off her skirt, blouse, and hair to make sure there weren't any remaining shards of glass.

"Thanks for being who you are, Emily."

Awkwardly, Emily replied, "Um...sure thing. It's what I...do. Now get out of here, you're holding me up."

Rebecca gave Emily a quick hug, nodded in agreement, and left toward her workstation. Sophie smirked as Emily grabbed the broom.

"Stop looking at me like that."

"Like what? I can't imagine what you mean."

"Weren't you going to put your feet up or something?"

"All right, off I go."

"Like a herd of turtles," Emily chided as Sophie waddled away.

Sophie found her favorite spot on the sofa and put up her feet. Her head sank into the cushion and she pulled a fleece throw over her lap, wishing she had the fire going. Quiet time had been her enemy, as it had usually ushered in thoughts of Sam. Lately, however, it brought something more. The realization had set in as she looked around the room when she saw Brady's sweatshirt draped on the back of a chair.

She loved him being there and missed him when he was away. It almost felt like "home"—that contented place, a happy place that made her feel safe and comfortable. Brady had become more than a friend; she knew this to be true. He'd earned her trust, and she was secure in where they were headed. She didn't know what she had done to deserve love twice in one life, but she'd found it, or it had found her. For the first time, she concluded that she had fallen in love with Brady Owens.

. . .

Brady's arms were full of firewood as he reached for the door. His fingers could barely catch the knob as he balanced the oak pieces, and bits of bark bounced off his L.L. Bean boots. He pushed the door open with his foot, then closed it behind him with his hip. Daisy curled around his legs as he tried wiping his feet clean.

"Scoot, Daisy."

She pranced away, leading him to the living room, where Sophie sat. Her legs were propped up on the tufted ottoman.

"Oh my goodness, you have no idea. I was just wishing I had a fire going and…here you are," she said with surprise.

"A little birdie told me that you were in here and I would do anything for my princess." He carefully set the pile of wood on the granite hearth, then arranged kindling, stuffed some newspaper under the rack, added two pieces of the oak and struck a match. Within moments, he could feel the warmth as the flames grew. Brady knelt and moved the logs here and there.

"Thank you, Brady. It's perfect."

He brushed off his hands and plunked himself next to Sophie, giving her a wide grin.

"You smell smoky."

"I'm sorry, does that bother you?" He started to move away as she grabbed his hand.

"I love it and…I love you, Brady Owens." Sophie leaned into him and brushed her forehead on his shoulder. He inhaled the smell of her hair, which he savored, and tenderly kissed the top of her head. She loved him. Somehow, this beautiful creature before him loved him. She'd found her way into his heart. A heart that had been cold and angry. Sophie had made it beat with calm and warmth, and words that he'd never dared to say before escaped his lips.

"I love you too, Sophie Anderson." She linked her arm with his and shut her eyes. He could feel her breathing settle into a rhythm that slowed until she drifted off to sleep. Brady stroked her hair, fearing that if he didn't play his cards right, it would be a short-lived love. Brady had earned the distinction of letting those that he cared about the most down. Daisy jumped onto the couch and curled up next to Brady's hip. She kneaded several times with a purr, and before too long, they had all dozed off.

CHAPTER 37

The sun had gone down, and Sophie groggily opened her eyes. The baby had been kicking her in the ribs and rolling from side to side. She placed her hand atop her growing baby to trace the movements of what she believed to be her foot.

"Time for you to eat, my little one? Is that what you're trying to tell me, baby girl?"

Sliding herself out of Brady's grasp, she pulled herself up using the arm of the couch. The fire was almost reduced to embers, with one log hanging on at a slow burn. She stirred the coals and added another log before heading to the kitchen. Brady remained asleep as she took in the sight and sounds of the moment. Daisy had maneuvered her way to his lap, and the two of them lightly snored in unison. *He loves me*, she thought as she watched him sleep. He was a gift; an unexpected gift that she hoped Sam would approve of.

It was nearing closing time at the shop when Sophie noticed that Emily's car was gone and Rebecca's was still there, along with another that she didn't recognize. Turning on the outside light gave her a better look, but she still didn't know the car.

"Eating will have to wait, little one." She tapped her belly. "We should see how Rebecca's doing with her first solo day. But first we shall go pee." She giggled to herself. The concept of talking to her stomach was still foreign to her, but she couldn't imagine not doing it.

Laughter sounded from the shop as Sophie approached. Rebecca's eyes lit up when Sophie entered the room. The customer sat at the table with her back facing the archway and didn't see her come in.

"Perfect timing, Sophie," said Rebecca with excitement. "I'd like to introduce you to our new bride-to-be that has booked our services for her and her fiancé. She's come all the way from New York to be here, which I guess isn't too surprising, as her fiancé lives right here in York. Would you believe his name is Brady too?" Rebecca stood and extended an arm to her new client. "Miss Lockwood, this is Sophie Anderson, one of the owners of Proposals. Sophie, this is Miss Cynthia Lockwood."

Cynthia stood up to face her with a wide, menacing grin. The look of gotcha gleamed in her cold eyes. The room swirled as Sophie felt the blood drain from her face before she hit the wood floor. She could hear Rebecca scream and scramble to her side, but the sound was muted, as if she were underwater. Rebecca sat on the floor next to her head and yelled for help. Cynthia's chuckle grew into a full-fledged belly laugh.

"Who are you and what have you done?" Rebecca demanded.

Cynthia's laugh continued as it echoed beyond the walls of the shop. Sophie's world went black.

. . .

Brady awoke. *Was I dreaming?* No, he could hear someone yelling for help, and a laugh that sent chills down his back. He flew off the couch and ran toward the shop. Skidding to a halt, he took in the scene before him. Rebecca was sobbing as Sophie lay unconscious on the floor while Cynthia had tears of joy streaming down her face.

"Oh, my God…what have you done!" If he could kill her and get away with it, he would, but right now he needed to focus on Sophie. "Rebecca, call 911!"

"Yes…of course. I'll call 911. I'm sorry. I wasn't thinking. I should have done that already." Rebecca scrambled to her feet to get to her phone.

"Oh, no, you won't!" Cynthia said in a panic while diving for the phone. "There will be no police."

Brady rose and grabbed Cynthia by the arm, bringing her face-to-face with him with a heavy-handed grip.

"You know what, Cynthia? Believe it or not, this isn't about you right now. She's calling an ambulance, not the police," he said through gritted teeth as he shoved her toward the door.

"What do you mean it isn't about me? If I get caught here, I'll go back to prison! I'm going to be your wife, Brady! You're supposed to protect me!"

"You are a delusional woman!" Brady looked up to see Rebecca still standing with the phone in her hand. "Rebecca, for God's sake, call the EMTs!"

"Oh, um, right." Rebecca raised the phone to her ear.

"Cynthia, you'll be going back to prison either way. Either you stay here and you get arrested, or I find another way to send your sick ass back. Regardless, I am going to get help for the woman I love, and that woman is not you."

"You've hurt me, Brady, but you're not yourself right now. I'm going to forgive you. She trapped you, that's all this is. I can see that now. She's having your baby, isn't she? That's why you feel you need to be with her. It's your bastard baby that you love, not her! Can't you see that?"

"Get out! Would you just get out of my life!"

"They're on their way, Brady," Rebecca said as she scooched down next to him. She whispered in his ear, "They'll be here any minute."

Brady was weeping as he stroked Sophie's hair away from her face. "I'm sorry, Sophie. I'm so sorry."

Within moments, they heard the sirens as the ambulance approached. Cynthia had slipped away when they weren't paying attention. Rebecca ran to the driveway and guided them through the back door. The paramedics swiftly loaded Sophie onto the gurney and whisked her away.

"I'll meet you at the hospital," Brady yelled as he ran out the door.

. . .

Brady sat in the waiting room for what seemed like an eternity. He could hear the large clock over his head tick each second away until the sound drilled into his head. He ran his hand through his hair in desperation. *What have I done?* The words played over and over through his mind in rhythm with the ticking clock as two police officers approached.

"Brady Owens?"

"Yes, that's me."

The officers introduced themselves and stated why they

were there—they'd just come from Proposals, where they'd spoken to Rebecca about what had happened there. Rebecca had been on the ball, and he was grateful for her quick thinking.

Brady filled the officers in on who Cynthia Lockwood was. He persistently offered his services, which they declined. They left with the reassurance that they'd find her. Brady gulped the hard lump that formed in his throat. Again, the clock ticked away until he couldn't take another second.

Emily burst through the doors with panic on her face. She was shaking and wide-eyed as she saw Brady sitting against the far wall between a stack of magazines and a plastic fig tree. Tears rolled down her face as she sat next to him on the plastic settee.

"Rebecca called me. What in the hell happened?"

"I never in a million years would have guessed that Cynthia would come here, Emily. If I'd ever fathomed that, I would have told Sophie a long time ago. I could have protected her." Brady grew pale as his lips tightened to a thin line.

"It's not your fault."

"It sure as hell is!" he retorted. "She's psychotic, and I should have known."

Emily sat silently, twirling her thumb ring around and around in time with the ticking clock. "Any news on Sophie?"

Brady stood and paced, then stopped in front of the clock with clenched fists. The next thing Emily witnessed was Brady tearing it from the wall, ripping the batteries out, and heaving all the contents in the nearby trash can. Emily sat back, biting her tongue. Onlookers didn't flinch. They just kept thumbing through magazines, pretending what they had just seen never happened.

A hand gently touched Brady's shoulder as a calm voice whispered, "Mr. Owens, I'm going to need your consent." Brady and Emily recognized her as the same doctor Sophie had seen the last time she was here. "The baby is in distress, and Sophie is still unconscious. I need permission to perform a C-section. Do I have your permission?"

Brady looked blankly at Emily as if in a fog, and words didn't come as Emily replied, "Yes, please do what you need to do to save her baby girl."

Tears rolled down Brady's cheeks in silence. Emily took his hand and gave it a reassuring squeeze. The connection to another human being helped to steady his pounding, racing heart as the sound of the doctor's footsteps got further and further away.

Emily continued to sit with her eyes closed, her head tilted toward the wall behind her, while Brady cradled his head in his hands, staring at the floor. Neither moved nor spoke as time quietly ticked by.

Brady could feel the air closing in around him. His throat was dry, and taking a deep breath was becoming more and more difficult. He needed to escape and breathe. Exiting through the door seemed too great a task. The faster he walked, the further away it seemed.

When he reached the outdoors, the cold hit him. He took in a gasp and began to sob. He collapsed onto a nearby bench without reservation. Sobs continued until no more tears would flow, but he could now breathe with anguish in each give and take of his lungs. Running his hand through his hair, then wiping away his salt-encrusted face, he stood and turned to enter the eternal waiting room once again.

Emily was no longer in her seat, so he sat where they had

been sitting as he waited for her return. He watched the ladies' room door open and close a couple of times before he realized that she wasn't inside. Looking for assistance, he approached the desk of a senior citizen with a gentle smile.

"I'm, um...Brady Owens. Can you tell me...is there any word on Sophie Anderson?"

"I'm sorry, sir, but I'm not able to relay what you request."

"Excuse me?" Brady's eyes widened with surprise.

"It seems Mrs. Anderson's wishes are being acknowledged. She doesn't wish to see you, sir."

"That means she's awake. She can talk! But, I don't understand. She needs me right now." His voice was raspy and defeated as Emily opened the door and stood face-to-face with a wide-eyed, smear-faced Brady. "Emily! She's okay, right?"

"She's doing okay, Brady."

"And the baby?"

"She's in the NICU, having some breathing and feeding problems. They're also having difficulty regulating her body temperature, and she's jaundiced. Might need a feeding tube, too, but not really sure on that yet."

Brady was now reeling with the overload of information. "I want to see them. When can I see them?"

"I'm afraid she doesn't want to see you right now. She's hurting, Brady."

"That won't bother me. I want to be there to help and comfort her. Surely she knows I can handle her recovery?"

"Not that kind of hurting." Emily looked into his eyes, placed her hands upon his shoulders and took a breath. "She doesn't want to see *you*. She asked me to tell you to leave."

When he didn't think he had any more tears, he could feel a trickle down his cheek. Backing away, he once again walked toward the door. He could hear Emily's whisper of "Sorry... goodbye," and the door shut behind him. Anger poured into his soul at what he'd allowed to happen. Confessing to himself that he might never gain the trust or love of Sophie again only pushed him to seek it anyway, regardless of the outcome.

CHAPTER 38

Tubes, tape, and tabs covered her baby girl. Breathing tubes taped to her nose, extending across her cheeks and into her hairline, didn't detract from Sophie's gift. She was perfect in Sophie's eyes. A full head of strawberry-blond hair contrasted with the white bedding. Her little angel was sprawled out on her back in a restful sleep. Sophie gazed upon her with a love that she never dreamed possible.

"Can I touch her?" she asked in a hushed voice.

"You sure can," said the kind face standing next to her.

Sophie's hand trembled as it gently passed through the protective circles. She could feel the warmth of her daughter's skin next to hers. She felt her tiny fingers and touched a couple of her own fingers to her little one's chest. Feeling her tiny heart beat released the tension that had been building. Tears of joy rolled down her face. She was all hers. A new life and a ray of hope. *Look at our sweet creation, Sam. Isn't she beautiful?* The kind lady stayed quiet at her side, rested a tender hand on her shoulder, and gave it a loving squeeze. After a few moments, the attendant went on to explain what each clip, tube, and electrode was for, which Sophie took in with great attention.

"In the next day or two, you might get to hold her. It has healing powers, you know, being skin to skin."

"Oh, really? That soon?"

"Yes, dear. Sure gives you something to look forward to, now doesn't it? You need to get yourself stronger, too; don't forget about that. It's easy to think only of your little girl here, but you must remember yourself too. She needs a healthy mommy, don't you know? Have you thought about a name?"

"I have, but nothing has spoken to me until now." Sophie paused to collect her thoughts and regain her ability to speak without a quivering lip. "When I look at her, I see an innocent sweetness, and the feel of her soft pink skin; I feel such overwhelming incredible love for her." Again, she paused to control her emotions. "A pink rose, a sweet little bud in this case, means innocence, healing and first love. I'm going to name her Samantha Rose, after her father, Samuel. I think he would like that." Sophie nodded to herself in agreement. "Yes, he would like that very much."

"It's a meaningful name that Samantha Rose will love as well."

"Hello, Samantha Rose…I'm your mommy," Sophie whispered, just as baby Samantha opened up her eyes to see her mommy for the first time. "I love you. Mommy loves you so very much."

Sophie never wanted the moment to end, but she withdrew her hand and nodded her head. She knew it was time to go. The ache of her incision and fatigue from her surgery was winning, and she asked to be wheeled back to her room. As distance came between them, a tingling sensation emerged from her breasts, soaking the front of her gown. She remembered too late to apply pressure to her bosom by crossing her arms and holding them to her chest. This phenomenon of lactation still blew her mind. Even though she couldn't breastfeed directly, she was still happy to be able to provide for her tiny newborn.

She rested her eyes as the rhythmic hum of the pump continued, and she once again thought of Brady. She was playing tug-of-war with anger and sorrow—or was it betrayal that was bubbling to the surface? Yes, she concluded. It was betrayal that caused the feelings of anger and sorrow.

CHAPTER 39

Elizabeth Lockwood threw the Lenox crystal glass, which smashed against the door just over Henry's head. The contents of red wine ran down the mahogany and pooled into the Persian rug at its base.

"When will you stop?" she yelled with clenched fists while Lockwood laughed at her failed attempt to strike him.

"When are you going to learn that Cynthia is my baby and that I will do anything to protect her—and I mean anything?"

"When will you learn that you are spoiling her beyond repair? You are not helping her, Henry. You're encouraging her, and she's ultimately going to be the one to suffer because of it! You are delusional and will pay the cost for what you are doing."

"Since when do you give a damn about the cost of anything? You don't complain when what I do serves you, but when it comes to Cynthia—oh, that's crossing the line. Face it, you're jealous of her because you've come to realize that no amount of cosmetic surgery can turn back the clock of your aging crusty soul."

"This will come back to haunt you, Henry Lockwood, mark my words." Elizabeth could feel the rug squish beneath her feet as she pushed the doors open with force to escape, but she turned back toward a grinning Lockwood. "Go to hell," she said with an intensity that even Henry had never seen before. The steely expression in her eyes was cold with contempt, and the look on his face suggested that he wondered if this time he'd gone too far.

. . .

Stevens took a swig of his scotch and poured another for Brady, finishing off the bottle. Brady wasn't feeling any pain as he swished the rocks glass to watch the golden liquid slosh against its sides over and over again, lost in his thoughts. Brady was lost.

"Hey, why don't we call it a night? A good night's rest will help, and tomorrow we'll figure out a way to put the bastard and his crazy-ass daughter away. Okay?" Stevens suggested.

Brady's glazed-over eyes connected with Stevens's, but there wasn't anybody there. Stevens nodded in understanding. "See you in the morning. Just try to get some sleep." He walked away, turning the lights off behind him.

Brady sat in the dark, feeling numb. He tipped the glass to finish it off and wiped the last drip from his lips with the back of his hand. He eased himself down on the couch pillow and pulled his legs up off the floor. He lay there staring into the darkness until he drifted off to sleep. Peaceful sleep didn't come. Dreams of Sophie, looking frightened and panicked with her eyes wide, stumbling, trying to escape a captor, played over and over like a broken record. Was he the one she was running from, the one who'd caused her pain? Was it Cynthia? He never saw the face of the captor, but he sensed it was him. She'd been trapped in his lie, never escaping her living nightmare.

He awoke with a cold sweat, his heart ready to jump out of his chest. The sun had not yet come up as he sat in the dark, unfamiliar room, forgetting momentarily where he was. His heart rate steadied, but the panic was soon replaced by self-loathing. He recalled the dream...he was the captor by making her live out her worst day over and over, never being able to put it behind her so that she could be released to find peace.

After fumbling his way to the kitchen, he flicked on the tiny light above the stove, causing a small glow just enough to show the coffeemaker. The grinding of the machine along with the steady stream of coffee flowing into his cup gave him promise. Soon he was back on the couch with a hot cup in his hands. Knowing he wouldn't be able to fall back asleep anyway, he turned on the floor lamp and loomed over the files that Stevens had collected.

All the pieces were there. He knew it; he just couldn't see the full picture. Wiping the sleep from his eyes, then running his hand through his matted bedhead, he focused on a still photo of Elizabeth Lockwood glaring at Henry, who was getting a bit too cozy with Gwen Palermo, the governor's wife. Gwen was wearing a plunging neckline, a glass of bubbly in her hand as Henry had, from what it appeared, said something to tickle her fancy—perhaps something a bit naughty from the sultry grin on his face—as he'd leaned in toward her ear.

Brady was more convinced than ever that he had to meet up with Liz Lockwood. He gulped the last drip of coffee and set his mug on the table with determination. He would get answers in order to make amends with Sophie, even if it killed him.

. . .

Brady watched out the window as icy rain bounced off the sidewalk in Midtown Manhattan. Nameless faces ducked within their scarves and collars against the freezing rain dodging in and out of the overhang that hung over the entry to the Un-wined & Dine, in which he sat. Patiently, he waited as taxis picked up and dropped off their fares.

At last, a limo pulled up. The driver ran around the front of the Town Car and jumped the slushy curbing. Umbrella in hand, he popped it open along with the passenger's back door. Brady could see a high-heeled black boot emerge, followed by the face of Elizabeth Lockwood. Taking in a deep breath, he stood to await her entry. He raised his hand and nodded to the server. Within seconds, a glass of Flichman Malbec sat at the table for two as Elizabeth approached. Elizabeth extended a cheek for a greeting and Brady obliged with a kiss and helped her with her coat.

Liz took a deep inhale of the Malbec's plum and oak aroma and breathed a calming exhale. She sloshed the wine around the crystal, then sipped.

"What brings this about, Brady?" she asked as she peered above the glass and looked into his eyes. "You looked aggrieved. Let me guess—my daughter is at it again?"

"Something like that," Brady said with reservation. "I'm concerned, really. Did you know that she drove to Maine?"

"Yes, she told me that. Wanted to see you and where you'd like your wedding to be. I don't know what goes through her head sometimes. It's as if she forgets or frankly doesn't care that she's on probation and can go back to prison over maneuvers like that. Can't blame her, though. Her father always manages to intervene."

"Intervene? I don't know. I think he's just a man who loves his little girl and wants to protect her."

Elizabeth downed the rest of her wine and raised her empty glass in the air. The server accommodated her quickly. Brady waited patiently for her response, hoping that this glass would go down as quickly as the other.

"Did I say intervene? I meant to say orchestrate. Yes, orchestrate." She nodded as if in agreement with someone else.

"He must have some pretty good connections to, as you say, to orchestrate her protection."

"Oh, Brady, you poor dear. You don't know the half of it! Trust me, if you're on his good side, there isn't a thing he wouldn't do for you, or for money for that matter. Get on his bad side, and he'll do everything in his power to make your life a living hell."

"I confess, Elizabeth—"

"Please, call me Liz."

"All right, Liz. I can only imagine what it must be like to be married to such a powerful man. Although, you are powerful in your own right. I can see that in you, Liz."

Elizabeth reached her hand across the table and gave his a tender squeeze, then lingered there. Brady hoped he was able to hide his discomfort as he turned his hand toward hers and responded with a squeeze of his own.

"I am the daughter of Robert Hurst," she said with pride.

"Of the law offices of Lockwood & Hurst? I'm listening."

"Yes, I am powerful, as you put it, but powerful people can be gullible and blind when it comes to love." She rubbed her finger around the lip of the crystal to make it sing. "You're a fine man, Brady, and I don't want you to do what I did."

"Meaning?"

"I too wanted to make a name for myself and, as you can imagine, being the daughter of Robert Hurst, I had a lot to live up to. But I had to earn my way, not have everything given to me."

"I never realized that you were with the firm." Brady saw that her glass was empty and motioned for another refill for each of them.

"Not in the way that you'd expect. Yes, I'm a lawyer, but I preferred the back office; I was the controller. Numbers were my strength, but Henry Lockwood was my weakness." Her sigh of reflection was soon doused with the return of a full glass. "After my father passed, I inherited his share of the firm and became more of a silent partner. You see, I was pregnant with Cynthia at the time, and my role changed somewhat for a while. However, being a mother isn't one of my strong suits. I don't have patience for spoiled brats. Henry would undermine my decisions at every turn. So, I figured, if I can't raise her the way I see fit, I may as well take on more at work and let him handle her upbringing. He'd have to deal with it. My mistake."

Brady could feel the wine taking effect and ordered a plate of assorted cheeses. To his surprise, he was the only one to partake. Liz Lockwood was well into glass number four and continued running at the mouth, for which he was grateful.

"It must have been hard all these years to see their relationship. I know I sometimes get envious of their closeness." He was hoping she'd take the bait.

"Envious isn't a word that I would use. Resentment, perhaps, but not envy. Honestly, what bothers me more than that is how he squanders the firm's money for her escapades."

"That must hurt, after all your father did to build a great firm. He brought Henry on and made him partner, am I right?"

"Yes."

"Seeing him, as you say, squander money from your father's firm, especially with you being the one to see where the money was and is going—well, I can't blame you for being angry, regardless of who it's being used for."

"Then you get it! His daughter has done nothing to contribute and only takes the spoils. My father built an empire, and I've worked way too hard over the years to maintain it." Her voice was rising in pitch and volume. Brady stroked her hand to bring her back. Elizabeth hushed her words as she continued. "Using my money for his illegal actions and payoffs. Well, I'll be dammed if I'll let him continue down that road."

"What can you do?" Brady asked, mimicking Elizabeth's tone.

"I will destroy him," she said with determination. "He thinks that I won't because he thinks I'm weak like Cynthia, but I'm not. I've seen and heard too much. I know about his little rendezvous with Gwen Palermo—the bribes he's paid to the powerful. I will take him for everything he's worth. I'll get majority ownership, and he'll be ruined."

Hoping he wouldn't jeopardize her position on the matter, Brady responded, "I completely agree with you and understand how you must be feeling, but won't that tarnish the image of Lockwood & Hurst? Isn't that what you're trying to avoid?"

"Don't you see? If I expose him, what he's done and with whom, then I will be a hero. Lockwood will be no more, and he and his daughter can deal with the consequences—consequences that they've brought on themselves."

The space between them became silent. Brady now realized why Cynthia was the way she was. In part, he'd felt sorry for her.

"I've said too much." She leaned back looking toward the ceiling. It was clear she could feel the effects of the wine. She sat back up and retrieved a slice of cheddar.

"No, no. It's okay. You needed to get it off your chest."

"We'll just blame it on the wine, shall we?" she said with a giggle.

"It will be our little secret."

Elizabeth reached her hand toward Brady with a tap. "You aren't going to marry Cynthia, are you?"

"No, Liz, I'm not."

"Well, good for you. You are braver than I was. We'll keep that as our little secret as well."

"What do you say we order something a little more substantial to eat?" Brady knew he had gotten what he needed from Elizabeth Lockwood for now. Serving her more wine would only open him up to her awkward advances. She was getting too close for comfort, and her eyes were looking too seductive for his liking.

They placed their order, and Brady continued, "How can I help you, Liz?"

"Why would you do that?"

"Let's just say...I want justice, too."

By the time they were done eating, they'd come up with a plan. A plan that included Stevens and a wire. He was giddy when he left for Stevens's place, but by the time he arrived, he was filled with doubt. What if it was just the wine talking? What if she wouldn't follow through with the plan? He pushed the doubt aside and leapt up the stairs two at a time until he reached the threshold and rang the bell. Stevens opened the door with a well-how-did-it-go expression all over his face.

"It worked, my friend, it worked!"

CHAPTER 40

Grounds was buzzing with the latest gossip as Mrs. Margo Bennington spouted off at the mouth. Emily blew into her cup, allowing the steam to warm her face. She'd needed to step away from baking and thought a walk could clear her mind. The bitter cold winds had penetrated deep within, nearly spilling her cup from shivers that she couldn't shake. Jillian pulled up a chair across the table.

"How are you doing, Emily?" Without waiting for a response, she rambled on. "Mrs. Bennington said that she heard Sophie nearly died and that her little baby was barely hanging on. I can't imagine what she's going through with all that, not to mention what Brady did to her." She shook her head side to side with downcast eyes and pursed lips. "However are you managing Proposals without her?"

Emily took a deep breath. "Mrs. Bennington doesn't know what she's talking about, per usual. It's true that Sophie gave us a scare, but the baby is doing great. In fact, she'll get to go home very soon."

"Well, that's wonderful news," she said without skipping a beat. "But, is it true about Brady Owens? Is he really having an affair with that woman from New York City? She came in here, you know…asking about Proposals and Sophie. She seemed nice, and she's really pretty…poor Sophie, she's a hard one to compete against."

"Jillian, you also don't know what you're talking about, per usual. I would suggest that you stop talking—"

"But I saw that woman with my own eyes, and Mrs. Bennington said—"

"Who gives a damn about what Mrs. Bennington said? She doesn't know shit!" The room fell silent as all eyes turned to Emily, then to Margo Bennington. Emily was amused that Mrs. Bennington's jaw was able to drop with all the cosmetic surgery she'd had done. "Margo, you might want to lift your chin. Your dentures might fall out, and we wouldn't want people talking about you, now would we?"

Mrs. Bennington remained speechless, and the oxygen was sucked out of the room. Emily walked up to the counter, grabbed a to-go cup, carefully poured her coffee in, applied the lid, and pushed the door open. A gust of wind shot through Grounds, which broke the ice. She could hear Margo Bennington's exasperated response of, "Well, I never!" as the door slammed, which brought a smile of satisfaction to her face that soon faded as she realized the now-difficult situation she'd put Proposals into. Mrs. Bennington's support over the years had boosted their business, for which Emily and Sophie were grateful. However, Emily just couldn't take the smug gossiping windbag any longer. Life was too short, Emily concluded, and the time had come to say her piece.

After walking off her anger, she shook her coat and watched plumes of snow fall to the floor, then proceeded to stomp it out with her weighty boots. Emily felt pensive as she tried to come to grips with what had been bothering her. Maybe it was the added stress at Proposals without Sophie there, or a guilty conscience. Either way, taking her stress out on Mrs. Bennington probably hadn't been the best thing to do. She owed her an apology, but more importantly, she owed Sophie an apology. She owned some of the pain that Sophie was going through with the revelation of Brady and Cynthia Lockwood. Brady was a good man, but he'd screwed up; they both had. She'd have to come clean before it ate at her another second.

. . .

Sophie sat propped up in a rocking chair next to Samantha's cart, holding her little one against her chest. Emily's eyes were wide as she stepped through the door. Sophie looked to her with an enormous smile.

"Can you believe it, Emily?"

"What a picture that is…what a beautiful picture. This moment is something I will never forget."

"Take one with your phone!"

"Okay, you asked for it, but I can't promise how good it will be; I'm not the trained professional."

"It'll be just fine," Sophie replied, glossing over the subtle plug for Brady.

Emily took a couple of shots, then scooched down next to Sophie, looking on at baby Samantha as she slept peacefully in her mother's arms.

"She looks so much bigger, and some of her attachments are gone." She wiped away a tear from the corner of her eye.

"I'm so happy for you, Soph." Emily stroked the strawberry hair that poked out from under the little pink hat. "You've got the best mommy in the whole wide world…yes, you do." She cleared her throat appearing to erase the baby talk that had just come out of her mouth. "Why do grown adults do that?"

A silence fell, with only beeps from monitors in the background. As the beeps continued, Emily fidgeted with her thumb ring and Sophie knew that Emily had something on her mind but didn't dare to ask.

"Seriously, once Samantha Rose gets home, you really should have Brady take some photos. This is a once-in-a-lifetime gift, Soph. She'll only be like this for a short time, and he's great at capturing special moments. Please don't let what happened make you miss it." Sophie remained quiet as Emily waited for a response, yet none came. "It isn't what you think. What happened…isn't what you think. He's a good man, Sophie, and you need each other right now."

Sophie's heart rate increased with each utterance of Brady's name. She loved her friend dearly, but this, she wouldn't put up with. "You know what, Emily? I think that Samantha and I need to be left alone right now. I'm going to have to put her down soon, and I don't want to waste my time with her talking about things that…I just think you should go home now, okay?"

"Sure…okay…I'll go now." Emily stood up slowly. "Um…is it okay if I come back tomorrow?" Sophie closed her eyes as she rocked. "I'm sorry, I didn't mean to upset you. You're my best friend, and I love you. I just wanted to—"

"Not now, Emily."

"Right. I'm going." She backed away, and a nurse opened the door and escorted her out with a tender smile and a nod.

Sophie gazed into baby Samantha Rose's eyes. They were wide as they peered into her own. "You would be photogenic, little one, but Mommy isn't ready to forgive." She was puzzled by Emily's openness to Brady and her willingness to allow him back into their lives after what he'd done. As he had bookings for photography at Proposals, it only made sense that he'd try to justify his betrayal and lies. She wondered what kind of tale he'd woven to get to Emily. She was gullible at times, but also acutely aware and cautious. *How could I have been so blind?* she thought as she rocked back and forth. *It had to have been right in front of me all this time.* The so-called work trips to New York City had seemed legitimate and believable. What she wrestled with was why; what was his deal? What was the point of seeking her out and living a façade, and to what end? She wanted to ask him, but the thought of being in the same room was more than she could bear.

She played their relationship over in her mind. He'd seemed so…genuine. So, good and kind. Was any of it real? She thought of them meeting on the beach, had it been random? Or, had it been on purpose? No, she concluded. He'd have no way of knowing she'd be there. *What am I missing?* She'd fallen in love with him and she believed he loved her. She shivered with remorse. She felt dirty and embarrassed by how she'd opened up to him. She'd allowed this to happen and the only person that should have received her love was Samantha.

Sophie sighed with regret and looked upon her bundle wrapped in her arms. "We're going home soon, my little buttercup. Yes, we are." She smiled to herself, realizing that she too spoke in the same squeaky voice she'd just heard from Emily. "Grown-ups are funny, buttercup…yes, they are."

CHAPTER 41

Brady and Stevens worked tirelessly day after day, piecing together a string of players in the twisted game of the Lockwoods. The top of the list included the names of the most plausible perpetrators: the father/son-in-law duo of Lloyd Becker, the warden, and Adam Libby, one of the guards at Bedford Hills Correctional Facility; the parole board members, Julie Barrows and Charles Denning; Governor Mark Palermo; and both Henry and Cynthia Lockwood.

Elizabeth Lockwood and her legal counsel listened acutely as Brady, Stevens and Frank Sinclair, Stevens's investigator friend, laid out a plan of action. They knew that, without the FBI's assistance, the evidence obtained by wearing a wire would most likely be inadmissible in court. However, that didn't preclude Elizabeth from wearing one. If they could at least record something incriminating, it could give them enough evidence to give the FBI, as accusing the governor without some kind of proof was sure to lead nowhere. The

FBI could then intervene with full knowledge of what had gone down, then record legally from that point on. It was concluded that if all else failed, Elizabeth and Brady would become key witnesses.

Brady was keenly aware that Elizabeth appeared enthusiastic about the prospect of playing such a role as this. She'd been leaning forward and nodding in agreement as the explanations continued, much to his relief, but still he had his doubts. Brady stood from his chair and leaned on the corner of the desk nearest Elizabeth. He clasped his hands and rested them on his thigh. Elizabeth leaned back and looked curiously at Brady.

"Mrs. Lockwood...Elizabeth," he said with a gentle tone. "I understand that we are putting you in a difficult situation, and we need to be sure that this is truly what you want to do."

"Brady, I don't do anything that I don't want to do." She stared at him with a look of determination.

"You could be put through hell...publicly. Are you absolutely certain that you want to do this?"

"What you don't understand, Brady, is that I am convinced that it's what's best in the long run. Some would call it revenge, or even betrayal. Others might even say it will be justified, but so be it. I need to save my heritage and the legacy of the firm. To me, that's all that matters. Besides, I know that when all is said and done, my husband—and my daughter too, for that matter—would have turned on me in the same way if it was to their benefit."

"I understand," Brady stated. "Thank you, Elizabeth."

Elizabeth clamped her hands together with a clap. "Let's get this done."

The first step was for Elizabeth to visit the warden at the Bedford Hills Correctional Facility to thank him for all he'd done to help get her beautiful daughter out and request the audience of anyone else there, like the kind prison guard, who had magnanimously assisted. She'd be sure to ask them not to say anything to her darling husband, with a promise of reward for keeping it their little secret.

Sinclair showed Elizabeth how to turn the recording device on and off. His hands fumbled as he attempted to show her precisely how to place the device on her person in an inconspicuous place. He'd been a private investigator for two decades, and maybe it was just her cleavage, which peeked out voluptuously from her half-unbuttoned silk blouse, but Brady noticed Sinclair's hands tremble. Elizabeth was kind enough to act like she didn't notice.

"Is this comfortable, Mrs. Lockwood? We don't want it to pinch or pull because then you might be tempted to fidget with it or not move naturally."

"Yes, it's fine."

"Great. Okay, so I'm going to remove it, and I'd like to see you do it yourself." His hands began to shake again as he attempted to pull her blouse open to access the device.

"Maybe I should practice taking it off myself, too, Mr. Sinclair," she said with a grin.

"I suppose you're right."

Brady and Stevens exchanged knowing glances. They'd be sure to tease Sinclair relentlessly after Elizabeth Lockwood was gone.

As evening came, Brady lay in the pitch dark on Stevens's couch, looking toward the ceiling. He'd been so consumed with trying to put Cynthia and her father away that he hadn't actually quieted his mind. Sophie flooded his thoughts as he lay there, missing her so much it hurt. He was supposed to be there for her and the baby, and he'd let her down. He would never forgive himself for allowing this to happen, so how could he possibly expect Sophie to? Regardless, putting the Lockwoods away would at least make losing her manageable.

The stillness of the night was unsettling as the nor'easter added inches of snow to the pavement. Stevens lived in the city, and Brady expected to hear noise, sirens, cars—anything to take his mind off his reality. Not tonight, however; tonight it was as if all life had stopped. *Are you sleeping, Sophie, or are you awake with the baby peacefully sleeping in your arms?* He longed to be with her as he pondered, as time stood still, in the quiet, in the dark.

. . .

Sophie slowly emerged from Emily's car. Proposals was in full swing as it was being outfitted for the last wedding of the year. "You didn't have to pick me up. I could have found another ride, for Pete's sake."

"You're kidding me, right? Like I would ever allow that, you silly woman."

"I know, I know, but you have to make sure everything is going smoothly—"

"Everything is going smoothly. Rebecca has really stepped up, and Brady will be here in a few minutes for pre-shots and anything else we need, so I have time to get you a cup of tea and get you tucked in."

"Okay, you win." She knew she was defeated and yet remarkably at ease considering everything going on next door. "Em, do you know if this is Brady's last booking?"

"Um, not sure, but I can check."

"No, no, don't bother. It doesn't really matter one way

or the other," Sophie said as if they were discussing the trash pickup, then cleared her throat and looked away.

"I know you were hoping that you wouldn't have to come home without Samantha, but it will be soon."

"Yep, soon." Sophie swallowed hard as if she had a lump in her throat. "There's my Daisy Girl…Momma missed you." The calico put her nose up in the air with indignation, making it clear that she'd been left alone for far too long. "It was just as hard on me, you know." Sophie opened the cabinet and retrieved a catnip snack, holding it out as an olive branch. "Am I forgiven?" Daisy rubbed her nose and cheek on Sophie's ankle, and she could feel the vibration of her purring.

"I guess you're forgiven," Emily said as Brady's BMW pulled into his parking spot.

"You know what, Emily? I think I'm just going to take a shower instead and maybe read for a while. I'd feel better if you were next door keeping an eye on things."

"Sure, okay. Do you want a fire? I can send—"

"Good heavens, Emily! Please! I don't want him here or anywhere near me! Why is that so hard for you to understand? You of all people should respect that!"

"It's just that I—"

"He betrayed me, Emily. I can't wrap my head around why they would do this to me. What was their scheme? It sickens me to think that I was that gullible. Don't you see? I was used for some reason that is beyond my comprehension. To think that everything was a lie, and it just pisses me off. I want him to be done here and gone from my life! So please, go next door and watch over things and keep him the hell away from me."

Emily's stumbled for her words and put her head down with a shake. It was Emily's turn to be defeated. Sophie never knew Emily to be at a loss for words and she didn't care. Anger gripped Sophie and she stiffened as Emily gave her an awkward hug. Emily turned toward the door, fumbled with the handle, and stepped out into the cutting wind. Sophie watched on as Emily flung her arms up in frustration, then stood on the icy pavement. Sophie could see Brady sitting in his car as Emily shrugged and shook her head as if indicating *not now* as Brady nodded in what Sophie assumed was some kind of understanding between them.

Sophie gripped the doorknob, about to give them both a piece of her mind, then hesitated when she saw Emily retrieving the multitude of floral arrangements, Sophie's overnight bags, and the box of well wishes from her car. Emily hesitated as if she pondered where to put them. She took a few steps toward her, paused, then marched on with a tentative stride. Sophie needed her personal items, but more importantly, she needed her best friend. Emily appeared surprised as Sophie opened the door for her.

"Sorry I snapped at you. It's not your fault that Brady is a scheming jerkface, and I shouldn't have taken it out on you."

"No worries. You've been through a lot lately." She set the items down on the counter and went out for more. Brady was still in his car, watching Emily go back and forth, which Sophie found insufferable.

"Doesn't he have work to do or something?" Sophie said, gesturing toward Brady, when Emily entered with the last armful.

"He's got it covered," Emily said cautiously as Sophie added water to one of the arrangements.

"He better. We've put everything into this business, and if he even thinks of letting me down with this too—I'll…"

Sophie's hands shook, and the wet vase slipped through her fingers and smashed into fragments into the sink. "Dammit!" Sophie pulled on the paper towel roll with hands trembling as she wiped the pieces of glass, paused, then threw the towels into the sink. "I can't...it's too much, Em...it's just too much."

"I'll take care of it. Why don't you head upstairs and get some rest?"

Without another word, she walked away toward her room. The place that used to be a sanctuary. Now, it was a place of memories that mixed with competing emotions. She passed the nursery at the top of the stairs. The door had been shut, but it drew her in. Sophie had vowed not to go in until Samantha was in her arms, but she needed the connection. She needed her baby girl.

Sophie turned on the mobile, then removed the quilt that her grandmother had made, draping it around her shoulders. She sat in the rocking chair and closed her eyes, imagining her baby's sweet powder scent and picturing her tiny little fingers around hers. Sophie could feel the detail of the silky stitched flowers roll along under her touch.

Sophie was lost in a sea of abandonment, which she couldn't climb out of. She ached with the knowledge of her kind and loving grandmother's passing, her mother's constant distance, Sam's death, and Brady's betrayal. Now, a part of her was left in a hospital room—alone—without her mommy.

Daisy pushed the nursery door open with her nose and squeezed through its opening. "Come here, Daisy Mae." Sophie patted the side of the rocker, but her furry friend only whined at the door. "Oh, I see how it is." Daisy continued to meow. "You're right. It's late and we need to get to bed and get some sleep. Don't we girl?" Sophie grimaced as she stood, feeling the effects of her C-section. She folded the quilt and gently laid it across the back of the rocker. Silence fell across the room, and the motion of the rocker and mobile came to an end. Feeling a familiar knot forming in her throat, she stepped out and closed the door behind her.

. . .

Sophie woke to the sound of laughter and celebratory music ringing through the night. She'd never experienced one of their events from the outside. She grabbed her pillow, placed it over her face, and pressed it firmly to her ears. She kicked the blankets in frustration as the merriment penetrated through the fleece casing of the down pillow and then tossed it to the floor in a huff. Daisy made circles on the comforter and tried once again to get comfortable.

"I know how you feel, girl. Should we take a peek?" She slipped on her furry slippers, threw on her robe and walked toward the palladium window that overlooked the grounds and the face of the barn. "Looks like everyone is having a great time, Daisy. I'd say it's another success in the books."

Snow was coming down, and as if it were the first snow, guests spilled out the double barn doors to witness the spectacle. The lights from the chandeliers bounced off the snow and it glistened with cascading splendor. Within moments, the bride and groom emerged, holding hands as he twirled her around like a ballerina in a music box. Brady stepped out to capture the scene and make it a lasting memory. Sophie realized that it was making a lasting memory for her as well.

This is the last time I'll be seeing him, she thought as she bit her lip, refusing to allow him to make her cry again; to her chagrin, it was too late. The beauty of the romance before her was in such contrast to the sadness she felt at seeing Brady. She'd had hopes of them together. He had been her rock, her safety, and her future. Now, that future was gone and she had to focus on getting her little girl home. Sophie retrieved a tissue from her robe pocket and wiped her dampened cheeks. She inhaled deeply, then released her breath with a four count. *One step at a time…just one step at a time.*

Tea sounded good, and she tentatively descended the stairs. Her abdomen ached at each stretch of the leg. Holding the railing steadied her footing, until Daisy made a run for it and bounded down the steps. Sophie grasped the rail tight as her feet slipped beneath her and she landed with a thump on her backside. Being more frightened than hurt, she turned to anger and sheer self-pity, which only made her angrier. Clenching her teeth with determination, she used her arms to pull herself up and proceeded toward the kitchen for her tea.

. . .

Brady couldn't help but feel envious of Emily's ability to turn off her emotions in front of the guests, like nothing horrible was going on in their world. He conceded that he could at least hide behind his camera for much of the time. Brady could see the happy couple gazing into each other's eyes filled with hope and wonder for the future. Their joy was evident with every gesture and caress. He held her with tenderness as she was enveloped in safety and security. There was an underlining trust between them that was palpable through the lens. He dreamed of this with Sophie. She still consumed his every thought, but his thoughts now turned to sadness and a sense of unattainable dreams. Still, he would keep moving forward with the hope of justice.

Brady saw the kitchen light turn on from a distance and caught a glimpse of auburn hair drifting by the window. He made a mental note to point it out to Emily and have her shut the blinds at night. He shivered at the thought of someone peering in and watching her. Granted, Sophie was usually at the events and not in her personal space, but he still wasn't comfortable knowing she was so highly visible.

The bridal party hurried back into the barn for warmth, but Brady lingered. The soles of his dress shoes made his feet ache as the cold worked its way in. Snow gathered around his feet as it intensified. He just stood there looking on, watching Sophie caressing Daisy and nuzzling her nose as the cat sat on the countertop. Sophie seemed content sipping her Sleepytime tea with one sugar and a splash of cream. He was lost in his thoughts, thinking about what could have been; it didn't register that Sophie had looked up and in his direction until it was too late. He'd been caught. Sophie was now watching him watching her. He was frozen, not knowing what to do, and yet part of him didn't care. They locked eyes through the now-light flurry of snow that glistened in the night. A soft melody played in the background as time stood still, and then the blinds shut in one quick motion and she was gone.

Brady sucked in the cold air and felt the ache in his feet up to his ankles. Realizing that his camera was now covered in snow, he brushed it off and retreated inside, faked a smile, and finished the job.

. . .

Sophie crept back to bed with the ache of loss in her heart. She missed Sam deeply, missed the hope of what she could have had with Brady, missed her baby girl, and missed the person that she used to be. Tears no longer came. Self-pity was no longer acceptable. Lying in her bed caressing Daisy, she vowed to be strong and overcome. Soon, Samantha Rose would be in her arms once again, and she could focus on being the best mom she could be. Proposals would continue to provide an outlet for her passions and creativity, and she would thrive. She had Emily in her life and was grateful for her unconditional love and support. She was safe, secure, and capable of writing her own story; it could be a tragedy or a happily ever after. It was her choice to make and hers alone. Closing her eyes, she nodded to herself. *I choose to be happy.*

CHAPTER 42

Elizabeth Lockwood paced the floor, with her hands actively wringing the pair of leather gloves that she held within them. She had a determined set to her jaw, and she stopped and stood her ground firmly as the door opened. Stevens stood with a questioning expression as he invited her in.

"What brings you in, Mrs. Lockwood? I thought we'd agreed never to meet here."

"Yes, well, this was urgent and couldn't be helped."

"Oh," Stevens said with surprise, "do sit down."

"No, I won't be here long. I'm just going to get straight to the point."

"Okay."

Elizabeth resumed pacing and wringing her gloves once again as Stevens sat quietly.

"I can't do it." Stevens clasped his hands together atop his desk and leaned back, waiting for further explanation. He watched her pace until she was ready. "I've thought about it a lot. I really thought I could do it…should do it. But she's my daughter, and even though I detest what she's done and what she's doing—and God only knows what she'll do—I can't do it."

Stevens stood and walked casually around the desk. Placing his hand on her shoulder, he guided her to a pair of swivel chairs with slight pressure. They sat side by side, and he turned his chair toward her. She was still wringing her gloves and looking down at her high-heeled leather boots.

"I understand. This must be an extremely difficult position for you to be in."

"Yes," she said wistfully.

"We wouldn't want you to do anything you don't want to do. It was only through your well-thought-out plan to save your father's hard work and name that you convinced us." Stevens lowered his head to peek underneath her wide-brimmed hat in order to catch her eye. "Don't you still want that?" he asked carefully. On the inside, however, he was near panic, praying that she would change her mind.

"Yes, of course I want that."

"Has he threatened you? Is that where this is coming from?"

"No. At least not any more than usual, or no more than I threaten him."

"I see. You're being a good mother, and I commend you for that."

"Thank you," she said with her chin up, regaining some of her usual confidence.

"Let me ask you something, if I may."

"Go on."

"When they do something, and from past experience we

know they will, will you be able to stomach the publicity and humiliation that it will cause if you don't get in front of it and take control?"

"I hear you. However, I would be looked at as a monster if I threw my own daughter to the wolves," she said firmly. "Yes, I want to destroy my husband. However, there's got to be another way." She placed her hand on his shoulder. "I trust that you will find it." With that, she stood up and abruptly left the room.

. . .

Brady was going through photos and placing the proofs online for the bridal party to see. He was surprised at how they had come out as he had been doubting his talents. Everything had appeared out of focus and uninspired at the time he was taking them. But after seeing them, he saw that each photo actually had more focus and care. Maybe it was luck, or maybe it had been his brokenness that sought the special moments, the tender looks, the sparkle of joy, a hope of a future. He clung to that hope as well. Soon he'd get the proof that he needed from, of all people, Mrs. Elizabeth Lockwood. He smiled to himself with that promise and the satisfaction that this situation was only temporary; it was in his grasp. There was still a chance that Sophie would forgive him once everything came out and he'd be holding her, and her baby, in his arms.

Brady's cell rang, and he saw Stevens's name pop on the screen. "What's up, my man? Making some progress?"

"On the contrary, Brady; we've hit a wall."

"What the hell are you talking about?"

"She backed out."

"Who backed out? Elizabeth?"

"Yep. I tried, man, but she was adamant."

"But why? She hates him. Did he get to her?"

"It's Cynthia," Stevens replied.

"Did she get wind and threaten her?"

"No. Apparently, she's decided to be a loving mother and refuses to throw her under the bus in order to seek revenge on Lockwood."

"No!"

"She insists that we have to find another way."

"How the hell are we going to do that? After what happened at Sophie's, Cynthia's not going to trust me. I haven't even spoken to her since then, and I bet my ass that she spilled to her darling daddy and he won't trust me either. My original plan isn't going to work. I don't have an in anymore."

"I don't know, Brady. I'm stumped too. But you can bet your ass that we'll figure out something."

Brady was shaking by the time he hung up the phone. It was all he could do not to rip every single joyous, happy, sappy, kissy-faced picture that lay before him to shreds.

· · ·

Sweet confections were piled high atop the counter in the shape of a whimsical castle of turrets with a gelatin moat. Emily stood back, examining her masterpiece. "All that's left is to add powdered sugar to create a winter scene." Emily gestured with a nod of satisfaction.

"It's really beautiful, Emily. You outdid yourself," Sophie stated with pride in her friend's talent.

"Thanks," Emily said with a smile and proceeded to heave the ten-pound bucket of powder off the shelf, then grasped the lid to open it. As quickly as the lid finally gave way, so too did her grasp of the bucket. The sugar bounded to the floor, which sent projectile sweet powder up and out, fully covering Emily from head to toe. She stood in the cloud of sugar.

"Don't you dare say a word," Emily chided as the dust began to settle. Sophie stood in the doorway, doubled over and squealing in laughter.

"Oh, it hurts. I can't...breathe."

"I didn't think it was possible to hate you, but right now, I do...in a really big way."

"You should see yourself. It's hysterical. Oh my gosh..." The squealing continued. "I'm going to pee myself. Never mind...correction. I just peed myself."

Emily was a powered mess. All that was visible were her eyes and her lips where she'd licked off the sugar. "Is there something you wanted?" she said with a deadpan voice and expression.

"Actually, yes. It's a bit perplexing, though." She was still trying to get the smirk off her face in hopes of not losing it again. "I got a card in the mail from Mrs. Bennington. She congratulated me on Samantha and said she wished me well. However, she said she'd miss seeing me. Not really sure what she'd meant by that. Strange, Huh?"

"Excuse me for a sec." Emily stepped outside just as a strong wind kicked into gear and blew the sugar into the wind. She was shivering as she came back in. "So, about that. I kind of screwed up. But you have to understand, I was emotional and maybe a little touchy...or better yet, bitchy, that day."

"What on earth are you talking about?"

"Well, I told her that she might want to shut her big fat mouth so that her dentures wouldn't fall out."

"You did what?"

"Like I said, I wasn't myself that day. She was in Grounds, running her mouth with her cackling hens, and I just couldn't take it."

"Emily, she's a valued customer and friend. She's been our cheerleader since the beginning. How could you?"

"She was spreading gossip about Cynthia Lockwood and Brady, and you too for that matter."

"Oh."

"And it was all lies."

"With a grain of truth, I'm sure," said Sophie. "Honestly, they get what they deserve."

"No, they don't!"

"Excuse me?"

"Well, not you and Brady anyway."

"Emily, I honestly don't know what to say right now. You're my friend, my partner. How can you keep defending him?"

"He's a good man and you know it. You should at least give him the benefit of the doubt...don't you think?"

"No, I don't. I saw it with my own eyes. He's been lying to me since I met him. He's a con man!"

"I'm sorry, but I just can't—"

"I'm going to the hospital to be with Samantha. I beg of you...please don't speak to me about Brady Owens again. And I don't care how you do it, but go make things right with Mrs. Bennington. She doesn't deserve your disrespect, and neither do I." Sophie's departure from her normal sweet disposition left Emily bewildered as she stood there amongst the powder, not knowing whether to be upset by it or proud.

"Fine," Emily said to the closed door through which Sophie had just exited. Then she whispered, "But I won't like it."

Before long, the sugar was vacuumed up and wiped down and her winter castle was complete. Glancing at the time, Emily picked up the phone to call Grounds. Jillian answered in a singsongy voice that made Emily want to cringe.

"Jillian, it's Emily Vassure. Can you just reply yes and leave it at that if Mrs. Bennington is there for her afternoon tea with the ladies?"

"Yes, she is. She's right here. Would you like me to get her for you?"

"Jillian...just a yes was all I needed. Would you please let me know if she leaves? I'm on my way there now and I'd like to see her."

"Oh, sure thing. Easy peasy. I can keep her here if you'd like?"

"Please don't. Please don't say anything or do anything. I'll be there in five." Emily collected a variety of pastries from the case and arranged them on a platter, then went to the floral fridge and picked a few yellow roses—*Friendship...crap. I hope that's what they frickin' mean anyway*—and placed them on the tray for an added touch. *Can't hurt.*

. . .

Emily saw Jillian inside with a big wide grin as she approached. "Good Lord," she said under her breath before pushing the door open. She could see Margo Bennington's back, too, as one of the hens stopped talking and looked up. At that, all the other ladies looked in Emily's direction. Then, Mrs. Bennington turned. Emily had never seen the hens this quiet. She could hear every creak in the wooden floorboards as she meandered through the tables and chairs until she reached their table.

"Mrs. Bennington, ladies." She nodded. "Would you please accept my deepest apology for my actions the other day? I was rude and out of line." She set the tray of goodies down between them. No one spoke for what seemed like an eternity. All eyes turned to Mrs. Bennington to await her response.

"Mini whoopie pies. Are they the maple or vanilla centers?" Mrs. Bennington asked with her gaze fixed on the treats.

"Maple, of course. I know how much you like them."

"Apology accepted."

Emily breathed a sigh of relief, not even realizing that she'd been holding her breath. "Thank you."

"Emily, I'd like you to pass on a message for me, if you will." She was acting as if nothing had ever happened between them.

"Um, sure."

"I'd like you to let Mr. Owens know that he'll be getting a call from me this afternoon. My Penelope is with child, and I'd like him to take some announcement photos. I'll be setting a date and time for the next day or two. I'm sure he can arrange his schedule accordingly."

"I'll be sure to let him know, but he's—"

"No excuses. This is far too important. Regardless of his imperfections as a man, I want the best photographer for my Penelope. I'm sure you understand...don't you, Emily?"

"Understood. I'll let him know right away."

"Oh, and do give dear, dear Sophie and her blessed baby girl our best."

"Of course. Well, enjoy the treats, and we'll see you soon," Emily said before backing away from the table, bumping a couple of chairs that had shifted into her path, and catching her foot in a coat hem. "Sorry," she said sheepishly, thankful when she'd finally reached the door to escape. Jillian yelled goodbye with an overly enthusiastic wave.

Well, that royally sucked, she thought as she rang Brady's cell. "So, this thing just happened," she said, not waiting for him to say hello. "You have another job and you can't say no."

"No. Emily, you know I can't."

"I said you can't say no, Brady."

"And yet I just did."

"It's for Sophie. Well, for Proposals really, but also for Sophie."

"What is it?" He sighed.

"You have to take baby announcement pictures of Penelope what's-her-name."

"I'm up to my armpits in shit right now and you want me to take a gig with Penelope Ashworth? What the hell does this have to do with Sophie?"

"I promised her that I'd get Mrs. Bennington back in our good graces."

"What did you do this time?"

"Nothing! Okay, maybe something, but I really need you to make this happen...please?"

"Fine, but it's for Sophie."

"You're the best. So, what's the shitshow that you're in?"

Brady explained the predicament regarding Elizabeth Lockwood and his non-plan as Sophie's number rang in.

"I gotta put you on hold," Emily said in haste. "Sophie's calling, and she's with the baby." She tapped to put Brady on hold, and Sophie's excited voice chimed in.

"She gets to go home, Emily! I'm going to be here for a few more hours until they get everything squared away, but she's going home!" Emily broke down in tears as she put the car back into park; sobbing was more like it.

"I'm so happy for you, Soph...so damn happy."

"Can you believe it? Do you think that you can get a fire going and turn up the heat a little? I don't want her to be cold. Oh, and turn on her wet wipes container so those will be warm, too?"

Emily was thrilled to hear Sophie so happy. It made everything else wash away. Her joy was contagious.

"Sure will, little momma. But, what's a wet wipes container?"

"Seriously? It's a...never mind, I'll take care of that. See you soon!" She disconnected and switched back to her other line.

"Brady, she's coming home!"

Brady, a bit confused, said, "But she's already been home."

"No, not Sophie. The baby! She's coming home!"

"That's really great news, Emily...really great."

Emily picked up his sad tone. "I'm sorry, Brady, truly."

"So am I, Em...so am I."

Chapter 43

Sophie watched and listened carefully as she was instructed on how the car seat worked and how to put Samantha in it securely. She was giddy with excitement, yet terrified at the same time, not quite believing that this was real.

"She's so tiny in that seat. Are you sure she's safe?"

"The seats always look huge with newborns. She's safe and snug."

"It seems so strange that I just get to leave here with her."

"She's yours, Sophie, all yours."

"But, am I ready? I don't know how to—"

"You're her momma and you will be great, I'm sure of it. Look how you've been with her so far. You've shown her love and care, and that's all any little one needs."

"Sure, but you're all here too and—"

"You don't need us anymore and, more importantly, neither does she."

Sophie gave hugs goodbye, then got into the car with her little Samantha Rose. "We're going home, my little one. Oh, you're going to love your room; it's magical and beautiful."

Sophie drove home under the speed limit and took every corner cautiously, fully aware of the precious cargo that she carried. Pulling into the drive, she saw pink balloons on the mailbox and then a huge banner over the door that read *Welcome home, Samantha Rose*, with a border of pink hearts and roses.

Emily and Rebecca cheered with excitement and ran to the car to help. Rebecca shared her congratulations and ran back inside the shop to work. Inside, the fire was going, which cast a warm glow across the room, and hot chocolate was being kept warm on the stove. *We're home*, Sophie thought as she took in the moment. "Em, if you wouldn't mind, I think I'd like to take her upstairs to show her the nursery by myself."

"Of course. If you need anything, anything at all, you'll let me know. Right?"

"You bet." Sophie leaned in for a hug. Emily gave Samantha a peck on the forehead and left them to themselves.

Sophie set the carrier on the counter, removed the knit blanket and held Samantha in her arms, taking in the smell of her baby. Daisy jumped up to see the creature that had just invaded their home.

"This is Samantha. She's your baby. Samantha, this is Daisy, your kitty." She gave Daisy a little time to get acquainted. "You will love her just as much as I do someday, girl. I promise. What do you say we show her the nursery?"

Sophie walked gingerly up the stairs. She could see that Emily had turned on the light, and as she got closer, she heard music playing. Brahms' Lullaby was just beginning.

"This is one of my favorites, my little rosebud."

Sophie sat in the rocker, rocked in rhythm to the lullaby and sang along softly.

Lullaby, and good night
With pink roses bedight
With lilies o'er spread
Is my baby's sweet head
Lay you down now, and rest
May your slumber be blessed.

Lullaby, and good night
You're your mother's delight
Shining angels beside
My darling abide
Soft and warm is your bed
Close your eyes and rest your head.

Sleepyhead, close your eyes
Mother's right here beside you
I'll protect you from harm
You will wake in my arms
Guardian angels are near
So sleep on, with no fear.

As she sang, Sophie traced every curve of her face and stroked her fine strawberry-blond hair. Then Samantha's tiny finger wrapped around her index finger until her little bundle of joy drifted off to sleep. Sophie didn't want to move, not because she didn't want to wake her, but simply because she wanted time to stand still. She was utterly and completely happy. In this moment, she felt joy.

. . .

Over the next couple of days, Sophie found a rhythm. The routine was going according to plan, which was an unexpected pleasure. So, when Mrs. Bennington arrived with Penelope for her photo shoot, she felt comfortable enough to step over to the barn to say hello. Of course, it took some begging from Emily to convince her that it was the right thing to do, regardless of Brady's presence. Fences needed mending with Mrs. Bennington, and Sophie's appearance was necessary.

For the first time since before Samantha had been born, Sophie decided to do her hair and makeup properly. She picked something out of the closet that wasn't maternity but was still roomy enough for comfort. She chose a green knit tunic with brown leggings, threw on a scarf, stuffed her feet into her boots, and called it a day.

The timing couldn't have been more perfect, with it being naptime. Sophie turned on the baby monitor, then headed toward the barn. Taking a slow pace, she could hear Margo Bennington kibitzing about everything and everyone under the sun to Brady. Just before Sophie stepped inside, she heard a hushed version of, "How tragic for Sophie, what that poor girl has been through. Of course, I don't need to tell you, now do I? I understand that your lover came for a visit. That must have been embarrassing for you."

"Mother!" snapped Penelope. "I am so sorry, Mr. Owens. Sometimes my mother just doesn't think before she talks."

Sophie stood outside the door to listen, darn well knowing she shouldn't but wanting to hear how Brady would respond.

Brady didn't miss a beat. "So, Penelope, I was thinking that the fireplace area would be nice. You said that your husband was bringing a banner to drape or hold? Maybe we could drape it on the mantel. Would you like that?"

"Yes, that would be perfect. He should be here any minute. He's coming from work and he got held up."

Sophie felt a pang of disappointment, wishing he'd flat out denied Mrs. Bennington's statement. She opened the door to greet the guests, but before she could get a word in, Margo burst out with, "Well, there she is! You hardly look like you've had a baby at all! Just a bit of a tummy now. Would you look at that, Penelope? If Sophie can look this good, imagine how you'll bounce back!"

Penelope rolled her eyes.

"You disappoint me, Sophie," Margo blurted.

"I'm sorry?"

"You didn't bring the baby with you. We've been dying to see her."

"She's napping right now, Mrs. Bennington. Maybe if she wakes before you leave, I can introduce you."

"That would be simply wonderful. Wouldn't it, Penelope, dear?"

"Yes, Mother, it would. But right now, we really should let Mr. Owens get back to work."

"Well, then," said Brady, "why don't we do some shots of the mom-to-be so I can test the lighting?" Sophie recalled when Brady had looked at her through the lens when she was expecting and tried to shake off the memory.

Margo Bennington didn't shut her mouth for what seemed an eternity, and Sophie was grateful. There would be no awkward silence and glances between her and Brady with Margo droning on and on. Sophie pulled up a chair as a headache began to pound.

Finally, Penelope's husband showed up to fully get the show on the road. Margo had to put in her two cents with every decision Brady made. "Penelope, turn to your left side. That's your better side. Don't you agree, Brady?" On and on it went until Sophie couldn't take it anymore. Between Mrs. Bennington's loud voice and hearing Brady's name continually, she'd had enough.

"Mrs. Bennington, I hate to interrupt, and I hope you don't mind, but I really must get back inside. Samantha should be waking anytime now."

"Of course, dear. We'll be just fine. You go right on ahead."

Sophie escaped the chaos. Her head was indeed pounding, and now she needed a nap, which was unfortunate as Samantha would be awake any minute. Walking past the shop, she silently cursed Emily for having chosen this time to run errands. A shadow caught her attention on the porch.

"Daisy, what on earth are you doing out here? I'm sorry, girl, you must have followed me out." Sophie picked her up and stroked her fur. "Let's get you inside and warmed up."

Daisy jumped out of her arms the second the door opened, then bounded through the house and up the stairs.

"Don't you wake the baby, Daisy."

Pulling off her boots was exhausting. For that matter, getting dressed at all was exhausting. She added a log to the fire and plopped down on the couch before drifting off to sleep for what seemed like a minute before Samantha's cries woke her. She gave herself a few quick slaps on the cheeks and shook her head to snap out of her haze. Still barely opening her eyes, she slowly ascended the stairs.

"I'm coming, baby girl."

Samantha lay in her bassinet, but something didn't seem right. She was no longer swaddled. She was just lying on top of her receiving blanket. *That's odd.* Leaning in, she picked Samantha up. *Even your stuffed animals look in disarray.*

And that's when she saw it. It was pinned to the receiving blanket, which was directly underneath where Samantha had been lying. A note. Sophie turned the light up to bright, then peered into the bassinet to read it.

You can't have what is mine.

Sophie began to shake, and bile reached her throat. With a panic, she held Samantha tighter and frantically ran around the room, looking for who could have done this, her eyes wide and heart racing as her panic increased. She was hyperventilating and feared she'd drop Samantha if she passed out. Sophie wanted to run for help but wasn't steady on her feet in her state. *Just sit down, Soph. Collect your breath and then go get help.* She took a few long, deep breaths in and out, clinging onto Samantha for dear life.

That was when she remembered that she'd left the baby monitor in the barn. Hopefully, if she yelled loudly enough into the stationary one, they would hear her, even if Margo Bennington was still flapping her gums.

"Help! I need your help!" Brady instinctively came to her mind, and without hesitation she shouted his name. "Brady, please, I need your help!"

By now, between Sophie's anxiety, the yelling, and mere hunger, Samantha wailed. Sophie heard Brady burst through the kitchen door and bound up the stairs three at a time. He was breathless when he saw them. Sophie was shaking uncontrollably, pale, and unable to speak.

"Is it the baby? Are you hurt?" Brady scooched down next to Sophie and took her hand. "It's okay, I'm here. Look at me, Sophie, and take a breath." Sophie obliged. "Good, now take another one and let it out nice and slow...great. Can you tell me what's wrong?" Sophie pointed to the bassinet.

"Don't pick it up!" Sophie protested.

A confused look crossed his face until he looked inside to see the note. "I won't, at least not until after the police can see this. Do you have your phone with you?"

"No, I left it downstairs."

"I'm going to call 911, and then I want you to stay right where you are. I'm going to take a look around."

"It was her, wasn't it?"

"I expect so." He opened the closet door to peer inside. "Promise me that you'll stay where you are. I'll be right back."

Sophie nodded in agreement, clinging on to Samantha.

. . .

Brady moved quietly from one room to the next, looking under beds, behind curtains, and anywhere else Cynthia Lockwood could be lurking. He crept down the stairs and looked through the den and the living room. He was working his way to the kitchen when he heard a loud bang, followed by several others that rattled the back door.

"Mr. Owens! Is everything okay? Mr. Owens!" Brady flung the door open to face Margo, Penelope, and her husband. "Well, thank God you answered. We're very concerned...is everything all right?"

"Yes...well, not really...but yes," Brady said in a rushed tone. "Sophie and the baby are fine, though. I think I got everything that I needed for the photo shoot, so it might be best if you head out now. I'll call you when the proofs are ready, okay?"

"Sure thing," Penelope said. "We'll get going."

Sirens screamed louder and louder, and then two cruisers raced up the driveway and screeched to a halt. Margo Bennington would need to be dragged out kicking and screaming before she'd leave now, Brady thought with regret. This would be the talk of the town with Margo Bennington in earshot. However, better to have her know what had happened than speculate, and then God only knew what turn her story would take. Besides, he thought, Penelope's husband, James Ashworth, had arrived late. He might have seen something. So, Brady invited them into the kitchen and decided he'd fill them all in at the same time.

Seeing the officers on their radios, Brady quickly excused himself to let Sophie know what was happening. Walking into the nursery made his heart skip a beat. Sophie was nursing the baby; they had both calmed, to his relief. She looked up to see Brady standing in the door frame. She motioned that she was okay, and he nodded in understanding. He bounded down the stairs in order to be there just as the officers got to the door.

Brady was relieved that they were the same officers that had been there before, which saved some time; he was anxious for them to track her down. James hadn't noticed any vehicles in the driveway besides the ones that were currently there.

"She must have walked from nearby," he added. "I can look around to see if I can track some footsteps. The recent snow should make it pretty easy if she did in fact walk."

"I tell you what," said the ranking officer. "I'll go look around upstairs, and you and my partner here can walk the perimeter. Sound good?"

"Sounds good." James suggested that Penelope and her mother head home. He'd be sure to fill them in after confirming that it would be okay with Brady. Margo Bennington was just about swooning as she was escorted to her car.

"Poor, poor dear."

Brady and the other officer approached the nursery. Samantha had just finished feeding and seemed content. Sophie lay her in the crib, then joined them by the bassinet. The officer went through a litany of procedures. Fingerprinting, photos, bagging the note, checking windows and doors for points of entry. Sophie kept her distance to allow the officer to work as Brady followed every step, adding comments and suggestions. Close to an hour passed before the two officers met up.

"Well, we found some footprints that stood out to us beyond the other side of the drive. There was a path in the tree line that led to the neighbor's yard."

Sophie chimed in. "That would be the Templetons' place. There's a path there that we take back and forth when we visit." One of the officers wrote down the Templetons' names. "They're senior citizens, a wonderful couple that I've been friends with since we moved here. Maybe the footprints were one of theirs. I'll ask my partner if either of them came over for a treat today." Then she hesitated. "Wait a minute. Come to think of it, they've been out of town. They've been visiting a niece down south for the holidays."

"The place must have appeared empty. No lights on, unplowed driveway, no tire tracks perhaps. We'll check it out as we head out." Making sure that they hadn't missed anything, the officers compared notes, then headed out the door.

Sophie had been quiet through the whole ordeal once

the officers had arrived, with the exception of the mention of the Templetons, and now she remained quiet. The only sound Brady could hear was the crackling of the fire. He couldn't help but notice that she hadn't made any eye contact with him either.

"Sophie, I don't know what to say except that I'm sorry. I had absolutely no idea that she was capable of anything like this." She refused to look at him. "Sophie, please hear me out—"

"No. I will not hear you out. You have put me and my baby in danger. I don't know what kind of game you're playing. For all I know, you're in this together. I don't trust you, Brady, which breaks my heart."

"I would never—"

"You would never what? Lie to me, deceive me, not tell me that your lover is the woman that killed my husband and destroyed my life! Is that what you're trying to tell me you would never do? Well, can you deny any of that?"

"No, but—"

"No?"

"That's not what I meant. I mean, yes, it is, but not really. She's my ex-lover from way before I met you. I didn't know who you were until—"

"Until when? A week after we met? A month? A month ago? When, Brady?"

Brady hesitated, knowing that he couldn't lie, but not wanting to make things worse. "A few weeks after, maybe it was a couple, but I can explain—"

"Oh my God. All this time you knew and didn't say anything? Get out, Brady!" She gave him a shove. He stood his ground. "I said, get out!"

"I'm not leaving, Sophie. An insane woman is out there, and I'm not going to leave you alone. Not until she's caught and behind bars."

Sophie stopped pushing at his chest as the reality set in. "She was in my home, in my baby's room. She picked her up, Brady. That crazy woman picked her up." Sophie began to sob. Brady grabbed her and held her in his arms. She sobbed until no more tears would come. "I'm so mad at you, Brady Owens."

"I know, and you have every right to be."

"You're damn right I do." She pounded him one more time on the chest for good measure.

Samantha began to stir and within moments was crying up a storm. "I never changed her diaper earlier. I'm sure she's wet and—"

"I'll tell you what. If it's okay with you, why don't you go lie down and take a nap, and I'll take care of the diaper changing?"

"I couldn't ask you to do that."

"Sure you could. Believe it or not, I know how to change a diaper. Besides, I'd like to introduce myself to her; we haven't officially met."

"Sleep does sound amazing...but it doesn't change anything. I'm still unbelievably angry with you. But I'm more scared of that crazy woman. You can stay and I'll take a short nap, but after I wake up, I'm calling Emily. When she gets here, you'll have to leave."

"Whatever you say."

"Fine," she said with her hands on her hips, looking up to read his expression.

"You don't seem like you mean fine."

Sophie lingered, fidgeting with her hands and pacing.

"I thought you were going to take a nap."

"I am."

"Then go! I've got this."

"Are you absolutely sure you can change a diaper? It's really kind of—"

"Yes, I'll be fine." He pointed to the stairs. "Go! Poor little thing's up there crying, and I need to change a diaper." As she walked away, he patted her on the behind. She swung around, ready to take a swipe. "Sorry...habit," he said with a wince.

Brady crossed the threshold into the whimsical world of *The Secret Garden.* He crept up to Samantha and gazed down at her. He scooped her up and held her with both arms in front of him so that he could take her in fully.

"Well, look at you. Aren't you just perfect? You look like your momma."

He carefully brought her to the changing table and gently went through the process of cleaning her up. She'd had a bit of a blowout, so a complete change was necessary. Feeling accomplished, only having gagged a couple of times, he sat down with her in the rocker. When she began to fuss, they strolled around the room.

"This is a picture that I took of your mommy before you were born. Now this over here is called an arbor. See all the pretty flowers?" Then, pointing to the wallpaper, he said, "Those flowers are called roses, but you're the prettiest one of all. Your mommy sure named you well, Samantha Rose." He turned the mobile on and hummed along to the tune as they did a little waltz around the room.

. . .

Sophie lay quietly in bed. Brady hadn't realized that she also had a monitor on her nightstand. She had heard everything, every single adorable moment of it. *How could such a good man be such a jackass at the same time?* she wondered. But she was still determined to follow through on her wish for him to be out of her life. She convinced herself that this lapse of judgment on her part was simply unavoidable given the immediate situation.

CHAPTER 44

Brady watched as Emily pulled up into the drive and proceeded to unload the car. Around the third load back inside, he surprised her when he stood just inside the door, holding a wrapped-up Samantha in his arms.

"Well, well," she said with her typical smirk. "Do tell."

"Absolutely, but first things first. Samantha should be ready to eat any minute, and Sophie's finally getting a good sleep in. Do you know where she keeps the formula?"

"She doesn't," Emily said while unpacking her supplies. "She gets the all-natural stuff."

"Come again?"

"Breast milk. She keeps some in the freezer in little pouches."

"Come again?" Brady's said as his face contorted with confusion.

"It's okay, Brady. Jeesh, you look like you've never heard of breast milk before. I'll show you how to get it ready."

"It's not that…you can buy it in little pouches?"

"Oh, for Pete's sake. It's hers." He was still confused. "She uses a breast pump, then puts it in little bags and freezes it."

"My niece used formula when she was a baby…at least I think it was." Right about that time, Samantha started to stir. "Let's do this thing, shall we?"

Emily walked him through the steps of thawing out the milk and pouring it into the Playtex sheets that lined the bottle. She handed the bottle to Brady, and he popped it into Samantha's tiny mouth.

"I'm still waiting," Emily said with her hands on her hips.

"Oh, right…of course."

Brady relayed what had taken place over the past several hours. Emily sat wide-eyed with her hand over her mouth.

"She could have abducted her, Brady!" she finally said, sounding horrified.

"But she didn't."

"But she could have. You have to wonder, was she referring to you or Samantha in the note? *You can't have what is mine.* Brady, this scares me to death," Emily whispered. "What do we do?"

"I don't know, Em. I was making headway, real headway, in getting her and her father behind bars, but it all fell through. Somehow, we have to prove that it was Cynthia who was here and wrote that note and broke her parole. The police found some tire tracks and boot prints, but who knows if it will be enough? I wish we could have caught her here."

"But we did catch her here before."

"We can't prove it, though. It's our word against hers, and she's got powerful people behind her." Emily slammed both hands down on the counter with so much force that Brady jumped and the baby began to cry. "What the hell, Em?"

"Follow me," she said with determination and purpose. Brady was intrigued and followed dutifully. The brisk walk to the back office of Proposals lulled Samantha back to sleep. Emily opened up her computer and clicked on a security system icon.

"You have surveillance cameras," he said, stunned.

"Yes, but just for inside the shop. Not outside and not in the main house. But—"

"We might have proof of when she was here before!"

"I don't know why I didn't think of this until now. We never look at the stupid thing. Never had a reason to, really, and I forgot all about it," Emily said excitedly. She clicked on the timelines from when Cynthia had her appointment with Rebecca. "When was that, Brady? I can't find it!"

"The day Samantha was born."

"Right!" She was scrolling when Sophie walked up behind them.

"What's going on? I heard a loud bang and Samantha was crying. Why didn't you wake me, Brady? Samantha's missed her feeding, and I told you I wanted you gone when Emily got home and—"

"I didn't want to wake you. You've been sleep-deprived. Emily helped me with the feeding, and I've been updating her on what took place."

"Oh," she said with a nod of understanding.

Emily shouted, "I found it!"

"What?" Sophie asked as she took Samantha from Brady's arms.

"Just watch." Emily played the recording of the entire event, including Sophie's collapse and Brady's tirade against Cynthia Lockwood.

Brady grabbed Emily, picked her up, and twirled her around. "You did it, Emily! We've got her."

"Okay, okay...put me down. We're going to break something...I have motion sickness...seriously, put me down." Brady obliged. Emily rested her hands on her thighs to steady herself. "I get your excitement, Brady. I really do. It still doesn't give us proof that she was here today, though."

"But it's a start to putting that woman away for a very long time," Brady said, reeling from the realization of actual proof. "Can we send this to Stevens?"

"Sure, but shouldn't we just send it to the police?"

"Not yet. Don't you see? She wears an ankle monitor, right?"

"Yes," Emily replied.

"Exactly. So how is it that she can make it all the way to Maine from New York and not have her parole officer know about it?"

"Her father!" exclaimed Emily.

"He pulls the strings, and we've known that for a long time. We've got to figure out a way to put all the pieces together with some proof, but how?" Without skipping a beat, Emily and Brady stated the obvious. "Mrs. Lockwood." Their enthusiasm and collaboration were suddenly halted.

"Hello. Am I invisible? I'm standing right here," Sophie said in exasperation. They looked at her as if seeing her for the first time. "How long have you known about this, Emily?"

"Umm..."

"You were both in on... whatever this is together?"

"Well, I...umm."

Brady spoke up. "It's not her fault. I convinced her because I thought it was what was best."

"Oh, really. And you know what's best for me?" She pursed her lips and closed her eyes as if contemplating whether to allow them to live or die. "You mean to tell me that the two people that I've trusted most in this world have been in cahoots, behind my back, and that was supposed to be good for me?"

Emily jumped in. "I thought he was having an affair, but it turned out that he was going to New York and meeting with Cynthia Lockwood so that she would go back to prison. Oh, and her father, too!"

"Oh, well now, that makes perfect sense, now doesn't it?" Sophie looked at the two of them like they were idiots. "If it was all so innocent, then why didn't you just tell me?"

Brady ran his hand through his hair. "Because I love you, Sophie. I knew that I screwed up by not telling you right away when I realized who you were. I didn't seek you out. Don't you see? We simply met. Me in a broken-down boat and you helping me out. It was chance, Sophie—pure and simple. I thought I recognized you from somewhere, but I couldn't place it, at least not right away. By the time I put two and two together, I didn't know how to tell you. I wanted to fix everything first and then tell you—for my own guilt, I guess, not because it was the right thing to do. It was the right thing to do, but more importantly, I wanted to do it because I'd fallen in love with you. Like Emily said, the only reason she knew what was going on was because she thought I was having an affair, and I couldn't have that."

Emily stood back, holding her breath with her hands covering her mouth as if in prayer. Brady just stood there with a firm jaw, head up, and hands to his side, facing Sophie. His heart was racing, and he concentrated on slowing his breathing.

Sophie replied, "What's the next move? How do we throw that murderous crazy woman back in prison?" Emily threw a punch up into the air in victory. "Oh, no, you don't, Emily. There is no victory here," Sophie said sternly, then reached out and took Brady by the shoulders.

"I'm still angry with you, you know."

"I understand, but can you forgive me?" He waited patiently for her response.

"Maybe," she replied, "but I'm counting on you. Please don't let me down again."

The word *again* stung as Brady replied, "I'll take a maybe."

CHAPTER 45

Christmas came and went with Brady still on thin ice. Sophie was distant, which was more than he had hoped for considering the circumstances. What was discouraging him the most was that there was still no real evidence that could prove Cynthia Lockwood's presence in Sophie's home. The tire tracks matched thousands of other tires, and there hadn't been enough detail in the tread marks in the snow to pinpoint what automobile they belonged to. Even if they could, Henry Lockwood would be damned if they could access any of his vehicles to test them. A warrant would be impossible to obtain without any kind of actual proof. Her boot prints ran into the same wall. There were no fingerprints to be found, and they presumed that she'd been wearing gloves. The only real evidence they had was from her previous visit—the recording.

Brady took a walk to clear his head. Before he knew it, he was stepping through the doors of Grounds. Jillian was obviously happy to see him. She greeted him with a "Happy

New Year" and an ear-to-ear smile. She brought him his coffee and pulled out a chair.

"Have you caught her yet?" she blared.

"Not yet, but I will," he said, trying to convince himself.

"When Mrs. Bennington and Penelope came here that night and told us what happened, I couldn't believe it! I can't imagine how scared Sophie must have been. Thank goodness you were there with her," she continued. "And to think that she'd been here that very day, asking about Sophie and the baby. I would have never guessed that—"

"Excuse me? What did you just say?"

"What? What did I say?"

"Exactly, Jillian. What did you just say?" Brady shouted, which caused Jillian to tense up and not say a word. "I'm sorry, I didn't mean to snap at you. Did you say that Cynthia Lockwood was here, in this very coffee shop, *that day?*" Jillian nodded her head up and down. "What did she say about Sophie and the baby exactly?"

"Umm, something like, how happy she was to hear about the baby being born and that she'd been worried about Sophie's health. She seemed genuinely concerned."

"Go on."

"Well, she asked if I knew when they'd be going home. I told her that they were already home. She was so excited to hear that."

"I bet she was. Continue, please."

"Brady, if I'd known who she was—goodness, I thought she was a *really* good friend of yours."

"She wasn't. Go on," he said with some impatience.

"Anyway, she hoped that the neighbors had been bringing meals. She said that was the polite thing to do, but I told her that the Templetons had been away and would be until after the New Year. Now that I think of it, I bet she already knew that they weren't home. Oh my, I never should have told her that, but I had no idea. She seemed so nice. Brady, I'm so sorry. If there's anything that I can do—"

"Actually, Jillian, you've just done a whole lot." He stood up, gave her a kiss on the cheek, and dug his hand in his pocket and pulled out a couple dollars.

"Oh, please. It's on the house."

"Thanks." He ran out the door and was back at Proposals within a few minutes, winded as the icy air left his lungs. He drew in a few more deep breathes, then searched around and found Rebecca. "Where are they?"

"In the house, they're—" Before she could finish, he sprinted toward the door. "Having lunch," she said with a shake of her head.

Sophie and Emily were gooing over Samantha's newest expression when Brady came busting into the room. "We have a witness!" They both stared with shocked looks on their faces. "Jillian talked with Cynthia that day!" He continued to fill them in on the details. "Emily, can you go to the police department and drop off one of the thumb drives with the recording on it, and then have them stop in to talk with Jillian? Oh, and I need a copy of the recording as well."

"Sure thing." She was still seated and waiting for more. Brady gestured for her to get up. "Right now? You can be so demanding," she said, winking at Sophie.

"Why aren't you going?" Sophie asked Brady.

"I'm going to pay a visit to Mrs. Elizabeth Lockwood."

. . .

It was a remarkably clear afternoon. He'd make it to New York by dinnertime. Elizabeth, with some coaxing, agreed to meet him at the same restaurant they'd met at previously. Brady ran his persuasive request over and over in his head a million times by the time he'd pulled into the underground parking at Un-wined & Dine.

After taking the stairs two at a time, he stepped out into the crisp air. As he turned the corner, he could see through the window that Elizabeth Lockwood already had a half-empty glass of wine. Her hands tapped on the rim of her glass as she fixated on the entry door.

Brady stepped through with confidence. He nodded and motioned to the maître d' that he was all set. He removed his coat and then hung it on the brass hook next to Elizabeth's. She didn't get up and didn't say a word.

"It's good to see you, Elizabeth," he said in a calm, reassuring tone. Elizabeth took a swig, swished it around in her mouth, and then nodded. "I suppose you're wondering why I asked to meet you. I wanted to give you something very valuable." He took the thumb drive out of his pocket and slid it across the table. Elizabeth inhaled, then looked into Brady's eyes. Brady stood his ground and didn't speak. He hoped she'd be the first to crack.

Mrs. Lockwood took another swig to finish it off. Her hand flew up in the air with a snap. The server scurried to refill her glass, then asked if Brady would like anything. Brady didn't speak. He just shook his head no, keeping eye contact with Elizabeth.

Elizabeth picked up the thumb drive, turned it over in

her hand once or twice, then balked. She squirmed a bit in her chair, then rolled her eyes to the ceiling. "Okay, I'll bite. What is it?"

"Proof."

"Oh, really. Proof of what?"

"That, Elizabeth, will get you off the hook from having anything to do with Cynthia's bad decisions." Her eyes perked up. "You need to know that the police have the same thing that you now do, and there's more."

"I'm listening," she said with anticipation.

"Are you still in? Can I count on you to do the right thing for Sophie Anderson and for your law firm?"

Elizabeth took her time to reply. "It depends." Then she went silent.

"Okay." *It's my turn to bite.* "It depends on what?" Brady asked sternly.

"I need to be one hundred percent sure that I will be protected from liability for any wrongdoing. I want immunity."

"I can't promise you that, nor can I grant that. I'm only a witness, just like you. That being said, if you weren't a part of anything, then you have nothing to worry about."

"What else do you have?"

Brady still wasn't sure he could trust her. "It can wait, but I assure you that you'll find out soon enough, and when you do, you'll know it will be time to do the right thing."

"I'm not sure I understand."

"Trust me, you will. For now, watch the video on the thumb drive and think about it."

"Fair enough." With that, Elizabeth Lockwood stood up and grabbed her coat. "I trust you'll pay the tab." She walked out.

. . .

The York Police Department notified the New York authorities about the situation. Within a couple of days, the FBI jumped in, with enough probable cause to justify obtaining a search warrant of Cynthia Lockwood's home, vehicle, and person. As luck would have it, her tires' tread matched part of the tracks found in the snow, and a notepad was obtained from her purse that matched the note left under Samantha Rose. There was no doubt that Cynthia Lockwood would be heading right back to prison.

Elizabeth Lockwood now knew what Brady Owens had meant. She would not have to be responsible for sending her daughter back to prison; Cynthia had done that all by herself.

While Cynthia was being taken away in handcuffs, Lockwood looked on as she shouted, "Daddy, I didn't do anything! You have to help me!"

Elizabeth Lockwood looked at Henry, then turned and ran upstairs toward her room, crying. She left the door open, and her crying continued until Henry followed.

"Henry, you have to stop this," she cried. "Do something!"

Henry was visibly taken aback by the emotion that Elizabeth was displaying. He handed her the glass of whiskey that he held in his hand and sat on the duvet next to her.

"I don't know what I can do, Liz. I've done all I can already."

"But you got her free the last time. Why can't you just do it again?"

"It's different this time."

"Why, why is it any different? Shouldn't it be easier this time? For God's sake, the last time she killed someone. This time all she did was cross state lines and try to plan a wedding."

"I've played all my cards already, Liz. There's no way that anyone will stick their necks out again. It's too risky."

"I don't understand. You're friends with the governor, for God's sake. You must be able to do something!"

"And he already did something, and so did the parole board."

"Okay, then. Have them just do it again," Elizabeth pleaded, clinging to Lockwood in desperation. "Just give him more money...anything! Our baby can't stay in prison, Henry! Why don't you tell me what you did before? Then we can brainstorm together. I can't have the reputation of my father's law firm destroyed, and we certainly can't have our baby locked away for God knows how long."

Henry told her everything—how he'd made huge contributions, both public and undisclosed, to Palermo's gubernatorial campaigns in the past and pledged to give big to his Senate campaign—effectively buying him. The governor needed to appoint a new attorney general before his term ended, and Lockwood had his heart set on being just that, the new attorney general. Then, Governor Palermo had positioned two new parole board members, Denning and Barrows, and replaced the chairman in order to secure her release.

When Charles Denning and Julie Barrows were working at Palermo's office when he was a district attorney, apparently, he'd caught them having an affair in the office. They were both married and begged him not to fire them and create a scandal with their spouses. Palermo didn't really care one way or the other, but he kept this secret to use as leverage someday when he needed a favor. Well, someday had come with the imprisonment of Cynthia Lockwood. All Denning and Barrows needed in order to secure a release was for Cynthia to be vouched for, and Lockwood had provided plenty of cash to bribe the warden and one of the guards to accomplish that. Elizabeth Lockwood sat quietly, listening to the entire confession.

"You did all that for our little girl? How come you never told me?"

"I didn't want to trouble you with any of it, my dear. I had it all under control until now. But you leave it to me. I'll figure something out. Don't you worry your little head."

Elizabeth laid her head on his shoulder as he stroked the hair away from her eyes.

"Everything will work out, Henry. You just wait and see," she said with a smile across her face, which Lockwood couldn't see.

. . .

That evening, Elizabeth Lockwood took a drive to a scotch bar in Midtown. Stevens sat at the bar, adding a drip of water to his glass of Talisker, when Elizabeth pulled up a stool beside him. "Stevens," she said in a whisper.

"Hello, Mrs. Lockwood. Brady said you wanted to meet me."

"I have something for you." She then slid a recording device across the bar. Stevens met her hand to retrieve it. "I think it should be everything that you need." She walked away.

Epilogue

It was April by the time all the trials had ended. Cynthia Lockwood had already been back behind bars for quite a while by the time her father was put on trial.

Henry Lockwood was sentenced to prison for bribery, fraud, and racketeering, as well as a handful of other charges. He'd also lost his law license. Elizabeth Lockwood had filed for divorce and become the largest stakeholder of her late father's firm. She took up the mantle with vigor to restore its reputation.

Governor Palermo was sentenced for bribery, extortion, and campaign finance law violations before being impeached and removed from office. The two parole board members, the warden, and the prison guard were convicted of lesser charges, but they would still be going away for a long, long time.

Brady looked for Sophie at the close of the final trial; she was nowhere to be found. "Emily, where's Sophie?" he asked, running his hand through his hair.

"She had to leave, Brady."

"But why? I don't understand."

"Oh, sorry. Not for good or anything. She got a text from her mom, saying she'd be waiting out front with Samantha. Sophie just stepped out to meet her."

Sophie stood at the base of the stairs leading out of the courthouse, holding Samantha and a bouquet of daffodils, as Brady exited the building. There were cameras, television crews, and craziness that surrounded them, but that didn't matter, as all they could see was each other. Emily held back the masses with a "no comment" here and a "no comment" there.

When Brady joined Sophie, she was smiling ear to ear. "You did it, Brady. You really did it."

Sophie broke off one of the daffodils and gave it to Samantha to hold, then handed her to Emily. The rest of the daffodils, she handed to Brady. "Daffodils mean a new beginning," she whispered in his ear.

"They also mean love and desire and affection returned," he said with a raspy voice.

"Yes, they do. How did you know?"

"I know because I know you, Sophie Anderson." Brady picked her up and twirled her into the air, then slowly brought her down to meet his lips. Emily let out a cheer as tears of joy rolled down her face; all was right with the world.

THE END

ACKNOWLEDGMENTS

I believe in dreams fulfilled. I have never shied away from a chance to better myself or my circumstances, as scary as it can sometimes be. We all have people around us that can be dream killers, dream fulfillers, or dream instillers. I have been blessed enough to be surrounded by dream instillers: positive people that believe in me and share in my joys, which is a blessing that cannot be measured.

Through the years, I've written drama sketches and published a short story. It wasn't until Lorrie Thomson, an author, walked into my women's boutique that I realized the possibilities of fulfilling my dream of writing a novel. The subject matter for *Hope from Daffodils*, came to me in a dream in the wee hours of the morning and followed me in a morning run. Wedding planning, flower gardens, and the New England seacoast are a few of my favorite things, so it only became natural to incorporate these elements into *Hope from Daffodils*. Thank you, York Harbor Inn, Ships Cellar Pub,

Bagel Basket, Union Coffee, and McCleod's Scottish Pub, for providing inspiration for some of the setting.

A huge thank you to my daughter, Sara, who tirelessly, yet patiently reviewed, provided feedback, and did the initial edits; you are my angel. I'd like to also acknowledge my husband, Michael, for his undying guidance and unwavering support. Additionally, my son, Douglas, and my kids' significant others, who became my living thesaurus and feedback tribe, and provided countless belly laughs during our biweekly family dinner night.

A big hug to Lisa, for listening and providing consistent, emotional support, and helping me with my lack of decision making. My gratitude to the Galucki family for instilling in me the ability to dream big and for their support. A special thank you to my brother, Dan Thornhill, for always being willing to answer my many legal 'what if' questions. Thank you as well to my sister, Kathy, and brother, Doug, for being my cheerleaders.

Additional thanks to the Weare Area Writers Group; ALLi; Sylvie, for your invaluable input; Sheila, for grounding me; Emily, for always saying yes; my editor, Eliza Dee of Clio Editing Services; and my book cover and interior designer, Robin Vuchich of My Custom Book Cover for helping to make this novel a finished work.

Hope *from* Daffodils

A NOVEL

KAREN COULTERS

Karen Coulters On The Book's Setting
York Harbor, Maine

York Harbor, Maine and its surrounding areas of Long Sands and Short Sands beaches have, since I can remember, been a source of comfort and tranquility for me. My siblings were born and raised in Maine, but I was not. I grew up in the small town of Woodsfield, Ohio and would spend summers visiting family members until I moved there in 1981 as a young woman. Fun anecdote, my husband and I kissed for the first time on York Beach...it was salty and wonderful. Anyway...back to why I wrote *Hope from Daffodils* to take place there. Not only does it bring fond memories; it also brings solace from sorrow. I've cried on those beaches numerous times over the years. Even now, I mourn the loss of my brother as I watch the waves lap up on the shore. His remains are of the sea and I feel close to him there.

I can still envision me as a child, running along the beach, digging in the sand, creating castles, and dreaming about what my future might hold. As an adult, the feel of the sand on my feet, along with salty mist upon my skin, and the sweet aroma of roses and lilac in the air; I am grounded in who I have become and who I am yet to be.

The main characters of Sophie and Brady grow from their past, the situations that they find themselves in, their pain, and find peace and purpose within the sights and sounds of York Harbor, much like I have. My hope, is that you too, should you find yourself in sorrow, will find a sense of comfort and hope for your present state and your future. I hope that you will be open to change, be it subtle or drastic, and dream of a new beginning in which you will find joy.

As to the specific locations within the book, there are some that are actual locations and some that were created by inspiration. For example: York Harbor and York Village are real, as well as the Ships Cellar Pub at York Harbor Inn, the Nubble Lighthouse, York Hospital, and sights from downtown Portsmouth, New Hampshire. However, Grounds Coffee Shop, was inspired from both the Bagel Basket of York Village and Union Coffee of Milford, New Hampshire. Proposals was born from the combination of historical architectural designs and landscapes of the New England coast and my imagination. I don't know about you, but I would love to attend a wedding there. The locations within Manhattan, New York, are all from my head; however, there is a scotch bar called Macleod's Scottish Pub in Ballard, WA that inspired the pub that Brady and Stevens met on occasion, and in case you were wondering, Aberlour Scotch Whisky is a nice virgin scotch drinker's scotch.

If you've never been to the coasts of Maine and New Hampshire, I hope that you will add them to your bucket list. Through the area's rich history and beauty, I promise you won't be disappointed.

QUESTIONS AND TOPICS FOR DISCUSSION

1. *Hope from Daffodils* opens with Sophie mourning the death of her husband, Sam. Sophie's feelings of guilt are revealed when she says, in thought, "I'm sorry, Sam." How does this feeling of guilt thread through the story?

2. What role does the symbolism of flowers play over the course of the story?

3. How are Emily and Brady's relationship with Sophie similar and what role do they play in Sophie's wellbeing?

4. Sophie's mother is usually absent from her life. How do you think this absence has affected Sophie's confidence in regard to motherhood? Do you see Sophie as a strong, independent woman or as vulnerable and weak?

5. Shame and perception of others tends to loom in Sophie's mind. Do you think her guilt is justified? Do you approve of, or think it was inappropriate of Sophie and Brady's relationship, being she was as a newly widowed and an expectant mother?

6. Brady ran away from his career, whereas, Sophie dug in deeper. What role did their pasts play in why they made these decisions?

7. Do you think Brady is right to feel guilty about Cynthia's role in Sam's death? When Brady realized the truth of who Sophie was, were you surprised at his response in regard to working on Proposals' expansion? If you were in his shoes, how would you have responded?

8. Sophie and Emily's friendship are a fundamentally based on trust. Brady asks Emily to keep his secret and she decides to keep it; do you agree with this decision? How would you feel if you were in her shoes? How might you have handled it differently?

9. Do you think that Brady was selfish or admirable in his decision to keep the secret from Sophie and including Emily in his deceit? Why? Do you think secrets can be a good thing in certain situations, or do you think honesty is always the best policy?

10. Brady's relationship with Cynthia and the Lockwoods brings out a side to him that he doesn't like. Why do you think he stayed in his relationship with Cynthia and in Lockwood's law firm for as long as he had? Have you ever found yourself in a situation in which you felt stuck but didn't think there was a way out of it?

11. Cynthia was clearly a troubled person. Do you think she was a victim of her upbringing or do you think she would have been manipulative and vengeful, regardless of her upbringing; was it just in her nature?

12. Do you think Elizabeth Lockwood was a good person or a bad person? Did you feel sorry for her? If so, when and where in the story line did you do so? Did you think it was good judgement or wrong for

Brady to involve Elizabeth in exposing her husband and daughter's behavior?

13. Forgiveness and guilt became crucial parts of the characters in *Hope from Daffodils*. Some need to forgive themselves while others need to forgive others. Name moments in the story where forgiveness was key. What role has forgiveness and guilt played in your life? Have these characters helped you to see forgiveness differently?

14. Would you have been so willing to continue a relationship with Brady had you been in Sophie's shoes? Why is it that Sophie can forgive Emily so easily compared to Brady?

15. What character did you connect with the most? If you could meet one of the characters right now, who would you want it to be?

16. In what ways do Brady, Sophie, or Emily change during the course of the book?

17. If you could be transported to any event or location in the book, what location or event would it be?

18. What were your favorite moments in the *Hope from Daffodils*?

19. Are you happy that you chose this book?

Inviting The Author To Your Book Club

Karen loves book clubs and you can invite her to join your book club @ www.KarenCoultersAuthor.com

She may attend personally within a limited geographical area

- Over the phone

- Facetime

- Skype

- Other

Before The Meeting

Contact the author at least a month ahead, if possible, and be flexible.

If you organize a public book club, such as in a library or bookstore, and want to publicize the event to more than just your regular attendees, you'll want to plan much further ahead so that you can publicize the event.

Agree to the details such as, what time zone, which book, duration the author is available, and provide at least two contact points in case the first one doesn't work.

During The Meeting

- Plan on discussing the book first before the author joins you, so that you know what questions you'd like to ask.

- Be sure the computer or phone is positioned so everyone can see and/or hear. It is wise to run a test before the conversation starts.

- If you are inviting the author to your book club in person, please be considerate of her time. You may wish to invite the author for the whole meeting or for just part of it. In the event that it's for the entire time, it is wise to discuss among yourselves ahead of time, so you have some questions ready.

- Most importantly, relax and have fun.

This guide may be downloaded for printing purposes from Karen's website @www.KarenCoultersAuthor.com

REVIEWS ARE ALWAYS APPRECIATED

Lastly, if you enjoyed reading *Hope from Daffodils*, please post a review on social media, Goodreads, Amazon, etc. Additionally, Karen would enjoy hearing from you directly @ KarenCoultersAuthor@gmail.com